# The DOPPELGÄNGER QUEEN

The
DOPPELGÄNGER
QUEEN
K.N.Fitzwater

# Dedication

This book is dedicated to those who we've lost to the
pandemic, war, and internal strife.
May we shine a light on their names.

# Table of Contents


## Act 1

✦ Chapter 1 . . . . . . . . . . . . . . . . . . . . . . . . . . . . . . . . . . . . . . . .1
✦ Chapter 2 . . . . . . . . . . . . . . . . . . . . . . . . . . . . . . . . . . . . . . . 12
✦ Chapter 3 . . . . . . . . . . . . . . . . . . . . . . . . . . . . . . . . . . . . . . . 20
✦ Chapter 4 . . . . . . . . . . . . . . . . . . . . . . . . . . . . . . . . . . . . . . . 31
✦ Chapter 5 . . . . . . . . . . . . . . . . . . . . . . . . . . . . . . . . . . . . . . . 43
✦ Chapter 6 . . . . . . . . . . . . . . . . . . . . . . . . . . . . . . . . . . . . . . . 54
✦ Chapter 7 . . . . . . . . . . . . . . . . . . . . . . . . . . . . . . . . . . . . . . . 63
✦ Chapter 8 . . . . . . . . . . . . . . . . . . . . . . . . . . . . . . . . . . . . . . . 73
✦ Chapter 9 . . . . . . . . . . . . . . . . . . . . . . . . . . . . . . . . . . . . . . . 82
✦ Chapter 10 . . . . . . . . . . . . . . . . . . . . . . . . . . . . . . . . . . . . . . 90
✦ Chapter 11 . . . . . . . . . . . . . . . . . . . . . . . . . . . . . . . . . . . . . . 102

## Act 2

✦ Chapter 12 . . . . . . . . . . . . . . . . . . . . . . . . . . . . . . . . . . . . . . 117
✦ Chapter 13 . . . . . . . . . . . . . . . . . . . . . . . . . . . . . . . . . . . . . . 129
✦ Chapter 14 . . . . . . . . . . . . . . . . . . . . . . . . . . . . . . . . . . . . . . 141
✦ Chapter 15 . . . . . . . . . . . . . . . . . . . . . . . . . . . . . . . . . . . . . . 150
✦ Chapter 16 . . . . . . . . . . . . . . . . . . . . . . . . . . . . . . . . . . . . . . 162
✦ Chapter 17 . . . . . . . . . . . . . . . . . . . . . . . . . . . . . . . . . . . . . . 175
✦ Chapter 18 . . . . . . . . . . . . . . . . . . . . . . . . . . . . . . . . . . . . . . 185
✦ Chapter 19 . . . . . . . . . . . . . . . . . . . . . . . . . . . . . . . . . . . . . . 195

✦ Chapter 20 . . . . . . . . . . . . . . . . . . . . . . . . . . . . . . . . 205
✦ Chapter 21 . . . . . . . . . . . . . . . . . . . . . . . . . . . . . . . . 215

## Act 3

✦ Chapter 22 . . . . . . . . . . . . . . . . . . . . . . . . . . . . . . . . 229
✦ Chapter 23 . . . . . . . . . . . . . . . . . . . . . . . . . . . . . . . . 241
✦ Chapter 24 . . . . . . . . . . . . . . . . . . . . . . . . . . . . . . . . 253
✦ Chapter 25 . . . . . . . . . . . . . . . . . . . . . . . . . . . . . . . . 264
✦ Chapter 26 . . . . . . . . . . . . . . . . . . . . . . . . . . . . . . . . 275
✦ Chapter 27 . . . . . . . . . . . . . . . . . . . . . . . . . . . . . . . . 286
✦ Chapter 28 . . . . . . . . . . . . . . . . . . . . . . . . . . . . . . . . 297
✦ Chapter 29 . . . . . . . . . . . . . . . . . . . . . . . . . . . . . . . . 307
✦ Chapter 30 . . . . . . . . . . . . . . . . . . . . . . . . . . . . . . . . 318
✦ Chapter 31 . . . . . . . . . . . . . . . . . . . . . . . . . . . . . . . . 329
✦ Chapter 32 . . . . . . . . . . . . . . . . . . . . . . . . . . . . . . . . 353

Book Club Questions . . . . . . . . . . . . . . . . . . . . . . . . . . 353

The Mannequin Queen Teaser
✦ Chapter 1 . . . . . . . . . . . . . . . . . . . . . . . . . . . . . . . . 357

Author Bio . . . . . . . . . . . . . . . . . . . . . . . . . . . . . . . . . . 363
Trigger warnings . . . . . . . . . . . . . . . . . . . . . . . . . . . . . 268
Glossary And Translations . . . . . . . . . . . . . . . . . . . . . . 365
Acknowledgments . . . . . . . . . . . . . . . . . . . . . . . . . . . . 371

The City of Freedom
Amaveriel
The Galliheah Mountains
The Iounese Desert
The Abby of the Rising Dawk
N
W
E
S
The Anglori Ju
The Market
Sulmain Street
The Pit
Eagle Nest
The Iron Lady
Madame Pompadour's
Western Gate
The Western Spire

# Foreword

From K.M. Rice

When I first encountered this novel in its early stages, I felt as if I had slipped into a world with tremendous breadth that felt familiar and strange at the same time. Fitzwater has constructed such a complex yet charming web of a society that, as fantastical as it seems, I feel I have been to before. Perhaps in a dream. Or perhaps Fitzwater has crafted a tale that seemingly does the near impossible in this day and age: *The Doppelgänger Queen* has carved itself its rightful place as its own realized vision for a mature audience while harkening back to the comfortingly familiar folklore and themes many of us first encountered in childhood. This blend takes the reader on a journey that is part mystery, part tragedy, and part action/adventure, woven together by the gravitas of the human heart. I am thankful that this manuscript once came across my desk, for I find myself recalling scenes and passages, even years later, as they were brought to life with such vivid, cinematic detail that the story has a life of its own. Every author hopes that their work will leave such an impression and linger in some way, and Fitzwater's tale of love, deception, corruption, and redemption does just that. What you hold in your hands is an entry into an engrossing tale, and I hope that, like me, you will turn the page. And the next. And the next.

# Act I

"There's no weight in gold worth
more than a pure soul."

~Mother Superior Justiania,
783 After Ascension

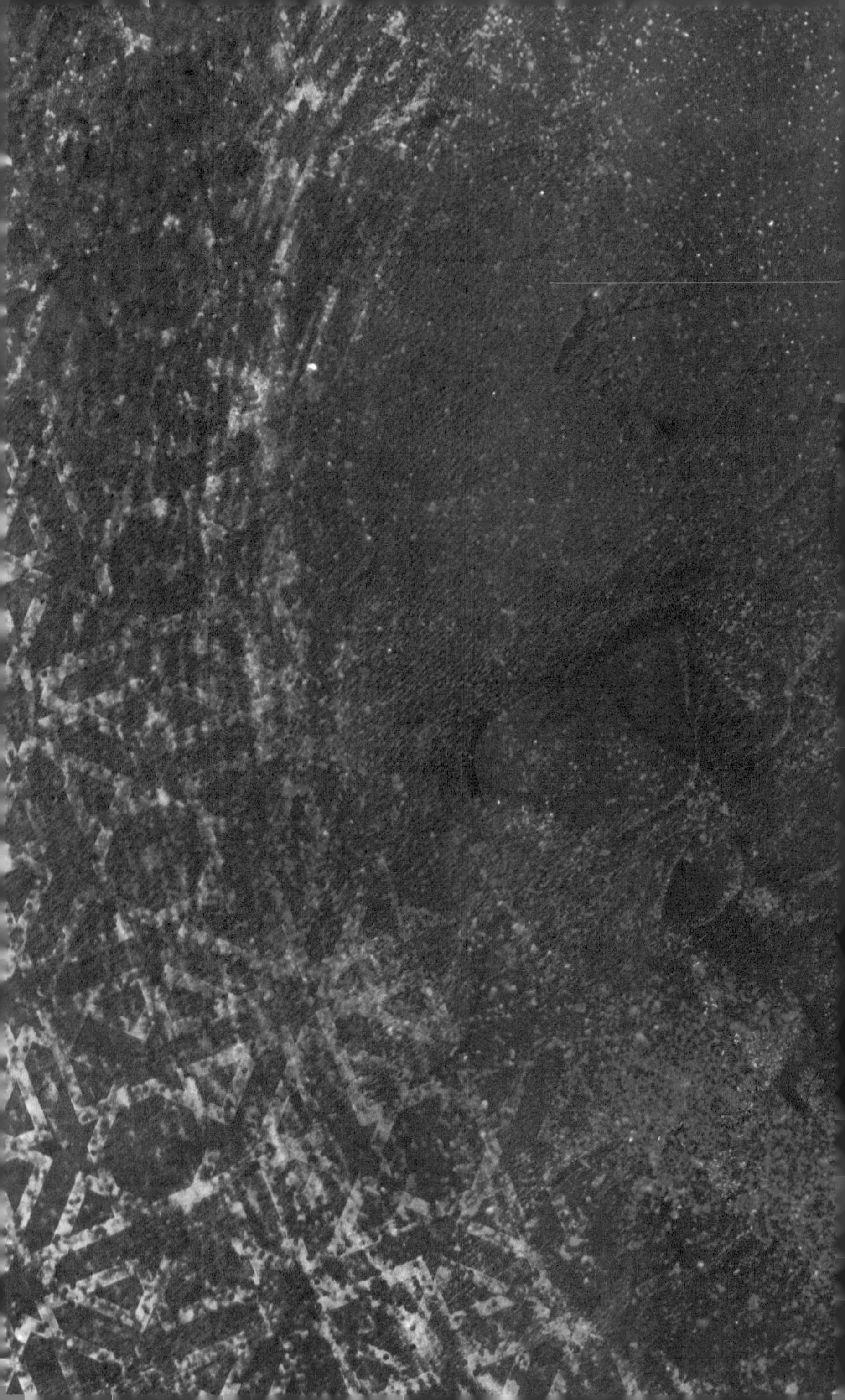

# Chapter 1

## M'THEALQUILÔK

EAST OF THE WIND-WHIPPED DUNES OF THE Iounese desert, lost in the jungles of Angloria, far in the ruinous depths of M'thealquilôk, under suffocating silt and haunted halls—a light. Quivering. Timid. Clinging to life against the oppressive dark. Illuminating four grim faces steeling to meet their fate.

"Call it, Ruth," Aramis, the one holding the light, whispered. His silver eyes burned fiercely in the flickering shadows.

"The tome is the key," whispered their company leader, gilded in splint mail, her tongue thick with a northern accent. "It is the source of Tellezard's power. If we can get it out of his hands, we can defeat him."

"And you expect me to do a wee bit of lightnin'?" The third, Joel, furrowed his brows, distorting the swirling woad on his face.

"No, we need your wind. We'll distract the villain while Aramis will go up top for the grab. Once we have it in our sights, we give the signal."

"Hail the Dawn?" queried the last, Rhyllae, priestess of the Morning Lord and sister to all friendly folk, her curls contained in a golden shawl.

Ruth nodded. "When you hear that, Aramis, you jump. Joel, you catch him and fly him at the necromancer. Tellezard won't know what hit him. Once the tome is plucked, we make our escape."

The silence was as stifling as the hall they were in.

"Ye sure you don't want me to do an itty, bitty lightnin'?" asked Joel.

"Not with these bombs, you don't," Aramis said, the handmade cigarette dangling from his lip. Gingerly, he touched the flame to the paper as he spoke. "Rudderbangers are for underwater. Once out of the water, any spark can set them off."

"Bah, Rhyllae can put you back together, right?"

The sister hardly stirred, save to give Aramis a look. Her brows pinched together.

Aramis sighed, smoke hissing from his lips. "I'll be fine. This isn't my first."

"Which one?" Joel jested.

Aramis rubbed his neck as he turned his gaze to the arched ceiling above, the ancient fresco still as stunning as the day it was made. "Seventeen for the bombs, three for the jump."

"Three?"

Ruth hissed for them all to be silent as she put her hand on Gleamwood's scabbard. It was a side hall, after all. There were no doors to run to. No alcoves or pillars to hide them. Joel had first wondered if this was the makings of the Ancients, humans who had once dominated the entire globe, due to its arched precision. But Aramis, ever the historian, explained it was once called the Hall of Peace. Elves and dwarves signed the treaty to "inherit the Earth" as one, which still stood to that very day, thus they commemorated the event with this hall. The Ancients would've used a different material, such as metal or cinder blocks, and had gravitated to rigid rectangles. The natural stone ceiling was curved, so the fresco encompassed all who passed through as equals. If only they could see it in better times.

"All clear," Rhyllae said after a few heartbeats. They could always depend on her elven heritage.

"Right. No fire. No sparks. Hail the Dawn, jump, catch." Ruth pointed at Rhyllae, Aramis, and Joel respectfully. "Grab the tome or die trying."

All nodded save for one.

The smoldering end of the cigarette blazed up to Aramis's lips before he spat out the words, "Fuck that."

"Aramis," Rhyllae scolded.

"I didn't free myself from Bazzuuport so I could die in this hellhole." He flicked the spent roll. "There's an old chute the builders used during the building's construction. Once I get it open, tome or not, we get out of here."

"But the ghouls!"

"Hell, Aramis, he can raze this entire city." Joel jutted his palms out, barely keeping his voice down. "The world would be doomed if we left it in Tellezard's hands."

Aramis covered the flame so it wouldn't go out. "We have the Jessenters. Ruth, I know it's not the Djinnasi, but they can help fight this."

Ruth cupped her chin and bowed her head in thought. Aramis held his breath. He knew the rebel fighters were spread thin throughout the entire Iounese desert, fighting to end the tyranny of their overlords. Surely they could convince their colonel, Korzha, to lend some of the troops to them. If not, then the treasure should persuade him.

"My sisters and mothers will." Rhyllae put her fist out in the middle. "For Bagheera."

"Aye, for Tamira and a pint back home." Joel slapped his hand on top of hers.

Aramis's grizzled expression softened into a smile for the first time since they had started this venture. His gloved hand covered the two. "For Amaveriel and the free people."

"For the good of the realm." Ruth grasped with both hands. "Come what may, we will end him."

They made their pact. They snuffed the flame, but not the fire within.

The grand hall. A humble title for what it contained. 15,000 feet of gigantic statues lined abreast. Their regal heads soared to the vaulted stone ceiling as they stood attention in the all-consuming darkness. A testament to the engineering prowess of the elves.

Lo, high above on one such head, a light. Dangling upside down from a slender cord, Aramis inched down like a silkworm from the vaulted ceiling. No guide wires. No safety nets. Bare rope and bare skin was all he needed. A feat that would be too intimidating to most humans or elves. But Aramis was no human, though he might look like it, he was a jhasin. A being constructed by the Djinnasi lords by magic and sin, as the saying goes. Dexterous and durable, they can withstand immense punishment and still perform incredible feats of acrobatics. All for the Djinnasi lords' sickening nighttime pleasures. To add to this pleasure, every jhasin lights up in the dark, he included. Though, his is of an older making, and only his eyes light up in a silver pall.

Aramis allowed his illuminating eyes to guide him to a safe purchase. He slipped on his special mask, concealing the silver light his eyes bore while allowing him the vision to see. There he waited among the monarchs, enveloped in the vast veil of slumber known as oblivion.

Whatever foul terrors lurking in the shadows witnessing him, Aramis secured all the rudderbangers in the air shafts enclosed above. He strung their fuses together into a singular cord. One strike and all would come crashing down.

*What a shame*, Aramis thought as he peered into the velvet dark. His inner historian would be amiss to have this place buried again, never to be discovered until the next unfortunate soul stumbled by.

Before him, across the void, was a carved statue of an elven face. Through all his memories of precious vellums, he never knew who was staring back at him there, in queenly judgment, majestic lips closed with elven secrets, keeper of history, never born to the light of day.

Would he have such a face when the time comes? A silent mask lost in the shifting sands of time? Or would he disappear as the Ancients did three thousand years ago, their skyward towers of glass fallen by avarice and vice? If these were to be his last words to a slumbering god, then it should be with illumination. He produced the flickering flame with a matchstick and cupped it close to him. His breath shuddered as the flame danced. As he bent down for his silent prayer, Aramis froze. From the corner of his eye, the light caught a shape on the wall.

It took his entire will to push the scream back down his throat.

It was a ghoul. A creature of the dead awakened by Tellezard's cruel magic. Like the rest of the mindless hordes known as inmorti, but with an insatiable hunger that drives them into reckless abandon. Clinging to the bare stone like a cicada ready to molt its flesh. The ghoul's head craned backward in an inhumane manner.

And it was not alone.

Aramis dared to raise the tiny flame closer and found the entire wall lined with millions of the dreadful creatures. All of them were crouching in wait with their eye upon him, rasping in anticipation. Had he ever drawn near the wall earlier, he would've lost his courage.

A cry pierced the walls surrounding him. In a flash, he enveloped the matchstick in his gloved hand.

*Rhyllae?*

Then he heard a dark cackle emit from far below.

*Tellezard.*

His assumption was confirmed as the hoarse voice mocked, "It seems that your Morning Lord is not as strong as your faith, priestess. Perhaps there is another worthier of your devotion?"

"There... There is no light greater than the Morning Lord," Rhyllae cried out.

Aramis readied himself by the fuse. This was all part of their plan, after all. Have themselves captured by these goons. Keep the necromancer gloating. Once the tome was in sight...

"Not even your Silver Fox?" Tellezard posed the question.

The Silver Fox. A moniker the free people had given to Aramis long ago when he was the shepherd of the desert, a hero worthy of their praise. It wasn't the question itself that gave him pause, though. It was her silence. How can he—a delinquent through and through—be brighter than their god?

*Why can't she answer the question?*

As if she heard his thought, Rhyllae's voice cracked, "He's ... dead. You killed him."

Aramis grimaced. Even he could tell the deception fell flat before Tellezard's cackle echoed to the ceiling.

"No, you elven mutt. But soon, the Fox will be."

It was decided in his mind. *Signal or no; it ends here.*

Aramis's fingers fumbled in the rough-hewn leather and found only one matchstick left. Crouching at the fuse line, he sparked the match. The flame licked the frayed end, struggling to catch from the suffocating throne room.

Then he sucked in his breath as he looked up before him.

A pair of eyes hovered before him. Dull. Clouded. Dead. Trailing his hand movement with hateful ticks. A foul voice disturbed the air, speaking in a tongue he couldn't understand. As the flame dimmed, the evil eyes grew brighter.

And closer.

Aramis reached for his twin daggers. But it was too late. The ghoul slammed into his chest, knocking Aramis flat on his back. Spittle flew from its inhumane maw as it raked his black linen shirt with its bony claws.

Grabbing the ghoul's throat, Aramis gave himself enough distance to reach for his dagger. With a flick of his wrist, he slid it into its armpit. A death sentence for any living man. Yet that was not his aim, for this was no living being. With the twist of his knife, he popped the arm out of the joint. Then he locked the leg, grabbed the arm, and rolled the ghoul to his right in one fluid motion. Now vertical, Aramis stabbed his dagger into the base of the skull, wiggling the knife until those dingy eyes stopped twitching. Its face melted back to its original death mask: a frozen scream of terror.

A shudder roiled over his spine. Easing himself from the still corpse, he glanced at the fuse line. Still there, though the blackened ends were free of any flame.

A clatter of steel rang out from below as Rhyllae's song "Hail the Dawn" echoed down the hall.

Aramis crawled on his hands and knees to the frayed line. He banged the two grit pads together. With every spark, his heart leaped. Sweat trickled down his brows before the cloth wicked it away. Bones popped from the wall as the ghouls shuddered from their stasis. They, too, hail.

"Light, damn you. Light," he said through gritted teeth.

At last, the tender flame licked the end, then sped off toward the dark void above. A smile and a half-hearted laugh were all the celebration Aramis could give. Springing to his feet, he dashed to the edge and freed his sweaty brow of the mask. A globe of silver light enveloped his head and shoulders as it streamed from his eyes.

"It's lit," came Joel's voice.

Then Aramis saw it. One by one, balls of flame appeared, encircling his compatriot, as well as the pack of ghouls. They broke off and circled around as hyenas would with a lone lion. Gleamwood, Ruth's trusted sword, met them in a flash. To and fro she moved as if dancing, parrying and ending their vicious hunger. Joel, in the meantime, crouched low to the ground, whirling his arms in circular motions.

A violet arc of lightning streamed from the right. Aramis could see the foul necromancer's contorted face in that chilling moment. Fortunately, the lightning crashed and showered over an invisible shield. Steadfast at the break was Rhyllae, the song still on her lips.

Then came a warble of a different sort. Hissing. Snarling. Groaning. Rising from below like a snake. In Aramis's silver pall, the abominations slunk down from the wall. Ridges of their scapulas rose and fell with each step as they stalked toward the floor.

He couldn't afford to wait for Joel's good time.

With that thought, Aramis squeezed his eyes shut and launched himself. Flipping backward into a somersault before twisting himself into a spear, he clasped his palms tightly below his head, piercing the self-made wind rushing over his form. It took everything he had to not lose himself to fear as he braced for the worst.

"By Lune's pointy tits, I lost him!" cried Joel.

"Aramis! Open your eyes, Aramis!" cried out Rhyllae, the last word a shriek of desperation.

At last, his eyes flew open, straining against the stinging wind—a silver meteor falling to earth. Only the ghouls were able to keep flight. One decided to leap off of their fellow toward Aramis. Thankfully, he squeezed himself into a ball, and the ghouls grazed past him.

Then he felt an incredible pull toward the earth below. The protocol would have him wait for the light of day to meet another officer. His incantation whispered in the very wind that caressed and carried Aramis into the magical vortex.

Everything sped past Aramis as he flew over their heads. Lady Ruth's hair looked like a flame on a thatch. Glints of light from her armor shone like stars. Rhyllae's saffron hijab whipped off her head, sailing with Aramis until it hit Joel's tattooed head.

In a blink, Tellezard was in his sights. His leprotic maw gaped as Aramis zoomed toward him. Aramis moved to bring his daggers to bear, but the wind carried him too quickly. His shoulder slammed into the necromancer's chest. Try as he may, Aramis couldn't stab the slippery devil as they rolled on the floor.

They came apart, and Aramis rolled down the throne hall, carrying with him the prized possession: Tellezard's tome. He had separated the flesh-bound book from its master.

"Aramis." Rhyllae came over, tugging on his arm to help him stand. "Hurry before they swarm."

A deafening boom shook them to their bones, forcing them to cling together as chunks of limestone fell from above. The bombs were meant for the vents, not the structural frame of this impressive room.

*That ... shouldn't be happening...*

"We have to get them out of here!" Aramis shouted so he could hear himself over the groaning of stone. He knew he could have whispered with Rhyllae's sensitive hearing.

As the ancient world collapsed around them, they raced back down the hall with the book in tow. Beams of light pierced through the dark corridor. Sand and silt mingled with the falling archaic stones. As they drew near, they saw Lady Ruth standing tall. Tellezard was pinned to the floor with Gleamwood through his chest. Joel covered her back with razor-sharp winds, slicing through any ghouls that came near.

The necromancer spotted the oncoming duo. He reached out with his gnarled, diseased finger, and the floor cracked before him, splitting toward them with incredible speed. Aramis thought his eyes were playing tricks; it seemed shadows flew from the unmade seam.

Rhyllae stepped in front of Aramis, forcing him to halt in his tracks. She mouthed another prayer against her two fingers before she stretched her arms wide. The crack bifurcated and encompassed them, creating a rough-hewn circle.

The island of stone shifted as the next blast sounded, causing them to fall to their knees. The vile tome slipped from his arms, opening to a series of arcane text written in blood. Its pages glowed with an eerie light.

"Keep the book away from him. He's trying to teleport out of here!" Joel cried out.

"Then let us go and be done with it!" Aramis shouted.

Then his heart sank.

A ghoul launched at the Mynx's backside. Bringing him down hard to the ground. His arms jerked up and down as more joined the feast.

"Joel!" Rhyllae cried, scrambling to stand.

Another bang sounded over their heads. Without a second thought, Aramis grabbed her by the waist and held her back. Boulders crashed before them, blocking their path.

"Ruth," Aramis cried to out their captain. "Get out of there!"

"No!" came her thick northern accent. "They call upon me. My mothers. My sisters. They bid me to take my place. I shall go to Valhalla, free."

A distinct snap within the earth sounded. The structure groaned in protest, vibrating through their bones as the floor rolled in waves. It was too late to leave.

In a futile effort, Aramis swept Rhyllae underneath him to shield her from the destruction he had wrought. Stones bounced off of his spine as they embraced. Her words of last rites shuddered in his ear as he rocked her in his arms.

*I'm sorry, Vanessa. I won't be coming home this time.*

Then he saw it through the sandy haze. The glowing tome slid across the floor. Without forethought, Aramis slapped his hand against the chartreuse page. All he could remember next was the smell of sandalwood in Rhyllae's hair as mists engulfed them whole.

# Chapter 2

## CHANGING OF THE GUARD

THE LOW-HANGING MISTS FROM THE SEA PARTED around Tavian Korzha's riding boots and the hem of his duster. His long legs allowed him to speed through the slumbering alleyways of Amaveriel without notice in the long hour of the night. There would be no sleep for him. Not with what he had read from Mariam's letter. He had come to the city as quick as his ship could against the wind.

A quick jog down a bend of stairs, and at last, he made it to his destination—a simple hovel of a door, sunken in the earth. At the other end of the alley, the market street was aglow from lanterns.

Two men jumped to their feet, one with a mop of copper hair and a pocked face. The other was a nervous, twitchy fellow with dark, curly hair. Both wore red sashes on their waists. Korzha knew them to be Jessenters under Captain Basil, Falçion, and Mudhi.

"Passwo—" Falçion started to say as he brought his halberd to bear.

"Tiki-bikini," Korzha's crisp northern voice cut through the air.

Without breaking his stride, he entered the base. The elders granted the rebels an ancient lava flow, a natural wonder lurking under the very streets where merchants hawked their wares. Twisting and turning in convoluted networks, it gave any intruder a dizzying orientation. If only they had such steel-trap security at the Karatow Mountains.

"Colonel, sir," Mudhi piped up, bringing a torch to bear. "We weren't expecting you to be back so soon."

"Clearly, you weren't expecting anything at all. Where are the men and women?"

"Asleep, if they're not at the Iron Lady."

"The Iron Lady, at a time like this?" Korzha whirled on the back of his heels.

Mudhi flinched from his steely blue gaze, which the locals considered unnatural. Then again, not all were kind to foreigners like him.

"It's three turns of the hour before dawn," Mudhi managed to squeak out of his throat.

"With no night watch?"

"Well, there's Falçion and me, um, sir."

Korzha gave the man a good, long, measured look. He heard how well the people spoke of him. Mudhi Nazir was part of a company that helped secure the Gallileah's eastern aqueducts, a lifeline for this coastal desert town. But most knew he lacked the bones in his spine when they were assailed by dwarven raiders immediately afterward. Some would argue—Captain Basil included—that it was wise to run to the city watch for backup. But Mudhi never journeyed back to join them. Even a yellow dog would have the gall to bite back with the strength of a pack. Throughout his military career, Korzha could discern a coward in their ranks. And there was one standing right before him.

"Where's Captain Basil? I need to speak with him," Korzha asked as he took off his long scarf, his blood too hot for such protection.

"Office," came a squeak. Then Mudhi cleared his throat. "In his office, sir."

Shoving his scarf in Mudhi's arms, Korzha took the torch and walked down a flight of stairs, quickly striding over the bottom three. All the while, Mudhi scrambled to keep up with the lanky foreigner, scarf trailing on the floor.

At first, Aramis thought he would splatter on the time-worn floor, but then he heard Joel's voice. Their ranks were a manner of favoritism, not based on merit, after all. To accost a fellow officer would be the same as accosting the general himself. But this was not the time for such pleasantries. His worst fears, that what the Sunset mother had said was true, were fast becoming a reality. The Jessenters in the Karatow Mountains, a small chain in the Gallileahs, were gone. It could only mean they were compromised. Part of him regretted discussing trade negotiations with the president of the Pirate Federation.

At last, they came to a wooden door fitted in a circular arch with a singular plaque bolted to the side.

## CAPT. EL'MUREED BASIL

"I apologize, but he did tell me he didn't want to be disturbed," Mudhi said.

"That will be all, Nazir."

Korzha then, with his left hand, twisted the knob and pushed the door open. As it swung open, he froze in horror.

There, strung high up toward the ceiling, was Basil himself. His entire cavity as exposed as a gutted boar. His face was purple, his entrails wrapped around his neck, hung by an unlit floating oil lamp, rotating freely behind his blood-soaked desk and papers.

"As you can see, he's all tied up." Mudhi chuckled darkly.

*It was all a façade!*

Korzha reached for his sword, Silver Star, at his right hip. But the fiend stopped him before he could unsheathe it.

With incredible strength, Mudhi wrenched Korzha's right arm high up as he body-slammed the colonel against the door. The force of the impact knocked the scabbard off its hooks, and the torch was snuffed out completely. Try as he may, Korzha couldn't shake Mudhi off.

"Why, Colonel, I didn't know you danced," Mudhi articulated next to his ear, spit dribbling down his neck. "Let's cut a rug, shall we?"

Mudhi shifted his body weight as if to move them into the room, which was all Korzha needed. He pushed against the threshold with his long legs, causing them both to fall.

Korzha rolled free. His back slammed against the wooden desk behind him. He found the Silver Star in the dark and pulled it out of its scabbard. The metal rang a continuous pure note, one of the few surviving singing blades.

Clearly disadvantaged, Korzha scrambled onto the desk for higher ground. Snaking up the slimy intestinal cord, he managed to find the floating vessel. Then, with one quick stroke, freed Basil from his tether as he held on to the lamp.

"Oh, Korzhy. Have you ever danced with the devil under Lune's pale light?" The voice appeared to morph and change with every word. "I have. It was a pleasure and a delight to revel in Hellfire's fright."

"Revel in this!"

Into the void, Korzha threw the lamp before him. A startled yelp came forth, then a clatter of metal against stone.

"Is that the best you can do?" He could hear the sneering with every syllable.

Korzha smirked and spoke in his native tongue, "*Ilumina.*"

The blue flame from the lamp's spout spread from the puddle, then onto the villain. In short order, all became a roaring fire. In the fiery glow, he saw Mudhi madly flailing his arms to put out the flames, to no avail.

Before he could bring his sword to bear, the coward ran, a plume of fire trailing in his wake, lighting the halls before vanishing from his sight. Taking a reprieve, the Töskan sheathed his weapon.

Remarkably, Falçion, with another Jessenter, came bounding in a short time later. Their mouths hung open as they took in the room, the flames dying.

"It was Nazir. Find him and bring him to me."

"Why would he... We'll find him." Falçion saluted and commanded, "Wake everyone up. Get the watch if you can. Shake the whole city down. I'll secure the perimeter. Go!"

Watching them run, sounding the alarm with every step of the way, Korzha wondered, *Why, indeed.*

The assassin was not expecting him to enter the room. Perhaps there was a reason to kill a low-ranking officer like Basil. Korzha scoured the papers on the desk, then the ones scattered on the floor. All were dispatch notices and supply requests, with no inkling of valuable information worth killing over. As the flames simmered down, he found nothing of significance—most of them stained by Basil's blood or burned by the blaze.

Kneeling, he pinched the bridge of his nose at a loss. The fire was now a single flame. Its flickering light made the shadows dance from the ceiling to the walls and to

Basil himself. His fist was clenched tightly in his rigid pose—only the one.

This odd detail stirred the officer from his thoughts. Coming to his side, Korzha eased Basil's fingers apart and was rewarded with a torn note.

"Your service was commendable, Captain."

As he read the slip of parchment, his stomach sank. It came from the dwarves, spirit guardians of stone, who combed the battlefield. Over and over again, his eyes took in the baffling news. It wasn't the devastation wreaked upon the land or the estimated dead—it was the names of the deceased, no one was spared.

Falçion returned. "We've locked it down, Colonel Korzha."

Slow and steady, Korzha stood and crossed the room. Handing him the note as he passed.

"It's General, now."

The smoldering light caved to the oppressive dark and withered away.

The sunlight filtered through the tall canopy leaves, dancing in his silver eyes. The dull ring in his ears faded into a gentle cacophony of Anglorian warblers and cackling lemurs.

*I survived?*

Aramis Feres closed his eyes as he felt the pleasing contrast between the cool earth on his back and the timid warmth on his face. With care, he breathed as much as his aching lungs would allow him, clawing the moist jungle soil with his free hand.

*I survived.*

He laughed to himself. Then the sharp pain sobered him into silence.

Squinting through the grit, Aramis found the flesh-bound tome close at hand, the leather bloated at the hand-sewn stitches running haphazardly over its cover. Even as he reached out to caress its ridged spine with his fingertip, it remained as docile as a lazy crocodile, even in the bright of day.

*Perhaps … there must be some use here. Somewhere between these pages. If this is the price to pay for all we lost…*

A whisper on the wind, carrying the cloying smell of jasmine, tantalized the bare skin on his outstretched arm. Goose pimples rose, causing the number 479241 imprinted on his skin to pucker. A lasting legacy of his former life when he was a slave and of a different gender. No matter what magic he commissioned, not even the transformative powers of the Zemzem Fountain, the stain couldn't be removed, always there to haunt him until the end of his days.

The cloying wind rushed again, and the canopies rustled. Aramis shuddered at the sudden chill and rocked his head to and fro. The view of jade and saffron blurred before the veil of sleep smothered it shut. In the dark velvet fold, his ears rang from the whispering wind, playing sweet words into his mind, conjuring the sweet embrace of his wife, Vanessa, raven-haired and pale as the moon, by his side in their pillowed bed. The vision whispered the words she always asked through her crooked smile:

*"Did you miss me, Aramis?*

*"Aramis…*

*"Aramis…"*

"Aramis, it's time to go," a new voice called out. Warm, gentle, and strained with impatience.

"I'll go when I say so," was his gruff response. Aramis could still taste the grit in the back of his throat from that death trap. The thought of it alone gave him a coughing fit. The jabbing pain from his left lower rib didn't help. He coughed and wheezed for clean air until he felt a chill at his side. Like being in a cold spring river, the pain washed away within minutes.

Taking a good look around, he found Rhyllae looking down upon him. Her kinky hair clung to her glistening, olive-brown skin. His head was on her lap with her fingers on his temples. He must have dozed, for the sunlight had shifted in a new angle, and all were basked in the warm hue.

Sitting upright, he muttered, "Thanks."

Rhyllae nodded and stood, wiping the dirt from her white robe. Though it was still smeared with earth and blood after she was done. A vivid contrast to the delicate embroidery of the Morning Lord's rising star trailing down the tunic's skirt.

"Did... Did Ruth...?" Aramis asked.

For several breaths, Rhyllae didn't answer. Even when she reached down to pick him up from the jungle floor, her brown eyes couldn't meet his. With care, she placed a smooth stone in his hand. It was etched with the image of a raven, Lady Ruth's prized treasure.

Aramis knew the answer before she spoke.

"You're the company leader now." Her voice cracked as tears streaked down her round face.

Aramis wrapped the sister in a tight embrace, hiding his stricken face in her curls, ignoring the mocking cajoles of the cackling lemurs above.

# Chapter 3

## A MEASURE OF WORTH

CIVILIZATION AT LONG LAST.

It was a two week trek before Aramis knocked down the last bush of the Anglorian jungle, revealing the city of freedom, Amaveriel, nestled in its coastal dale.

The whitewashed buildings, etched from the cliffside, glowed orange from the setting sun. It cast purple shadows in its twisted, narrow alleyways. The protective ridge of the city extended beyond its walls to the sandy inlets of the shallow bay, providing refuge to man and bird alike. Farther south, the Shining Sea glimmered as specks of triangle sails danced for the last catch. Behind the city, to the west, the cliffs rolled into the sweltering Ioun desert, the haze of the day still lingering on its white sands.

Despite all this beauty, his eyes lingered upon the backside of Amaveriel's western gate. He remembered his first arrival at those gates almost twenty years prior—the day he stopped being the shepherd of the desert.

*It had been a dangerous trek, spanning through the entire length of the vast Ioun with three thousand in tow. Some of them he had managed to hand over to the ever-migrating tribes, others succumbed to heat or old age. All the while, he beckoned the rest to move ever toward the dawn and the rising moon until they reached the legendary free city. Stories and rumors of Sulmaith's Chosen founding of the hidden city spurred him to carry them here.*

*Low did his spirit drop when they told him he could never leave. The elders of amaveriel vowed to keep this place a secret in order for the people to remain free. Nestled at the foot end of the Gallileah mountains, where it meets the sea, diving jungle from the desert, one would think of the city as formidable to any assault. Yet, it could only remain safe if the Djinnasi lords never knew its location. They were, after all, the embodiments of the natural elements. Mountains and oceans were toys for their use.*

*And so he had remained, leaving the gates as a hired specialist for the Jessenters.*

"At what cost?" Aramis murmured aloud to himself. Ruth's etched stone, heavy in his hands.

The snapping of foliage drew him out of his thoughts. Rhyllae emerged from the brush, the tome stuffed in a bag hung on her back, coming to his side on the high bluff. Weary, sweaty, and grimy as he, yet fitting to her character. Ever the vigilant one to get her hands dirty to help the downtrodden wretches, himself included.

Rhyllae sighed in relief at the sight. "Home."

"To whom?"

"Must you?"

"What?"

"Every time? It's home to every free people."

"Free for some." Aramis punted a small stone by the toe of his dusty boot, watching it tumble end over end, dislodging others to join the merry chase.

"You broke the law. Twenty-six times, mind you."

"All for coin. Come on, let's collect the blood money."

Aramis slid down the slope, spreading his feet apart to keep himself upright. Landing on the large rock jutting out, Aramis turned back to find Rhyllae lingering behind. Her perfect face twisted in a scowl.

"You can't eat or drink gold, Aramis," Rhyllae said. "You can't breathe in gold dust. You can't survive with it out in Ioun. When are you going to learn?"

It puzzled him. It wasn't the first time they exchanged such words. Yet, Rhyllae's words bit worse than any flea this time.

"Not all of us live in the mercy of the Morning Lord, Rhyllae," Aramis said. "I should know, having lived on the streets before Rhum came along. Fighting for the 'Greater Good' doesn't fill an empty belly. It didn't save our friends back there."

"You can't purchase our friends back."

"No, but it can sure bury them." Aramis pointed back at the city. "Their blood is on their hands, Rhyllae, as much as it is on mine. They better pay for it."

Much to his surprise, Rhyllae decided to join him after all. Her weight carried her faster than he, and she crashed into him, causing them to fall upon the rocky stone. Red-faced from such a blunder, she separated herself from him.

"Their blood is on my hands, too," she said as she looked back at the Anglorian jungle.

Aramis sighed and held out his hand. After clasping on, he lifted her upright. Hand in hand, they walked through the western gate. As they were led through the gates, Aramis could not help but notice the dejected faces of the watchmen. Overhead, flags depicting a phoenix against a starburst flew at half-mast.

"Did they think we were dead?" Aramis asked the sister, but she didn't return his gaze. Her honey-brown eyes were cast down, lost in gloomy thought, much like the people on the street. Slouched shoulders. Vacant stares. Shuffling past them in a numb stupor. One woman openly wept in front of her door. The rebel flag of the red phoenix clutching red sabers against white served as her handkerchief. It was then Aramis connected the two together.

Something terrible had happened to the Jessenters while they were away. At first, Aramis thought they might have lost one of their higher officers. But as the two traveled farther into the city, Aramis found that every house hung a red ribbon by every door. And every person had a similar red ribbon tied on their biceps. Then he froze at the intersection.

"Rhyllae, I don't think we're the only ones who lost people," Aramis said.

Stirring from her thoughts, the morning priestess gasped and gripped his hand tighter.

The city was weeping blood.

Everywhere, they saw red ribbons tied to posts, doors, and even wagons, flapping in the unsettled wind. They stood still, lost for words. Hands clasped together for fear of flying apart in a spinning world.

"I need to go home," Aramis murmured.

"You need to see Korzha," Rhyllae murmured simultaneously.

"Wait, what?" Aramis blinked and turned to look at her.

"You're the company leader now. You have to see him."

"I have … other matters. Why not you?"

"I have duties."

"We just came back. Tell your mothers they can wait."

"They're … for our friends."

Aramis sighed and ruffled his salt-and-pepper hair. The market, where the rebel base lay hidden underneath, was in the opposite direction from where he called home.

"Besides," Rhyllae continued, "I don't think they would appreciate talking to a—"

"Heretic? Blasphemer? Infidel?"

"Someone out of date."

The Silver Fox laughed in surprise. Aramis heard it all, from believers to atheists, concerning his archaic religious belief. Historically, the Sleeper was worshipped far and wide, acquiring numerous names from all cultures. Now, no one, but Aramis, gives the Sleeper prayers anymore. Most claimed They were defunct and had no powers to grant, while others said They didn't exist. But this was a first ... and was kind.

"Just because the Sleeper gave the entire kingdom over to Their Sun doesn't mean I should hop over with the rest of the congregation."

"Aramis, that happened fifteen hundred years ago." The priestess tilted her head at him.

He shrugged. "Yeah. Well, I need more time."

"Then it's settled." Rhyllae gave him the knapsack. "You go to the colonel, and I go to the abbey."

Aramis opened his mouth, then shut it tight. She had him.

"Fine. I'll go to see the Töskan."

Korzha's office was dim enough for Aramis's eyes to glow, even with the floating oil lamp. Rarely did the colonel stay longer than a week at a time, thus the space was spartan at best. There was a bare desk deprived of secrets, and Aramis should know; he checked often enough. Behind the desk, the clay seeped through the boards nailed against it. The bricks meant to rebuild the wall were held off for immediate expenses. Situated in the corners were two hip-high vases, stuffed to the brim with loose sheets of parchment and tubes of maps and charts. One of these was spread over the desk at that exact moment. Poring over the chart was the man himself, the one who had sent Ruth's expedition to their doom.

Octavian Augustus Korzha.

He was not the sort one expects to be a military man or even a rebel fighter. Korzha was as tall as the legs of a crane and just as thin. His sandy blond hair was slicked across from a severe side part, with shocks of gray at his temples perfectly framing his razor-sharp cheekbones. Despite wearing the red regimental sash around his waist and desert coat, he still clothed himself in a Töskan doublet and riding boots. His ice-cold eyes regarded Aramis the moment he stepped into the room, never wavering as he eased from the table to clasp his hands behind his back.

"Of all the people to survive the expedition, I am the least surprised it was you," Korzha said to him.

"I take it you heard." Aramis twirled one of the wooden chairs so he could lean on the top railing.

"Your appearance is merely confirmation. You wouldn't dare slink in here unless Ruth and the others are dead."

"Save for Sister Ghalédale."

"That should appease the Mother Superior," Korzha grumbled. He flung the quill on the desk, next to the red X at the Karatow Dunes. Its white-and-brown feathers covered the rest of the letters.

"How many?" Aramis's silver eyes fixated on the mark.

"More than 30,000 of our best, including General Tackett. We are all that is left of the resistance."

The number gave Aramis pause. The rebel army was reduced to a fraction of its size. "Which son-of-bitch do we follow now?"

Korzha glowered at him. "I'll have you know my mother was a respectable lady of the court."

Aramis leaned far forward on the chair. "You?"

"Yes." The now-general sat behind the desk, his long fingers joined to form a hollow triangle. "I hope you did not come back empty-handed from your frolic in the Anglorian jungle. Chessentari's wares do not come cheap."

In response, Aramis slung the makeshift knapsack from his shoulder onto the desk. Sand and dust from the ruins puffed into the stagnant air.

Glancing up at him, General Korzha produced the tome. Running his hand down the haphazardly sewn leather, the general spoke with his nose in a twitch. "This is bound in elven hide."

"We encountered a necromancer named Tellezard. This was used against us."

"Hmm. Then it could prove to be of use for our own gain."

"Then it's worth its weight?"

The general eyed him. "We shall see." He straightened himself up, keeping his left hand behind his back as he stood. "You have cleared the entire dungeon?"

"Yes."

"Every beast?" He paused for another affirmative nod. "And every trap?"

"I took care of all of those hazards myself."

"Good." General Korzha scribbled on a paper slip and handed it to him. "Here, take this to Dido for the payment of your services."

Aramis glanced at the sliver of parchment and crumpled it up. "This is not the agreed amount."

"You are absolutely correct. It is not. It is the payment you and the priestess have earned thus far. You will receive the full amount when the wealth of M'thealquilôk is hauled back with no casualties."

"Casualties were made," Aramis spoke tersely. "Two of my compatriots lay smoldering in those accursed ruins while the rest were dismembered. You expect me to bring them back and set their funeral pyres with a meager stipend?"

"No. I expect the wealth of the ruins to account for those expenses."

"So, they lay without rest."

Korzha cocked an eyebrow at him. "Rest for the dead, from what I understood from those fanatics, is for eternity. They can stand to wait a little while longer." Then he wrote on another slip and sauntered up to Aramis. "Of course, the original payment was meant for six members. This should be plenty for the two of you to do whatever you desire." He waved the parchment at Aramis's face. "Before you set out once more."

After all the horrors, it was all Aramis could bear.

"You can go clear out the ruins yourself. I'm done." Aramis snatched the note from his hands and turned on his heels to leave.

"Pardon?"

"I quit!" Aramis kicked the chair out of his way, not caring that it crashed against the wall.

"So be it," Korzha called out after him. "We're not a charity house for the destitute!"

"Could've fooled me." Aramis leaned back on the threshold frame. "Only the lowest scum of the Earth would think freeing slaves an expense."

Seeing the Töskan steaming brought his heart a small measure of joy. "Take your payment and never return."

"Gladly."

In haste, Aramis sped through the maze-like hallways, passing officers and informants in the tight corridor with ease, not caring about the stares that followed. The treasury office was simply a hall dead-ending into a large metallic door, sealed shut with four levers and two wheels. Guarding the corridor was a little wooden booth covered in colorful doilies of dyed cotton. Pushing his way to the front, Aramis slammed the sorry excuse for a slip down on the stand.

Before the startled accountant could utter a word, he barked, "Fill it out so I can leave this hellhole."

He should've felt sorry for the little lady as she fumbled with the vault wheels without question. It wasn't her fault—hell, it wasn't anyone's fault. But this mockery of a military establishment wasn't helping his mood either. When the two bags full of gold and silver were tied off, he took them without uttering a word of gratitude.

"I'm sorry for your loss," a meek voice spoke.

Aramis glanced back and noticed the accountant had opened the booth door ... and was a satyr. The lady looked minuscule in an oversized tunic with a rough, red robe dragging behind her. Her brown furry legs and glossy hooves cocked inward as she stepped around, her palms clasped to her chest. Huge, black-rimmed spectacles parked halfway down her broad nose. Her large horns swept far back and curled into a Q at her cheeks, like a ram. But it was her eyes that he could not turn away from; red as a rose and just as sweet.

Ashamed, Aramis shied away from her pity and slipped away.

The street vendors had closed shop by the time Aramis emerged from the alleyway entrance. The overcast now orange from the setting sun, creating a dusky, yellow tinge to everything around him. Shifting the pack on his shoulders, Aramis started making his way home when he saw Sister Rhyllae heading his way. She covered her face with a new golden shawl, protecting her from the sand blowing through the marketplace—her pace quickened when she finally spotted him in the crowd, waving an envelope in the air.

"You're back soon," Aramis said. "Does the church need the money that badly?"

"What?" When her brown eyes spotted her earnings in his hand, she waved it aside. "Oh, I don't care about that. I found out my sisters were fulfilling our wills."

"They don't wait around, do they?" Aramis snorted as he pocketed her share.

Sister Rhyllae shook her head. "They were supposed to wait until colonel—"

"General," Aramis corrected. "Tavian Korzha is now a general."

"Well, at last, some good news." Rhyllae smiled until he looked at her like she sprouted two heads. "Someone had to run the operation."

"I would rather have the entire force run by pirates than a man like him."

"Aramis, he's the only one with formal military training."

"He's a Töskan, Rhyllae. They love to decorate their pine trees with their victims' entrails. I wouldn't be surprised to find a spunky recruit with a spruce up his ass for Shab-e Yalda."

The sister of the Morn sighed and shook her head. "Well, as I was saying, my sisters were ordered to wait on General

Korzha to fulfill the will and testaments. Why the Mother Superior would allow such a thing to happen, I don't know. I had to stop them from delivering this—Hey!"

Upon recognizing that the envelope she was waving around had his name on it, Aramis snatched it away from her. "Did you read my will? That information is—"

"Addressed to the survivors of the party. It's from Tamira..." Her face was crestfallen. "Well, was."

Aramis looked at the envelope's face to see it was addressed to each member of Ruth's company. They must have been the only family their dwarven friend had. He gently opened up the letter and read aloud:

To my fellow gut busters,

If I should return to the stone, my only wish is to have all ya lucky bastards drink long and hard for your health. I mean everyone, and that includes you, Sister Ghalédale. I shall be watching from the stone.

Tamira Blackstone.

Aramis kept his head hung low as he folded the letter by its seams. A wish made by the dead is not something to dismiss. No matter how long one yearns for home or the comfort of a lover's arms. What few words of protest were hanging by the edge of his lips fell when he returned Rhyllae's gaze.

"The Iron Lady?"

Dabbing her eyes with her yellow headscarf, Rhyllae could only nod. With his arm around her shoulders, Aramis guided the sniffling priestess down the road, led by the torchers lighting the candled lanterns dotting the main road.

# Chapter 4

## THE IRON LADY

THE IRON LADY. THE ONLY PLACE WHERE EVERYONE could drink their fill and crash upstairs. A popular establishment for the rebels and any sailor that missed the hookah pubs near the docks. The building's entire length was the bar, with racks of stolen spices, wines, mead, ciders, whiskeys, and liquors lined up behind it. A massive barrel of the finest stout was safeguarded at the far end, between the bar and the racks. On the same wall, a fireplace big enough for three burly men to stand abreast blazed. Three black cannon-size cauldrons steamed over the flames while "shut-eye" skillets were blazing red-hot among the embers.

None paid the two any mind when they arrived, which was fine by Aramis. The chair he was looking for was the one by the lone clavichord. It was painted in cream with blue geometric designs and gathering dust for weeks with nary a finger touching its keys until then.

"Bagheera begged me to make this for her," the Silver Fox told Sister Rhyllae as he ran his calloused fingers along the curved side. "Just like how the sylvan elves used to have it. Did you know it took me two months to figure out how to shape this wood alone? And now..." He couldn't find the words, stuck behind the lump in his throat.

Rhyllae placed her hand on his shoulder and laid her head on his arm. "Her music will carry on in our hearts."

"But not on this. At least, not after tonight."

Scooting the bench back, Aramis eased himself in front of the keys. He could never play like their late moon elf, making the black keys bleed, but he was trained long ago during his youth. It was one of the plethora of instruments his former master demanded he play until boredom again took hold. The brass tapped on the gut strings as Aramis stroked the notes from its belly, mingling with the murmurs of the dinner crowd.

Then some blubbering old fool cried out, "Firebird," and cheers erupted.

"Are you serious? Halfway through the song and they're crying out 'Firebird.'" When Bagheera told him she always heard this request, Aramis didn't believe it. Perhaps this was why she wrote what he must do next in her will.

He reached up and yanked down one of the floating lamps. "You want 'Firebird?' Then you shall have it."

The fire trailed the oil as it poured into the painted organ. Strings popped, and the soundboard cracked as it roared into life. Then Aramis ushered Rhyllae far from it, up the stairs. Though she gave him a concerned look, she didn't interfere. For it was indeed what was in Bagheera's will.

At first, only one cried out, "Fire!"

Then they were joined by others waking up from their stupor. Those nearby tried to put it out with their drinks and cloaks, but others cried out to throw it outside instead. Before the flames could lick the walls, two men wrestled the inflamed clavichord from its resting place. Patrons rushed out of the way as they started swinging the instrument in front of the window.

"Not when it's shut, you fools," Bashir, the owner, cried out, ripping out what little hair he had.

Medea, his daughter, crouched by the sill, unlatched the glass panes in the nick of time. Allowing the clavichord to sail through unhindered. Broken wood and popped strings sounded as it crumpled outside. Then they heard a cackle that grew into a full belly laugh. Everyone swiveled their heads to Aramis sitting on a step, wiping a tear from his eye as he quieted his laughter.

"Of course, it would be you to incite mischief and mayhem." Clara, the barkeep's wife, threw her towel on the floor. "Silver Fox, indeed."

A great clamor broke out as soon as the name left her lips. Many were happy that members of Ruth's company came home. Others were mystified—what happened to the rest? A miserable few returned to their drinks. Grumbling about what new terror the Silver Fox would inflict on the under-market trade.

"Well, it's about time you graced us with your presence," a red-haired youth spoke above the crowd, his pocked face smiling as he waved his mug high over the people. "Too long have you dared to mingle with us lowly common folk."

Aramis peered through the crowd and spotted the red-headed youth. "If that's you, Falçion, you can trade places with me. I would gladly drink and smoke to my early grave than face another dragon's maw."

"Well, get your ass over here—if you still can."

Smiling at Sister Rhyllae, Aramis led her to the bar. The faithful Jessenter guard was working on his third ale by the time they arrived. Every night before his shift, Falçion could be seen in his corner, a smoldering cigar in his left hand and his favorite stein in his right. Aramis could always trust him to know everyone and everything in the rebels—and then some.

As soon as the two sat down, Bashir gave them their usual: honey wine for Rhyllae and Mynx coffee for Aramis.

"How's the general, by the way?" Falçion asked between puffs.

"Alive, sadly," Aramis quipped. Rhyllae swatted his arm and gave him a scolding look.

*If only she knew...*

"I heard someone beat you to it. Well, tried."

"Who?"

"Lieutenant Nazir."

Foam sputtered over the counter as Aramis gagged. "That gutless pig?"

"Perhaps not as gutless as you like to think." The pock-faced guard drew back before continuing, smoke escaping through his nostrils. "Did it on the general's first night back, he did, with nothing more than a toothpick of a blade."

"Why would he do such a thing?" Rhyllae asked.

"Why not?" Aramis interjected.

"What is with you tonight?"

"Let us say I've been ... emancipated from their services."

Aramis tried not to look at the sister as he helped mop up his mess, but he could feel the daggers shooting at him. He glanced quickly at Falçion, his ruddy eyebrows raised high on his forehead.

"You have three counts to clear," Rhyllae spoke too loudly for his liking, "and you left?"

"The man is heartless as stone."

"Do you know what they will do to you if you stop right now?"

"What is done is done. I'm not going back."

"Aramis..." Rhyllae pinched her nose and rested her elbow on the bar.

Aramis waved his hands out wide before he clasped them. "The Jessenters can't be my only option. There are other ways to 'serve.' Right?"

"You can always join the abbey," Falçion jested as he puffed on his cigar.

"Oh, I would pay to see you in that getup." Then Bashir placed five mugs on the counter between Rhyllae and Aramis.

"I didn't order this," Aramis said.

"I did." Rhyllae put the coin in the barkeep's hand, her face still in a stormy disposition.

Placing a hand on hers, Aramis spoke in a lower tone. "I'll find a way to pay for my crimes. Promise."

Before another word could be spoken, the door burst open. Several people, adorned with the same red sash, marched in, carrying casks of nectar and alcoholic delights. Others brought in bushels of fruit and caskets of herbs for smoking. They took it all straight to the cellar under the stairs. The last one brought in an enormous ale barrel— bigger than what was wedged away in the Iron Lady. Yet, it was who was carrying it that boggled the mind. A woman, no taller than Sister Rhyllae, cradled the giant barrel on her back without a tremor in her lean muscles.

Leaning back, the Jessenterian woman slipped the giant barrel by the bar, quaking the entire establishment as soon as it landed. She waved at the patrons, who were busy gawking like fish on dry land.

"Where did y'all get this from?" Clara asked with her palms stuck to her cheeks.

"From our most generous Djinnasi neighbors," the lady spoke gaily. She unfurled the turban that covered her entire face, revealing sandy blonde hair and sunbaked skin.

The young woman hopped up on the bar to address the whole tavern. "Wenches and wretches, we plundered the Glass Plain Caravan." Everyone roared in delight. "All of the goods have been equally divided among the food stores, pubs, and taverns. No favors, Bashir. Everyone's gotta have their share. All medicines have been given to the Abbey of the Rising Dawn." Rhyllae hooted in approval. "And drinks are on me!"

The entire tavern burst into song and dance as she took a crowbar in hand. Flinging off the pried board as the greedy patrons clamored around with their raised hands—Falçion included.

Clara yanked on the lady's trousers. "What would be ye name for the tab?"

"Lieutenant Dawn," she answered once she switched out with Bashir.

"That can't be your last name." Clara put her hands on her hips.

"It's not." Falçion put his arm around the woman's shoulders. "Her true name is Lady Lover. And you best keep your knickers on guard."

The bar owner's wife sputtered as Dawn gave her a wink. Soon she stomped to the back, muttering, "There goes the neighborhood."

As soon as she left, the surrounding patrons filled the void. Many patted the lieutenant on the back. Others shook her hand. One person handed her a cigar from the stash and lit it for her. Then Aramis found himself being passed one as well. Tonight's crowd is in a celebratory mood, despite the calamity that had befallen prior. Or, perhaps, it was because of such horrors that they looked for any excuse for such an escape. Aramis smelled the length of the cigar: hints of chocolate and cranberry. The finest fare hailed from across the ocean, Valentra.

"That's bad for your health." Sister Rhyllae tried to snatch the lethal stick from him.

"How could a bit of smoked herb be bad for you?" Aramis shimmied to Falçion's seat with his boot propped on his prior occupation. Safely out of reach, he struck the match. The flame sputtered out as soon as he tipped the slender cigarette in it.

At the corner of his eye, he saw her thin eyebrows flatten into a line over her honey eyes. "You'll die if you keep that up."

"Faster than a blade?" he said as he tried again. But the flame flickered out when Rhyllae knocked his boot off the stool. "Rhyllae, I'm not going to leave you anytime soon."

"Hopefully not before I get to say 'hi' first." The strong woman stepped in. Her smile shone brightly against her tanned skin. She kindly lit Aramis's cigarette with her cigar. "Name's Dawn."

Aramis Feres took a long draw from the lit cigarette. "The name's Feres, and this here is Sister Ghalédale, but I call her Rhyllae."

Rhyllae scowled when he accidentally blew the smoke in her face, swatting it away as Aramis gave a sheepish smile as an apology.

"I know—I mean, I'm a big fan of your work." Dawn gave a nervous grin.

"My work? By the Sleeper. One month away, and they're martyring me."

Rhyllae cleared her throat at him, and he shrugged as he showed his hands.

"You must've lived under a rock, sir," Dawn said. "You've been renowned by many here for years."

"Depends who you talk to. I prefer to keep to myself and not to be called 'sir' by anyone."

That raised a chuckle from Rhyllae. "You may join us. We're about to drink for our friends."

Dawn looked around. "Are they late coming in?"

The question was enough to knock the wind out of Aramis's sails. He turned to face the back of the bar, not knowing what to say to a complete stranger. Should he tell her the terrible news so she could join their miserable company? Would it be wrong to let her carry their burden? Should he lie for her sake, one who seemed to idolize them much? However, doing so would be a disservice to their friends by not recognizing their death. Try as he might, he could not find a way out of the situation.

Rhyllae gave him a warm touch on his arm, drawing him out of his thoughts. "They're not here right now, Dawn. They fell at M'thealquilôk."

The young officer's smile was dashed. "Damn. Er … my condolences to you both." Dawn looked at the set of tankards in front of them with puzzlement.

"Our dwarven friend, Tamira, wished for us to have a wake in her honor."

"A drinking competition?" Falçion, who was not at all eavesdropping on their conversation, bellowed. Before they could do anything, he whistled at the whole room. "Hey! There's a drink off. Who will win? Sister Rhyllae Ghalédale or Aramis Feres? Everyone, place your bets."

Everyone stopped what they were doing and stared at the two at the bar. Then, one by one, people start naming their bets. Some bet on paying for the next tab or their next meal. Others went for the gold, others for silver. So far, the Silver Fox is in favor.

Aramis squinted at the redheaded youth. "Was that necessary?"

"Don't look at me. My money's on you." Falçion started counting the coins in his purse to see how much he could spare.

Aramis sighed and drew the last bit of his smoke before he flicked it away. Taking the steins, he kicked his stool out from underneath himself and led Rhyllae to a nearby table.

As Falçion called out the rules of engagement from a comfy seat, Aramis quietly withdrew a tiny paper bindle from a small pocket in his left cuff. Hiding it underneath his right fingers, he gently opened the bindle with his thumb. He casually laced her drinks as he pretended to arrange the steins between the two of them, right under everyone's noses. When he finally completed the underhanded task, he put his hands on his hips. Then secured the paper bindle under his belt.

The mention of clean, good fun from the soldier made him smirk. *Too late for that.*

He knew cheating was wrong, but he wanted to do this in private. Now that it was out in the open for all to see, his pride could not allow himself to lose without making the playing field level between them. If it was an ordinary man competing against a common woman, the man would win. But this was Sister Rhyllae.

The priestess of the Morn could draw out any poison from any wound and never shied from the gory mess to save their lives. She alone withstood the devastating maladies that inflicted them during their trek through the Anglorian jungle. No, Rhyllae, in Aramis's eye, was no ordinary woman, which required him to have a handicap.

Aramis gave a wink to Dawn, who was holding her own tankard. She blushed as she betted on him to be the victor. Sister Rhyllae eyed Aramis for his teasing. He held up his foamy mug, waiting for her to clank against it to start them off.

"Ready?" Aramis asked.

"Ready." She gave a swift clank and swigged the drink in one motion.

Aramis took his time as she gulped down the stuff. She coughed and sputtered, her eyes almost bulged, and her olive face took an unusual red color. Aramis prayed that she wasn't allergic to his concoction.

But no, she made a face of disgust. "How can you drink this?"

He tried not to laugh as he gulped the rest of his drink. "Ready to call it quits?"

Rhyllae harrumphed at his statement and finished the rest of her drink. Aramis expected her to start feeling woozy any minute, but she stood resolute. They paused while everyone exchanged bets, then they started again.

*This time, she should start feeling it.*

But he was wrong; she didn't sway or flush at all. Truth be told, the sister scrunched up her button nose as she stuck her tongue out.

*Adorable.* The thought flickered through his mind. Aramis shook himself awake. *My wife would kill me for that.*

When Rhyllae finally opened her eyes, she laughed at him with great delight. "You're getting red, Aramis."

*Uh-oh.*

Aramis knew he was not as stout as any man; he was ashamed to admit that he could barely keep two pints.

Already, his fingers and tongue were starting to feel numb. The heat was bothering him, and he loosened his ragged scarf.

Yet, there she was, dandy as a spring chicken. Aramis knew for sure he had laced her drinks. One cup of the substance was enough to make a man groggy. Two were enough to knock someone of her size right out. His concoction always worked, his life depended on it.

He observed her as they took on their third bout. There was nothing out of place he could detect. No prayer was muttered to purify her drink, which would have canceled out his powder. No finger waggling to pull off any spell. Her clothing looked relatively normal. By all rights, Rhyllae should have passed out, and her looking unfazed was irritating him. With three rounds gone, Aramis leaned heavily on the table, his face flushed.

"How could you possibly be fine after all that?" he slurred.

Rhyllae shrugged. "I'm blessed with good constitution?"

The drinks took a while to come to their table, letting some furiously switch their bets. Now she was the expected victor of the night. Only a few, including Dawn, kept with Aramis.

Rhyllae absent-mindedly pulled out an amulet from underneath her robes. It was a lovely necklace of red jasper flanked with two fangs on a long, dark cord. As he gazed upon it, he realized it was a periapt of some sort.

He tilted his head like a confused puppy. "Rhyllae? When did you get that?"

"Oh? This old thing?" she waggled the stone between her fingers. "The Magionni shaman gave this to me a few years back, remember?"

Aramis racked his befuddled brain. He knew it was no simple trinket for decoration. Dozens of necklaces were used to ward off evil or to fight against ailments. Could this be one of them?

The bartender finally slammed the next set of tankards down. Without forethought, he downed it as he flipped through his mental archive of precious items and their history. It finally dawned on him.

"You're cheating," he slurred, pointing his finger right at the tip of her nose.

"What?" Her honey-brown eyes were wide in disbelief.

"That there is a periapt against poison. I demand a redo." He twirled around, pointing up toward the ceiling.

Somehow, he tripped over himself and fell on someone's table. Cold drinks and hot soup flew as the table flipped over. One soup in particular sailed across the room and landed on the lap of a minotaur mercenary. Like a tiny spark landing on a powder keg, the reaction was explosive.

# Chapter 5

## THE POWDER KEG

THE SICKLE FACE OF LUNE WANED IN THE INKY void of the night, providing little comfort to Dido as she made her way back to the underground base. Then again, she was a satyr who didn't care for any excitement. Neither did she care for the desert conditions. The air was too dry and gritty, making her nose itch insufferably. And the sand. An absolute nightmare for her furry legs.

Yet, a life debt is a life debt.

Thirteen years of service, far from home, in a quiet job as an accountant, were not unbearable for a fae. It provided her with the means to escape the Bramble Court and their cruel machinations, as well as granting her protection from the Djinnasi's magi assassins. No, not unbearable for her for such a life among these mortals. So long as she kept her magic a secret, Dido could exist in that space in peace.

Traipsing down into the base, Dido took care not to bang the long box's end against the steps behind her. She scurried along with the twists and turns toward the general's office until her acute hearing picked up something unexpected this late in the hour—a conversation.

Dido froze, her heart pumping faster than a hare's. Standing there, she found none of the voices sounded like Korzha's. As she inched toward the conversation, she heard metal scraping on metal. In the direction that would lead to the vault.

Panic ran through her heart, and she gripped the delicate package a little tighter. Despite the comforts provided, the Jessenters had a traitor in their midst. What if another was there? What if they brought friends? Or worse, called by that nefarious tome brought by the Silver Fox. Try as she may, she couldn't convince the new general to eliminate the terrible thing.

The metal scraping continued to echo. Cursing her loyal heart, she ran toward her office, taking the package with her. Tiptoeing around the last bend, she found there was indeed a group of men clamoring around her office door. They must have been mercenaries-for-hire by the looks of their attire, foreign to the region, and a bit slipshod. Dido gently put the box of flowers down next to her. She felt her knees knocking together, and her hands started sweating.

*Oh, I really hate this. Why can't someone else do this? I haven't done this in a while. What if I mess up?* Then Dido shook her head. *No. You've got to do this, Dido. There's no one else here to stop them.*

As she peeked around the corner, Dido gave a nervous squeak and slammed her back against the wall. Over and over in her mind, she rambled, *I'm a coward. I'm a coward.*

Finally, she calmed down and mustered enough strength to hop around the corner. Dido pointed her finger at them, exclaiming, "St-st-stop it right there!"

They looked straight across with puzzled faces. Then they looked at her. She had thought there were only three of them inside her cramped office, but she realized she was wrong when she noted five heads looking back at her through the booth's door. Her knees start knocking again as they start unsheathing their swords and daggers.

But she managed to continue on, "Don't come-come any closer or I-I-I—"

"Or you will what, Little Bo Peep? Ya gonna blow the house down?" a gaunt, slender man taunted.

"Yeah, or bleat at us to death?" another spoke up. He looked crossbred between an ogre and a troll with his large hands and twisted face. The rest of the men chuckled darkly, making her heart a little faint.

"Or maybe you would like to join us and give us a good ol' time?" a broad-jawed brute asked with a malicious grin.

"Mmmmm. I do like 'em lamb chops." A bald dwarf stepped forward, his battleax ready to swing at a moment's notice. He licked his lips as if he saw her as tonight's dinner.

They inch toward her, one by one—the goons cackling to themselves, thinking of her as a mere toy to play with.

Dido froze for a moment or two, then she closed her eyes. Looking deep within, Dido recited phrases as ancient as time itself. Words of creation and flame. When she flicked her eyelids open, they were lit with determination.

"Or I'll incinerate you all."

When they laughed, her eyes locked onto her mark. Dido adjusted her finger centered at her desk and let her spell fly. A tiny molten marble sailed over their heads like a lone bird in the sky. The thugs looked on with their mouths hung open, like a carp out of water. None of them had a chance.

Dido ducked behind the wall before it landed. The roar of flames rushing forth stifled their surprised screams. The heat baked the wall behind her, and the flames licked around the bend. In a few seconds, the fire dissipated. Leaving behind five smoldering corpses with their bones showing through the charred surface. What had once been clay mud was now baked stone. What was wood and cloth became cinders. Farther down, she saw the vault's metal door welded in its frame. Misshapen and warped like a circus mirror.

"Oops," Dido whispered as she took off her glasses. It had, indeed, been a while.

Dangling off a meat hook by his ankles in the storage basement was not what Aramis had imagined when he suggested the Iron Lady. He figured it would be a couple of drinks, some good wishes, then off into the starry night to claim the sweet comfort he so desired.

From the flying soup to dangling here, the memories came in a blur. Most of it was due to drinking, the rest because of the raucous stirred up by the minotaur. Despite Dawn using half a table as a shield, she couldn't deflect the man flung toward the trio. And Aramis, unlocking the door under the stairs, was struck from behind like a marble at the back of the line. That part he remembered well. If he hadn't known how to do aerial dancing, Aramis wouldn't have been quick enough to secure himself on the meat hook.

Curling up, he switched to his hand, rotating himself to scan the place. The silver light from his eyes, somehow free from his mask, revealed all the smoked meats and herbs hanging next to him. Crates of the stolen goods the Jessenters brought were piled high against the walls, barricading the way out.

"Oh, give me a break," Aramis grumbled.

"Gladly," replied a deep voice.

The next thing he knew, something slammed into his back. A grunt escaped him as he met the floor. An inhale alerted him that another powerful hit was coming at him from above. Aramis commanded his aching spine to bend backward on the floor. Dust flew into his face as two burly fists hit the ground, inches from his nose. Through the dust, Aramis saw shining green eyes staring back at him.

Aramis swung his legs far behind his opponent's head. Crossing his ankles to create a vise-like hold on his thick neck. Then he pushed off the ground and sat on his shoulders.

"Enough," Aramis cried. "I'll let go if you—gah!"

The burly man lifted him into the air with ease, swinging him backward, slamming them both on the stone floor. Aramis grunted as he felt the air escape his lungs. The strong man hoped to dislodge him from the suffocating grip, but he never let go. Instead, Aramis brought his left ankle around and behind his right thigh—a tighter and less-forgiving hold for his dancing partner. The man squirmed in a panic, gasping for air.

"If you give up now, I'll release you," Aramis told him. "Tap me if you've had enough."

The short, burly man grabbed at his knees, futilely trying to tear Aramis's iron hold off of his neck. Aramis couldn't believe that this man would refuse to give up. This strongman would die for the sake of pride.

"Tap!"

Three slaps against his thigh later and Aramis quickly released him. As the man hacked and wheezed for breath, Aramis found he wasn't a stout, burly human—but a Dwarven man of the Gallileah mountains. By the looks of his dreads and his flat, broad nose, he was the same dwarf who had the minotaur pinned against the wall earlier.

The dwarf coughed for air on all fours for a little while, then he chuckled. "By me lady's beard, never had anyone put me in that position before."

Aramis smirked. "Clearly, you never have tangled sheets with a jhasin."

The dwarf looked up at him with awe, never expecting to meet a former harem boy. He laughed mightily. "Oh, is that so? If that's how Djinnasi make love, I would hate to see how they dance a jig."

"Poorly." Aramis offered his hand to lift the dwarf up.

The dwarf clasped his arm and eased himself off the floor. "Name's Lockjaw."

"Aramis."

"Yer shitting me, the great Silver Fox himself?" Lockjaw's bearded jaw dropped. Then he burst out with a belly full of laughter. "I better be careful who I drink with now. Would hate to ruin yer reputation with our little … dance." He then gave a wink.

"Hate to ruin yours, Lockjaw."

A thunder of footsteps roared above them. Sure enough, three of the city guard, the watch, rushed down, their chain-mail gleaming from their torchlight. Aramis nudged his new-found friend to raise his arms as the three surrounded them.

"Why am I not surprised to see you here, Feres," said the watchman with a filigree hammered into the metal of his armor.

Aramis squinted against the torch's glaring light. "Just having a good brawl, Tristan."

"Captain Tristan. I'd appreciate it if you recognize my rank once in a while."

"Oh, excuse me, I forgot you were the elders' peon. Tell me again, how much are they paying you to kiss their ass?"

Tristan grabbed his collar with one hand and lifted him up to his gilded helm. "I have a special room reserved just for you."

"Put it on a rain check."

Swift as a leopard, Aramis yanked the visor down. As expected, Tristan released his hold on him, allowing him to crouch low on the ground. Aramis knocked the captain back into his fellow watchmen with a spinning kick.

One of them managed to pull himself out of the dog pile, but his head was knocked back by Lockjaw's forehead on his way upstairs.

Light-footed, Aramis danced off of their armor to follow. Halfway up, he felt his foot pulled from underneath him, knocking his chin on the step in front of him as he fell. It was Tristan, his ironclad gauntlet wrapped around his ankle. There was no way Aramis could shake him off as he pulled down on him hard. Managing to dislodge him from the stairway, they tumbled to the floor together. Two lackeys sped past to chase down Lockjaw.

Landing on him, Aramis brought both fists together and hammered them onto Tristan's helm. Instead of seeing him wilt underneath him, Tristan growled and threw him to the floor. Rolling on top of him, he let him kiss his knuckles—twice.

In a brawl, there's a choice one makes—spill blood or admit defeat. Often Aramis chose the former for the sake of being a free man. But that night, he raised his hands above his head and gave in to the dizzying stars. Imprisonment was not the worst thing in the world. He knew that now. With a snap of Tristan's fingers, one of the watchmen came to his call. They lifted Aramis off the floor, having him trail behind Lockjaw, who was smiling ear to ear.

As they were carried up, he whispered to Aramis, "Ye get around, don'tcha?"

"Ms. Dido?" a crisp voice called out behind her.

It made her jump out of her skin, and she shrieked. She spun around on her hooves, holding out her two index fingers and thumbs in the shape of an *L*. Luckily, she didn't let out a single spell before she realized it was the general himself standing there.

Dido straightened herself out, embarrassed about how she presented herself in such a manner to him. "Oh. Good evening, sir."

Korzha cocked an eyebrow at the lady satyr. "Pray tell me, how is it a good evening if we're being robbed?"

Dido cleared her throat while hopping from one hoof to another. "Well, as you can see, the robbers have been vanquished by the ... trap that I had laid while I was away. Yes. There was no expense on the account since it was ... donated. Yes, donated by the um ... ah..."

Her voice trailed off as Korzha unsheathed the rapier by his left hand, a detail she didn't miss. It must have been an enchanted sword, for the silver blade sang in the air as he approached the nearby corpses.

"Have you ever dealt with the inmorti before, Madam?"

"No, sir. I must say I have not."

"Then, I hope you never will." Korzha stabbed through the eye socket into the brain of the burned cadaver. "It is a nasty business. The 'dead that walk' are the most difficult to take down. One must be swift with every stroke lest they become one of them. Especially when facing one that used to be your colleague." After scrambling the organ with the tip of his fine blade, he gave Dido an icy glance. "Now, are you done spinning your yarn, magi, or would you prefer to cast it on the loom?"

The little satyr gulped. "Why, yes. I did use … um … well…"

"Arcana," Korzha responded dryly.

"You're not surprised?"

"The late General Tackett had mentioned you in the confidential files as part of the company's bargain with the fae."

"Well, not the whole fae, just me." Dido let out a nervous laugh.

Bidding her to continue, Korzha moved to each corpse, stabbing them as he listened to her tale. And told a tale, she did. Through her nervous energy, she gave every detail she could muster: what occurred, the actions taken, and why she had made her decisions. As she spoke, she found Korzha was perhaps the most patient of all the generals she had ever worked for.

"What of their armor?" Korzha enquired.

"It was simple, worn," she said. "Patched by metal straps. They seemed to brand their leather with an eye high on a scepter."

Korzha made a simple nod with a thin scowl on his face. He must've heard of them before. He tapped the vault door with the pommel of his enchanted rapier.

"And the necromancer's book?" he asked.

"Locked inside the vault, sir."

"Knowing your skill set, I hope you have unearthed the book's contents?"

Dido looked down at her hooves. "I can't. The tome can be only opened by 'hands that deal wicked deeds.' General, this… Nothing good can come from this."

The general gave a frustrated sigh as he sheathed his singing sword. "We're at war. Nothing good ever comes from the hand we are dealt. I need you to relocate the treasure and hide it properly this time. I shall rally a more vigilant watch for our quarters."

"Excuse me, sir, but I can't open the vault without resorting to extreme measures."

"Then acquire a detonation specialist. The sooner we bring ruin to the Djinnasi, the better."

Her shoulders sagged. "Yes, sir. Oh, I almost forgot." Dido skirted past the slain villains and returned with the package. "As you ordered. One pink gladiolus stem."

Slipping off the pale-blue ribbon, Korzha uncovered the box to reveal a three-foot-long stem with flowers the size of his fists trailing into a diminutive cluster. It looked like a sword with the bottom portion of the stem left bare. And the flowers, making the blade, looked like swords them-selves; they had three large petals arranged in a trinity with two secondary petals like a hilt. The gladiolus was a rare iris symbolizing strength, courage, and a warrior's death.

"The Mother Superior would thank you, madam, for obtaining this for the ritual." Korzha took the delicate package in his slender hands.

Dido smiled a little. "Happy to help, sir. When are they planning to hold the ceremony?"

"The local's Sabbath."

"May I ask… Why do you keep this vigil every year?"

"No, you may not." And the general closed the lid shut.

Fortune must have been smiling upon them that night. Of all the eye sockets he had pierced, the new general had man-aged to miss one. The one enchanted by a magical lens by fey magic. The one being scried by them.

They, who resided deep in the catacombs, where two braziers blaze and a lone stone sarcophagus lies between them. Where a corpse, still in her silent scream pose, upon it. There, they sat, musing and cackling at this turn of events, as they held the scrying orb aloft. To think all was considered a loss when the greedy fools found the vault instead of the general. Indeed, it was what mother had always said, 'there's a silver lining to every mushroom cloud.'

"How considerate to offer another alternative for your rebel's demise, Korzhy. A necromancer's tome? That only wicked hands can open?" they asked aloud, for no one dares venture this deep down where they were.

The corpse on the sarcophagus gave no comment save for the terror fixed upon them, her perpetual death mask. Her arms raised in feeble self-defense with curled, bony fingers.

"Well, thank you for the sweet compliment. One should always be true to themselves."

# Chapter 6

## PROMISES

THE IRON LADY LOOKED AS IF A HURRICANE blasted through. Tables were overturned with cutlery, knives, or whatnot pinned to their surface. Aramis and Lockjaw were led out into the open night sky, where a wagon stuffed full of bruised-face patrons was parked. Through the barred window, Dawn smiled broadly and flashed two fingers with an extended thumb. One of the numerous victory signals of the phoenix.

Lockjaw was in the wagon when Rhyllae, holding a bandage in her hand, hustled out of the Iron Lady. "Captain, you don't have a reason to jail him."

"I have every reason to lock a scum like him away." Tristan did, however, slam the door behind Lockjaw, leaving Aramis out of the wagon.

"You made a promise."

"Causing a public brawl is not part of the list, Sister Ghaledale."

"But a private one would," Aramis quipped.

As Tristan glared at Aramis from under his helm, Rhyllae mouthed at Aramis to stay quiet. Then went mum when the captain turned around. Her cheeks puffed out as she stifled her grin when she caught Aramis miming what the captain would say next.

"I know you believe every soul needs saving," Captain Tristan said, "but this two-time, despicable, son-of-a-whore—"

"Needs all the help we can give," she finished for him. "He is, after all, the Silver Fox. And free for employment."

"Is that so?"

"He's ... retired. Aramis is a resourceful man and knowledgeable about the common folk. He'll be a good asset for the watch."

"You'd have me hire a criminal to give watch?"

"Who watches the watchers?" Aramis interjected. "Besides, there may be some deadbeats that need a good shaking down."

The captain removed his helm and groaned as he pinched between his eyes. Then, at last, he spoke. "So be it. I have a task for you, and you alone. Report to me before this week is done."

Then he snapped his fingers, and the two men released Aramis and mounted their horses. Before the wagon pulled away, Lockjaw called out to him, "If ye ever need me, head to the Salt & Battery. That be me shop."

"I can't wait to see it with my own eyes," Aramis said.

They clasped hands, then parted as the wagon rolled off into the heart of the city. He half expected Rhyllae to stay and chat, but she turned and left.

"I take it you're on healing duty?" Aramis asked, following her back into the bar.

"That or go to jail? Yes," the sister quipped as she returned to the man she had been mending before.

Aramis slowly nodded as he watched her wrap the remaining cloth tightly into a ball. It irritated him that Rhyllae kept her back to him as she moved to the next patient. Looking down at his feet, he flipped one of the knives over with the toe of his boot.

"General Korzha would love to hear they're jailing his people," Aramis commented.

"That and when he hears you're the one who started all of this."

"Me? I didn't start this."

"Please, Aramis. You were the one who tossed the soup." She snugged the knot on the man, making him wince.

"I tripped." He kicked the knife away.

Aramis looked her over as she hastily healed the patient's nicks and bruises, ignoring his wincing. This was not the first bar fight they went through together. In all those times, never had Aramis seen her this upset over such a ruckus. Then it dawned on him.

"You're mad that I caught you red-handed."

"What? I wasn't cheating."

Aramis laughed as he shook his head. "You were wearing it the whole time."

"I didn't know what it was."

"You never suspected? Now, I find that hard to believe."

"I would never dishonor our friends to save face."

"There's always a first time." The words slipped through his lips before he could stop them.

Rhyllae looked like he had smacked her with a brick. "Would you?"

Aramis felt a pang of guilt in his heart. It was true, he wouldn't deny it. He was so caught up in winning the competition that he had forgotten the original purpose. Yet, he couldn't find the words to say that.

He didn't need to. Aramis could see the realization dawning in her gold-flecked, brown eyes as the answer hung in the air.

"Rhyllae," he said when she turned her back on him.

"Go home." The words stabbed him right through.

He almost reached out to touch her, to explain himself, but the damage was done. Aramis left without another word, leaving the Iron Lady behind.

"This will cool your heels." The city guard pushed Dawn into her cell.

The rough handling didn't bother her. This was not the first time she had been thrown into the brig; decking her fellow officer for cheating at cards, roughhousing, and sneaking in ale for the recruits were the tip of the iceberg on her record. However, this was the first time she had been jailed in there.

Dawn, the last one rounded up, was transferred to the city watch instead of the brig. The difference between the two prisons was hardly noticeable. Both were made of stone walls with iron bars that enclose the cells save for one minor difference. The city's was made entirely of solid limestone— no clay to dig oneself out if anyone would dare.

Not that Dawn would. The way she figured, this was a perfect time to exercise. Shrugging her shoulders into circles, she found they were not too sore from the fight. With the end of her boot, she dragged the cot to the center for her pushups.

"Who's there?" a man's voice called from across the way. A shambled figure leaned against the bars, torn and bloody. "Dawn? What are you doing here?"

"Mudhi?" It took a while to recognize him, but there was no denying it once Dawn looked past the swollen lip. "Guess the bar fight was too good to pass, huh?" she smiled at him.

"Bar fight?"

"At the Iron Lady. I admit I took a few good licks myself. Without returning a few." She gave him a wink, but he didn't seem to care.

"Iron lady? I haven't had a drink in a while..."

"A while? How long have you been here?"

"A couple of weeks? I've lost count. One moment, I was minding my own business, then next—wham—I was jumped by the watch."

"The watch doesn't jump people for kicks, Mudhi. What the hell did you do?"

"Nothing." When Dawn squinted her hazel eyes, Mudhi sputtered, "They keep saying I tried to kill the general. But I didn't do it. I wasn't there."

"You were with Marilyn, right?"

Mudhi hung his head low. "She refused to even see me here."

"Why would she unless... No, you didn't." When he looked away, Dawn banged her fist against the iron bars, making them chime like a bell. "You son of a bitch. I hitched the two of you together, and you pull this shit?"

"I know, I hate myself—"

"Shut up. Who?"

Mudhi paled. "What? No, you can't know."

"For Marilyn's sake, you better give up their name."

"He'll... He'll kill me."

"You're dead meat anyway for being called a traitor. If you were with them that night, you have an alibi, Mudhi. Look, I won't tell anyone, I promise."

"No. Promises won't do me good. Not with who will be after me. You must swear that you tell no one."

*Crap.*

Breaking an oath made under the Morning Lord is condemnable for any soul. But she had no choice. The idiot would get himself hung if he kept this up. How could she face Marilyn when that happened?

"Fine. I swear by the golden crown of the Morning Lord, I won't tell anyone." *And help me keep my word*, she mentally interjected. "Now, who are they?"

Mudhi Nazir nodded in approval and told Dawn the full name.

Dawn's eyes widened in surprise. *Oh, by the Morning Lord's shiny ass, he is a dead man!*

The clouds parted, allowing the starry night to illuminate the sand-ridden road. Vendors were now replaced by beggars coughing for alms. One by one, Aramis silently dropped bits of silver in their tins like a nameless phantom. Aramis pulled his cloak tighter around himself, remembering how it used to be, cold, hungry, with a gutter to call home. Blessings and promises don't fill an aching belly.

*If I can make it, they can make it, too*, Aramis consoled himself. *They just need to hold on.*

Aramis gazed at each passing window, looking for the basket of roses that would mark his home. Taking off his right glove, he ran his fingertips over the limestone as he passed. Pockmarked and worn by decades of sand, wind, and rain. He knew every crevice at his fingertips, as he did on her skin. Aramis closed his eyes, remembering every freckle, dimple, and curve of her body. Oh, how his body ached.

Aramis took off the other glove, massaging the finger adorned with the golden band. The moonlight revealed every scratch and ding etched these past three years. Clenching his fist tight, he kissed the ring. He'll make it up to her tonight.

The apartment building was no different from all other residences: built with limestone—plain and rectangular. A small set of stairs ran up to the front door with an wrought iron sign hung in the corner toward him. The sign creaked in the wind, humbly displaying "Eagle's Nest Apartments." Behind it would be their window, with roses as red as blood in a basket and gossamer curtains floating out to the night. Within, awaiting his return, was his one and only safe-guarded treasure, Vanessa.

Yet, no curtains floated in the moonlight sky. Aramis was taken aback. The roses she always watered were nothing but black stalks.

He dropped his gloves. *She cannot be...*

Fearing the worst, he ran up the side of the building and leaped up to the creaking sign. Swinging from the placard to the rose basket, he pulled himself to the windowsill.

Peering into the darkness, he found the bed they shared stripped bare. The walls were naked of the pictures and curtains that used to hang there. All the rugs they had on the floor had disappeared. Two pieces of furniture were left: a dresser, the attached mirror reflecting the waning moon, and a pedestal table with something bound on top.

Aramis's heart sank as he silently crept toward the table. There before him was parchment, covered by several weeks' worth of dust.

*She cannot be dead. Not her. Not Vanessa.*

His hands trembled as he slipped off the red ribbon, the same ribbon she used to wear, and unfolded the paper.

Scrolled in elegant writing, Aramis found something worse than death:

> *I, Mother Superior Frianul, free the bonds of matrimony on the two souls, Aramis Feres and Vanessa Magionni, on the twenty-third day of Ikthal in the year of the Wasting Moon. The separation of the two is based on gross negligence on the husband's part. The duties he hath not fulfilled are as follows:*

Aramis couldn't read beyond that point.

*This is insane! A hoax!*

But the words were there, stained in the fibers of the parchment. Stained like his name. Aramis gazed at the dark, dusty room around him. Happy memories of care and devotion were gone like a spring breeze.

*This must be a dream. This can't be happening.*

Sinking to his knees, he clasped the table to steady himself.

*Why?* Squeezing his eyes shut, he held his breath.

Aramis could recall the first day they had met. Vanessa twirling near the tribe's fire. Her laughter and cymbals bewitched him, body and soul.

*O, Sleeper, why?* He looked up, tears escaping down his cheek.

Her vivid green eyes elated on their first night together.

*I had loved you with my whole being.* Aramis blinked away the tears, looking down at the golden band on his finger.

He was so nervous during their wedding that he'd spilled most of the water on his knees instead of her feet. Her laughter had soothed him.

Aramis took off his wedding band. *Was it all for nothing?*

The wear-worn jewelry provided nothing but a promise. A promise that was broken.

"Is there nothing sacred anymore?!" Aramis hurled the golden band across the room. Shattering Lune's pretty face in the mirror.

Voices stirred from the hallway and the room next to him. He had overstayed his welcome.

In his haste, the table tipped and fell over. Aramis grabbed the wedding band before he slipped out of the window. From the windowsill, he hopped to the corner sign outside. Then he hesitated before dropping down, so his boots wouldn't sound. Then he ducked around the corner.

After a few breaths, he felt the sharp pain in his hand. Opening his fist, he saw his wedding ring, mingled with broken shards of glass that were piercing into his skin. Gingerly, he picked out the glass, letting them fall to the ground like tears. Once free, he forced the ring on to the finger on his right hand, despite the dent. It was a poor fit, but it would have to do. He needed answers, and dawn was fast approaching.

Aramis headed down the boulevard. Not minding the gloves left in the gutter.

# Chapter 7

## THE ABBEY OF THE RISING DAWN

THE NIGHT WAS CHILLY FOR THE MORNING priestess as she headed back to her cloister. Rhyllae pulled the yellow shawl tighter around her, mulling over the words Aramis had said. Her fingers lingered on the jasper necklace.

*It's still not my fault.*

The thought did little to comfort her. What would their long-gone compatriots think of their sad display of respect? How dare Aramis cheat in the first place? Then again, should she be surprised that he had done such a thing?

When they first met, Aramis worked for a sleazy merchant, Pondo Rhum. He was doing all sorts of underhanded tasks, from smuggling to blackmail, usually restocking Rhum's wares by stealing their competitor's inventory. When she asked him why, Aramis stated that freeing slaves didn't pay the bills.

Yet, there were lines one couldn't cross.

On that fateful night, he had discovered that they were selling people into slavery, even the ones who were once freed from such shackles. Aramis slaughtered them all. If it hadn't been for Lady Ruth's rescue—she was following Rhum's paper trail—the act would've cost his life.

In the abbey's hospice ward, he'd woken up to Rhyllae dressing his wounds. Aramis thought she was an angel that had fallen from the Heavenly Court and tried to woo her. Impressive, since he barely could speak from his swollen lip. For the "compliment," she doused him with a bowl full of cold, holy water.

Yet, the man persisted, sweet-talking her to come along as he worked off his moral debt with the Jessenters. Perhaps the best decision she had ever made. Otherwise, Rhyllae would never have befriended Ruth, Bagheera, Tamira, and Joel. They had gone through so much together. From crawling through the belly of forgotten ruins to rescuing slaves from desert slavers, Aramis would never do anything to bring them harm, let alone smear their name.

Perhaps their friends, watching from above, knew that, too? No doubt laughing at the ridiculousness of the whole situation while taking bets?

No, Rhyllae shouldn't be surprised that Aramis had used his tricks in the drinking game. He was trying to put on a good show ... and to save face. Sister Rhyllae stopped at the intersection and shook her head.

*What a piece of work. What am I going to do with you?*

Her eyes lingered upon the street sign: "Sulmaith Street." Long ago, the Grand Magi of Ioun unlocked a magic portal, letting the djinn Bazzuu into the capital. He offered each of them powers beyond belief. In return, they crowned him as the supreme ruler. One by one, they all transformed into the Djinnasi lords they suffered to this day. All but one.

Sulmaith the Wise never kneeled to the black-hearted fiend and threw all his magic upon them. He failed. Thus, the founders declared him the first martyr.

Almost all the Jessenters joined him. Her sisters had told her the death toll from the Karatow mountains was catastrophic. Mother Myrrh, one of their two sunset mothers, took a legion of priestesses to reclaim the people's fallen warriors. Though it was the new general's task to organize the fighters, the people of Amaveriel saw Ruth's company as a beacon in the dark. How could Aramis and she guide them when they were stumbling in the dark themselves?

*What are we going to do?* Rhyllae hoped against hope to hear guidance from the venerated spirit.

A breeze flitted through the street, chilling her neck, reminding the Morning sister that soon a new day would dawn. Sister Ghalédale pulled the yellow shawl tight and hurried home.

This time, the sister followed the parishioners' route, passing under the saffron-painted entrance into the nave, the breathing belly of the abbey. Pillars, striated in black basalt and white limestone, soared high, as if to touch the stars. Her slippers padded the geometric tiles as she took in the serene incense. Clinging to the closest pillar, Rhyllae took off her shoes to let her olive feet feel the cool marble, swept clear of the day's dust.

The sunlight would dance on the floor in green, blue, orange, and red colors during the day. Now, in the still of the night, flickers of prayer candles dotted the way to the chancel's warm glow. A hair larger than a slab of rock, the altar was a broken piece of the heavenly palace fallen from the Great Fight. Every night, it would glow brilliantly, then fade with every dawn. The sisters protected it in a lattice dome as they sheltered the people of Amaveriel within this city and as it had nurtured and cared for Rhyllae.

She didn't know much about her parents beyond that she was born from a Southern Isles woman whose heart was too great to deny the affections of a sun elf. And he loved her as much in turn. The ship crashed on the black shores close to Amaveriel, and Rhyllae was the lone survivor. If it hadn't been for the manifest, Mother Celia had said, they would have called her Farrah because she was full of joy and love. Rhyllae never saw those islands, nor saw a fellow sun elf. But she knew deep down that they loved her as much as her sisters and mothers of the order. Perhaps more.

Oh, how she needed their love more than ever.

Cutting across the cloister garden, her olive feet padded up the stone stairs toward the prayer balcony, and she flung the saffron door wide open. Rhyllae bounced through the painted threshold into the cold starry night, getting goosebumps as she reached the balcony's edge. Greeting the dawn's light with a song was one of her joyous duties. Her fears and sorrow were cast aside when the sun crawled over the horizon as she felt the embrace of those who passed. Rhyllae pushed her honey-brown curls behind her pointed ears, scanning the night sky for the morning star. The dark side of the moon was far behind her, allowing the constellations of ancient heroes to sparkle above. She never noticed the figure lurking in the shadows.

Aramis climbed the minaret, skillfully picking footholds from the pockmarks and edges within the stone. Finally reaching the top, he paused to catch his breath. Then a yellow door slammed him against the wall. Violent thoughts crossed his mind when he pried the door off of him, then flew when he spotted Rhyllae standing there, her back to him.

He had never seen her that way before, her olive-brown skin glowing under the starlight. The gentle breeze teased her golden-brown curls and played with the tassels on her shawl. Aramis held his breath. It was like watching a desert flower in bloom.

Then the morning star shone brightly over the horizon. The herald of the coming dawn.

"Ruth, Bagheera, Tamira, Joel, this is for you," Rhyllae whispered to the wind. She raised her arms, beholding the star before her, and began the morning prayer.

The prayer was no a chant as one would expect to hear, rather words strung together in melodic praise. Timid at first, then growing in strength as the sun crawled over the horizon's edge, reaching a climax of glory and renewal. It was Rhyllae's personal creation, and she was the only one who could sing its full potential.

Aramis was awestruck as she sang into the night like a lark. He had heard this song several times but never knew it was her. He leaned back against the wall, enchanted by the purity of her voice, sweet as water from a hidden oasis. He wished that he could drink from her well of hope.

The sun finally broke through the distant canopy of the jungle and far-flung mountains. Its warmth cast over their still sleepy town. Happy colors of dawn turned away the shades of violet and indigo. It was as if Rhyllae was the rising dawn, the beacon of his dreary and cold world, showing the way to a better and brighter tomorrow.

Aramis reached out to her, to join her in her song even though he didn't know the words. To hold her hand and stand by her side. His one and only friend. Then a gleam caught his eye. There, upon his finger, his wedding band.

Despite its scrapes and dents, it shone as brightly as the first day he'd laid eyes upon it.

Remembering his promise, Aramis snuck away. With one last look back at Rhyllae, he slipped through the yellow arch into the dark stairwell. Arriving at the second-floor threshold, Aramis froze. He ducked behind the arch as a pair of chattering sisters passed. He cursed himself for dallying. With everyone waking up, getting to the Mother Superior would be problematic for him. She was the one who could provide the answers, after all.

He peeked both ways. The coast was finally clear. Aramis took a right, hoping it was the way to Mother Superior Frianul. The windows gave a pleasant view of their garden. He crept close to the statues lining the wall, depicting the rise and fall of the sun. Halfway down, he heard echoes of bare feet pitter-pattering against the stone from behind.

Ducking behind the statue of the setting sun, he saw Rhyllae running toward the dormitory. Slippers in the clutch of her hands, her curls bouncing as the yellow sash trailed behind her. He let out a sigh of relief when she was out of sight. Aramis didn't want her tangled up with his personal affairs.

Farther down the hall, a modest wooden door was ajar. Aramis let himself in and found it was the ladies' laundry room.

*Drats! A dead end.*

Aramis turned to leave when he heard the bells ring. The laysisters would start their chores soon. It would be nigh impossible to pick his way through with them shuffling about—no doubt, starting with this room first.

Touching the robe closest to him, he mused about if he could hide behind the cloth since it was the largest of them all. *Big enough for a man.* Then a mad idea hit him. A mischievous smile crossed his face.

A few minutes later, Aramis emerged from the laundry room wearing the robes of a Morning Lord sister. He kept his eyes low while carrying the water bucket and brush as the sisters greeted him as Sister Gertrude, and he grunted in reply. He had to wonder if she had a beard like his, it was in a ragged mess, after all. Hers would be impeccable, as all aspects of the sisters in service would be.

After multiple greetings and a lot of fake scrubbing, he reached the office of the Mother Superior. The polished wooden door was locked, a minor obstacle for the Silver Fox. A flick of a wrist and it was done.

There before him was an incense-scented room filled to the brim with ledgers, lore, and manuals. Illuminating the room was a beautiful stained glass window of the sun in its glory over the land and sea. It took up most of the room's width, looming from the floor to the next floor's ceiling. Even the second floor made an overlooking balcony to not limit the grand staircase. A tidy desk was set in front of the stained glass window, flanked by a shoulder-high tower of candles.

He approached the desk and found an iron spiral staircase tucked behind a red velvet curtain at the left corner. He removed his disguise as he climbed the ironwork to her bedroom.

Aramis snorted. *She certainly is living well.*

The bed was made of red silk, with a canopy of red velvet and golden fringes. Pillows were embroidered with golden thread. Even the prayer rug was embellished with an ornate design. Perusing the Mother Superior's possessions, he noted the incenses were of the highest quality from the

Imperial Chessentari. One was a hallucinogenic derived from a five-petal poppy, illegal in Amaveriel.

Below, he heard the door open and close.

"Who's there?" a female voice called out.

Aramis ambled down the stairs, letting the heel of his boots ring out on the iron steps. Tossing and catching a poppy box as he descended. "Lord of Mornings, renew my heart, body, and soul. Lead me not to the temptations of these worldly pleasures, for no gold or flesh would ever satisfy the warmth of your holy embrace."

To his satisfaction, he found the Mother Superior giving him a sour look. "So, it is you who are desecrating these holy chambers."

"Oh, I'm sure you are doing a fine job of that yourself." Aramis bunted the illicit incense toward her.

As she looked over the box, he shimmied over to her seat and plopped down, propping his dusty black boots on her desk as he leaned back.

"Only the Devil would know, for the Lord's love is blind." He flashed a facetious smile at her.

Mother Frianul's face turned a shade of red. "How dare you speak blasphemy here?"

"How dare you disavow something sacred to me?"

The Mother Superior narrowed her eyes at him. "I was expecting to discuss the matter with you upon your return. Though, not so soon."

Mother Frianul moved to her desk, glowering at him to relinquish the chair. In reply, he interlocked his hands together and stared back at her, steeling his gaze as the seconds passed. She decided to look out the window instead.

"It was an urgent one, Mr. Feres," she said. "We thought we lost you like those who fell in Karatow. It was only a matter of time before your wife ran out of money. She was desperate."

"A resourceful woman like her, desperate? Vanessa could've found a job."

"Who would hire her based on your reputation as a smuggler, robber, and, if I dare say it—"

"Murderer. I know who I am and my sins, Mother Frianul." Aramis stepped over to the Mother Superior, her perfume cloying the air between them. "If I recall right, you had named all those who serve 'holy warriors fighting for a true and just cause.' I may have a dark and twisted past, true. I have sworn to destroy Djinnasi slavers not to redeem myself, but to continue to free those still in their clutches. If you had any pity in that ironclad heart of yours, you would have taken her into your care. Not break our vow and toss her out like yesterday's catch."

"I would if I had the power to do so, Mr. Feres. It was she who asked for the divorce."

Still was his heart in the suffocating quiet of her office. The only thing that stirred in that silence was the dust floating in the prismatic light. Calmly, the Mother Superior reclaimed her desk chair, allowing him time to process.

"You mean," his voice cracked, "she had no choice."

"No. We explored all options, but your wife insisted this was the right course to take."

"The right course to take?" Aramis whirled on her. "Since when is a divorce even an option?"

"When the marriage as a whole threatens the integrity of one."

"Lies!" He sliced the air with his hand, knocking one of the conical candelabrums to the floor. "I have done everything I can to provide what she asked for. Hell, I still remember saying my vows like it was done yesterday: 'None shall come before you, for I will remain true 'til my soul rests in the grave.' I stayed true to my word." Aramis slammed his hands on her desk. "I loved her with every fiber of my being. I gave her my all. I gave her … everything."

His vision spun and his hands shook. Aramis bowed, trying to keep himself upright.

"Oh, Mr. Feres, you don't look well," the Mother Superior cooed with a smirk.

Aramis muttered, "What did you do?" Beads of sweat formed on his forehead.

She never did answer him.

The door opened behind and a melodic voice called out, "Mother Superior Frianul? I heard a commotion—Aramis?" Rhyllae rushed over to him. "What are you doing here? Are you all right?"

Aramis firmly removed her hand from his shoulder. "I'm fine." Though his heart beat like a mad drummer. "Tell me where she is, and I'll be on my way."

"Sister Ghalédale, the Silver Fox is not feeling well. Please escort him out," the Mother Superior coolly said as she brushed the dirt off her papers.

"No." Aramis grabbed the collar around her neck and lifted the Mother Superior up from her chair. "I'm not leaving until I know where my wife is."

Unfazed, Mother Frianul shrugged. "Only the Morning Lord knows."

"Bull sh—" Aramis's legs collapsed underneath him before he could say anything else. The strength in his arms gave out, letting her slip through his fingers. Aramis wheeled backward into the enveloping darkness.

The last thing he heard was Rhyllae's words. "I'm sorry. It's for your own good."

# Chapter 8

## GHOSTS

"—IT," ARAMIS SAID WHEN HE WOKE UP. "Hell" was next when he started feeling the throbbing in his muscles and the ache in his bones.

No matter where he looked, everything was ninety degrees, double, and blurry. It felt like he was hungover from the Iron Lady's vermouth without the enjoyable benefits. Aramis rolled over to his side, but the bed gave way underneath him, and he fell to the floor.

He rolled back to stare at the shadows dancing on the ceiling from the sickle flame. Flickers of figures and images danced among the cracks of dried paint. Dancers, masks, jesters, skulls, and daggers flashed like puffs of smoke before his eyes.

Closing his eyes, he could feel Vanessa's weight upon him, nipping at his earlobe. Her intoxicating scent wafted from her locks. Lifting his hand to tangle his fingers in her raven hair, he grasped nothing. He opened his eyes to find empty, itching fingers hovering before him. The mocking shadows continued their dance on the ceiling behind them.

Aramis clenched his hand into a fist and touched his forehead. *Where could you have gone? Alive? Dead? Worse?*

Jesters, masks, daggers, drops of blood. His mind swirled with horrors. Chained and bound in a dark, forgotten cellar. Vanessa stabbed endlessly with a heated fire poker, her screams muffled by the gag in her mouth.

"No!" He sat up, finding it hard to breathe in the still room.

*Lock it away, Aramis. Lock your fears in a chest and throw away the key.*

He pulled himself vertical with the nightstand. Wobbling to his feet, he knocked over the candlestick. It fell, with the flame flickering to hold on. He reached to grab it before the darkness swallowed it.

He blinked.

And lo, he was reaching not for the candle but for Bagheera. Their fair elven guide was falling into the inky pit. His heart raced as he fumbled to grasp her. He felt her fingertips as she reached out. Then she vanished. The candlestick clanked on the wooden floor, the wick smoldering from the snuffed light. Yet, he could still hear her wails.

Falling to his knees, Aramis groped for the candlestick. His vision blurred as tears fell. When his calloused fingers found the metal, he cradled it in his arms, rocking back and forth.

*It's all my fault.* Aramis could've saved her from such a simple trap. Hell, he could have rescued everyone from those ruins. He didn't care what Rhyllae told him during their trek home—he should have found a way for them. For all of them. *Bagheera, Joel, Tamira, and Ruth. I have failed you all.*

There he wept, his shoulders shuddering with every broken breath. Far too long had he steeled himself from unwanted eyes. To be the pillar of salt in a world on fire.

Then, what at first felt impossible, the tears lessened, and the breathing came easier. Deep down, he knew he couldn't stay this way forever. Not when there was a chance to fix what was broken.

Staggering to his feet, Aramis headed toward the door, dropping the candlestick as he slapped the latch open. He must be out at sea in the belly of a ship, for the ground lurched and swayed underneath him. Determined to move topside, he weaved to and fro down the hallway.

A few of the doors were ajar. Through one, two demonic figures were entangled in combat. Through another, a shriveled old hag rocked herself, wailing melodic nonsense. Aramis wondered what type of ship it was to have such occupants in those quarters. He continued down the listing corridor until he found stairs leading down instead of up. No vessel would have such a design.

His mind whirled. Could he still be in M'thealquilôk under some sick illusion?

Fearing enemies nearby, his hands whipped back for his twin daggers and found his hips lacking his lethal instruments. It was then he noticed that his shirt was gone, as well as his belt and boots. He patted himself all over at a frantic pace until his fingers brushed against the metal on his right hand.

His wedding band was still where he switched it on that night.

His head spun.

*But it was a lie. Coming home was a lie. Those papers—every-thing. All an illusion. It had to be. She would never leave.*

Yet, try as he may, he couldn't bring himself to see the ring as part of the illusion. Aramis was indeed free of the wretched ruin. As he was free of his home and wife. Placed somewhere foreign after whatever the Mother Superior did to him.

The unexpected smell of white flowers tantalized his nostrils.

*Vanessa?*

Aramis approached the open room to his left, letting the fragrance guide him. The orange flickering of light on the walls made the shadows swirl like a couple dancing the minuet. Around the corner was a fireplace. Standing in front of it was a woman cloaked in a yellow shawl.

He found her. Aramis was elated and terrified. He stumbled across the room and turned her around. "Vanessa?"

Instead of seeing a pair of smoldering emerald eyes, he found amber eyes with flecks of gold. Clear and bright. When she called his name, her voice wasn't the husky purr of a sphinx but the melodic voice of a lark.

Aramis shut his eyes. "No, wait … you're not … her."

He felt her comforting hands lead him to sit by the fire. He opened his eyes to see a familiar lady of olive skin and golden-white robes, her curls peeking out from her yellow shawl.

"Forgive me, Rhyllae, I thought you were—"

"Your wife," she finished for him.

Aramis nodded. They said nothing, listening to the crackle and pop of the fire-licked logs.

"How long was I asleep from that spell?" he asked.

"Twelve hours, give or take. I tried to diminish it, but I guess your body demanded more time to recuperate."

"Recuperate? Ha. Cure me of this insomnia and call me in the morning."

For as long as he could remember, Aramis had always been an insomniac. No matter how weary the day had been, he would be wide awake well past sunrise. If he could help it, Aramis wouldn't bother in the first place. He would gaze at the heavens above, counting the stars until dawn.

Rhyllae sighed. "You know that's beyond my skill."

"Doesn't mean I have to suffer for it."

Despite his grumbling, Aramis had to admit his body felt rested. With his vision finally cleared, he discovered the perfume's source was a vase of orange blossoms, white roses, and lilies on the mantlepiece. The vase was shaped like a woman in armor, holding the bouquet like a war banner. How could he not recognize they were on the 2nd floor of the Iron Lady? He felt like a complete fool.

Hanging his head low, Aramis fiddled with his wedding band. "I'm sure you want to badger me for all I know."

"Yes, but not here." Sister Rhyllae offered her hand to come with her, which he took.

As they walked back to his room, he realized not all was as it seemed. The listing of the ship came from his stumbling. The withered hag was a dingy mop lying on the floor, fallen over a chair while he was passing by. Yet, the wailing still persisted farther down the hall. When they approached the jarred door, Aramis had to cover Rhyllae's eyes and guide her to his room. He dared not wish to disturb an intimate moment between two minotaurs lest he had a death wish.

Back in the room, Aramis found the rest of his clothes folded neatly in a corner chair above a pair of boots, his belt hung over the chair railing with care, and his daggers still sheathed. Waving Rhyllae to the bed, he pushed his clothes over on the floor so he could sit down to dress. Aramis felt like a nitwit for not seeing them earlier, despite the heady state he was in.

Rhyllae spoke first. "It was when I was treating that viper bite on your arm." When Aramis widened his eyes, she interjected, "You were hallucinating something fierce. I had to put you to sleep."

"Ah, I see. You took a peek under my gloves."

"The poison was going into your hand, I had to take off your ring. I put it back on when the swelling went down." She paused, gripping the metal tightly as she searched for the words to say next. "Is... Is Vanessa ... a man?"

Aramis raised his eyebrows. He did say wife around her, or so he thought.

"There's nothing wrong with having a husband. Or spouse if they're khanith. You alone have convinced me that all love, of all types, is pure and sacred. There's no shame in it. You didn't have to hide it from anyone, let alone your friends."

"Oh, Rhyllae." He would've laughed if the circumstances were different. To think how far she had come.

"We love you, Aramis. Why didn't you tell us?"

"I... Look." Then Aramis sighed and buried his face in the sock, collecting his thoughts. "Vanessa is a woman borne from the Magionni tribe. I hid her because I didn't want her life in danger. Though, I'm glad to know it's okay to be me around you."

"Was this when we escorted the freemen from Ryothun's compound?"

He nodded. "Three years ago. Almost to the day."

"How?"

Aramis opened his mouth, then shut it tight. Instead, he jammed his foot into the sock and reached for the next. It didn't take long for Rhyllae to put two and two together. When it clicked in her head, she slammed the candlestick on the side table.

"That's why they dragged you out of the tent. You drank Vanessa's cup, didn't you!"

He waved his hands off to the sides. "Vanessa was a skilled dancer. It's not often someone could pull off the 'Fire Rite' with one sash."

"Aramis, we almost barged in to save you."

"I had it under control. I convinced the chief that we should get married. We got hitched a week later."

Rhyllae crossed her arms. "Just like that?"

Aramis reached down to pick up his shirt and halted. A twinge shot up his back. "Just like that," he grunted out his reply.

"Here, let me help you."

Rhyllae eased him out of the chair and had him face the window. Her fingertips trailed over the scars on his back as she searched for the spasming muscle. Part of him felt guilty about not telling her. Still, the thought dissipated when he felt her magic penetrate his muscles. They loosened from their vise at her healing touch.

Aramis looked back. "By the way, what stopped everyone from barging in?"

Rhyllae reached around and turned his head forward. "Ruth. She thought you stole something. Which wasn't too far from the truth."

"There wasn't much to steal. Vanessa's port was already boarded by other ships. Ow," he yelped as she poked a tender spot between two vertebrae. The same place he had the spasm, no less.

"I was checking. Hold still." Once again, Rhyllae's buttermilk palms straightened his face to look out the window.

Sighing as he rolled his eyes, Aramis let the healing power melt away the strain in his spine. It felt like being immersed in a crystal-clear waterfall. She slowly moved the positive force up his vertebrae, touching each bone and connecting rib as she went.

"If anything, she was the thief. I had never met anyone as wild and funny as her. She's got a tongue that won't quit and is smart as paint, too. Sure we fought, who doesn't? But Vanessa always knew what to do in a pinch. She was resourceful when things were tight; fished for food, weaved baskets, and painted shawls."

The clouds in the sky parted to reveal the stars in their glory, surrounding the faint silver halo that was the moon's shadow. It had been a complete cycle and a half since they left Amaveriel. His ring clacked at the windowpane as he pressed his hand against it.

"We have been married for three years, Rhyllae. It may mean nothing to others, but it's everything to me. I swore all of my oaths and washed her feet. I have been true to her ever since that day. We have been through thick and thin, and never had she asked for more. There's no reason for her to leave me. I don't care what your Mother Superior says… I love her."

He balled his hand into a fist in a futile attempt to hold on to the ever-changing moon.

Rhyllae stopped her healing efforts, her fingertips trailing down the numerous scars he endured. The price of freeing others.

"Aramis, what if she doesn't feel the same way you do?"

"She's not like Bagheera. Or Joel, for that matter." He turned himself so he could lean against the windowsill. "They only see a one-trick pony to play with until their curiosity is spent."

"No, Joel is the one-trick pony, not you. And Bagheera—"

"Don't." Aramis cut through the air like a knife. Then, ashamed, he said in a quieter tone, "Just don't. I have no qualms against them both. They weren't the first I tangled sheets with, and they all ended the same. I'm a fascination to discover—a doll to wind up and play with. No matter how hard I try, I remain broken." His fingers lingered on the numbers stained on his skin. "Vanessa, being broken herself, has been the only one who understands."

Rhyllae put her hand on his. "Aramis, even my sisters thought we were dead. What if…"

"Vanessa moved on? Then why send the letter? Why leave in the first place?" Aramis gazed at her, his silver eyes pleading. "Something is wrong, Rhyllae. I need to know what happened to her. I can't lose her. Not when we lost everyone."

With her hand on his cheek, Rhyllae looked into his eyes. "*Muel lausel sa'wauji*, Aramis."

"What is lost will be found…" Aramis muttered, then a light shone in his eyes. "That missing person case."

"You think it could be her?"

"Who else, Rhyllae? Who?"

She tightened her lips and instead focused on his hand. "What happened here?"

"It's … nothing serious."

Aramis averted his eyes to look at the bedding. The cloth, he found, was made of cotton and was a poor attempt of the forest green shade. It should be bluer rather than yellow. Then he felt her tugging on the ring on his right hand, revealing a cut that lay underneath it. He held his breath as she took the left to compare. A pitiful pout crossed her face as she put two and two together.

"I… Vanessa wasn't there," was all Aramis could say.

"*Muel lausel sa'wauji*, Aramis." Putting both hands on his, Rhyllae let her last healing reserve flow into him. "*A weyad*."

"*Shaka un*."

Moved by her promise, Aramis bent his head low. His salt-and-pepper hair touched the golden curls on top of her head, never parting as the light from the new dawn shone upon them.

# Chapter 9

## EXILE

HE RED DAWN ROSE, HERALDED BY SONG. THE chill of the night vanished wherever the light touched, leaving a hint of dew in its wake. The white limestone buildings and streets would soon bake in the ever-oppressive heat of the sun. For the time being, the walls were cool to the touch and the roads not blinding to see. Safe for a foreigner to linger in the dawn's glow.

From the city wall's eastern spire, next to an unused banner anchor, Tavian Korzha gazed upon the sun rising over the jungle canopies. His duster and scarf were cast aside by the steps, his doublet untied around his neck, exposing his sweat-stained cotton shirt. After seven years, Korzha still found it difficult to adjust to the dry and barren desert nation Ioun.

His icy-blue eyes perceived horizons of beige, dunes of white, or canyons of dusty orange and clay throughout every engagement. The only saving grace of green in this forsaken country was the Anglorian jungle hugging its eastern border.

Its viper-infested edge hung close to Amaveriel's cliffs. A constant reminder of the danger that lurked in wait.

Closing his eyes, Korzha could still see the lush hills and valleys of his homeland, Töska, past the Gallileah mountains up north. A rich and vibrant empire crisscrossed with rapids and magnificent waterfalls lay beyond. Every square inch covered with the tallest trees, rugged bushes, and golden wheat fields. Even the stones were covered with the daintiest of moss and fern. No fruit tasted sweeter, and no flower smelled fairer than those hailing from Töska. Not even the gladiolus, with its trailing flowers, lying on the wall next to him.

A timid breeze from the south ruffled the gladiolus's pink petals, letting loose yellow clumps of pollen from its stamens into the wind. They danced around his blond-and-gray hair, gently depositing a few grains on the strands. As good a breeze as any before the heat set in.

Korzha held his trusted sword across him, the Silver Star. The entire blade was made of the most precious material, Mithral, forged with magic as old as the world surrounding him. The intricate guard was inset with diamonds representing the stars of the midnight sky. Its handle spiraled like a unicorn's horn, ending with a pointed dome pommel. Attached to it was a silver threaded tassel that never frayed. The magic made it so it would never tarnish or be broken by any mortal means. The Silver Star had been in his family for generations, passed down to those who could make the sword sing its ethereal song. Much like how his beloved had made his heart sing until that fateful day. This day, seven years ago.

Pushing such thoughts aside, Korzha began his annual vows in his mother's tongue.

"<Lo, there do I see my father. Lo, there do I see my mother, my brothers, and my sisters. Lo, there do I see the line of my people back to the beginning.>"

With one fluid motion, he unsheathed the Silver Star from its scabbard, cutting a single flower from the base of the gladiolus's stem. So quick was the cut that the flower lay still in its spot with no damage to its petals, the others left behind. Firmly, he pierced the middle of the flower with the tip of his blade. Korzha held the warbling rapier erect, the light shining upon the blade finding no fault upon its edge. The dew trickled down and landed on the signet ring on his left hand.

The wind strengthened as he recited the ancient words.

"<Lo, do they call to me. They bid me to take my place among them in Valhalla. Where thine enemies have been vanquished. Where the brave may live forever.>"

Into the gust, he swung his rapier out in front of him. The gladiolus's flower sailed several yards, straight and true, before arcing down to the jungle floor.

Then he heard an eagle's piercing cry. The mighty hunter rose from below. Its dark, majestic wings stretched out wide. As it banked near the eastern wall, it snatched the pink flower in its talons. They locked eyes in that instant before the black eagle soared over the city, toward the west.

"<Never shall we mourn, but rejoice for those that have died a glorious death.>"

His voice hushed with awe.

Korzha had never been a man of blind religious devotion. Though he embraced the traditions of his mother's people from the Great North, he regarded their superstitions with equal skepticism. Yet, as the black eagle faded out of sight, he took it as a good sign.

"Thought I would find you here, sir."

Glancing back toward the stone steps, Korzha spotted a strapping young woman saluting him with a wry grin on her face. Her short, tousled mane freed of the traditional coverings. *This must be the late Captain Mosul's rising star, Dawn.*

Clicking his heels, the general saluted her back with his rapier. "I hope you bring good news, Lieutenant." He sheathed the Silver Star, ending the song.

Bringing her hand down, Dawn gathered up his coat and scarf. "Thirty caravans ransacked from the Glass and Purple plains, with goods dispersed as ordered, sir."

She balled up the clothing and tossed it to him. He caught it with ease. Korzha patted his forehead with the scarf and then wrapped it around his head. Already, he felt the heat of the day starting to set in.

"Casualties?"

"Minimal," Dawn said at first, but the icy-blue stare made her reconsider her words. "Fifty."

Korzha nodded as he donned the coat. "Never expect for an instant, Lieutenant, that victory can be bought without sacrifice. Simply turning a blind eye to that fact will only lead to failure."

"Like General Tackett, sir?"

The general paused in his movements and took a good look at the young officer. Underneath that brash visage, he could sense her nerves were shaken. How could they not be? 35,000 plus had perished, and his regiment was the only one remaining.

"Mourn not for those who have died in glory. Duty, honor, and, yes, self-sacrifice are tenets upon which we stand. General Tackett understood that in ways none could ever comprehend." With one hand, he covered the gladiolus stem's box with its lid and handed the package to Dawn. "While he may have lost the battle, we will not lose this war."

Dawn took the package as he passed by. Peeking inside, she told him, "That's still a lot of men to bury."

Once again, Korzha paused and sighed. "No. To burn."

"I will not have you destroy what little remains of their dignity, General." Mother Celia frowned as she crossed her arms into her robes.

The mother of the Sunset didn't hold her rank well. The vibrant colors of purple, red, and orange made her skin ashen. The vestments were far too big for her stature, making Mother Celia mousy compared to the grand architect of the abbey surrounding them.

Mother Celia pulled them aside to let the sisters pass. Dawn nodded and winked at the pair. One giggled while her friend stuck her nose up in the air. General Korzha gave her a look, a keen reminder they were here for business. In a flash, she straightened herself up.

"Mother Celia, please." Korzha turned his attention to her. "You know as well as I do the dangers of pestilence from decay alone."

"Which is why we embalm and treat our dead with considerable care," the Mother retorted.

"En masse? With one mistake, you will be overrun with disease, or worse."

Mother Celia narrowed her eyes at him. "Our procedures have been handed down by generations of skilled mothers of yore. And I would not have a pagan like you nitpick it to suit your sensibilities."

"I will not have this city overtaken by an army of inmorti."
He spoke in a measured tone.

"This is not Töska, and you are far out of your league."
Mother Celia also spoke in a measured tone. "If you wish to
discuss this matter any further, wait for your precious Myrrh.
I'm sure the two of you have much to discuss."

With that, the mother turned and left them in the check-
er-tiled hall. Korzha clenched his gloves as tightly as his
slender fingers would allow it.

"Sir?" Dawn asked, caution in her voice.

"Clearly, common sense is lacking as of late, don't you
agree?" the general quipped before speeding away with his
long legs, past the idle priestesses and muttering parishioners into the open, arid air. Korzha fumed like a black
kettle, leaning upon the stone wall overlooking the city
stretched out below. *How long can this dale stay hidden from
our unyielding foe?*

"Commander?" Dawn asked when she finally found him.
"What does Töska have to do with this?"

He couldn't give her a response. The anger still held fast
in his throat.

"Does it have to do with the inmorti?" Dawn slowly
approached until she was by his side. "Is that why you left?"

Korzha winced. Collecting his thoughts, he gave her a
measured look. "You have never left the confines of this
desert, have you?"

Dawn shook her head.

With a wave toward the city's northern ridge, he continued, "Beyond those mountains of Gallileah lies my
homeland. A verdant paradise, more beautiful than any
oasis you have ever seen. There, in its beauty, is an infestation unimaginable, the never-sleeping dead.

"Ghouls, ghosts, vampires, these beings are not conjurings for bedtime terrors. They are as real as you and me. Every sunset, peasants and nobles alike shutter themselves in—praying feebly to let themselves be spared for the coming morn. For that is when they hunt. When the light gives way to the long hand of shadow."

Dawn nodded. "So, with the infestation out of control, they have to get more warriors. Is that why the Töskan Empire expanded its borders?"

"That was an added bonus, but not the sole reason. The countries surrounding those boundaries were being decimated by the infliction. We took them under our wing for their protection." Korzha leaned against the wall on his elbows. "I had spent my entire military career studying those foul creatures and swore to hunt them down to the bitter end. From Açeron to Mesieh, I had battled those vile armies until the land was stained by their ruin."

"Are they still alive ... um, around?"

Korzha shook his head. "I threw down the Dread Lord Atanase, and their activity has since waned. Any traveler will be hard-pressed to find such creatures now. Though, I'm sure such tales will continue to endure. It was at that moment I decided to retire. As a result, I was given my ... reward."

Then Korzha paused as his eyes glimmered with a far-off gaze. Pain and fondness wrapped together in melancholy. Then he blinked and awoke to the present day. A twitch of a smile, a clearing of his throat, and General Korzha donned his veil of authority.

He finally said, "'Tis fate that brought me here and 'tis duty that keeps me bound. Though I shall not impose such restrictions upon you. You are given a month's worth of leave. Go home, recuperate. When you return, you will be given your new orders."

Dawn looked over the west longingly. The way she chewed on her lip made him wonder what ailed her. Then she sighed. "Sir, I must decline. There's a matter of Lieutenant Nazir—"

"Ex-lieutenant, you mean. I understand that he was once a friend of yours. Let not your feelings cloud your judgment. He is a traitor and a Djinnasian spy."

Dawn squared her shoulders. "Sir, I disagree. I believe he was framed. We may have the wrong guy."

"Do you have any evidence to back your statement?"

"I have a lead. I request permission to follow it, sir."

The general gave her a scrutinizing stare and found her resolve unwavering. "Very well. You have my permission to investigate the matter." He stepped forward, towering over the petite officer. "Don't return without sufficient information, Lieutenant. I do not wish to spend what few resources available on a wild-goose chase."

Dawn nodded and saluted him. "I won't disappoint you."

Korzha saluted her back. "Dismissed." She took a few steps before he spoke again. "And, Lieutenant. If you do find the true traitor, you have my permission to kill."

The order stunned her, but the lieutenant accepted it with a bow. They were low on resources, after all.

# Chapter 10

## SALT & BATTERY

"**G**OOD NIGHT, RUSTY, ME BOY, AND THANKS AGAIN for the bail."

Lockjaw locked the door behind his clerk. Taking the lantern by the door, he made his rounds. Snuffing out the candles and securing the latches on the windows. He attached a simple deterrent for any nighttime visitors to every window sill: a trigger plate saw. Taking the wet blankets, Lockjaw threw them over his merchandise. Any specialist would be shocked by such an act, for it would weaken their quality. But the mad genius knew his clients and guaranteed all products were 100% waterproof. The blankets prevented any sparks from competitors who would upend his business.

Once Lockjaw secured the first floor, he made his way to the top of the steps and pulled a lever. In a blink, the steps unhinged and became a steep ramp. Then the crafty dwarf secured every bookcase with a net, sticky with anti-flammable wax. Finally, he secured every window with the same insurance.

The last light snuffed, Lockjaw tightened the screw on his lantern. He didn't want his night to end with a bang. He had to work extra hard to get his latest invention out in production. Especially now that the famous Silver Fox knew about this place, he could waltz in the next day for all Lockjaw knew. Both of them had worked in a frenzy earlier to make the place spick-and-span with nary a grain out of place.

Approaching a sealed cabinet on the wall, he felt a chill on his forearm. A window was open wide down the aisle to his right, where he had already secured it shut.

He rolled his broad shoulders as he crept over to the window, still sore from that rumble in the Iron Lady. Out the window, he found no one down the alleyways of the pier. Down straight below, he found no movement from the shadows cast by the moonlight.

"No need to get yerself in a tizzy over it, Lockjaw," he told himself as he closed the window again. Turning back, he found the secret opening was open wide, his lantern still on top of the small cabinet.

*Someone after me keyhole?*

As insurance, Lockjaw grabbed one of the brightly wrapped candles from the nearby shelf and struck the match. The fire licked at the wick before he drew it away. He had spent a whole year perfecting his latest creation. Was it worth blowing it all to smithereens because of one lousy intruder? Lockjaw looked back at the passage in the wall, then back to the flame withering on the matchstick.

"What's one intruder?" And he snuffed out the light.

The morning light softly filtered through the crack of the window shutters, dividing the room in half, separating the bed and the chair. Aramis occupied the latter, leaning back so it balanced on the back of its two legs. The whetstone rang out rhythmically on one of his blades as he lowly hummed a verse from Rhyllae's morning hymn. Curled under the burlap sheet and yellow shawl was the sister herself, blissfully oblivious.

Watching her sleep always brought a smile to his face. She would often toss and turn, flinging her curls in every which direction. Sometimes a rogue strand got into her mouth, making her snort and snore until it became too much to bear, setting off another round of tossing. She couldn't decide whether she was hot or cold, either. Twice he watched her throw off the covers, and thrice she rolled around in them like a caterpillar spinning a cocoon. Right now, Rhyllae seemed content wedging the pillow between her right arm and head, allowing her left arm to drape over the side. Drool oozed from the corner of her tender, open lips. Her snore was syncopated to Aramis's humming.

A knock came on the door. Rhyllae snorted and muttered as she rolled onto her belly, submerging her head under the pillow. Flipping the dagger parallel to his arm, Aramis walked to the door, toe to heel, hardly making a creak from the floorboards.

He could barely hear the timid voice behind the door saying, "Excuse me, Master Feres?" Such a style of speech couldn't be that of a dangerous villain.

Opening the door ajar, while keeping the dagger out of view, he looked out, then down to find the treasury satyr curtsying before him.

"Good morrow," Dido said with good cheer.

A moan came from Rhyllae behind him. "Put the lime ... in the coconut," she mumbled between snores.

*She says the weirdest things,* Aramis noted.

Holding an index finger up at Dido, he mouthed at her *one moment* before returning to collect his items. He finally emerged fully dressed, with his dark cloak folded on his arm.

"I'm sorry to disturb your wife, Master Feres."

"Call me Feres, and she's not my wife." When he saw Dido's eyes grow wide, he added, "It's not like that. I was guarding one of the sisters of the Morn. She needed protection for the night."

What he said was almost true; nothing untoward had happened between them that night. When Sister Rhyllae had finished healing him, she finally succumbed to fatigue from the day, having been put to work as soon as possible by the abbey. However, she was fully capable of dealing with any intruder coming through that door. If Dido barged in without him being there, the poor faun would've wound up in their hospice ward.

"Oh, I see. The Iron Lady is not much of a place for a proper lady," Dido said, taken by the tiny fib. "Well, Ma—Er, Feres, I'm here to offer you a job as a detonator. A one-time commission, without conscription necessary. Would you like to have breakfast? It would be my treat."

A glint in his eye twinkled when Aramis glanced back at her. "No holds barred?"

Dido trembled from the hungry look in his eye. "Um... Anything you wish to order."

"In that case..." Aramis opened the door and yelled down the stairs, "Clara, we need the deluxe—double portions."

The Iron Lady's cook was happy to oblige. Clara gave the two a generous spread of falafel, hummus, pickled yogurt balls, nuggets of grilled hard cheese, olives, and a small tower of flatbreads smothered in zaatar, a paste made of thyme, oregano, sumac, and toasted sesame seeds. Since there were no chairs to sit on, they had it all to themselves in the upstairs sitting room.

Aramis shoved as much food in his mouth as he could. It had been a few days since the bar fight, and he hadn't eaten since. All the while, the little satyr gaped in amazement as she mechanically put together her own spread. Perhaps there was a cause for not setting a budget for their meal.

"I promise not to eat you," Aramis said between mouthfuls.

Dido shook herself awake. "Your record as a demolitionist is remarkable, to say the least."

"I don't see why you need me. Unless," Aramis took a heaping amount of hummus from the bowl and slathered it on his flatbread, "you have a buyer and a deadline to meet. In which case, my rates have doubled."

"Mr. Feres, I would never!"

"I would. Can't blame you for chafing on such a tight leash. Especially when Korzha is the one holding it."

"Well, the problem is the vault door, sir. Our anti-thief mechanism was triggered a couple nights ago. It proved too effective and welded the door into the frame."

Aramis paused from spreading the hummus on his zaatar. "How? That was a Manchester model eighty-nine with nine layers of metal sheets and twelve pump locks."

"Yes-yes! How did you know that? Was it the handles or the relief on the side?"

"That and you opened it right in front of me. Do you honestly think I wouldn't notice? No trap can get through all of that material, no matter the engineer."

Dido looked around to see if it was all clear, then she snapped her fingers. In an instant, a flame danced on her fingertip. The satyr looked diabolical with the horns curled on either side of her head.

Aramis stopped chewing and leaned back. "Okay, Firebird, take it easy. What did you do? Sneeze?"

"I got carried away while fending off those thieving hoodlums. If you can open the door, I'll pay your hourly rate. Plus the rest owed to your company for your silence."

He raised his eyebrows. "How generous. I take it you acquired extra from those amateurs last night?"

"From whatever I scraped from the floor, yes." Dido answered a little too cheerfully for the veteran's taste.

He had to admit the price was fair and would keep him afloat for a while. A new home. A fresh start. Even better, a proper funeral for his friends. The fragrant bouquet on the mantelpiece reminded him of dire matters.

"The answer is no." He tried not to look at the satyr as he focused on his cigarette case, but he could feel her beady eyes upon him.

"I don't understand." Dido adjusted her glasses. "Is the pay not worth your while?"

"Look, the answer would still be the same even if you offered me the entire world's weight in gold. This is a personal matter. Unless someone is dying or the world needs saving, your little treasure hoard can sit and wait."

Then Aramis, for theatrics' sake, started packing away his part of the spread in a cloth napkin. He gave a salute of sorts and headed down the hall.

"The tome is seeking a new master." The words chased after him.

Aramis seized his movements.

"That's why the thieves were there. It will continue to call any corrupted soul until a new master takes hold. Relocating it will only slow the process."

Aramis looked over his shoulder. The satyr stood in the dim light without a tremble in her bones.

"You're doing this behind Korzha's back, aren't you?"

"It needs to be destroyed, Silver Fox. The book is evil beyond measure. Anyone who falls prey to its whims can lose their mind and soul. I can't lose this opportunity. Believe me, it's better this way."

Aramis looked down and mulled. Then, after a resigned sigh, he spoke. "You know, you're wasted as an accountant. Fine, I'll help. No one should go through the same misery as I have."

Dido clapped her hands together joyfully. "Thank you, Mr. Feres."

"Don't thank me yet."

He scribbled a message in elvish script on a paper and tore it in half. He handed the bottom half to the lady satyr as he continued down the hall, smiling when he heard Dido gasp.

Taking care not to let the door creak when he opened it, Aramis peered inside. Rhyllae had hardly surfaced from the pillow's depths, save her foot dangling from the sheet's protection. Aramis was half tempted to wake her, but her soft snorting was too adorable to interrupt. Instead, he left the upper half of the note on the nightstand and snuck out of the room.

"Ready to go to the base?" Dido asked when he returned.

"Not yet. I need to get a few supplies first. And I just know the place."

The sea salt was palpable as Dido and Aramis walked down the pier. Despite the rebels' calamities, the pier was jam-packed with travelers seeking long-needed services or exotic flavors. Dido counted eighty-three pirates among the tourists. Seventy-two of them had scars, fifty-six of them had piercings, and forty-three had visible tattoos. Most of them paid them no heed, but some managed a scowl at them as they passed. One enormous fellow winked at her.

The skittish faun clung to the unshaken Silver Fox. "What are we getting from this place?"

Aramis merely shrugged at her. "Maybe a few candlesticks or some bath balms if they ran out."

"You sure she's not your ladylove back there?"

His silver eyes flashed at her underneath his cowl, causing her to shirk back. "It's strictly platonic. Ah, here we are."

The store looked shabby in between the cleaner and the upstanding brick-and-mortar stores. The dark wood warped with colonies of green algae. The windows were noticeably thicker at the panes' bottoms, giving their reflections a pear-shaped distortion. The shingles on the roof could use some repairing, and it was clear that a seagull nested on top of the chimney. The shop didn't seem that impressive, except for the sign. The extended board from the roof was a massive head of a battering ram in the shape of a fierce dragon's maw. Underneath it hung a white board with clear black letters: "Salt & Battery," with the edges chipped away by the weather.

Once they opened the door, Aramis and Dido were stunned. It was bigger than what they expected, and gleaming.

The entire store was polished to an incredible shine, making the floor and walls look like they were laid with freshly cut golden wheat. The first floor was a deep, open space filled with circular tiered displays showcasing cuts of jungle wood, metal rims, and cords for battering rams. Along the left wall was a series of black cauldrons filled with variations of "salt." Some of them were mottled, such as the one called bone salt, which held a white powder with black and yellow specks. Others were a single color, like the powder kindling, a solid red powder with a cautionary sign stating: "Highly flammable." Hanging from these cauldrons were scoops, tied with string, laid on top of the burlap bags stacked below. On the far back wall were jars of individual ingredients for hand-mixing improvised bombs or fireworks. In the back corners, spiral metal stairs were polished to a shine.

Hanging from the second-floor railing was an assortment of grappling hooks with barb variations that Aramis had never seen before, and high in the vaulted ceiling was the rest of the titan-sized battering ram that extended the entire length of the building, fit to take down any castle door in one fell swoop. The Salt & Battery was a candy store for marauders and detonation enthusiasts.

"Candlesticks and bath balms galore." Aramis waved before him and smiled at Dido.

Dido frowned. "You mean bo—"

"Hey, are cha comin' or goin'?" The shout came from the polished countertop to their right.

They quickly shuffled in at the request of the man behind the counter. The burly man was quickly tying some sample ropes in various sailor knots. His muscles flexed the fair maiden on his forearm, giving the illusion of her swaying her hips. He also had stupendous mutton chops, and his jaw jutted out to keep his pipe fixated between his canines. A tiny sign next to him stated, "Free Milkshakes Per Yard."

"My apologies, er, Rusty," Aramis said after peering at his name tag. "I am looking for some candlesticks."

The counterman didn't stop his tying as he answered, "We have all sorts of sticks. Which would ye be needin'?"

"Enough to blast a hole in metal as thick as this," Aramis said, holding his fist up in the air.

The retired sailor nodded and smoked on his pipe for a while before he spoke. "Have ye ever heard of the 'beeswax'?"

"No, is it new?"

"Been out for a while now, but 'tis difficult to make. Only Lockjaw can mix the swill … and live."

Dido shirked back while Aramis leaned forward. "Do tell."

Rusty smirked in approval and walked them up the stairs to the second floor. "'Tis the best thin' since liquid fire, the beeswax. It can detonate on any surface, dry or wet, wood, stone, or metal." He picked up a sample brick and smeared a dollop of the green goo on it with his pocket knife. "Ye apply it like a salve, mind not with yer fingers, to any surface ye like. Insert the cord like so." He pierced the goo with a black cord as thick as a normal candlewick. "When ye be ready, light it. The beeswax gives ye the oomph ye need to knock down doors four times the strength of any dynamite without riskin' yer limbs. And the performance—one hundred percent."

"In the rain?" Aramis asked.

"Aye, and in the 'ery depths of the sea, too."

"In any crook or cranny?" Aramis's fingers twitched as he reached for the jar.

"Ye can write yer name on it for show if ye like."

"And the blast radius?"

"The bee's knees," the store clerk proudly announced.

Dido groaned at the terrible pun while Aramis chuckled darkly.

"I would love to have a sample of your wonderful product if you would please," Aramis said.

"No can do," said Rusty. "But since this is your first-time purchase, I can give you a twenty percent discount and a free sample of our esteemed cherry bombs."

"Fifty. I know Lockjaw. He can vouch for me. Where is he, by the way?"

"Thirty. Workin' overtime on his latest work. 'Ery secret. Can tell ye no more than that."

"Thirty-three. I'm sure he doesn't mind me coming over to say hi."

Rusty gave him a good look over. "Deal."

Motioning them to follow, Rusty led them past rows of shelves meant for scrolls repurposed to hold thousands of colorfully wrapped dynamites. The stock transitioned to stacks of colorful bombs of various shapes and sizes; some like giant golden stars, others like tiny red gumballs.

By the farthest bookcase was a panel in the wall. Rusty touched a nearby nook, and the panel opened, revealing a metal pole. One by one, they all slid down two floors, by Aramis's estimate, until they reached the bottom. When they arrived, Rusty was unhinging the last spring-loaded wire on the metal door. Then he popped off a metal façade, revealing small, round, metal buttons with numbers painted on them.

Aramis went on his tiptoes as he peered over Rusty's shoulders when the clerk punched in a sequence. "So, what is Lockjaw working on these days?"

When the clerk looked back, the Silver Fox rolled on his heels, averting his eyes. Giving one last push of the button, gears clicked before them. Then the door fell into a slit in the floor, revealing a long and dank hallway. Rusty waved his hand to follow him as he took a lantern from a nearby post. Their voices reverberated back as they ventured down into the cold earth.

"'Tis called the keyhole," Rusty said. "Imagine a black cloth, if ye will. Slap it against any bulwark 'n now it becomes a black hole. Ye can shove the entire wealth of Valentra into yer hull. Or sink any Blackdog without firin' a cannon."

"Sounds great, but how deep of a wall can you punch through?"

"We don't know. We haven't reached the limits. The keyhole can go through three brick walls by our reckonin'."

They finally came to a door at the end of the stairs—a simple vault door with a standard wheel at its center.

Rusty whirled the wheel into a series of left and right turns, whistling a simple canon. The echoes cackled and giggled back the melody, distorting the cheerful tune into a disquieted one. Then the gears made a resounding *clunk*.

"Here we are, the workshop. What do you think?"

When he popped the door open, the acrid smell of sulfur and copper punched their senses, causing Dido to lose her falafel and Rusty's eyes to water. Covering his nose with his cloak, Aramis peered through the haze to find the bodily remains of poor Lockjaw, plastered and burned on all six sides of the room.

"I think it was a hit."

# Chapter 11

## DARK BLESSINGS

**T**HE RISING DAWN'S BELLS RANG. THE CLANGING bounced off every curve of the dale, through every twist and turn in the Jessenter tunnels, then pealing out to the docks and sea, telling all of Amaveriel it was time for midday prayer. At least for those still awake.

Drifting off to faraway shores and sun, Rhyllae continued her gentle slumber. Dreaming of a place where everything was cool in the shade, and the breeze pleasant.

*Everyone is there to greet her. All of her sisters and mothers of the abbey. As well as all of her friends from the Jessenters—including Lady Ruth and Tamira. Bagheera and her moon elf lover, Renigeld, sing in delight as the children play. Rhyllae feels like she has arrived in the Heavenly Court's garden—gorgeous and peaceful.*

*But something is missing in paradise. In all the sea of people, none of them is the familiar grizzled face with silver patches through his hair.*

*"Aramis?" Rhyllae calls out. "Aramis!"*

*No one in the crowd seems to care as Rhyllae continues to shout his name. They all turn to a large, dead tree. The show is about to start. She can't see anything as they press together. They woot and laugh as she pushes through, their faces changing into something sinister—some into beasts unimaginable, others much worse.*

*"Aramis!" she cries out again.*

*They all jeer at her, no longer the friends and family she once knew.*

*"What's wrong, Doll? Missing someone?" Falçion leers at her with red, glowing eyes. His teeth are crooked, and the pocks on his face transforms into eyeballs.*

*Then the entire crowd claps in unison. Above their heads, a rope is flung over the tree against a sudden backdrop of the midnight sky and torchlight. A slender fox, covered in mercury, is lifted by its throat. The poor creature kicks and yelps as it is hoisted higher.*

*"No!" Rhyllae pushes her way through the crowd. They claw at her, shredding her vestments as she passes. Still, Rhyllae per-severes, finally reaching the poor creature.*

*Knocking the shadow holding the rope to the ground, Rhyllae catches the fox. Then a singular tone sounds. Turning around, she sees the morning star shooting down from the heavens. The sound crescendos as it arcs toward both of them. Fearing it will kill him, Rhyllae hugs the fox as the cold light pierces her heart.*

Then her eyes flew open. The bright light of day struck upon them, reminding her that she was alive.

In Amaveriel.

In the Iron Lady.

Sweat clung to her bosom as she gripped the sheets, the yellow shawl tangled up among them. The dream faded fast, as dew on the sands.

Rhyllae fell back to bed, slapping her hand on her forehead. Mother Celia would not be pleased that she missed morning prayers. Rhyllae dreaded what chore Celia would force her to do. Perhaps she'd let her restock the medicinals rather than toil at the garden. But knowing the Sunset mother, she would be archiving the library, always a mess after devotionals. Sometimes, Rhyllae wished she could be mentored by Mother Myrrh instead. Even though she was a bit doleful and prim, at least she was forgiving—with the proper excuse.

*No point in waiting. The sooner I get it done, the sooner I can help track Vanessa.*

Rhyllae opened her eyes and found no sign of Aramis. Rolling over to her side, she noticed a note on the stand written in an elven script:

DEAREST FRIEND,

I'M CALLED AWAY. JESSENTER BUSINESS. YOU WERE RIGHT ABOUT THE TOME. IT'S TOO VILE TO LINGER. PLEASE CALL UPON CAPT. TRISTAN FOR ME. I'LL MEET YOU DURING VESPERS.

I AM AND ALWAYS SHALL BE,
YOUR ARAMIS

Her heart beat faster than it should have when her eyes trailed over his signature. This was the first she ever saw "Your Aramis" in any letter addressing her. It used to be "AF" or "your obedient servant" or, if he was being tracked, "*Theliad*," the elvish word for fox. Yet, he wrote "Your Aramis." Could it mean something beyond mere friendship?

Rhyllae dashed the notion. *He wrote "Dearest friend," and if that isn't a clue, I don't know what is.*

She shoved her boots on and readied herself to meet the captain of the watch. Her mind sifted through various excuses for their meeting.

Dawn threw her hands up toward the cloudy sky before she brought them back behind her head, puffing up her cheeks as she walked back toward the Pit. The fishermen were impossible. All of them were surprised to learn Mudhi's alibi had been fishing with them this whole time.

It wasn't because of the alibi's name—it was her gender. They had never suspected a woman was working among these sticks-in-the-mud the whole time. Worse, they were aghast to discover that Dawn herself was a Jessenter, fighting for their freedom no less.

*Is that really that hard to imagine?* The lieutenant punted a stone the size of a coconut, not caring if it squashed someone's innocent eggplant.

The fishermen sounded like all the old geezers back in her tribe:

"Fishing and war are dangerous for delicate flowers such as yourself."

"Warfare is a man's duty and burden."

"Why would you throw your life away when you could settle down with a good man?"

It took everything she had to restrain herself from popping them into the sun. That was until the last guy jested, "I could be your man." He got the shock of his life when Dawn decked him clear off the pier.

*That felt good.*

But it also left her at a dead end. They hadn't seen his alibi for two moons. Dawn figured she couldn't have run out of town before Mudhi's arrest. Somehow, somewhere, this woman was getting by without fishing with them. The lieutenant didn't blame her, not one bit.

So, it's back to the Pit for Dawn, once again, to request an audience with Mudhi. Getting anything out of him would be like pulling a stick out of tar. Promise or no promise, things were looking grim for the fool.

A warble of a melody tantalized Dawn's ear, echoing from a winding walkway to her right, a few blocks away from the center of the Pit. Half-hoping to get a lucky break, Dawn strolled down, still keeping her hands behind her head, weaving among the potted herbs and wash buckets by the colorfully painted doors.

Then she saw the source. High up on the wooden balcony was a lithe woman in a white gossamer robe, washing her long, onyx-black hair. It shone like a polished stone. She sang a foreign melodic phrase, then paused. The word reverberated all around Dawn and the petite beauty continued with another verse. A duet of sorts all by herself.

The young lieutenant, staying in the shadows, leaned against the brick. Forgetting all the worries she experienced. Drinking in the beauty of the moment.

When the maiden reached for a glass vial, it escaped her soapy grasp and rolled off the wooden edge. Without hesitation, Dawn caught it with ease. She lifted it high in triumph. But that feeling diminished when the foreigner ran back inside.

"Wait. Don't go. I'm not going to hurt you," cried out Dawn.

She spotted a small stack of barrels and decided to climb up. As Dawn clamored up, taking care not to damage the perfume, she could see the maiden peeking from the doorway with her crescent-shaped eyes.

*Her skin is as pale as the moon.*

She cleared her throat and continued her ascent. Despite her best efforts, Dawn came up short. The top barrel was too unstable for her to stand. Thus, she leaned forward, presenting the prized perfume.

"Here, don't be afraid."

Perhaps she noticed that Dawn, too, was a woman, for the maiden came forward, her lengthy hair dragging on the floor like a cape. Her warm brown eyes glanced away, and a faint warmth came to her cheeks. The sight took Dawn's breath away. Then, leaning over the balcony, the maiden reached for the bottle. Daring to stand on the wobbling barrel, the young lieutenant gave her the fragile glass. She even guided the maiden's hand to cup the crystal before letting go. The foreign maiden stepped back on the balcony and bowed with a smile on her face. Dawn couldn't help but smile back at her and let out a sigh, leaning toward the wall.

Which was to her error.

The barrel rolled out from her feet, and the young lieutenant toppled to the ground. The empty drams proved challenging to overcome for Dawn; when she removed one, another would roll in to replace it.

A lilted laughter echoed about her, despite the maiden covering her mouth with her hand. "Aw, you poor thing," she said before ducking out of view.

*She knows the prophet's tongue?* Dawn slapped her palm against her forehead. *I must have sounded like an idiot to her.*

Then she saw a pomegranate fall from the sky, hurtling toward her. Catching it with one hand, Dawn strained her neck to see the maiden waving her goodbye. Then she disappeared inside, leaving Dawn breathless once again.

Perhaps not every dead end is a dead end.

*Dark blessings.*

That phrase had been running in Rhyllae's mind since she left the Pit. Often learned when Lune hides her face, sometimes terrible things occur to reveal the light in others. Such as strangers helping strangers after a natural disaster. Or, in this case, when Aramis broke into the Eagle's Nest Apartments.

Captain Tristan didn't know it was the Silver Fox, of course, but the gloves dropped at the scene were his—grit pads and all. The noise from the attempted burglary led the tenants to ask for the apartment owner, Fanteen Dada. When there was no immediate response, the daughter checked in to find her elderly mother missing.

It wasn't Aramis's wife, as she would have hoped, yet the lead may turn for the better.

*A dark blessing,* she realized, *just as Aramis had been.*

If it hadn't been for Aramis, she wouldn't have been able to live through the dungeon. He had been her shoulder to cry on as they traversed their way back to Amaveriel. Even now, he still looked after her, tucking her into bed last night with her shawl, kissing her good night. How gentle his lips were on her forehead as she drifted away to dream. Did Aramis ever use those same lips on Vanessa? Touching his wife's head, trailing down her cheek. Then her neck. Lingering on her collarbone.

Rhyllae dashed the thought away and pulled the robe tightly around her. How embarrassing for her to think such impure things. Yet ... is it a sin for a married couple to do what they were blessed to do?

*Why would anyone want to leave a man like him?*

The thought lingered in Rhyllae's mind until the Eagle's Nest Apartments came into view. From this side of the entrance, the whole upper left corner was utterly gone. Something, or someone, must have been playing with explosives the way the wall caved. Standing on the tip of her toes, Rhyllae could see the kitchen in the next room. Leaning too far forward, Rhyllae stepped into a pile of mud and straw. There before her were rows of mud bricks drying in the sun on their vertical ends. Well, minus one, thanks to her. It wasn't unheard of for cheap contractors to make the bricks on-site, though it would delay the project for weeks.

"Sister Rhyllae?" a woman asked her.

She twisted on the spot to hide the muck on her boots. Rhyllae faced a lady of her age, with a long, sculpted face, perfect cheekbones, and dark circles underneath brown eyes clutched in anxiety.

"You must be Salina Dada," Rhyllae said.

"Yes, I was told you are now taking on the case. Have you learned anything? Do you know what happened to her?" Salina asked.

"The captain of the guard gave me the rundown, and I'm afraid there's not much to go on. But together, we can unearth some answers, starting here. I would like to see all the vacant flats first."

"What are you going to find there? They're completely bare."

"From all my years of travel, I learned you'd be surprised what secrets an empty room can reveal."

Salina Dada led the Morning Lord sister on a brief tour of the apartment, allowing the Morning sister to inspect every suite available. Then they came to one far down the second-floor hall opposite the blown-up suite.

*Aramis's suite*, Rhyllae suspected.

"I'm not allowed to tell you the names of the previous owners of this flat," Salina told her as she pulled out the key. "But I can tell you this was the one that was broken into a few days ago."

The smaller-sized lot was stripped bare like all the others, with the standard table, bed, and dresser next to an open window. A small layer of dust was disturbed from the window to the table and the entrance door. Yet, the table was wiped clean, and despite a shattered mirror, there were no glass shards on the dresser surface.

Rhyllae frowns to herself. *It's been cleaned. How is this going to help?*

"What position was the table in when you discovered it?" Rhyllae asked.

"Why, on its side—toward that wall."

"Like so?" she asked after she laid it away from the dresser.

The landowner's daughter nodded. Glancing behind, Rhyllae noticed a large void in the kitchen area.

"Was there supposed to be an oven over here?"

"Yes. The previous tenant's husband requested it to be removed after his wife tried to burn herself."

"Burn herself?"

Selina nodded. "He used to leave his knives with my mother whenever he came home from his … er … work. The neighbors oft complained of them being loud. Please don't judge me when I say I'm glad she has moved out. I met the woman on a few occasions. She was … odd."

Rhyllae understood why Aramis wished to keep it a secret or feared for her safety—the woman was disturbed. Whether it was by shame or for her protection, she could not tell. However, there is no denying his love for her. Bless him.

Returning to the broken mirror on the dresser, Rhyllae could see that most of the pieces had fallen, caused by a singular impact. As she approached to take a closer look, something on the windowsill caught her eye. A light piece of white clay, dried from the heat. The only type of clay found in this city would be from the Jessenter base.

*This must have come from Aramis's boot,* Rhyllae surmised.

Attached to the windowsill was a garden box of roses shriveled into black husks, their beauty long since gone. A stalk crumbled in her hand when she plucked it from the garden.

"How long?" Rhyllae asked.

"Oh, not too long ago. Almost a week. The resident asked me if I wanted her rug and items. She didn't ask too much for their price."

*It doesn't make sense. Vanessa should've been gone as soon as the divorce was filed a month ago. Why would the Mother Superior lie?* The wind stole the crumbled pieces from her hand into the darkening sky.

"Did she say where she was going?" Rhyllae asked.

"Well, sort of. The owner said she was taking the 'last train to Clarksville.' Whatever that means."

"I know what it means."

The Morning priestess recognized the phrase as one of the songs from Havik's tomb. That song was contained on a black disc and that could only be heard by scratching it with a needle attached to a trumpet, one of Aramis's inventions. He promised Lady Ruth he'd put it in the vault after he was done researching it. In truth, he enjoyed the music and shared it with whomever, wherever he could. Rhyllae forgot how often he would sneak in at night to let her and her sisters dance to the archaic music. Perhaps, he shared it with Vanessa before Ruth forced him to hand it back. By the look of it, she took the contraption as well.

"I can't blame her for leaving," Salina said. "They arrested the traitor right here in this house."

"So I've heard. But not to worry, we won't let your reputation be marred by this."

"Yes, the city watch has tried to keep it hushed up before his trial. But she found him right here, of all places. It was unusual."

"Yeah, that is odd." Rhyllae looked at the white clay on the windowsill and wondered who it belonged to. If not Aramis, then who? Perhaps there was more to this room than met the eye.

The dresser didn't look damaged, though the handles had been worn from use. The mirror was held aloft by two thin poles attached at its center: no blood and no sign of damage beyond the glass. The cracks radiated from a single hit at the lower half of the mirror. The impact must have caused the mirror to tilt forward. Rhyllae tried to move the mirror to see if the back had a clue, but found it stuck in place. She peered at it from the side and noticed the bottom seemed sunken in the wall, like a stick stuck in the mud.

*Mud!*

She pushed the dresser away from her. The bottom of the frame scraped against the wall, etching a line in its wake. Rhyllae stepped back. The entire wall was bricked by uncured mud.

"Salina, we're going to need a bucket here. Or three."

Hours they toiled. Pulling the mud with their bare hands like pulling a garden rake through pudding. Finally, a hole emerged. Despite their muscles screaming, the two women feverishly tore away the portion. The smell was horrendous, and the wind outside did not help wick the offensive odor away.

Salina pulled off a chunk of clay, then shrieked as she fell to her knees. Covering her eyes with caked hands. Peering over the lump of clay, Rhyllae felt her stomach drop to the floor. Inside was a dry and shriveled female corpse. Her bony fingers stuck on the clay from her end as her skull rolled back to show her teeth in a silent scream.

They found her.

# Act 2

"Upon witnessing their avarice, their lust, their malice, the Sleeper, Creator of All Creation, called upon the angels to bring their trumpets ... [A]nd with a great wind, they laid the towering glass cities low."

~Book of Sun 32:36

# Chapter 12

## HABOOB

"TEN COCONUTS. FRESH FROM ALLEPO. GET ALL for a dinar," the burly vendor roared from his stall, his voice mingling in the den of Market Street. Colorful canvases of vibrant yellow, purple, and red stretched over the vendor's stalls, sheltering the choked pathways crowded by hagglers and beggars alike. Spices and citrus filled the air as dapples of sunbeams shone on the riches spilling forth. Rugs from Chessentari. Nagano silk. Precious furs of the Great North. Elven jewels unearthed from Angloria's ruins. Wherever the pirates plundered, they dumped it all here. Then laded their ships with fruits, meats, spices, and rum for their "customers."

Pirates became merchants. Merchants became kings. After a night of splendor, kings were reduced to paupers, then rose up to be pirates once again. The wheel continued to spin on Amaveriel's spinning wheel. Much like the hoop rolling past Dawn, chased by a flock of barefooted children. The slowest was all too concerned with keeping his kippah on his head. The beaded motif of the morning star flashed a reflective white from every sunbeam peeking through.

*Why the star of the Morning Lord and not the Phoenix? Don't they care about their martyrs anymore?* she wondered.

The young lieutenant caught a glimpse of a mother slapping her child's hand, scolding him in her thick accent while waving a ring fashioned as a flying phoenix. A trinket to encourage future recruitment.

*Are they turning their backs so soon?*

Her suspicions were confirmed when the mother tossed the toy into the street. Picking up the glasswork in her fingers, she marveled at how they made the fiery tail as the base so Sulmaith's little pet could spread its wings.

Strolling down the congested street, she twirled it between her forefinger and thumb, then made a sharp turn into a sliver of an alleyway. Most would pass it in a blink, but as an extra measure, one of their own would wheel over a cart of goods to block it. The ring slipped through her fingers when she spotted the lone guard on duty. Wings broke from its crumpled body.

"All of them?" General Korzha queried. "Every single one of them?"

"Affirmative," Dawn confirmed.

The fib worked, for he rolled his eyes heavenward and sighed. "Zealots," he muttered under his breath as he fetched a long box with a bow, no doubt the gladiolus for the ceremonial rite.

"Alert the others, Lieutenant. We have a long day ahead of us."

Then he paused and sniffed. Dawn stiffened and held her breath as he leaned forward. Following his eagle eyes, she noted they beaded on her unkempt collar, brushed with a bit of rouge.

"I'm afraid Madame Pompadour will have to wait for another night," he remarked with a knowing look. "I expect my officers to hold themselves to a higher standard than the soldiers they lead."

"Yes, sir." Her face flushed red for good measure.

Satisfied, Korzha gave a curt nod and left her behind in his office. The blonde officer strained her neck until he passed the bend, then smirked. Stepping back, she closed the door.

*That was a close one.*

Twirling to the center of the room, she stretched as high as her petite form would let her. Then beyond.

Her bones elongated, and her frame broadened, towering past six feet into a willow of a woman. Her fingertips bumped into the lamp, hovering near the ceiling. Batting it aside like a kitten, she rocked the lamp into an orbit around the room. Casting a swirl of shadows with its spinning light. Swaying her hips in a belly dance, she ran her fingers down from her shoulders to her waist, feeling her soft breasts harden into pectoral muscle. Her flat stomach tightened into a muscular rack, followed by the squaring of her hips.

Then, flipping the gender inside out, what was a she was now a he. A tall, thin man. Much paler than the sun-kissed tan of Dawn. How fortunate the real lieutenant was too busy questioning the dock workers. Rolling up his sleeve, he flexed his forearm, receding the muscle definition and allowing the veins to pop.

*Should I add the sun damage?* he mused.

With a quick stride to the desk, he rifled through the drawers until he found a bottle of dark liquid wedged next to a teapot and cup.

*A spot of Captain Montague's dark rum in your breakfast tea? High standards, indeed.*

Catching the oil lamp with one hand, he looked at himself in the reflection in the glass. *No need to rouge the cheekbones, but the hair simply won't do.*

Smoothing his long thin fingers through his hair, the tousled blond hair lightened to a paler shade, shortened in the back, with a dash of gray at the temples. Then he slicked his bangs from a deep, severe part at his right temple.

He wrinkled his sharp nose. Something was missing; he changed his jaw and cheekbones to feline angularity. Korzha had no freckles, though he had crows-feet a mile wide.

*Ah, the eyes.* With a snap, the hazel-green eyes shifted to a pale-blue frost. *Perfecto.*

A knock on the door. The imposter cleared his throat, allowing his vocal cords to loosen like a string on a viol. Hiding the rum behind his back, he greeted the officer coming in.

"General." Falçion saluted. "I request leave to aid the sisters in preparing our fallen."

"It's denied. I need you to guard the entryway. A depleted base is a vulnerable base." The voice was as brisk as an autumn wind.

The Jessenter's face was crestfallen; then he solemnly nodded and left.

The chameleon smirked. *Don't worry, you'll join your fellows soon enough.* Then he plopped the rum back in the drawer and slammed it shut.

The fallen brethren of the freedom fighters, all 36,774, returned home.

They were laid in rows and columns before the western gate as far as the eye could see—some of them in boxes no longer than two feet. For the less fortunate, their ashes were diligently parsed out in ceramic jars by holy mystic powers. Carefully on the sandy floor, the caskets were staged for the procession to be visited by Jessenters and priestesses.

An impressive undertaking, directed by Mother Myrrh no less, one of the Sunset mothers, second in command of the Rising Dawn, and ex-baroness of the Töskan moorlands. She was a woman of various accomplishments; she was the first to document virulent transmissions of the inmorti, published a manifesto of disease management, and was named "Mother of Anatomy." The list could go on, for she always found a new cause to follow. Yet, to Tavian Korzha, she was Mariam, his childhood friend. And the one whom he swore to serve as her knight in their expatriation. It was she who encouraged him to put forth his military expertise in the Jessenters.

Before the Western Gates, she stood there waiting for him. The priestly red and orange robes of the sunset ripple against her maternal frame from the wind. Her delicate, dark-brown hand held her shawl of indigo to ward off the flying sand. The other had the intertwined cords of service, salvaged from their fallen warriors.

Kneeling on one knee, Korzha presented the gladiolus's trailing flowers before her.

"<For me?>" Mother Myrrh asked in their native tongue, trailing her fingertips over the large pink petals. Her head tilted in curiosity as her thick, dark locks framing her face danced in the wind. The indigo shawl flapped between the two.

"<You asked me to bring them forth for the dead,>" he replied back in Töskan.

Her thick brows furrow up in surprise. "<Only as a fore-thought in my mind. I only had hoped you obtain it for the procession. Though...>" She looked back at the caskets behind her. "<Your intuition has always been on the mark. It would not be a bad idea to begin the blessing now.>"

"<T'were not intuition that brought me here. T'was Lieutenant Dawn.>"

"<Odd. Never have I met any of your officers with that name before.>"

A gust of wind came between them, taking her shawl in flight, leaving her head covered by the small circular hat distinctive of her rank. Impishly, the thin fabric teased their outstretched fingers as they chased it downwind. Then it caught itself upon a casket. Korzha freed it from the snagging corners and paused to read the name carved on the wooden cover: "General C. K. Tackett."

"My apologies, old chap." He replaced the shawl with the sword lily stem upon the casket. Turning back to Myrrh, he wrapped the silk shawl upon his lady's head and neck, careful to capture any loose strands flying in the breeze from her bun. Her gray-lavender eyes, Töskan blue as they called it, gazed upon his face. It had been over two months since they last met, but he felt it had been forever the way she studied him.

Tucking in the last strand beneath the cloth, Korzha asked her, "<What do your eyes see, my lady?>"

"<A brow heavy with the burdens of this world.>" Myrrh traced her fingertips on his forehead, then down to his temples. "<With much more still to come.>"

Taking his long and broad hands, she laid the salvaged cords of service into his palms. The metal chains had been twisted and knotted into an intricate braid, with every link secure. The bone tags, etched with their names, lay outside like shingles on a roof. Dangling at the end as if they were strings of a tassel.

With the weight of the dead in his hands, Korzha wondered if any commander in history had this many. Never had Korzha thought he would ever see acres upon acres of caskets lined as far as his blue eyes could see.

A gentle touch on his cheek drew his gaze back into her soulful eyes. "<Burdens you do not have to face alone.>"

"<That is where you are mistaken, madame. You have command of the dead—a stoic guard against all of the supernatural evil of this world. Whereas I command the living, who may soon join the ranks which you keep watch. This is a burden I must face alone.>" Taking her hand, he bowed to grant a single kiss and departed.

Treading among the silent soldiers beyond the city wall, he brushed the gladiolus over every casket he passed. Brothers and sisters. Fathers and mothers. The honorable and the wretched. All were given his acknowledgment of their ultimate sacrifice and the courage to stare down death.

Though no tear did his eyes make. Nor did he rejoice in their glorious deaths, as his mother's people would have dictated. He was lost in the monotony of waving the gladiolus's stem as custom. Devastated by the overwhelming numbers, he neither heard the mourners cry from the wall nor regarded the saluting men and women he passed by. Korzha didn't even notice that he was the only one walking among the dead. Nor even took note of the wall of sand and doom coming from the west.

"Everyone inside," Dawn urged the street folk lingering in the Pit.

The wind was picking up quickly as the storm approached them. Dawn escorted them toward the city watch's building, the only place she knew that wouldn't have open windows.

A beggar, sitting in a small niche on the roadside, pulled his ragged blanket over himself.

"You too, pal." She reached down and pulled him to his feet. "This is one you can't sit out. C'mon."

Letting him lean on her small muscular frame, Dawn guided him through the biting wind, drawing strength with every step she took. With three solid pounds of her fist, the double doors creaked open. Dawn spotted additional stragglers stumbling around as she waved the people in, their arms raised to protect their eyes from the wind's sting. Wrapping her desert turban over her nose and mouth, Dawn ventured out to round them up.

As the last of the herd crossed the threshold, a gust of wind pushed the doors wide open, flinging the two young men back. Four guards, including Captain Tristan, joined to assist them. They struggled to gain traction in the depositing sand.

Their weight was lifted when Dawn jumped in to push on the right. The giant door moved smoothly with every step she took. Soon, the lieutenant was able to grab the other door. Holding one in each hand, Dawn paused to take one deep breath and stepped forward. Her lean muscles bulged from the weight, but they didn't break. She grunted and pushed against the battering winds spraying sand upon her entire body. The thick, massive doors creaked and moved with every step she took, gaining more ground than the eight men combined. They stood in amazement as she narrowed the gap to a close.

"Bar!" the young lieutenant cried, leaning with all her might.

They snapped to it, securing the front portal with a heavy beam. Once in its purchase, Dawn eased up. The doors moved to rest on the bar and not an inch farther.

"I've never seen anything like it." Tristan voiced the sentiments of his watchmen.

"Living on the edge of the desert, I'm not surprised you've never seen a haboob before. Well, as often as I have." Dawn unwrapped her turban caked with sand, ruffling her blonde hair to remove the grains that had slipped through.

"I meant you."

Her hazel eyes blinked as the young officer looked upon every wide-eyed face. She laughed and put her hand behind her head. "I'm just a kid from Bedouin."

"I highly doubt the rest of your tribe are as strong as you are."

"Wouldn't you like to know?" She threw a boyish grin at him. "You don't mind if we stay here for a little while?"

Hearing the storm's roar raging behind the doors, the captain of the watch felt there was no other choice.

A haboob was as devastating and as powerful as any hurricane or tornado. Like a tsunami heralding the earthquakes from afar, they came from massive storms that collapsed within themselves. The wall of sand stretched across the visible horizon. Towering high enough to blot out the sun.

The wind sprayed sand in Korzha's face, ripping the sword lily from his grasp as if the dead spited him. Korzha stopped in his tracks, furtively wiping the grains from the creases around his eyes. His view was obscured with colors of clay.

Then he heard someone calling his name. At first, he thought it was the low howl of the western wind. Yet, he heard it, distant at first, then becoming distinctive with every call. It grew to a deafening volume, louder than the roar of the storm itself.

"Spirits. Ghosts. I hear you," Korzha cried out into the sandy wind. "Speak. I will listen."

A figure formed before him through the blinding storm; it coalesced into a broad-shouldered man with a long beard and a hooked nose. The uniform was cut like his own but decorated with honors and valor of services unknown. It wasn't until Korzha spied the ranking on his neck that he grasped who it was—the ghost of General Tackett.

Protocol would have him salute his previous commander, but the force of the haboob was too great. Korzha had no choice but to lean into the wind, shielding his eyes with the service cords, slowly being unraveled.

"General Tackett, sir. Forgive my break in protocol. I am constrained in this mortal shell and bound to the hardships of this plane."

The past general's ghostly visage appeared unmoved by his pitiful excuses, unhindered by the gale-like forces whipping him. The ghostly Tackett simply produced a club and, upon it, lit a flame, white with blue on its outer edge.

"The torch," the apparition said to him. "Take our torch. We the dead throw it to you now." And he flung it toward him.

It defied all common sense of the world that it would sail end over end against the maddening wind. The flame did not sputter nor flinch as the torch rotated in the air.

Regardless of logic, Tavian Korzha stretched out his hand and managed to seize it. It felt unearthly in his hands. The sensation coursing through his nerves was utterly indescribable.

"Raise it high," the ghost continued. "Raise it high. And take our quarrel to our foe. We will not rest if ye break our solemn vow."

"I will not break," pledged Korzha, raising this flamed torch high as well as he could muster. "I will not bend. I will not rest until they meet their end. This I do swear upon my very soul."

He could not tell if the spirit was pleased with his words. General Tackett dissipated into the wind with the rest of the tempest-tossed earth. Gradually, the wind ceased, and the dust fell. Tavian Korzha found himself the only one standing among the field of caskets, barely visible in the deposited sand. He realized he was several feet away from the city wall, farther than he anticipated when the storm hit. Korzha looked to see if he still held the torch given to him but found nothing save for a lingering sensation tantalizing his senses.

"Tavian," someone called to him again, this time not from the dying western wind.

Squinting through the sand clinging to his lashes, he could see his old friend ambling toward him as fast as she could over the disturbed earth. Her vivid colored robes were muted by the sand covering her from head to toe.

Korzha attempted to straighten himself but fell to his knees due to the shifting sand under his weight. When she came to his side, he tried to wave her away. "<I am well, Mariam.>"

Waving her hand before his face, she shook her head. "<Please, for once, let me help.>"

Myrrh, standing over him, produced a small empty jar with a wide mouth from her frayed silk purse. Humming a prayer, she tilted the clay jar, and out poured clean water, pristine as dew on a flower. It splashed upon his face, washing away the dirt and moistening the ground around his knees.

"<You're lucky it didn't suffocate you.>" Myrrh paused to let him wipe his face with his handkerchief.

"<It could not be helped. The dead demanded my attention.>"

Myrrh tilted his face toward her again, her brows furrowing in scrutiny. Her fingertips traced over his brow once again. But this time, they moved over the bridge of his nose and swept over the apple of his cheeks.

"<They could wait 'til the morrow. You require medicinal aid.>"

"<'The dead could wait.' What a fool I am to say such things. Oh, how blind I was.>" Korzha spoke aloud to himself rather than to his dear companion. "<Am I any crueler than the very enemy we fight against?>"

"<Why say such things about yourself?>"

"<I say such things because they're true.>"

"<You say such things because you are tired. You need rest and care.>"

"<How could I rest when they could not? Or how could he?>" Korzha grabbed Mother Myrrh's elbow with a sense of urgency. "<Mariam, I need to find him and rectify my mistake. There are still those lost that need to be found.>"

"<Tavian, you're as mad as a mallard. I have never seen you this way before.>"

Before he could explain, a boom clapped the sky. Smoke billowed over the city walls, hovering over where the market should be. They exchanged worried glances and took off, running toward the cries for help.

# Chapter 13

## FAUX

"**I** FEEL SORRY FOR MR. RUSTY," SAID DIDO, TROTTING next to Aramis. "That was a horrible sight to see."

"Mhm," Aramis grunted as he weaved them through the crowd.

Everyone and their third cousin were rushing to the western gate. Perhaps it was a survivor. Or one of the dwarven merchants sporting their wares. Whatever it was, they ran out of time. The storm would be upon them soon. The wind gusts had ceased minutes ago, and there was a stillness in the air that was too stifling, like being in an enclosed tomb. The thought of those claustrophobic halls of M'thealquilôk came unheeded. No matter how hard he tried to dispel it, he could never forget how endlessly the corridors seemed to stretch beyond his sight. It was as if it all led to the dreadful throbbing heart of the abyss.

Then he felt a chill on his hand, colder than the ocean and biting. Snapping to attention, Aramis found himself in the middle of the street. The cart pushers gave him the evil eye. Dido was holding his hand, pleading for him to finish crossing the street.

*Did I blackout?*

Aramis felt guilty as the little satyr pulled him to the walkway, causing him to hunch as they hustled out of the way. Once to safety, Dido let go of her icy grip. Part of him wanted to ask how long he was out, but by her worried looks, it was long enough to cause a fuss.

"So that's how you stay cool," Aramis said as he rubbed his hand. "Explains why you're not in your skivvies."

"Humph, it shows what little you know about magic." Dido folded her arms across her chest. "I'm just preparing for whatever comes our way, that's all."

"Fair. It's not every day you see a brain plastered to the ceiling."

"Despite what Rusty said, I don't think that was an accident." Then Dido lowered her head as her rosy eyes tracked one of the men limping past them.

Once he passed, Aramis stooped to put a hand on her shoulder. "Neither do I."

It was all for the keyhole. The Silver Fox was convinced of it. Lockjaw was too skilled to slip up, especially if he was the one who could create the beeswax. It was done by a thief with an ulterior motive. If an ordinary thief had done a smash-and-grab, they left behind plenty of goodies at the Salt & Battery shop. No, someone in Amaveriel needed the keyhole. They knew where it was, and Lockjaw was in the way. For what purpose, the Silver Fox couldn't care less. Another friend was gone, and he wasn't there to stop them.

Aramis muttered, "I'll hunt the bastard down. I swear it."

The wind was screaming in Aramis's ears as they made their way to the huddling guard. He barely could hear Dido as she said, "Humperdink," next to his swaddled head. The clothed man slightly turned the secret knob before the door was flung open inside. All three stumbled into the cold, earthy shelter. They patted themselves down, sand falling from their clothes.

They snaked through the halls as they headed toward the treasury. Aramis couldn't help but notice something was off. As his silver-gray eyes darted from shadow to shadow, he noticed how hollow the lava tunnels sounded. Numerous candles in the carved niches were spent without replenishment.

*Where is everyone?*

"Why are you two here?" The question came from a slender man down by the dead end of the hall.

"General Korzha, sir." Dido saluted him as he came forward into the light. "We were on our way to the vault."

The general waved his hand in the air. "Never mind that. We have far more pressing matters to attend to."

"More important than the tome, sir?"

"We cannot leave our fallen brethren unattended, now can we?"

"But what about the treasure? You gave me explicit orders."

"They have changed. Time is wasting. We can't keep the dead waiting."

"Funny you should care," Aramis said bitterly.

Korzha's frosty-blue eyes narrowed at him. "We must honor those who made the ultimate sacrifice."

"So why hurry?" Aramis closed the distance between them as he spoke. "What difference would two people make from a hundred score? 'Rest for the dead is for eternity. They can stand to wait a little while longer.' Your own words."

He came nose to nose with the man, the scent of the man's lover sickening him. Then again, much of Korzha sickened him to his core.

"You know, for a man of honor, you sure have double standards."

Korzha didn't flinch from his unwavering glower. Instead, he smirked as the reflection of the torchlight danced in his eyes. "So sayeth the man who lived a double life. To claim a pair in my hand would be telling a royal flush in yours."

"Takes one to know one, General."

"Truly? Then tell me. What do you know of honor? Why would anyone give their life for someone like you, a vagabond sifting through the gutters of the moral high road?"

There were no words. The muscles in Aramis's jaw were too tight for him to retort back at the smiling Töskan.

"Now, you are dismissed." He shouldered his way past the Silver Fox and snapped his fingers at Dido to follow him.

The little treasurer hesitated in going with the general. She mouthed a word of apology to Aramis and turned to follow Korzha with her shoulders in a slump. With every step she took, Dido looked back at him. Her gentle rose eyes mixed with dismay and sympathy.

Watching them go, Aramis noticed something off. Korzha's hip was lacking his trusty Silver Star. A dark smile crossed his face as he considered the temptation. Then it widened when he suspected why it was lacking in the first place. Only one way to be sure. Unhooking his cloak, Aramis wadded the fabric into a ball and unhooked the daggers from their scabbards.

"I do have one question for you, General."

The man paused and cocked his eyebrow at him. Then those pale-blue eyes widened when he saw a dagger flying straight for him. His right hand snapped up in the nick of time, revealing a white silken purse tucked under his sleeve.

"I guess you're not left-handed," Aramis jested before he sprinted down the hall, past the stunned satyr, sliding halfway across the sandy floor, feet first.

The fake Korzha moved his arm back to spike Aramis with his own blade but was blinded when the Silver Fox flung his cape up. As the imposter wrestled with the dark cloak, he slid between his legs and popped up behind him. Aramis grabbed his left elbow and pinned the man's arm against his back. With each struggle the man made, Aramis pulled his forearm up, threatening to pop it from its hinge. Dido stood there in disbelief at the chaos unfolding before her eyes.

"Dido, knock him out!" Aramis pleaded.

"Are you crazy?!"

"It's not him—oof!" he groaned as the imposter lurched to slam him against the wall.

Reprieved momentarily, the lanky man climbed the wall in front of him with his long legs. Using Aramis as a fulcrum, he continued to run from the wall onto the ceiling. Up and over, he landed behind the Silver Fox like a spider. The tip of the dagger rushed down toward the base of his neck.

Taking the twin knife still in its scabbard, Aramis managed to hook the incoming blade in time.

"That's it. I'm done playing nice," Aramis said as he pushed it away.

Spinning around, he crouched as if to kick the man's knees from under him. But it was a feint to mask him leading with his knife. Flicking his dagger around, Aramis reached to slit his throat open wide.

The smiling imposter simply leaned back, seeing the move a mile away. He rushed Aramis. He grabbed his wrist and contorted it to the ceiling, while the other hand slid the blade into his soft underbelly. The cold steel felt heavy as it twisted among Aramis's intestines, forcing him to double over, clinging to the chameleon's shoulder helplessly.

In the back of his mind, he kicked himself for leaving himself wide open. And another kick for giving this actor his blade. What did he expect him to do, cower? All thoughts of regret flew when the imposter tightened his embrace around him, smothering him with the sensual scent of jasmine.

"Did you miss me, Aramis?" a familiar female voice whispered in his ear.

His silver-gray eyes dilated. The dagger fell from his numb fingertips. Aramis needed air, but all he got was their cloying natural scent.

*Vanessa!*

Before he could assess how or why, a flash of light streaked across his view. The magical bolt crashed upon Vanessa, sending them both flying down the hall.

Holding the dagger in place to not let his contents spill out, Aramis fell back to the wall. He wanted to cry out, *Why are you doing this?* but all that came out was a pathetic, "Why?"

Dido clipped-clopped down the hallway to his side. "Mr. Feres, I'm sorry I didn't believe you—leaping lima beans! That's a lot of-of..." She trailed off when she saw a sheen of wet maroon on his dark shirt radiating from the dirk's penetration.

Aramis pointed at the white coin purse with the Morning Lord's sunny emblem. There, peeking from the magical opening, was the corner of the tome's flesh-stitched spine. Dido dove for it, but the accessory was snatched away before her tiny fingers could grab it.

Vanessa reached deep into the tiny coin purse, up to their elbow. Then pulled out a rectangular box with a shiny red knob in the middle, a relic from ancient times. With crooked teeth, they extended the thin metal stick.

"Ah-ah-ah. Finders keepers," they sang, waving the relic side to side like a metronome, in the baritone voice of General Korzha, their thumb resting on the shiny button.

Creating a circle in the air, Dido let her nervous energy through her fingers, sparks arcing like tiny lightning bolts. A heavy hold on her shoulder broke her concentration.

"No, don't," Aramis told her, still keeping the dagger in his gut.

He recognized the artifact. The Ancients had used it to detonate their explosives from a safe distance. If they were waving that around, Vanessa must have rigged the place to blow sky-high.

"Oh, please do. I love big booms, I cannot lie," the cruel imposter jested.

"You don't have to do this." Aramis shuffled in front of Dido, preventing her from shooting off any of her spells at his beloved. He reached out with his bloody hand, offering to take the device from their hand. "Whoever is making you do this, please, let me help."

Vanessa snickered at him. "Oh, but I must. Who else will knock down these paper dolls and their house of cards?"

Closing his eyes, he cursed. Of course, Vanessa would stop taking their medicine when he was away. Hobbling forward, he continued to plead, "The world is not a paper moon. Please, stop this. You're not well."

Vanessa guffawed. "Not well? I've never felt better!" They stretched out their arms wide, swinging their hips as they nimbly stepped back. From their lips, they sang one of the ancient's songs about feeling good. Then, Vanessa pressed the button on the beat and tossed it away.

The ground rumbled underneath them, and a loud boom echoed down the hallway behind them. Skipping away, Vanessa pulled out a floppy black cloth and slapped it against the ceiling above. The black circle stuck like glue, becoming a hole leading to who knew where.

"The keyhole." Aramis grunted as he pulled his dagger out of his ragged belly, poised to fling it down to stop them from escaping. But he couldn't let it loose.

Smiling at him, the face of Korzha blew a kiss at him before running up the wall and pulling themself through the portal. Another ground-shaking explosion, and the fabric peeled itself off.

Snatching it in the air, Aramis realized he couldn't follow them. The wallboards moaned around them. The soft clay would come crashing in soon; he needed to act fast.

Gritting through the pain, he rushed back to pick up Dido. "Hold on."

The hissing sounds of the sand spilling down roared behind them like a raging basilisk. Turning the bend, Aramis spied the molten vault door ahead. Aramis threw the keyhole with all his might. The black fabric sailed through the air, sticking onto the dark metal like a spider's web.

Still running down the hallway, Aramis cradled the little satyr in his arms toward his center of mass. The ground slipped underneath his heels, threatening to swallow him into the abyss below. Throwing all his energy into his legs, Aramis pushed himself to run faster, hoping to reach the hole.

On a good day, he could jump almost a yard. Feeling the weakness in his gut, Aramis hoped he could clear one foot. He felt the shifting earth nip on his heels once again.

*Here goes nothing.*

He eyed the dark fabric on the black vault; it was difficult to discern the portal's edge. With one hop, he leaped forward. He gritted his molars, the pain screaming from his stretched abs as he straightened himself out like a javelin.

The hissing sands crashed all around him, knocking out the last torch. Leaving all dark as pitch.

It was nightmarish seeing the bewildered citizens rush past Korzha and Mariam. All were coated in a fine white dust from head to toe, hobbling, smote with red streaks. Some had the wide-eyed craze of panic's fervor.

Soon as the two neared the site, they found they weren't the only ones racing toward Market Street. Men, women, khanith, humans, elves, dwarves, fae, and everyone in between were running to Market Street. All humble people with no great regard other than selfless charity. They all joined those who were already there, neighbors and pirates alike. A relay line quickly formed to snuff out oil fires, while others dug with buckets and bare hands.

Upon reaching the scene, Korzha halted, for he couldn't believe his eyes. There were no stones left standing. No color canvas in the sky. All was swallowed by the earth. What hadn't sunk had toppled over like a red oak's farewell. Right before Korzha's eyes, one slab of a two-story wall broke from the foundation and slipped down. When it hit bottom, it veered over. Those in its path scrambled to escape before it fell. The cloud from its destruction plumed, shrouding the living and dead alike. Some fled while others rushed toward them, scrambling to re-create the relay and pull survivors free from the rubble.

Korzha spotted a familiar redheaded Jessenter, flagging others down for help. Grabbing him by his shoulders, he turned him around to face him.

"Falçion, what happened here?" Korzha asked.

The man's eyes were still wide in disbelief, and it took him a while before he could respond. "Shits blown to pieces, sir."

"Details, Private," he said tersely as he shook him.

A hand on his shoulder gave him pause. Mother Myrrh nodded toward the man's sleeve, soaked in red. Stepping back, he allowed her to tend to his wound.

"What has occurred here?" he asked again once he collected himself.

"I was standing guard at the door as you had ordered, sir, when I heard explosions deep in the trenches. I opened the door, and the next thing I knew, I was hit by flying rocks. Everything fell on top of me. And they … they pulled me out."

Falçion waved toward the people at the rubble. Korzha saw a strip of flesh hanging from where his two last fingers and the edge of his palm should have been. Mother Myrrh caught Falçion's wrist and started binding his hand. The man must have been too stunned to notice the pain.

"Who had passed under your watch?" Korzha asked.

"None save for the treasurer and the Silver Fox, sir."

"Where are they?"

As if to answer his question, the ground beneath them gave way, forcing them to move back. Like a gopher, Dido popped her head out, gasping for air. She tried to climb out of the hole, but the sand dragged her back. Quickly, Korzha and Myrrh pulled her to safety as she coughed the sand from her lungs.

Immediately after was a bloody hand groping the edge of the man-made burrow. Korzha reached down to pull the man out and found himself face-to-face with Aramis Feres, pale from stone dust.

Korzha glowered at the Silver Fox. All previous thoughts of making amends flew out of his mind. Of course, this disaster would occur. What did he expect to happen when Dido asked for his services? His anger simmered to the surface, but Korzha could not find it in himself to lash out. Pain was etched all over Aramis's face. In his silver eyes, terror.

Taking one step forward, Aramis fell forward into the general's arms. Turning him over, Korzha found his belly sticky with blood, slowly oozing through the cloth. His silver eyes implored him to listen as Aramis tightened his hold on his shirt. Korzha cradled him as Aramis mouthed a word he couldn't understand—still not used to the local dialect of the desert land. Over and over, he mouthed the word as blood crept to the corner of his murmuring lips. The chaos surrounding them muffled the sound he was trying to make.

Korzha sank to his knees in all of this déjà vu. The screams of chaos rang in his ears. Knees deep in the sand as the heat beat down upon him. The weight of the dying man in his arms. The sounds, the smells, the sights. It all came back to him like rolling thunder.

*On that fateful day, his knees sank into the muck. Screams of terror cried out in the distance before being silenced by a blade. Horses whinnied in confusion, galloping far away to safer fields. The heat from the crumbling estate evaporated the sweat on his brow. All he could breathe was ash from the burned pastures and copper from the slain. In his arms, his dearest husband gasped for breath.*

*Try as he may, Korzha couldn't stop the blood flowing from his belly with his hand. Brushing his delicate copper hair aside, he'd cradled him during his final moments. His husband tried to tell him something, but it was an elvish word he had never heard of before. His lips slowed to a stop as a ruby river flowed out. The mottled skin shared among the sylvan elves turning pale before his eyes.*

Korzha shut his eyes. Only to have them open to the same hell before him.

Alone in the eye of this storm of panic and helplessness. Then something occurred that he did not expect. Something which never happened when he needed it the most. A tender touch of a helping hand.

Myrrh. Her lavender-gray eyes implored him to let her intervene.

"<Please,>" he begged as he shifted Aramis into her arms.

Aramis's blood stained her sunset robes, but she did not care as she cradled him in her arms. Like a mother with a babe, she lowered her lashes as she gazed upon him. Still, the Silver Fox struggled to speak, though his lips began to slow.

Mother Myrrh shushed him with a wave of her hands and brushed her fingertips over his silver eyes. "Rest. You've done all you can do for the day."

Aramis's eyes fluttered to a close. His head tilted toward her breast. As his breathing slowed to a deep slumber, she began her work. Drawing from the well of Creation, she mended the rips and tears within him with every solemn word and touch.

For once in Korzha's exiled life, he felt something stir within the cockles of his heart. Meeker than righteousness, yet more potent than all the steel in the world.

Hope.

# Chapter 14

## CONFESSIONS

Est mea culpa.

Li'nim me'khatra.

It's my fault.

Mea maxima culpa.

A'nim khashra.

My most grievous fault.

Paeniteo.

A'nim shurri.

I'm sorry.

...Can no one hear me?

ESPITE HIS BEST EFFORTS, ARAMIS COULDN'T seem to get through to Korzha. Instead, the general stared at him in bewilderment. He knew the general spoke elvish—Töska was teeming with elves if not the inmorti.

Aramis tried again, this time tugging on his shirt, pulling him closer. "*Li'nim me'khatra, a'nim shurri.*"

Yet, Korzha didn't say a word as pity crept through his features. He even wiped aside his grizzled hair clinging to his face.

*Why?* Aramis numbly wondered. *Am I dying?*

He must be. His breaths felt more laborious by the second, and his eyelids were too heavy to keep open. For once in a long time, Aramis felt like he could sleep. Never to wake, as he blissfully drifted into a blanket of dreams.

*No!* he told himself, forcing himself to stay awake. *Not now. Not when Vanessa's out there. Not when she has that book!*

Breathing as much as he could, he forced himself to hold on.

Aramis wanted to say, *Just forgive me. I can fix this*, but the words jumbled together in a murmur.

He blinked and found himself speaking not to the general but to a mysterious, dark woman clothed in red and indigo. Her lavender eyes were soft, and her thin lips pursed to quiet him.

"Rest. You've done all you can do for the day."

*No, you're wrong!* he wanted to tell this dark beauty, but the all too familiar spell was cast upon him. Against his will, Aramis slipped into darkness.

*There's more I could have done.*

*I could have prevented all of this.*

*My wife... My friends...*

*I'm sorry. This is all my fault.*

*The dried leaves crackled as Aramis crushed them in his hands. Then, he placed them in the mortar and covered them in olive oil. The soothing, earthy smell filled the air as tiny droplets of*

oil emerged from the leaves, bruised from the pestle he'd turned. It would have been a calming experience if not for the sound of shattering wood in the next room. Aramis closed his eyes and pestled faster.

The shaman boasted of the magical properties of elven silkweed, bragging that it was the cure for all ails. Aramis didn't believe it would solve all the world's woes, but it did mitigate her behavior. He wished he didn't have to make this on the fly. Then again, Aramis never expected Vanessa to take the jar out of his hands. Hearing the glass shatter on the pavement outside almost brought his hand to her.

Almost.

After several long minutes of grinding, he plopped the contents onto the cheesecloth. Twisting it into a ball, Aramis squeezed as much oil as he could into the cup, praying he had enough of the expensive herb. A small amount went into the bronze cup, while the rest was secreted in another jar. Hidden in a hole behind a tapestry depicting manna falling from the Ancients' view of the heavens.

Taking the cup, Aramis took a few steady breaths to calm himself. The banging was still going on but slowed with additional nonsensical cursing. Pulling back the curtain, he found chair legs at his feet. Not too far off, a seat leaned against the wall, cracked beyond repair. Vanessa held the second chair up, frozen in place. Her blazing green eyes locked onto his.

This senseless destruction used to upset him during their first few months of living together. How many excuses had he made for the welts that came from Vanessa's thrown bridal dishes? Or the ones that came after that? Aramis was losing his mind; the cost of replacing everything exceeded his income.

That was until he learned the cause of her fury: an abnormality of the mind. A condition that had no cure with a treatment beyond his financial means.

When he discussed it with her father, unbeknownst to her, the chief was surprised yet sympathetic. He was willing to absolve their marriage. But Aramis couldn't bear to do it. How could he betray someone he loved, especially when this illness was not her fault? A broken woman for a broken man. That was his lot in life.

So, he adjusted to the norm to the best of his abilities, metal bowls instead of ceramic pottery, woven tapestry instead of paintings. Taking every precaution for both of their safeties. Even abandoning his love of tinkering so she wouldn't harm herself with anything sharp. He should have considered replacing the wooden seating with pillows.

Looking at the splinters on the floor, Aramis took another deep breath. "I guess we'll be standing for dinner tonight."

"Like we ever ate in this setting." She tossed the chair on the floor, and the rug wrinkled as the furniture skidded to a halt. Vanessa flipped her dark hair back over her pale shoulders and put her hands on her hips. "Not that the food would taste any different. Wax fruit is still wax fruit, after all."

"When a cigar is just a cigar, yes—but you claim otherwise," he flatly replied, holding the cup out to her.

Vanessa eyed the shot glass as if he was holding a bomb, then shifting her gaze from it to him and back to the cup again. "But this is not real. None of this is."

"No, this is real. This is not some fantasy concocted by a maestro behind the scenes. That chair," he pointed to the splintered pieces at his feet, "was real. I'm real. And so are you." He gestured with the cup again, daring to take a step forward.

With hesitation, Vanessa took the cup in her hands. Once again, she looked at him with pleading eyes. "What do I have to do to make you see the truth?"

Sighing, Aramis gazed at the wreckage around him. The curtains were torn away, the mattress flipped up and over, and the table wedged underneath the dresser. The entire room was littered with their fresh laundry. To think he's going to leave at dawn tomorrow to help look for M'thealquilôk.

"Maybe you should try knocking the walls down," Aramis jested.

"Hmph, quite a request," Vanessa mused, toying the cup in her hands. "Consider it done."

Aramis stared at her with a dropped jaw, too baffled to speak. For the first time ever in their marriage, she wasn't joking. And the prospect frightened him.

Vanessa pouted. "Do you still love me?"

Averting his eyes, Aramis blamed himself for letting her see him worry. Vanessa wouldn't do anything that dangerous; she wasn't that crazy. Closing the ground between them, he let his finger caress her arm, leaving a trail of the medicinal oil on her scented skin.

"Of course I do. You drive me absolutely insane," Aramis said.

Vanessa guffawed, almost spilling her medicine. "I'll drink to that."

After taking a swig, she rose on tiptoes to kiss him. The herb's earthy aroma was fresh on her tongue as it mingled with his own. At first, he hesitated to embrace her as she teased him with her fingertips. Snaking them down his shirt to his tight love handles. Her lips curved into a smile as he pulled back to gaze at her—pale like the moonlight shining through their window. Lips twisted and flushed red with anticipation. The fire in her green eyes smoldered. The medicine was working its magic.

Pursing her lips, Vanessa cooed while trailing her nail from his knitted brow to the tip of his nose. "No tricks, I promise."

"Last time you said that—"

"I promise." She brushed his lips with that same fingertip to silence him. "So long you come back to me." Taking his chin, she led him to her lips.

The cloying scent on her neck overpowered him, rekindling memories of their first night of passion. Pressing her body against him, he cradled her nape as Vanessa wrapped her arms around his. She drew back, nipping his bottom lip as she parted. Then Vanessa hoisted herself up higher in his arms. Wrapping her legs around his waist as she smooched from his lips to his ear. Whispering, "Promise me," as she clawed on his shirt.

Closing his eyes, Aramis leaned her against the wall. Pressing himself against her and unlaced his longings. His rough hands groped her round cheeks as he eased himself in. Moaning "Yes" to her every "Oh" as he dove into the depths of her sea. A pearler searching for long-lost treasure.

I should have seen this coming. I was blind, and everyone paid the price for it. I should have had someone watched her, cared for her, helped her. Vanessa. My love... My desert rose...

Why did you leave me?

I must have failed you somehow.

As I failed them...

The air reeked of decay, stifling what little clean air there was in the tomb. Aramis slunk to the top of one of the four gigantic statues along the wall. He'd glanced back to his compatriots down below, making sure the movement of his cloak hadn't given him away. Ruth and Tamira worked in perfect unison, creating a circle of destruction as bones and limbs flew everywhere. Sister Rhyllae was on her knees, deep in prayer, as Joel protected her with magical flames. Yet, none of it would matter if he didn't get into position.

As he often did, the necromancer would appear in the middle of the horde, mocking their efforts with magical destruction. It didn't matter to the mad sorcerer if his ghoulish minions perished from his ferocity. Tellezard had plenty to spare. Every time they managed to reach him through the horrific throng, the wretch disappeared in a wink.

After losing Bagheera, they couldn't afford to let him escape. A promise the Silver Fox intended to keep.

Like a fleeting shadow, Aramis leaped from the top of the statue to the next, stopping once to make sure the deadly horde didn't catch wind of him before he leaped again. When Aramis landed on the final statue, the walls reverberated from Rhyllae's prayer.

"Though I walk through the Shadow, I will raise my candle high. For the Light within me shall shine, like Fire of the Sun."

And Lo, did she shine.

A light, as pure as the stars, enveloped her. Wave upon wave of the holy light pulsated from the Morning Lord sister, dispersing all the desecrated dead as it filled the room. Yet, it warped around the sickly hooded figure, Tellezard. The hunched figure raised his boil-covered arms, widening his void. The sister of the Dawn waved her arms in front of her, lips moving in prayer, glowing white as molten steel. Joel, Ruth, and Tamira shielded their eyes from the spectacle. The dark sorcerer didn't budge as he muttered his incantations, becoming hazy as shadows gathered around him.

Aramis was transfixed by the sight. Light and dark warped and twisted into eddies like galaxies clashing in the midnight sky. Sparks flew from their mighty clash as both of them intensified their incantations. An arc of lightning headed straight for Aramis, causing him to fall onto his belly.

He must have cried out, for he heard Rhyllae call out, "Aramis!" and the spell was broken.

As the light dissipated, the room was filled with a dry cackle. "Is that any way to treat a host? After all, I have brought a gift for you." Lifting his cloak, he let a pale figure walk forth toward them.

Cursing at his delay, Aramis scrambled to his feet. He spotted an archway in the adjacent wall with a wide enough frame for him to use. Leaping from the statue's slope, the ball of his foot touched the top of the frame, giving him enough traction to take another step. Then, curling into that step, he pushed off like a diver, twin daggers in hand, contorting his body to flip and twist in the stifling air.

The hooded sorcerer gazed at Aramis coming down upon him, his leprotic face twisting into a rotten grin. Then he was gone.

"No!" Aramis struck the air before him as he landed, feebly hoping it would nick the elusive foe. A shriek cried out behind him.

Turning around, Aramis could not believe his eyes. Bagheera, as he lived and breathed, stood there before him. Her naked, elven form turned away from him, clutching a pulsing, ruby organ in her deathly paled hand. Tamira lay on the floor, still as stone, as her lifeline pooled from her bosom. Rhyllae shrieked again in horror in Joel's arms as Bagheera turned to face Aramis.

Somehow, her lopsided head was held up by her broken neck. Her eyes, glazed over by death's veil, pierced into his soul.

"Why did you not save me?" Bagheera asked in a raspy voice.

In a blink, Lady Ruth's sword cut her down like wheat during harvest.

In another blink, he woke in a jolt.

The air was clear and crisp, yet Aramis found it hard to breathe. His hands shook, and his salt-and-pepper hair was drenched from a cold sweat. His eyes darted feverishly around him, lighting on the long shadows with the soft silver glow from his eyes.

All about him, people in cots moaned and muttered softly in their sleep. He was laid among them in a long hallway. Across from him, a beautiful railing opened to the evening sky and the garden below. All was calm and quiet in the holy abbey of the Rising Dawn.

With tremoring hands, Aramis buried his face in the blanket. Not caring how much it scratched his eyelids or how the wool was soaked by more tears than sweat.

# Chapter 15

## VESPERS

THE CLICK OF HER BOOTS ECHOED IN THE TORCH-less catacombs as she sauntered down the spiral descent as if she owned the place. In a way, Frianul did—being the Mother Superior, after all. None dared to oppose her in her descent, slinking among the holy saints and beloved priestesses of old.

Then something caught her eye—a wisp of hair peeking from the mother's funeral caps. Stopping by one of the priestesses of old, Frianul twirled the dead hair strands around her finger lovingly. Then yanked it off. Tying the long lock into a lover's knot and tucking it into the mouth of another deceased mother.

"Now, I bind you two in holy matrimony," she said in a singsong fashion before she broke off the mummified fingers. The Mother Superior twirled in the hallway, crumpling the desiccated bone in her hands. "Ashes to ashes, 'til death do ye part."

And did they rise up to stop her defiling, these watchful dead?

No.

They lay still, unmoved and uncaring. The thought of it made Frianul's black heart sing with glee.

Hiking up the pristine white-and-golden robe, Mother Frianul skipped down the cobbled floor, rhythmically clapping while tapping her boots on the stone floor. It would seem ridiculous if anyone saw her dancing in this fashion, dressed in the highest station. But there was no audience, no judge, no one, save her and the silent dead.

On and on, she danced to the rhythmic echoes as the floor curved into a spiral. Down into the depths of the earth until she came to her destination. The holy crypt of Justiania, founder of the Rising Dawn. After picking up the soiled hat, she rapped on the tomb door three times.

"Honey, I'm home."

With a flick of the lock, she bounded into the small tomb. A lone stone sarcophagus rested in the middle, flanked by braziers at both ends. Laid on top was a corpse that was not even two months old. The cadaver was stripped of any clothing it once had, exposed to the suffocating air with no shroud or linen. But this bothered her not. It was precisely where she had left her.

"You won't believe who I bumped into at the market today," the old woman casually said to the female cadaver. "My old flame."

The cadaver stayed motionless, fixed in its silent expression of terror. She approached the corpse and caressed her withered face.

The same face they wore now.

Vanessa enjoyed gazing down upon the real Mother Superior Frianul in her contorted state. Her death was a joy to watch. Oh, how she had screamed, calling for anybody to come and save her. But none had heard Frianul with her vocal box plucked out of her throat. It was a beautiful death as she draped to the floor like a falling curtain. The thought of her struggle stretched Vanessa's wrinkled lips across their cheeks into a wicked grin.

"But don't worry, I told him I only have eyes for you."

Their fingers extend into dark skewer-like points around her neck. They severed the skull from the atlas bone with a pinch and tossed it into the air, then deftly caught it and spun it around to face them. Like a puppeteer, they moved the jaw, clacking the teeth together in syncopation.

"Oh? What's that?" Vanessa brought the skull to their left ear and let it clatter again. "Did I bring anything for you? Why, of course, I did, my dear. I would never leave the store empty-handed."

Stripping the white robe to reveal the Jessenter uniform underneath, Vanessa lifted the white silk purse from their belt with their needle-like fingers. Setting the skull aside on the iron spike brazier nearby, Vanessa reached deep into the bag up to their elbow. After fishing for a while, they produced a giant tome bound in rune-etched flesh, plopping it down on Frianul's remains. The impact cracked a rib.

Vanessa continued to undress as they transformed back to their favored form. The one that they had kept up for the past three years. The chieftain's daughter, the real Vanessa, was easy to mimic in voice and movement. It was even easier to ensnare the great Silver Fox into their loving arms that fateful night. The disguise was manageable, to say the least, since Aramis never knew the original. They could entirely be themselves. Well, as much as one could with the façade, and he fell for them entirely.

*It's a shame he must die, they thought. Aramis would have been beneficial. But not as he is, though. Oh, no. He has yet to see what I could see. Once I tear this house of cards these dolls have built, then—only then—will Aramis see beyond this papier-mâché stage. See the cruel world. The sinful world. The world of the Shadowhand.*

"Here we are, Falçion," Dawn told Falçion as they reached the steps of the abbey.

Not hearing a response from him, she looked back to find him asleep. His drooping head nestled on the nape of hers, with his bloody arms slouched over her shoulders.

"Lucky bastard," she muttered while shifting his weight on her back.

The whole situation felt surreal to the lieutenant. She felt the ground shake underneath her feet when she stepped out of the watchman's building. The smoke clamored toward the heavens from the marketplace. She started running and never stopped. Dawn was one of the few transporting the injured and dying to and from the collapse. To her grief, the Silver Fox was included. Falçion would've been next if he wasn't such a stubborn mule.

Taking care not to hit his head, Dawn bowed before entering the long, saffron-painted archway to find General Korzha at the end, looking worse for wear as he leaned on the threshold. That was until Korzha spotted her. He stood straight as a rod with his hands firmly behind his back, his steely gaze piercing.

"General." Dawn saluted quickly before Falçion could fall off of her.

"Lieutenant." Korzha saluted back and stepped aside to allow her into the nave. "How many more do we have left to bring in?"

"He's the last of the bunch. Well, until they clear the rest of the debris."

The general nodded and frowned as his eyes drifted in thought.

"Sir?" Dawn asked. "Do you think the Djinnasi did this?"

His icy-blue eyes whipped back to her in a snap. "I will not make any speculations until I have more to work with, Lieutenant. Since you are here, I want you by Feres's side when he wakes. Gather all you can concerning the incident and report straight to me. He almost died relaying the information. I want to know what it was." As if he read her mind, he whipped his index finger up in the air. "No exceptions. This matter is a top priority."

Dawn deflated. She wanted to investigate the Mudhi case further, but orders were orders.

"Yes, sir." She saluted once again.

General Korzha gave a curt nod and departed through the archway. "I shall be at the wreckage." His words echoed back to her.

To hear the main base of operation called a "wreckage" gave an unusual chill over Dawn—as if someone walked over her grave. Looking upon the warm glow of the altar within the chancel, she prayed aloud, "Morning Lord, let your Light guide us through the Night."

"Shine on, sister," a voice from the shadows spoke.

Dawn almost dropped Falçion to draw her sword until she realized it was Sister Rhyllae.

"By the Lord's bloomers, don't scare me like that."

"Sorry." Rhyllae flashed a smile, only for it to vanish seconds later. "How bad is he?"

Easing Falçion into Rhyllae's arms, Dawn listed the injuries from what Mother Myrrh told her. Falçion had lost half of his hand and suffered grisly wounds along his arms. The mother closed them, but his digits couldn't be saved. He'd be up and running as long as he didn't develop an infection. Dawn knew the last thing Falçion wanted was amputation. But, if she were to choose between life or limb—she'd pick limb any day.

"I have to clean this up before he's settled for the night," Sister Rhyllae said after looking under his shirt. They carried him down the hall and stairs to where the rest were laid. So numerous were the wounded that the Morning sisters had to resort to resting them in the corridor.

Settling him at the corner of the turn, Dawn took off his shirt as the Morning sister fetched the necessary supplies. Dawn hadn't realized how pale he was until the lieutenant peeled the fabric off of him. Sister Rhyllae finally came back with a basket of supplies. With a green jasper stone, spotted red all over, in one hand and touching his thigh with the other, she muttered a prayer. After what felt like an eternity, the sister finally let go.

"That should help him, for now," Rhyllae said as she sponged the blood away. "He lost too much blood. I could only encourage his bones to speed up the process, nothing more. It's up to him to pull through the night."

Tears burned Dawn's eyes, and she turned her face away.

"I'm sorry."

"Yeah, well, don't be." The lieutenant sniffled. "If anyone can get through this, it's Falçion. Hell, even the pox couldn't snuff him out. He'll make it."

*He fucking better.*

Falçion was, for the longest time, the only one who had befriended her when she came into the Jessenter's fold.

Never had she thought she would stop seeing his smiling face. Dawn tried to dismiss the dark notions as she wiped the lone tear with her forearm. Silence fell between them as she watched Rhyllae collect the items into the basket.

"How's the Silver Fox?" Dawn finally asked.

"I can show you to him if you would like. But mind, he's not awake yet."

"That's fine by me. I need a rest."

Taking all of Falçion's blood-stained clothes into the basket, Rhyllae walked Dawn down the entire length of the hall, then around the corner toward the hospice door. It was a sobering sight to see her fellow men swaddled in their makeshift cots, where she had once stood with the general in the early morning. Oh, how the sand shifts as the day passes.

Then Dawn saw Aramis, asleep with sweat beading on his forehead. Aramis looked dissimilar from the fateful night of their meeting. The low light from the prayer candles drew shadows upon his furrowed brows, etching wrinkles upon the already graying man. Dawn would've skipped him over for another if it weren't for Sister Rhyllae kneeling by his side. Taking the hem of her wide sleeve, she carefully dabbed the sweat beading on Aramis's face.

"He's stable, for now." The sister spoke quietly. "I'm glad you brought him in when you did. He lost a ton of blood, even for a jhasin. When we moved him to this spot, his lung collapsed. That was a nightmare. Not to say that Mother Myrrh was a horrible healer. Of all the mothers, we turn to her for guidance. I'm sure he was in worse condition when she saw him."

"Any visitors?"

When she shook her head in mute reply, Dawn nodded and rubbed the back of her neck. *Worth a shot.*

Dawn watched the sister pick at the hair clinging to his face with tender care. Though he was the Silver Fox, Dawn, the biggest hero-worshipper of them all, wouldn't touch him in such a manner. Perhaps there was time, after all, to pursue her original task.

"'Tis a real shame his wife didn't take the time to see him," Dawn said, looking out to the starry night sky.

"Perhaps it's for the best. The last thing Aramis needs is stress in his condition."

"Yeah, it's a good thing he's got you."

The young officer glanced at the sister, taking in the changing shades of emotions that crossed Rhyllae's face. From pity to confusion. Realization to surprise. Then, finally, to the ruddy embarrassment that stormed into wounded pride. Hastily, the priestess snatched the basket into her arms and hopped to her feet.

"Visiting hours are over. Now, if you excuse me, I've got work to do." Then Rhyllae sped down to the medicinal storage room.

Dawn jogged after her, passing under the shadows cast by the towering pillars. The morning glories, showcased in the large vases, shook from their wake.

"Look," Dawn called out, "I'm not going to tell her what's going on between you and him—"

The sister halted so abruptly that Dawn almost collided with her. "I'm the daughter of the Morn. We don't commit such lewd transgressions."

"You wouldn't be the first to fall in love, sis."

"Oh, you're just like him!" She whirled away.

Turning the corner toward the lone wooden door, Rhyllae kicked it open. Dozens of glassware shook on the shelves when the door slammed against the wall. The delicate clinking arose once again when Rhyllae slammed the wicker basket down on their folding table, her back to the Jessenter as she unpacked.

"Nothing is going on between the two of us," Rhyllae stated.

"Yeah, like rain's in the forecast." Dawn crossed her arms as she leaned against the frame.

"Aramis and I survived horrors you can't imagine. We have seen what no one should ever have seen. If it wasn't for him, we would never have survived M'thealquilôk. He's my friend, my comrade, my..."

Rhyllae halted when she unfurled Falçion's shirt from the basket. The stains darkened into a matte maroon, stiffening the fabric where they landed. Dawn crossed the room to put a hand on her shoulder.

"Brother in arms. I get it," Dawn said.

Rhyllae rubbed the stain with her thumb and finger. "He asked me for help. His wife, Vanessa, went missing. Aramis has been looking for her ever since we came back. I've never seen him this troubled before. He thought—we thought—she was kidnapped. I explored his home for answers, but it was empty." She twisted the shirt so roughly that Dawn feared it would tear in two. "She took everything and left him with nothing. No coin. No food. Not even a pillow to lay his head down at night. Nothing but the shirt on his back." The sister threw the clothing into the laundry basket. "It's like their marriage never existed."

Dawn stood in awe. Her greatest idol—homeless, penniless. Even the wealth of friendship whittled down in such short order.

*Is that why he almost died back there? He had nothing left to lose?*

Rhyllae cradled herself in her arms. "Why would she do this? It's not the first time we have been gone this long. I believe Aramis when he says he's been good to her. I don't understand."

Dawn sucked in her breath. She fully knew why, but a promise was made. Sealed by the Morning Lord's name, no less. Yet, when she turned to leave, she stopped herself short. If she walked out of the room right then and there, Mudhi wouldn't have a chance to avoid the noose. Hell, if the Silver Fox couldn't find this woman, how could she? If there was another way to help Mudhi, Dawn must take it. Oath or no oath.

"I think I know why. You might have heard what happened with Mudhi, right?" Dawn asked.

Rhyllae turned to her with raised brows. "Yes. He was arrested for treason, from what I heard."

"Well, he's got an alibi."

"And you think she is that? Mudhi was found and arrested in that apartment. He ran in there to hide."

"C'mon, sis, you honestly believe that?"

Rhyllae didn't say a word, but instead busied herself with sorting the medicinal jars, arranging them against the wall in mechanical motions.

Dawn pressed on. "Mudhi was there that night when it happened. He had been fighting with Marilyn and took solace there. All the way to morning. And now you're telling me she up and left him. Him? The Silver Fox?"

Rhyllae shoved the last batch back against the wall. One glass clacked too hard, creating a delicate web upon the jar. "Look, Mudhi may not be as innocent as you think. I found a deceased woman buried in the wall of that apartment. She died when we were still in M'thealquilôk. Mudhi could've killed her after he confronted Korzha. And then Vanessa found him. Who can blame her for leaving?"

At first, Dawn didn't know what to say. She remembered when she brought Aramis on her back to the abbey. She spotted Sister Rhyllae carrying a body on the stretcher with another woman. As soon as the sister laid eyes on him, she dropped her end and threw herself upon him. Her lips never ceased in prayer as the rest of the order came rushing over. The body, free of its covering, was affixed in a cowering position. A pitiable of a death mask as Dawn ever saw one.

Dawn shook her head and focused her thoughts. "If he attempted the assassination and failed, then why go to that building? His family lives elsewhere! Rhyllae, they were found out."

"You can't know that. We haven't—"

"Think, Sister Rhyllae. Mudhi wouldn't be able to block up that wall. It's got to be Vanessa. Why go to all that effort? He was found out. Unless she knew. That lady you brought in knew they were drinking each other's cups. All behind Aramis's back—this whole time! They killed her for it."

*And someone else attempted to assassinate Korzha,* Dawn thought, but a bottle shattered—how, Dawn couldn't tell— preventing her from saying anything more.

The priestess of the Morning Light bowed her head into her shaking hands. Red were the tips of her ears and temples. To Dawn's surprise, she spewed forth obscenities in the elvish tongue and stomped her foot. Dawn came over to hold her as Rhyllae trembled with fury. Then the sister wilted in her arms, to the lieutenant's relief. The storm that took hold of her finally cleared away, leaving a broken voice. "How can anyone be this cruel?"

Dawn's response was to turn the priestess around for a stronger embrace.

*I hate to see how Aramis Feres deals with this.*

A break of ceramic woke them both.

Running to the hall, they found a single cot rumpled and empty. Across, a vase of morning glories lay shattered on the stone floor. The tapestry behind it pulled out of the open window into the starry sky.

Sister Rhyllae ran to the stone sill and shrieked after the moving shadow below. "Aramis! Come back, Aramis!"

But there was no answer save for the echoes of the coming night.

Spinning to Dawn, the sister grabbed her shirt. "You must go after him before it's too late."

"But Mudhi is guarded by the watch."

"That won't stop him." Rhyllae dragged her down the hall toward the entrance. "He can fool the Djinnasi and free hundreds of slaves. A handful of watchmen is nothing to Aramis."

Letting her go at the archway entrance, the priestess of the Morn waved her fingers over the lieutenant while incanting words Dawn couldn't understand. Then she pushed her out of the door.

"Run!" Rhyllae cried out. "Run like the hurricane before it's too late!"

Dawn jogged out of the door and sped into a run, thanks to the slope's steepness. Then she felt herself running faster than she ever could before, as if a weight had been lifted from her soles.

Dawn's heart flew. *So this is how a cheetah feels.*

Looking back, she saw the sister holding her splayed hand up in blessing.

*Don't worry. I won't fail you.*

She turned back to the road ahead, growing dark in the ever-creeping night.

*I swear it.*

# Chapter 16

## CALL OF THE DEAD

"QUIET," DRAKE, A CRESCENT MOON ELF, CRIED OUT. Silence fell over all who worked upon the man-made mountain of sand and stone. Dido held her breath, straining to hear any sound underneath the rubble. It was one of the few advantages they had in the enveloping night, especially under a faceless moon. Then she heard it; a clatter of stone, not too far from where she stood. She bounded over to the spot with the grace of a mountain goat.

"What is it, lass? Heard somethin'?" a weary dwarf, affectionately called McGruffin' by all who knew him, asked.

"Shush." Dido wanted to be sure. It was worse to send them on a wild-goose chase than to be wrong. There was another clatter right underneath her cloven hooves.

"Here," Dido told them all and bounded away so they could come over.

Drake kneeled by the spot and yelled down the crevices between the stones, "Hold on, we're going to get you out of there!"

McGruffin' scanned the area. "Lassie, if you could move that slab out o' the way, we can dig 'em out."

"I'll do my best." Closing her eyes, Dido swung her arms out wide, feeling for the stir in the cooling air. She let the current curl around her hooves, playfully billowing her jacket. "*Vjetar oko mene, podigni moj teret.*"

Dido brought her hands together with her palms up and then lifted them toward the sky. The current left her side and swirled around the stone through the magical connection. Sand and rocks fell away as the limestone floated skyward.

"Okay, hold it right there. Now to the right." Drake started waving his arms in circles as he guided her to the discard pile. As she moved the slab away, the team rushed in with shovels and buckets, racing against the sand sifting back into the hole.

"Clear," he warned the gawking bystanders. They scattered from the incoming slab.

As gentle as laying down a Fabergé egg, the little satyr eased the slab onto the rubble. It may have been the umpteenth time she had to cast the spell, but some bystanders were still bewildered by the little satyr's power. It was not surprising considering how long she had hidden the secret close to her breast.

Cheers erupted as they pulled an officer from the wreckage. His entire body was coated white from the sand and clay. A beam of joy splayed across Dido's face as she watched them lead the wobbling man into the arms of a waiting sister. Perhaps she was mistaken for keeping her magic hidden from these mortals. Ultimately, good can only come from good, no matter the consequences.

"<My work is not yet done,>" Mother Myrrh said in their native tongue, bringing Korzha's gaze away from the joyous scene.

In the lone alley were the ones who had not escaped the clutches of death, covered in the market's colorful canvases, Jessenters and civilians alike. Keeping watch was the ever-vigilant Mother Myrrh. Kneeling by a boy, she held his limp hand while her other was on his forehead—the child's kippah with the beaded star lay upon his still chest. Mother Myrrh draped the purple canvas upon him after her song faded. Her throaty hymn of his final rite still echoed in the stillness.

"<Tell that to Lune herself,>" Korzha retorted. "<She won't show her fickle face at this hour.>"

"<I have no need for her light,>" Myrrh said.

Pointing with two fingers, she drew the name of the Morning Lord in the sky. Trailing behind it was a golden light that hung still in the air. Then the mother waved her hand, and the letters burst into tiny flames. They jumped and darted away like a thousand fireflies, climbing toward the sky at her beck and call. With another wave, they halted and twinkled in place.

"<Your dedication to my men is highly appreciated. But not at your expense. I beg you rest from such a long journey.>"

"<Your concern should be placed upon yourself. Go, I have much to do here.>"

"<Not without you.>" Korzha bent his head down as he lowered his voice.

The mother's thick brows were raised in amused curiosity. "<Have I been away for far too long? I never thought you would miss our nightly tea conversations.>"

*Please, not the teasing.* Korzha wanted to quip. But she didn't know of the attempted assassination, so he remained cordial. "<There is much to discuss.>"

"<And tomorrow is too late?>"

"<The matter is vexing at best. I need someone who can dig deep to the root of it all. Someone who can keep pace and stay completely loyal. I need you, Mariam, and you alone.>"

The mother of the Setting Sun stood there in thought, then shook her head. Placing her hands upon his face, the stark contrast between her dark complexion and his pale skin was evident even this late of an evening.

"<I need you to rest. Exhaustion does little for the working mind. Sleep, lest you become one of the dead.>"

Korzha uttered, "<Grace,>" in protest before Mother Myrrh's lips pressed against his. Seconds felt like eons before they parted. He stared at her sphinxlike face, eyes wide.

*She broke her vows! Mariam... What did you see out there?*

"<Take my room for the night, Gus. I won't be needing it 'til midday. We'll discuss the matter tomorrow... As well as for myself.>"

Then the mother kneeled to the next one in line, a girl with a purple headscarf, signifying her coming of age. Once again, the echoes resounded the throaty song of last rites, trailing after him as he left her to her duties.

What duties were left for him alone? Ghosts, imposters, and a battered cause. The weight pulled his shoulders into a slump as he clasped his hands behind his back. His mind was a turning wheel, unending.

"General, sir?" Dido meekly called out to him, causing him to pause. "I was with Mr. Feres when it all happened. It may not be much, but..." She looked down at her cloven hooves.

"There is a saying in Töska that even the tiniest crack can break the strongest dam." General Korzha turned back to her with a sliver of a smile. "Any information, no matter how small, will be invaluable to me."

Dido opened her mouth to speak but closed it again, scanning the crowd. She had every right to be wary. What if the imposter disguised themselves as McGruffin', Drake, or any citizen here in Amaveriel? She would be endangering them both if they knew what she desired to confide in him.

Korzha bade her follow him to the abbey. Her little cloven hooves echoed down the stone streets, chasing away the dead's call.

The Call of the Dead.

The most essential component of every necromancer's repertoire, yet it was surprisingly tiny in Tellezard's volume. But there, nonetheless. Vanessa had no need for the rest of the tome. It was filled with rituals utilizing their awakened bodies and a myriad of mind controls.

Yet, they mused. *No use for them—yet.*

However, Vanessa had been fooled before by the glamor of magic. All talk and no show was not much of an opera. Time to see what the tome could do in these catacombs full of shriveled wombs.

"<Awake, ye who slumber in the Earth.
"<Awake, ye shrouded in Death's veil.
"<Awake, I give you breath.
"<Awake, I give you a feast.
"<Awake and Rise.>"

The dark speech echoed up the catacombs past the forever-sleeping mothers and sisters, bouncing off the spiraling walls, projected and reinforced by its odd acoustics. As the words neared the top, they faded like a tidal wave hitting the coastal shelf. The archaic words were barely a whisper when they reached the foot of the door.

None of the sleeping matriarchs heard the call.

Save for Fanteen Dada. She heard them well.

A bundle of incense fell to the floor, making a soft echo in the empty hall. Kneeling on the floor, Sister Rhyllae picked up the pieces. Yet, the individual sticks separated from the pack and slid across the floor, teasing her trembling fingers. Try as she may, she couldn't get the nerves out of her system. Rhyllae doubted she would get any rest for the night to soothe them.

Mother Celia demanded she assist her in the ritual of speaking with Fanteen Dada. It was the only way they would ever know who killed her and why they encased the poor old landlord in the wall. Better to do something than to toss and turn with all the thoughts swarming in her head. At least by Mother Celia's standards.

*Please,* Rhyllae prayed, *Light of my Life, keep Aramis on the straight and narrow. Lead him to the light. So let it be done.*

Sister Rhyllae headed down the hall to the catacomb's preparation chamber. It was cramped with a flight of stairs that hugged the left wall and curved at the bottom to the floor. The floor had a raised dais that granted enough space to do the embalming and final rites before the burial. A convenient place for Mother Myrrh's studies on diseases, and a secure place to commune with the dead. She remembered the early days of Mother Myrrh's anatomy lessons where the sisters crowded these stairs overlooking the operation. They had spilled out to the garden, through the door at the floor level. Now, new initiates could assist in the operations—if they had the stomach for it.

Sister Rhyllae ran halfway down the stairs without even closing the door behind her. "I'm sorry I was late, I was—" She stopped dead in her tracks.

There on the dais lay Mother Celia. Her throat was torn as if a jungle leopard had ripped through it. Blood oozed down to her bosom, saturating the once pure fibers with its maroon ichor. But the grisly sight wasn't what disturbed Sister Rhyllae to her core.

Crouched on top of her was a sickly, naked creature with parchment-like skin, eerily showcasing the pale working muscles and dark veins underneath. Hunched over, the beast licked its paws.

*No,* Rhyllae realized. *Those are hands. Human hands.*

The creature stopped and turned her head like an owl, not caring if its neck cracked and popped from the movement. The face was that of an old woman, shriveled like a prune. Her eyes were glossy white, like mothballs, with lips drooling fresh blood.

"Fanteen?" Sister Rhyllae asked in disbelief.

Never had she ever expected to see a ghoul here in Amaveriel beyond M'thealquilôk, let alone the old lady be one of them.

The old corpse's face shook with seething rage and let out a dry shrill. Bent down, the sister cupped her hands over her pointed ears to muffle the worst of the sharp pain, the only reason she regretted her elven heritage. When the shriek finally dissipated, she found Fanteen crouching above her on the stone railing, swiping at her with her bony fingers.

Rhyllae ducked from her raking. Then she slipped on the hem of her tasseled robe and went tumbling down the cold, hard stairs.

Ignoring the hard landing, she recited the holy words she knew by heart. "Though I walk through the Shadow, I will raise my candle high, for the Light within me shall shine, like the fire of the Sun."

Feeling her soul blossoming with holy light, Rhyllae willed it forth to her hands as a shield. And in the nick of time, too.

Fanteen leaped from the edge of the stone railing then halted as it was slapped by the holy power. The creature shrunk back as a part of her chest and arms sizzled. Shrieking nonsensical cries, Fanteen bashed through the door leading to the cloister garden.

"No, no, no." Sister Rhyllae scrambled to her feet and chased after her.

"The world is not a paper moon..." Korzha gazed up to the night sky above, devoid of the Morning Lord's beloved sister, Lune.

"His own words," Dido said, walking as fast as she could to keep up with the lanky general. "Then the thief sang a song about a new beginning and activated the artifact."

"Ignoring the Silver Fox's pleas to stand down. And the book?"

Dido cast her rosy eyes down. "The imposter grabbed it before I had the chance. It will take me hours to sift through the vault to see what else was taken."

As sudden as lightning, a blonde rebel soldier officer sped toward them. As she passed, she raised a hand in salute, leaving behind a billow of dust in her wake.

Out of habit, Korzha had his hand raised to his temple. "That was Lieutenant Dawn."

"How strange. She's not going back to the base."

"No, she's going to the watch." He frowned, touching the hilt of the Silver Star on his right hip. The sword felt it, too—something wicked.

"But why?"

"Trouble. Hurry."

With adrenaline rejuvenating his senses, Korzha took off toward the Abbey of the Rising Dawn, with the little satyr trailing behind.

Korzha was the first of the two to make it to the yellow archway of the abbey. The metal gate at the end of the archway barred the way. He noted nothing unusual among the nave's limestone and basalt pillars.

A nettling sensation agitated his right forearm. He slapped it, thinking it was a bite from a noxious fly. But the feeling didn't cease.

Then, out of the corner of his eye, a shadow separated from the darkness, ambling out toward him. He could distinguish her humanoid arms and legs. Her naked, pallid skin, marbled and streaked with dark veins, was plain to see. In the pit of his stomach, Korzha knew standing before him was one of the inmorti, a ghoul.

The creature quickly fell forward on her hands and sprinted toward him on all fours. It leaped incredibly fast to his left, then hopped to his right, disappearing from his limited view.

Drawing his heirloom, Silver Star, Korzha's nape prickled with anticipation. With bated breath, he waited for her to emerge. Yet, he heard nothing save for the crystalline note from the sword's hum.

Daring to step closer to the wrought iron gate, he furrowed his brows.

*Come out, you damned creature of death.*

Dropping down from above, the gate shook as the reeking ghoul grappled it like a spider monkey. The shriveled creature gave an unearthly roar at him, letting the spittle fly from her human maw. The dried-parchment skin popped at the cheeks like an overused seam.

Dodging her bony hands raking at him, Korzha lunged the singing blade through her droopy breast. She shrieked in surprise and leaped back. The ghoul swatted his sword aside and clambered onto the left striated pillar toward the ceiling, out of view.

Korzha tried to open the barred door in vain, but it was locked. Against hope, he shook the iron door for someone to come. Grimly, he wondered if the foul being had gorged itself on his men in their sleep. The idea made him rattle the iron door again in a fury.

Thankfully, someone arrived; a priestess with kinked, golden-brown curls wielding a shovel. As she neared the door, Korzha could see that her white robes of the Morn were soiled, leaving no doubt, she was in pursuit of the creature.

"Sister Ghalédale?"

She lowered the shovel, realizing he was not the creature. Then her honey-drop eyes widened. "General Korzha? What are you doing here? It's not safe."

Before he could explain, Korzha spotted movement on one of the pillars. "Behind you!"

The ghoulish woman leaped off of the pillar, falling toward them.

Then met the blunt edge of Rhyllae's shovel.

The metal kissed the temple of the vile creature, skidding her across the marble floor to crash-land into the candle offerings at one of the window niches. The blow left a gash from her left temple to her jaw, shattered her cheekbone, and dislodged her jaw.

Yet, she stood up again.

"Open it, quick!" Korzha begged.

Rhyllae cradled the shovel as she fumbled with the locks. With a clang, the gate squealed in protest as she swung it open.

Furiously, Fanteen let out a long shrill, reaching the highest registers as she exhaled. Rhyllae dropped to her knees. Korzha soon joined her as they both cried out in agony.

When it was finally over, the inmortus stretched its maw wide, showing her crooked teeth with its twisted and unhinged jaw. Horrified, Korzha realized it was grinning as it took its wobbly steps forward. Familiar to the mindless throngs from his homeland, such a feat shook Korzha to his core.

It stumbled forward before being blocked by the small satyr.

In between puffs, Dido produced a tiny red feather from a small pouch. Dido spun in a circle with her arms out wide. "*Vatrena ptìca.*" Then she stopped and blew against the ruby plumage like a pinwheel. To their amazement, a stream of fire shot forth from her breath—engulfing Fanteen in its blaze. In a poof, she lit up like kindling.

Oh, how she shrieked and howled.

Fanteen didn't know what to do. She spun, rolled, and flailed about. Tearing at herself, she ripped at pieces of her own burning flesh. Tissue was strewn all around her. Then Fanteen fell to her knees, flinging her arms up in the air. Crying out in agony.

They stood dumbfounded, their eyes transfixed on the gruesome spectacle. Never had they seen such a sight—all in their own personal experiences with the inmorti, or lack thereof, in Dido's case.

It was Korzha who moved first.

With grim determination, he passed the satyr, gazing into Fanteen's eyes as her face burned away to the bone beneath, her jaw falling to the wayside. The melted eyeballs dripped down her cheekbones as she stared at him with hollowed sockets. Stretching forth her flaming limbs to him, she seemed to plea for this to end.

Lifting his blade to his face, he whispered to the Silver Star, "<For those that walk in twilight, grant them rest for the night.>"

With one smooth motion, he slashed the blade through her throat. The sword sang out a clear note in the still air. To the ladies' eyes, it seemed to have no effect on the creature. Korzha sheathed the heirloom, straightened himself up, and did an about-turn. As if on cue, the head fell forward, rolling past the general to settle at Dido's hooves, much to her dismay. The burned corpse fell to the side, crackling from the magical flames.

Korzha felt the adrenaline fading as he walked back. The events were taking their toll, from the previous night's vigil, the battering of the haboob, and the Jessenter explosion crisis. Still, he would not dare to break protocol. He was, first and foremost, a nobleman, no matter his current banishment.

The general nodded to Dido in thanks, though the lady satyr gave him a concerned look before he turned to the priestess. "I hope you don't mind if we ask for your hospitality for the night?"

The Morning Lord sister pushed her curled bang over her pointed ear and dusted off her robes, even though they were slashed by the ghoul. "Is that why both of you are here?"

"No, but I fear … rest … is in order." Before he knew it, the dignified Töskan fell into her arms from pure exhaustion, stirring not one bit when the rest of the sisterly order clamored down from their quarters to gawk at the scene.

# Chapter 17

## COMFORT AND JOY

"**B**RING HIM IN HERE," MYRRH, MOTHER OF THE Sunset, urged.

Sisters Rhyllae, Gertrude, Prell, and Joivre shuffled into the mother's austere bedchamber. Each one held a corner of the makeshift stretcher, burdened by the general's limp body. The Sunset mother disdained using the public bath and had requested a tub to be made for her private use. Otherwise, they would have to make do with the root cellar.

Dido was there with the Sunset mother. She pinched the air with her forefinger and thumb, then "pulled" down. As her hand moved down, a gnarled stick appeared, floating. Scooping it into her tiny palms, Dido tested the wood on her hand. Sparks lit the dim room as she tapped it against her palm.

Dido gave a big yawn. "Oh, pardon me, it's been a trying day. Please do open the windows."

The mother nodded at the ladies to do as she said as she continued to light the room. Once open, the satyr bounced the stick as a conductor before his ensemble. And, to Rhyllae's amazement, a creeping fog rolled into the room, swirling past them as it vortexed over the metal furniture. Then she waved her hands together, and the entire surface was covered in tiny dewdrops. Astoundingly, by the snap of Dido's fingers, stars of beautiful white lace blossomed. They unfurled in majestic strokes until the metal was coated in its splendor.

"What is this?" asked Sister Prell.

"Frost," replied the satyr.

"Joel was never able to pull this off," Rhyllae said.

"I can create ice, but there's not enough water."

"There will be more yet to come." Mother Myrrh then blew out the lighting stick.

Then the rest of the sisterly contingent brought in buckets of water. They were as astonished as Rhyllae was at seeing the beautiful frost covering. But by the mothers trailing after them, they were urged to empty their pails. Once the tub was filled, the satyr did her magic and transformed the top layer into a glistening mirror.

The beautiful transformation didn't last long, for the Sunset mother took the heel of her shoe and smashed the wooden block upon it. She was soon joined by two Dawn mothers, Vyreal and Gysea. Rhyllae remembered they had been sent from the far northern regions of the realm. Fissures ran deep along the length of the ice until it shattered into floating motes of ice.

Meanwhile, the four sisters undressed the Jessenter general to his shirt and pantaloons. Once the fuss was over, they laid him in the bone-chilling tub. Rhyllae couldn't fathom how any normal being could sleep in such a thing. Given the frown upon Mother Myrrh's face, this is not expected of Korzha.

"Thank you. I shall keep watch for the night. You may leave." Myrrh bowed to them all as they moved to leave the room.

"Not you."

Rhyllae froze as the rest of the contingent moved past her.

It had been frightening when the mother discovered the commotion upon her return. Her voice cut through the gaggle like lightning in the pouring rain. It was rumored she had once been a noblewoman of a great Töskan house. None would ever doubt it again. As soon as her purple-blue eyes had found Fanteen in a fiery heap, Mother Myrrh started giving orders in a calm but commanding voice, rallying the rest of the mothers and having every sister fall in line.

Then again, Sunset mothers were no wilting violets. Mother Celia was a stern taskmaster; until now, Rhyllae had never understood the severity of their duties. They guarded the dead, not in morbid reverence but to protect the living. If only Rhyllae had spared the time to mend her follies with Celia sooner.

Sensing her hesitation, Mother Myrrh removed her vibrant red hat and shawl. Her locks, as dark as the color of her skin, fell down the length of her back. Then she kneeled by the low-lying tub and raised her palm for Rhyllae to join her. In a sign of good faith, Rhyllae took off her yellow shawl and kneeled by her side. Though she had to admit, her garments were worse for wear compared to the mother's. Everything needed to be rendered into rags.

"I fear your duties are not over yet, my daughter," Mother Myrrh said.

"Even if they were, I won't be able to sleep a wink this night," replied Rhyllae.

"Indeed. 'Tis another to hear of the inmorti than to see it with thine own eyes."

"I've seen plenty from the ruins of M'thealquilôk. I never thought to see one here."

"Have you? Yes. I can see it in your eyes. Your steel has been tested in the fire many a time. You have done well in your service to the Morning Lord."

"Have I?" Rhyllae blurted. "Mother Celia and I were to speak to Dada's soul to know who killed her. If I hadn't been delayed, I could've—"

"Been killed."

Rhyllae would protest such a blunt statement if it weren't for the mother's sphinxlike gaze. The sister broke it as she bowed her head in shame.

Myrrh placed her hand on top of hers. "The strange event has occurred by no fault of your own. You were spared, by the Grace of the First Mother, Lune, alone."

*Dark blessings...*

Once again, Aramis, albeit through coincidence, had saved her life. If only she could do more for him.

*Unless...*

"Mother Myrrh. The dead were not the reason I couldn't rest this night."

Mudhi couldn't rest. Not when he heard the news. He never expected the Jessenter base to be hit in a million years. And it was all his and that wicked Vanessa's fault.

Ever since Mudhi had laid eyes on the woman, he wanted her. Oh, how her green eyes would smolder through her veil every time she looked his way. With one bat of her long lashes, he would follow her to every dark alley of the city. Letting their hands wander until they were lost in the shadows. He would do anything for even a whiff of her perfume.

And she knew it.

All it took was a whisper in Vanessa's ear, and she let him have his way. Mudhi told himself in their afterglow that she was concerned about her indifferent husband or curious about how the Jessenters worked. But in the end, what was done was done. He let all the secrets the freedom fighters wished to keep slip through his grubby fingers.

Perhaps he was a traitor, after all.

A guard came in to collect his meal.

"Hey," Mudhi croaked, his voice raspy from long disuse. "Did my wife ever come to see me?"

"Why would anyone want to see a louse like you?" the guard retorted.

With a slam and a click of the lock, the guard was gone, leaving Mudhi alone in a carved limestone room, deep in the earth. Alone in an iron-barred cell with only a cot for company. Alone with his thoughts, he knew there was no way it could be undone.

The ex-lieutenant sighed as he sank back onto the thin and lumpy cot. This was what he deserved, he figured. Why should he expect anyone to visit him? Even his wife never showed her face here. The only friends he could rely on were the chamber pot, the clothes on his back, and the sickle flame from the floating oil lamp.

Every evening, it would rise from its little perch, levitating close to the ceiling, burning the midnight oil until dawn. Never judging as minutes crept to hours. Providing enough light for him and the empty cell across from him. The cell that Dawn had once occupied for the night.

How long had it been since Dawn left, promising him she would set him free? Two days? Five? He shouldn't hold his breath for any flimsy attempts of salvation. She could be tangled up in another bar fight, for all he knew. Yet, Mudhi shouldn't count her out. She did swear under the Morning Lord, after all. Who but she would come to his rescue?

The flame fluttered out, leaving him in total darkness.

"Who's there?" his voice cracked.

But none responded. Mudhi held his breath, straining to hear anything—anything at all. Still was his heart as he looked into the inky darkness.

At first, he only saw the bars of his cell. Then he saw a shadow looming over him. A man cloaked and hooded, his head bowed like a monk in prayer. But no sermons or hymns left his snarled lips as he stood there.

"Wh-wh-wh-who are you?"

The cloaked man lifted his head, revealing twin silver stars piercing his soul. "Comfort and joy."

"No," was all Mudhi could say, holding his hands up before him. He was doomed. No one, not even Dawn, could save him now.

In one blink, the cloaked man squeezed through the bars with ease.

*Inhuman!*

Mudhi crawled away until his back pressed against the wall. He tried to beg, but all that came out of his lips was incomprehensible gibberish.

Another blink, and the man towered over him. His baleful eyes glared down at him as he brought his hand before him, beholding a singular golden band.

Mudhi let out a cry of horror that came deep from his belly before the man swiftly put him out of his misery.

Dawn felt her magical speed wearing off as she made it to the crowded city's watch plaza. People of all stripes clustered around the stockades to listen to Captain Felix. The courageous Mynx commanded a small Jessenter pirate crew. He stood on top of a stock as torches, pickaxes, and shovels were distributed by watchmen. On a rare occasion, the Jessenters and the watch worked hand in hand. A warm glow lit against the dimming twilight as the redheaded Mynx of the northern isles gave the volunteers instructions one by one.

"When ye discover a body, don' remove the tag. That falls under the sisters' duty. We'll have no nameless ghosties walkin' abou', now will we?"

Standing off to the side, Dawn saluted, which caught his attention. They locked eyes, and she could see dread flirting across his rugged features.

"Samson, I'll let you take 'em on up," Felix told the officer before turning to her in salute. "What is it, lass?"

"We have a situation," Dawn said.

Both officers raced down the jail hall with the captain of the watch in tow. Echoes of their heels clicked on the floor, filling their ears. They ran through the entire yard of the prison. Kicking the door open, they filed into the small room. The oil lamp still hung in the air but gave no flame.

"Illuminate." Dawn gave the command.

The flame magically returned to the lamp, revealing the cells on both sides devoid of occupants.

"He's gone!" Tristan cried out.

Refusing to accept the truth, Dawn reached to touch the cell door. It swung freely when her fingertips pushed it. Searching the cot for any clue, she found a folded, square, paper slip. Opening it, a single silver coin dropped to the floor. The note, written in mercurial silver, contained a single word: "Theliad."

Felix picked up the coin with his plaid handkerchief. "What does it mean?"

"It means the Silver Fox was here—"

"And he gave his thanks." Dawn slammed the jail door shut.

Mudhi Nazir woke up to the wind whipping his face. His hands were bound to his knees, making him hunch over. The remaining rope crisscrossed his legs, lashing his hands down to his ankles, forcing him to curl into a fetal position. He would be in that position anyway when he opened his brown eyes. Looming before him was a long drop to the jungle threshold below. He realized then this was the eastern spire of the city wall—the second highest point of Amaveriel.

"Comfortable?" he heard from behind. Boots clipped on the ground as Amaris walked toward him. "Cozy?"

Mudhi wanted to be the brave man and demand answers or lash back at him with a witty retort, but he whimpered like a dog instead. He was never good with heights.

A *shhh* sounded over him as the man turned Mudhi's face toward the midnight sky above. The Silver Fox gazed down upon him. His masked face contained the silver light from his eyes. He cooed, caressing Mudhi's cheeks with the back of his two fingers.

"I only need a few minutes of your time. A couple of questions, and I will let you go."

"J-j-just like that?" Mudhi managed to ask.

"Just. Like. That." He tapped Mudhi's nose with the tip of his finger with every word. "Though, should you ever lie to me…" He placed his index finger on his lips while the rest of his hand cupped his chin. Forcefully, Aramis squished Mudhi's cheeks between his fingers like a vise, making him peer over the edge. "We will see if Man really can fly."

Mudhi started to panic, wiggling as he tried to escape from Aramis's grasp. He slipped, and his heart leaped when he felt nothing underneath him. The Silver Fox grabbed him by the shirt to hold him steady. However, keeping him precariously on the edge.

Once again, the Silver Fox shushed, caressing Mudhi's cheeks with the back of his hand. "Don't worry. I promise to be gentle."

Backing off, the Silver Fox unfurled the rope stemming from the knot at Mudhi's ankles, coiling it to an old banner anchor, tying it down quicker than any sailor Mudhi had seen. Standing over his handy work with his hands on his hips, he nodded as if he were going over a mental checklist.

"Let's do a test run."

Mudhi's heart stopped when he heard the words. Before he could protest, he felt the heel in his back, shoving him over the edge toward the clawing jungle below. The wind rushed past his body, carrying his cry of terror.

Music to the Silver Fox's ears.

"Ahmed, Gunther," Tristan called to attention as he entered his office. "I want you to search the docks. Barryn and Nethia to the slums in the southeast quarter. Dilgur, I want every man not on tonight's rotation to sweep the walls."

"Captain. This is a Jessenter matter." Felix followed Tristan just as swiftly. "Stealin' a treasonous bastard falls under our jurisdiction, not yours."

"No, but murder does."

Tristan donned his helm and reached for his sword by his desk, only to be blocked by Felix. They locked eyes.

"Feres wouldn't go that far," Dawn quipped at the door frame, her arms crossed in front of her chest. "He's the Silver Fox. Nazir will be left maimed, not murdered."

Tristan narrowed his dark eyes at the woman. "You're naïve to think so. How did you think Feres made his living before he worked for the Jessenters? It wasn't by freeing slaves. His history with Pondo Rhum's schemes is enough to condemn him to the gallows. He would still be swinging if it wasn't for Lady Ruth."

"Yet, you would turn a blind eye to a traitor?" Felix's face turned as red as his tartan. "A traitor not just to the Jessenters, but the whole of Amaveriel? *Is e gobhar a th'annad.*"

Grabbing the Mynx's tunic, Tristan brought him to his face. "I don't care what rank you have, but you speak the prophet's tongue around here."

"Which one?"

Dawn clasped Tristan's arm, causing him to lower the steely Mynx to the ground. "We're on the same side here. We'll help you find Feres, but leave the rest to us."

Once he released Felix, Tristan grabbed his sword as he headed out. "Then you better find him first."

# Chapter 18

## THE SILVER PRICE

"**H**E MEANS TO MAKE AN HONOR KILLING?" MOTHER Myrrh asked.

"Upon Nazir, yes," Rhyllae said. "Dawn will stop him. I have faith, but I fear it will not be enough. What if he tries it again, this time to his wife? I have spent too many of my efforts to have him free of his past charges to have him swing from the gallows."

"If what you say is true, then your friend is in grave danger from himself. You must be the one to stop him from this path of destruction, not this lieutenant."

"But how?" Rhyllae waved her hands out in front of her. "How can I stay his hand?"

Then the general stirred within his icy tub, muttering something in his native tongue that she couldn't comprehend. Myrrh fished out his right wrist and pressed her dark fingertips upon it. She nodded to herself.

*His condition must be improving,* Rhyllae speculated.

Turning to Rhyllae, Myrrh took her outstretched hand and gave it a gentle squeeze. "By holding it and never letting go. As I have. And many who came before."

It was then Rhyllae looked between the two. She wondered if it was all true. Often, tongues had wagged since they had received Mother Myrrh into the abbey, accompanied by the exiled nobleman and his vassals. They wagged whenever he paid a visit in the early evening, having discussions over tea. The gossip worsened when the mother visited the general when he returned or to see him off before his next campaign. All the while, Rhyllae, the eldest of the sisters, dismissed them as petty rumors. There were plenty about her and Aramis, as well. The insomniac loved to disturb her slumber for any grand discovery he encountered on his nightly wanderings. No doubt that was how Dawn had come to such conclusions. Yet, Rhyllae couldn't be sure she could dismiss rumors of the Sunset mother.

"I take it you and the general are … close?" Rhyllae asked.

"Close?" the mother asked. But then her eyes lit from realization. "Oh, I see. The wickedness of gossip can taint even the purest of hearts."

"I'm sorry, Mother Myrrh, I mean no offense. But it sounded like you were asking me to—"

"To love." Upon seeing a wide-eyed Rhyllae, Myrrh sighed. "From the heart, not the girdle. Do you remember the history of how our Order came to be?"

Rhyllae tensed up her shoulders. "When the Morning Lord took the throne, he asked his sister Lune to watch over the flock."

"And?"

"When she took the title, she became Lune, mother to all. That's why we called her the First Mother?" Rhyllae cringed.

Truth be told, Mother Celia wanted her to be a civil servant rather than a sacred historian.

"Yes. And Lune was married to her dearest friend. They were both ... barren and took in lost children. The Morning Lord asked her to be a guide to the people because she understood love and compassion. Thus, as a mother would, Lune dispenses this knowledge of love to others. Mind you, it was a dark time. Many had forgotten back then and thought it merely a performance of the two bodies intertwining."

"I didn't know. Forgive me."

"Hmm. It seems my suspicions were correct. Mother Celia must have spared you from this knowledge to maintain your chastity. You are the only one in the whole order to hear the call since infancy. Never have you known life before service."

"But you did with the general?" Rhyllae asked.

"Yes, for a lifetime now. I was his childhood friend." Then she paused and took a deep breath, as if to overlook an ill thought. "Eventually, his wife." Myrrh gazed upon him, then sighed. "Those times were joyous but fleeting. I was called to serve and had to sever our ties. It was the strength of our friendship—our platonic love—that prevails to this very night. Love beyond the mortal coil, beyond all boundaries of nations and petty law. Love, pure and true. Without it, he would never have found it in his heart to forgive. Nor found the courage to marry again, one who was his greatest treasure. Even I wouldn't have had the compassion to bring him here for safety without this virtue of love."

Rhyllae raised her eyebrows. "So it was a cover?"

"If he had remained, he would've been persecuted to the highest sentence. Exile was an act of mercy. I volunteered to bring him here."

"You sacrificed your position to be here?" Rhyllae thought all the mothers and sisters were sent here due to neglecting their duties. The Abbey of the Rising Dawn was one of the few isolated sentries of the order. But then, she had to wonder...

The mother smiled. "You have a task of your own, though much more difficult, I fear. Feel the virtue in your heart and use it as a light. Guide the Silver Fox back to the path before he is lost forever."

"What if," Rhyllae whispered, "I'm too late?"

"Then drag him back and remind him who he truly is."

Though she understood the task ahead of her, her shoulders slumped. "I don't think I have the power to do this alone."

"Oh, my daughter, you're never alone." Then Mother Myrrh signed a blessing in the air and tapped it on Sister Rhyllae's forehead with two fingers. Radiating from her touch was a warmth that settled her nerves.

Then the mother encouraged her to rest, exempting her from singing for the dawn. Though Rhyllae laid her head down, she couldn't help but remember the tree, the fox, and the blinding light.

Mudhi landed like a sack of potatoes, though he felt heavier. After Aramis had him dangle at the end of the line, he heaved him back up to the top. His shoulder still smarted from the long haul.

*Perhaps a shorter length would do it.*

Aramis turned to adjust the rope—for his sake, not Mudhi's—when he spied the man inching away like a worm. With a flick of his wrist, he snapped a knife in front of Mudhi's face, halting him in his tracks.

"We've just begun, and already, you turn to flee?" Lifting Mudhi's chin with the tip of his blade, Aramis bent low to Mudhi's ear. "Pathetic."

He didn't care that he nicked the man when he drew back his knife. Scratching the side of his rugged jaw with the back of the blade, Aramis gazed toward the moonless horizon. As a jhasin, his eyes could see the subtle shades of the coming morn. A myriad of questions spun in his mind, and there was little twilight left to explore further. Returning his silvery gaze to Mudhi, he scowled, knowing every question he asked would be like pulling teeth.

"I could ask you when, how long, or even why you chose to seduce my wife. But I doubt I would get anything more than 'why not?' So, let's cut to the chase. What did you want from her? The book?"

"Book? Wh-what book?" Mudhi stammered.

As fast as lightning, Aramis crouched low, face-to-face. "The tome of Tellezard. The one the necromancer used to kill my friends. The book Vanessa stole and blew up the entire base for. That book!"

Mudhi's eyes bulged wide in the silver light. "I know nothing about no book."

Snatching Mudhi's tangled mop, Aramis slammed his head against the stone. "Lies!"

"I swear on my ancestors' grave, I don't know."

"The dead can't help you here. But you can join them if you wish."

Standing up, Aramis once again put his heel on him, nudging him over the edge of the eastern spire.

Quaking underneath his boot, Mudhi spoke in sporadic spurts. "No! I had nothing to do with it. I swear! She did it all her own."

"Bull!" Though it was enough to make him pause. "You used her. You knew her mind was addled and seduced her for your own gain."

"Seduced her? She seduced me!" Mudhi cried out.

"Why would she fuck a witless worm like you?"

"She was lonely."

"Married to a jhasin, I seriously doubt that."

"I was having trouble with my wife—"

"That I don't doubt—"

"Vanessa let me drink from her cup … for a price."

Mudhi yelped as Aramis grabbed his shirt and swung him onto his seat. The cool air wicked the sweat off his stained shirt's back.

"To dare call her a whore to my face," Aramis said, "you're braver than I thought."

Then Aramis let his fingers slip, enough for Mudhi to rock back before gravity took hold. Then grasped his collar a few lazy seconds later.

"It wasn't for coin. Vanessa wanted information."

Grabbing his collar with both hands, Aramis brought Mudhi to his face again. "What information?"

"Battle formations, locations, numbers, people—anything about the Jessenters. By the Morning Lord's light, I swear I thought she was concerned about you. But then it became too much. I asked her why. And, this is the truth—by the Light, it's the truth!—she's working for them."

"No… You didn't." The stone in Aramis's stomach dropped below his knees.

Mudhi lolled his head to the side as he cast his eyes aside. "She promised to spare my family when the time comes. If I complied, Marilyn would be spared."

"At what cost?" Aramis's voice trembled with fury. "Blowing up the base, killing hundreds—no—thousands at the Karatow mountains?!"

"I didn't think—"

"Of course you didn't! The only mind you had was the one between your legs!"

Aramis pulled the traitorous bastard to his feet the best he could since Mudhi's hands were still bound to his knees. Aramis could end this now and be rid of him. He had every right to. Everything—everything!—that his friends sacrificed themselves for was now null. A devastating effort marred by a spineless worm groomed by negligence and idiocy.

"You... You condemned us all," Aramis said through gritted teeth. Yet, he cast him aside, far from the edge, watching him weep and shudder in his hempen bonds.

"You were the one that brought her here." The retort squeaked out of Mudhi between sobs.

All of a sudden, Aramis couldn't find the air to breathe. He snaked his trembling fingers under his mask, letting his blade fall as he slipped it off. His fingers continued to run through his hair as he paced to and fro. His silver eyes cast shadows as they darted in maddening confusion.

All doubt was thrown out the window. Aramis could not press himself to think this weasel was behind all of this. It could be none but his once-endearing, manic lover, Vanessa. Between the two of them, she was crazy enough to pull it off.

No... not crazy.

Clever.

Clever enough to trick and seduce him with lie after lie. Seamless was their art that Aramis couldn't begin to remember when the real Vanessa ended and the façade began. For all he knew, everything had been false. Their marriage, their condition, even their gender—often disguising themselves as Ashabar to sail among the fishermen. Even their love could have been a falsehood. A fool he was to think anyone would love a man like him.

Was he wrong to think he could change everything?

Wrong to step long ago into the waters of Zemzem?

Wrong when he emerged with this masculine veneer?

At the time, he wanted to be his own man and claim himself free of anyone else. Then he found Vanessa. For three years, he thought they were the one. To have both of their broken halves fit into a whole. Only for Aramis to be, instead, taken apart piece by piece for their own uses. A target for their schemes. Was he wrong?

Perhaps there was still time to redeem what had been lost.

Kneeling next to Mudhi, Aramis scraped the point of his dagger down the man's right cheek. "You did more than spill the beans, didn't you? You were working together. Otherwise, why else would Vanessa have you do the dirty deed?"

"For the last time, I didn't do it," Mudhi said.

*A master of disguise, indeed.* Aramis then said, "Then it is Vanessa, and you took the fall."

"I didn't know that was her plan, honest. I was with her that night—it's not what you think. She told me it was our last time together, and we toasted. But the drink knocked me flat on my ass."

"She drugged you."

*The medicine. I should've known Vanessa would use it on someone else.*

Mudhi nodded a little too enthusiastically. "She poisoned me. Vanessa laughed at me as I lay there. And... And ... her face changed. I didn't believe it at first, but her entire face shifted. Before I knew it, I was staring at myself like in a mirror."

"Had she done anything before she changed in front of you? Put on a ring. Chanted. Sung a song. Anything?"

Mudhi half-smiled, perhaps glad to know someone, at last, believed him. "No, nothing at all. She laughed at me until I passed out. I woke up to the watch hauling my ass to jail."

"Never to see her again... And you know nothing about the book?" When Mudhi could only nod, the Silver Fox sighed.

Perhaps Vanessa was magically gifted this whole time? Or had obtained another magical device for their transfiguration? It would explain a few things when it was her turn during their lovemaking. Aramis looked to the jungle horizon. His eyes searched among the rose and lavender of the breaking morn, but no answer could be found. Another sleepless night. Another dead end.

"In the end," his voice whispered to the wind, "nothing more than a toy to play with."

"Am I ... free to go?" came Mudhi's cracked voice.

Aramis smirked. He regarded the fool over his shoulder with a dark twinkle in his eye. "I suppose I am done with you."

He pulled the ex-lieutenant to the edge once again. This time propping him on his feet. When Aramis cut the bonds around his hands, Mudhi wept. The cretin was sure that his end was nigh.

"Your wife must have missed you. Though a wretch like you doesn't deserve her," Aramis continued as he crouched down to cut the bonds around Mudhi's legs. "But I'm sure you will find another way to disappoint her."

Finally, the rope unraveled, a tangled mess around Mudhi's ankles.

"Perhaps with another man's wife," Aramis said, locking his steely gaze upon him.

Mudhi quaked as his words hung in the air.

Then Aramis smiled at the nervous wreck. "Or perhaps not."

The Silver Fox then produced a small pouch of silver and calmly placed it in Mudhi's hands.

Mudhi blinked in disbelief and smiled. "For ... For my troubles?"

Aramis grabbed him by his shoulders, pulling him toward himself so Mudhi rolled on the balls of his feet.

"For your funeral." Then Aramis shoved him over.

# Chapter 19

## TEARS OF KATHRÉFTIS

SAILING THROUGH THE INKY VOID, KORZHA FELT his body falling, tumbling end over end. The wind was hot and abrasive on his skin as he continued to plummet. There was no end in sight, and there was nothing to hold to slow his descent. No sound. No time. He was free-falling through the darkness.

He flipped himself over and saw a clear blue light, like an evening star. He tried to direct himself toward it but felt helpless as he tumbled and pivoted in the steaming hot darkness. Despite his feelings, it seemed to work. The star started to swell in his view. Then it dawned on him. It wasn't a star, but a pool of water.

Not wanting to drown, Korzha tried to redirect himself away from the fast-approaching disc of water. But it was too late. He splashed down in its icy embrace on his back.

The shock woke him up. He was not in an ocean but fully clothed in a tub with chunks of ice floating in the water around him. It was merely a room, adorned with a small wardrobe and a bed, with dried flowers pressed in the shape of the sun and hung on the wall. A crack ran diagonally on the wall, a hair above the pressed motif, highlighted by the noonday's light. And there, by his side, was Myrrh.

Despite the chill from the ice, the Sunset mother's arm draped upon the metal rim to cushion her drooping head. Her thick dark locks, free of the red shawl-like habit, fell into the water, reminding him of the Romani falls back home. Clasped around his left wrist were her long fingers, monitoring his condition.

*Oh, Grace.* Korzha reached for her pointed chin with trembling fingers. *You care too much for me.*

His knuckles quivered as they brushed her skin. Her lips parted, and she let out a sigh. Long had he hoped for such a tender greeting. And yet, these same lips had granted him a kiss hours before without forethought, defying all convictions of her dogma.

And defying all of his oaths.

Letting his hand slip back into the water, he closed his eyes. As long as his late husband remained unburied, Korzha was bound to him. For seven long years, he had dutifully stayed by his vow. Never wavered by any man or woman. No matter how strong the longing, he stayed true.

And there he found himself quaking. That kiss, no matter how innocent, reawakened the kindling inside him. Memories long snuffed out, from when life was simple and carefree, were now lit. From before the war. Before he had to choose between country or family.

Korzha buried his face upon Myrrh's shoulder. *I cannot endure this any longer. Release me. One of you, please, release me!*

Then a cry broke his internal suffering.

Above, he spied a black eagle on the stone sill of an open window. The day's warmth shone on his dark plumage, casting an orange sheen upon his wings, a pink, five-pointed lily in his talons. It cocked its head, its amber eyes studying him. Then the black eagle, with its great wings, took flight. Leaving the blossom behind.

Was it a sign from his dearly departed? Or was it nothing but a strange coincidence, a mere temptation of a weak mind?

Korzha gazed back upon the dark beauty not once stirred from her slumber.

*If it is wrong to pluck this flower, then let me be damned.*

With his now steady hand, he cupped her cheek as he locked his lips upon hers. What chill he had fled with her warmth, soothing his senses. He only paused when he felt a smile creeping from the corners of her mouth.

Heavy lids fluttered to reveal two sleepy Töskan blue eyes. "<I know you.>"

"<And I know you.>" Korzha leaned again to kiss her. She placed her fingers on his lips.

"<Gus. I must explain myself. I...>" Her words halted when a knock came at the door. She muttered, "<Stay put.>"

Securing her hair into the habit, Mariam opened the door to find Dido bowing. "Good morrow."

*I think I stayed here long enough, thank you.*

Grasping the rim, Korzha began to lift himself out. But he slipped and fell back in. Not only had the ice coated the edge, but it also lined the bottom of the tub. The clumsy effort, worsened by his soggy clothes, caused the water to slosh out of the container to the stone floor.

"<I thought I told you to stay put?>" Myrrh said.

"Oh, he's finally up?" Dido asked through the open door.

"I will be once I get out of this accursed thing," Korzha retorted. Again, he tried to pull himself out and failed.

"Oh, allow me."

With a snap of her tiny fingers, Dido willed the ice away to the Shining Sea, the metal tub along with it. The water, free from the container, splashed all over the stone floor. Leaving the drenched general on his rump in the middle of the bare floor.

The Sunset mother, now deprived of her tub and her sleeping quarters flooded, verbally dressed down the satyr. Meanwhile, Korzha pulled his sodden shirt off his back before donning the rest of his trappings.

With all the commotion, another priestess of the Morn poked her head through the portal. It was Rhyllae. Her golden-brown eyes flashed in mirth before she hopped back into the hall. No doubt to laugh at his expense without the mother noticing. Finally, the young priestess came back in.

"I see the general is on the mend, Mother Myrrh. Unless you need me, I shall join the others downstairs." Rhyllae bowed and turned to leave.

"Before you go," Korzha spoke up. "What do you know of the creature last night? What caused her arousal from her grave?"

Dido, while magically blowing away the assaulting puddles, coughed vocally. For no apparent reason, save to give him a knowing look over the rims of her glasses.

"And thank you for your assistance," Korzha eventually said.

"I should thank you," Rhyllae countered. "If the two of you hadn't shown up, I wouldn't have been able to stop Fanteen. I brought her here to see if I could find her murderer. Mother Celia planned to commune with her until..." Then her honey-brown eyes veered away.

"She awoke."

"Yes." She bowed her head in shame. "I was busy with other affairs and came too late."

Mother Myrrh put a hand on the sister's shoulder. "As we all were. There's no shame tending those who still draw breath."

"Speaking of which," Korzha said, "what of the Silver Fox? Is he awake? Did he say anything?"

Both the mother and sister exchanged glances.

Even little Dido stopped her magical cleaning as the silence drew out. "So, the thief had felled him after all." Dido bowed her head.

"What? No! He's alive," the young priestess's words spilled forth like a broken dam. "Aramis sped off as soon as he awoke. I fear what he will do. For good or for ill, I just know blood will be spilled. I should've kept better watch over him and never strayed from his side."

"Sister," Mother Myrrh urged. "Have faith. Not all is lost. You have sent this Jessenter after all."

"Who?" queried the general.

"Dawn," Rhyllae replied, her face flushed from the emotional outburst.

"That's right. We saw her speed by last night," Dido spoke up.

*But can she wrangle the elusive Fox?* Korzha kept the thought to himself.

"And we shall attend the mourners while we wait," Myrrh interjected. "There's much to do before the ceremony tomorrow."

"Very well. I thank you." Korzha nodded to them both as they left the general with the satyr.

Dido closed the door behind the two departed priestesses. "Do you think Mr. Feres went after the thief?"

"Perhaps. Or perhaps not." Korzha eased himself to the edge of the bed, donning his socks. "'Tis folly to follow him. 'Once his mind is set, he is loose in that direction like an arrow,' or so Lady Ruth used to say of him. There is no telling where he is in the shadows. Though, if he does know who the thief is, it's a wonder he didn't linger."

"You think they're still hiding here, the thief?"

"The purse, the one with the golden sun, is our only clue. A common item for all traveling priestesses, but difficult to obtain. We can still pick up their trail here if the rogue has long deserted this haven."

"That may be more difficult than you would like to think." Dido pulled up the vanity stool, then hopped up to sit on it. "I couldn't sleep last night, so I perused their library. It bothered me to no end that I couldn't detect any sort of magic from the disguise. It would require a great deal of it to produce, yet there was nothing. I finally figured out why."

From the pocket within her robe, Dido pulled out a scroll and handed it to him. The elegant script was plain to see when he unfurled it: "Doppelgänger."

"They're creatures of the fey like I am. Akin to chameleons, doppelgängers mimic others by transforming their own body. It can take days to perfect the entire form and voice from memory. Always they resemble those who surround them, but never have their own image. It's a bit sad now that I think about it. No matter how close they get to someone, they will never be completely understood. Never knowing who they truly are under all those layers of falsehoods."

"So, they're like Fylgia—a spirit twin?"

Dido shook her head. "No, those are sprung from the afterbirth and possess any animal that ate it. Doppelgängers are sprung from the tears of the cursed maiden, Kathréftis. It is said she had seduced Uranus by disguising herself as his wife, Gaia. When Gaia returned from harvest, she caught them in the act. Kathréftis was flayed alive and left wandering the Earth for all eternity. Ashamed, she clothed herself with a beaded cloak that reflected light—hiding from the world. It is written that wherever a tear fell from her eye, a doppelgänger will appear."

"And you believe we have a doppelgänger wandering in Amaveriel?"

"It's the only creature I know of that can pull off such a disguise without any magical means. The imposter fooled me with your likeness, down to your very voice! It was impressive."

"So they can transform into another person in the blink of an eye." Korzha snapped the scroll's bindings shut. The situation was much worse than he cared for.

"Almost. Doppelgängers require intense study and practice to mimic the person. Even then, they may not get all of it right and usually don't speak."

"But this one did. As you said, 'Impressive.'"

Dido sat mum in anxiety-ridden thought. When she spoke in a hushed tone, a tremble clung to the edge of her words. "There is one who can pull off such a feat with perfect precision at the drop of a hat. A superior being of the species—a doppelgänger queen if you will. Legend has it that they unlocked this great expertise by revealing their true nature outward. Discarded all refuse of any influence and memories from others. But... It cannot be them! It's said, once they achieved this spectacular feat, they looked at themself in the mirror. Upon seeing their visage, they succumbed to madness and tore themselves into shreds..." Once again, Dido fell silent.

The general paced the room, his mind reeling from the information brought forth. He glanced into Myrrh's vanity mirror with each pass until a thought struck him.

Walking up to the mirror, Korzha pondered aloud, "To know one's true self is to accept all you are—vice and virtue. If it's possible for such a creature to accept who they truly are … then it is possible for one to know them … and to understand them."

Korzha slammed his hand down on the vanity, snapping Dido from her thoughts. "That's it! How else did he see through it all?"

"Pardon?"

"'The world is not a paper moon.' Feres knew the doppelgänger, personally, to be able to make such a remark. Knew what their likes, dislikes, and all of their habits."

Then Dido hopped out of the chair in excitement. "And if they are a creature of habit…"

"The thief would have a tell, and the Silver Fox can confirm it for us." Korzha donned his coat and trusty Silver Star. "I need to inquire further with Sister Ghalédale. We must find out his closest associates besides herself."

The little satyr nodded and opened the door. Then slammed it shut once again.

"General Korzha, what if she's the doppelgänger queen?"

The thought gave him pause, but he finally shook his head. "No, for if she was, Aramis would not have left her behind alive."

Rhyllae ran her fingertips on the palm-sized wooden box. The decorative floral lid had been freshly carved and stained yesterday, with no years to wear down the edges or blacken the relief. After a while, she eyed the woman waiting. Her blonde hair, braided in her northern heritage, was high-lighted by the stained glass's prismatic colors. She looked like she could hold her own in a fight, but Ruth often said her sister, Naomi, was a peaceful soul.

After a while, Rhyllae handed the box to her. "Lady Ruth stood tall and proud to the very end. She died with honor and courage."

Words failed her when the box opened. It had been a short time since she laid eyes on the smooth, oval stone painted with the raven, their family sigil, yet it felt like for-ever. Much had transpired since that fateful day.

The woman took a great sniff, and a tear escaped from her lashes. "Then she is welcomed into the halls of Freye to sit with my mother and sisters. Thank you for your service, sun priestess."

Rhyllae was taken back, for the Great Northern people rarely showed thanks or emotion. "You're welcome, Naomi. I'll inform you when we finally recover her from the ruin. Shine on."

With a curt nod, the tall woman left. Leaving Rhyllae behind in a sea of parishioners. Some huddled together as they touched the trinkets and medals with tender care. Others waited in lines leading up to their tables to claim their loved ones' belongings. Many a tear fell, sometimes flowing into a heart-wrenching sob. A sobering moment for all. For none expected this grand of a loss. Not one.

Rhyllae felt numb, lost in the work laid before her, steeling herself into stone from every low whimper. Her eyes tried to steal the happy colors streaming down upon them whenever they flitted heavenward. But even she could feel as dour as the Sunset mother working two tables down from her.

Donned again in the autumn hues of her matronly habit, Mother Myrrh was in discussion with Mother Vyreal. The former made a cupping motion with her dark hands while the latter shook her head. It seemed they were missing an ingredient, but of what, Rhyllae couldn't make out through all the somber chatter.

The blue daze was broken. Wailing came beyond the narrow arched entrance. Fresh mourners led the way: a mother with her children in tow embraced by an elderly woman. The men escorted them with bare heads bowed in sorrow.

At first, Rhyllae wondered if these were the family members of Fanteen Dada, but Salina wasn't among them. Then, as she watched one of the women rend her clothes in passionate grief, she thought perhaps a Jessenter had fallen into the clutches of death.

But no.

Rhyllae felt dread as she laid eyes on a familiar ruffled blonde at the saffron entrance. The crowd dispersed to let Dawn through. Her muscled arms were draped with a heavy burden as she trudged forward, not even locking eyes with Rhyllae.

Mother Myrrh, the sole evening priestess in the abbey, stepped forward. Halting the lieutenant, she waved her to lay the body before her.

Dawn set the tightly bound bundle on the black-and-white marble tiles with her head hung low. Untying a knot at the head, she revealed a face. Broken and swollen, with bulging eyes wide with fear.

Upon seeing the gruesome display, the fresh mourners shrilled like banshees. The priestesses prayed, and the rest of the common folk were aghast. Through all the cacophony echoing in the nave, Rhyllae heard Dawn say as clear as night, "I fucked up."

# Chapter 20

## CLOY

THE AIR WAS STIFLING, CLASHING WITH THE PRO-saic colors filtered from the stained glass windows above. As the lights shifted from one spectrum to another, Rhyllae's senses spun from the earthy notes of sandalwood to the putrid taste of death. She needed air—pure air.

Letting her feet guide her, Rhyllae didn't care if Dawn or Mother Myrrh called for her. Not caring that she bumped into the general in the hall when her feet picked up a swifter pace. Not caring about the lingering stares from the injured soldiers' and her fellow sisters as she sped past them.

They had failed.

She had failed.

Running into the cloister garden, she tripped, falling into the deep recess of the eastern garden bed, made half a foot deep to contain the precious soil. A soft layer of rose petals broke her landing as she caught herself on the lap of Lune's statue. The torchbearer for all wandering aimlessly in the shadow. Sister, mother, wife, it mattered not. All the sister needed was a comforting hand.

Sobbing, Rhyllae hugged the statue and buried her head against the stone.

*How could he do this?* she asked Lune. *Fighting for the Jessenters was the only way to avoid the noose. And he threw it all away for a woman who couldn't care less.*

The pang in her heart redoubled as she remembered how Aramis had looked at the night sky as he told her, "I love her." How he clenched his right fist, the wedding band on the wrong hand.

*He will die a broken man. A soul lost and alone, far out of my reach.*

Gazing up at the serene face of Lune, Rhyllae begged aloud, "Please help Aramis. He's my friend, my dearest companion, my..."

*Love?*

The thought surprised her, ceasing her tears from falling.

And still, as she turned the word in her head, it felt right. If it was love, then it felt purer than the sun and truer than the gospel. Love, pure as flame and warm as sunlight.

How often had Aramis given Rhyllae his shoulder to bear? Put himself in harm's way in their battles? Giving his all for her through thick and thin. Always holding her hand and never letting go. Warm as the Sunset mother's blessing.

She felt the warmth radiate throughout her body, seeping into the fiber of her soul, breaking the gloom like the sun after a storm. Giving her the strength to do what must be done.

Wiping the tears from her face, Sister Rhyllae stood up. She brushed off the rose petals clinging to her skirt and wrapped her yellow habit firmly on her neck and shoulders. There was one place he always visited before he leaves

Amaveriel, no matter which gate. Passing through the back door used by the laysisters, Rhyllae ran through the streets of Amaveriel, praying she could make it in time.

There was no stopping Sister Rhyllae the way she came barreling down the hall from the nave. When Korzha raised his hand, she slammed into his shoulder, knocking him back against the wall.

"Ghalédale," he cried out, but she didn't flinch from her path.

"Oh no," Dido moaned as she peered into the heart of the abbey.

Fearing it was the Silver Fox, he joined in her viewing. There, Dawn kneeled before Mother Myrrh, cradling her shorn head. Between them was the bloody mess of Mudhi Nazir. Perhaps Aramis was onto something after all.

"It's my fault," Dawn said. "I swore to her I would stop him. I didn't mean to break my promise."

Mother Myrrh gave a comforting hand on her shoulder. "You did all you could with the power within you, Lieutenant. Even you could not save him from the error of his ways. Mother Vyreal, please."

The mother swooped to Dawn's side, urging her to follow. With a somber nod, Dawn picked up the bloody remains and trailed behind. She paused when she spotted the general at the door. Forgoing the salute, Korzha stepped back to let them pass.

"Especially a traitorous fool." He spoke to the Sunset mother once he entered the nave.

Before he made his way to Myrrh, a woman clothed in a black shroud, her shoulder bare from the ripped seam, confronted him.

"How could you say such a thing? How can you call him a traitor when he has served under you for eight years?" Marilynn shrilled at him before the priestesses gently pulled her away to join the rest of the mourners.

"How, indeed?" A grandiose maternal voice filled the spacious room.

All of them, the mourners, the sisters, the mothers, bowed, for it was Mother Superior Frianul who graced their presence. Well, all but two. The general stood erect with his hands clasped behind his back. Glancing down, Dido shied behind his crane-long legs. Not all favor a being with horns, no matter how kind.

"How callous you have been, General, after what they have been through." Mother Superior Frianul caressed Marilynn's chin as she passed. "What a tragedy."

"I'm surprised you would call this a tragedy when numerous have fallen in the Karatow mountains," Korzha said.

"And not of the destruction of your freedom base?" She circled him like a lazy vulture. "Blown by the true traitor, not this poor, foolish man, mind you."

"Who?"

"Why Aramis Feres, the Silver Fox himself." Mother Frianul waved her arms out wide, high above her head. Gasps and murmurs broke out among the parishioners and the priestesses.

"You lie!" Though meek, Dido's voice broke through.

"I would never lie, vile creature. That would be a sin in the eyes of our Morning Lord."

"Perhaps a mistake, Supremacy?" Mother Myrrh stood up from her bow. "Is it possible one spoke falsely toward you?"

"I do not doubt the honesty of a dying man during his last confession." Frianul waved her hand with fingers splayed while her eyes were cast upward.

"Who was this soldier?" the general asked.

"Forgive me. I have forgotten the soldier's name. But he had brilliant red hair and a pox-scarred face. One of your guards, I believe? He was there when the cave-in occurred. The man told me all he could before the Lord took him into his arms. As a matter of fact, he did mention the Silver Fox was not alone. Accompanied by a satyr, I do believe. And look, we have one here before us."

And just like that, all eyes fell upon Dido, and she trembled from their heated gaze. Korzha's left hand crossed over to his pommel. His blue eyes darted to and fro to gauge who would come first. He noticed Mother Myrrh mouthing at him to stay his hand with clasping hands brought before her chest.

"That is quite an assumption to make." Korzha spoke with a careful measure.

Frianul smirked before bellowing down the belly of the abbey, twisting her wrists while twirling her fingers in intricate gestures. "I command thee all: any who brings the satyr and the Fox before me shall be granted salvation and a ticket to heaven. In the name of our Morning Lord, amen."

The entire room shifted before him. A veil of milky haze crept into his vision, distorting everything into shadowy figments. His movements felt not of his own and unusually sluggish. No matter how much he willed it to be, Korzha couldn't unsheathe the Silver Star.

Then a brilliant light shone, streaming from the chancel itself. The blinding light pierced through the fog, and his vision became unclouded as a blue ocean horizon. He found himself surrounded by glazed eyes and lips murmuring, "Salvation." Dido begged them to wake, to no avail.

"Go. Go!" he heard Myrrh cry.

Crouching low, Korzha scooped Dido into his arms and bolted to where he remembered the narrow entrance to be. The light was so brilliant that the daylight appeared dim when he emerged with her in tow.

"It looks like we found our doppelgänger," Dido voiced as he ran down the sloping road.

"Yes, how fortunate." Looking back, Korzha spied the rabid horde filing out of the narrow arch.

"Turn here." Dido pointed to an alleyway off Sulmaith Street.

Following through, Korzha carried her down the constricted path until they reached a dead end. Putting Dido down, he waved the Silver Star in front of him. "Hide yourself, Ms. Dido. I'll fend them off—"

"Oh, get down."

Leaping up with her powerful goat legs, the little satyr grabbed him by his shirt and dragged him behind a smelly compost bin. With a wave of her hand, Dido sprinkled sand in front of them and crouched with the general.

Two blokes ran down the alley, well ahead of the small group at the mouth of the alleyway. As they came closer, Korzha stirred to end them with his blade. But Dido slapped her tiny hand over his mouth. His heart was set into a panic when one of them walked up and turned to look at them. But he simply blinked, wiggled his finger in his ear, and looked around.

*Are we invisible?* Korzha looked upon the satyr, impressed by her magical skill.

"I think we went down the wrong way." The man put a finger in his ear and gave it another wiggle.

His friend slapped the back of his hand against his chest. "Oi, what's the matter with you?"

"I dunno, it keeps ringing."

Dido gaped and gave Korzha a bewildered look. The singing sword was still unsheathed. Slowly, the general slipped it back into its scabbard, silencing the blade. Neither one of them dared to draw breath.

"And now it's gone," said the slack-jawed man.

"C'mon, we're losing daylight."

Once the men were gone, Korzha and Dido poked their heads out of their hiding hole.

"Oh, we will never get rid of the doppelgänger at this rate," Dido moaned.

"Indeed," Korzha said. "They're clever to disguise themselves as the Mother Superior. The elders wouldn't dare touch her, nor resort to violence to remove her."

"Not without hard evidence. Or magic. Or a coup."

"The latter should suffice."

"How? The elders won't allow it."

"Feres. He can verify the villain, and through him, we'll have our proof for them. Then we'll be sanctioned to do what's needed to be done."

"It will be a challenge to find him without being noticed." Then Dido's eyes lit up. "I do have the means to make myself invisible. That leaves you without, though."

"Better you than me since you're the target. Go. Find Feres. When you do, bring him to me."

"Yes, but where should I find you?"

*Where indeed?*

His options were limited with the base of operations gone. He didn't have much in the way of friends, and any inn or tavern was too likely a spot to hide. However, he did narrow it down to the one place where none would expect him to venture.

"Madame Pompadour's Teahouse."

*CLICK*

Myrrh shifted her eyes down both halls. The master key turned too heavily in the lock for her tastes, but none was there to deter her. As swift as she could, Mother Myrrh let herself into the superior's office. With a gentle hand, she closed the door without making a sound, breathing easier when it was locked again.

The Mother Superior insisted on overseeing the preparations for Mudhi Nazir's final departure. Another oddity since the mother would only let Mother Celia, *May she rest in peace*, and Mother Myrrh handle all of such duties in the past.

No, something had been amiss since Mother Myrrh left, and she needed to find the root of it. Perhaps the reason for Korzha's plea the prior night.

*Morning Lord, keep him safe*, she prayed as she searched through the desk.

The only significant find was a snuffbox of illegal herbs. Though deplorable, not something that would reveal Mother Frianul's true nature. Still, she took two leaves to further her investigation.

Climbing up the spiral iron steps, Myrrh found herself dumbfounded by the bedroom's opulent display. Her silk curtains were of Chessentari make, along with the pillows and the plush rug on the floor. The bed sheets were of Nagano, made with their unmistakable woven pattern. And Myrrh would know, being a former baroness herself.

Running her slender black fingers on the sheets, Myrrh felt the thin fabric. It had clearly been used, judging by the fray of the hem.

*Oh, how garish.*

Disgust boiled within her as she tucked the sheet back into place. After Mother Myrrh jabbed the silk underneath the ornate red pillows, she smelled something peculiar on her fingertips. It was cloyingly sweet, as if a bouquet of exotic jasmine were rubbed into its very fibers. Never would the superior, always an advocate for natural beauty, have such a scent.

Such a distinct odor must be enough of a clue about who the imposter could be.

Taking a scalpel from her medical pouch, the sunset mother cut a palm-sized portion from the underside of the pillow. She took out her handkerchief and hid the offending cloth.

*I'm sorry, my dear Gus, but I have no choice.*

Tucking it into her sleeve, Mother Myrrh worried whether it would seep through her garment. Then the bells tolled a melodic phrase. Evening mass was upon them. Returning the pillow to its original state, she hurried down the stairs. Taking some scrolls from the shelves as her cover, the mother rushed out of the office.

A thought occurred to her when she turned down the hall to the stairs below. Mother Myrrh wouldn't be able to go out to search anytime soon. She would have to lead the evening mass in the superior's stead and had a large work-load waiting for her in the preparation chamber. How could she follow the lead?

On the first floor, Myrrh found her answer across the way.

Down the hall, alone among the soldiers laid last night, was the young officer from earlier. Crouched with her back against the balcony pillar, the lieutenant had her head on her knees. Her shoulders shuddered as she wept. As the Sunset mother drew nearer, her eyes beheld a man with brilliant red hair lying in perfect stillness. The color of life drained from his skin.

*So it is true. Oh, the poor dear.*

Mother Myrrh stood behind the lieutenant and draped her handkerchief next to her. With a murmured thanks, Dawn took it and brought it to her nose. She almost retched when she caught the scent.

"What the hell is this shit?" Dawn whirled around but stopped her fury when she saw Myrrh. "I mean… Uh…"

Waving her to be silent, the Sunset mother kneeled before her. "A task, if you are willing to take it."

The young Jessenter officer narrowed her eyes, trying to discern the ever-sphinxlike face of Mother Myrrh. But to no avail. Averting her gaze, Dawn looked upon her fallen friend instead.

It was then that Mother Myrrh saw the reason for her hesitation. A hole smaller than her thumb was in the groove between the collarbones. Mingled among his ebony tag, the once ruby life-force was reduced to a cracked maroon stain.

Touching her arm, the Sunset mother whispered to her, "There is evil here that cannot be vanquished by the sword alone. Your general knows this. He seeks to draw it from our cloister, as should you."

The words snapped her awake, her hazel eyes wide with clarity. Dawn took the pungent cloth and shoved it in her pocket with a single nod.

"I can't make any more promises, but I will do what I can."

Then the hour struck.

# Chapter 21

## ELYAMAMEN

**T**HE BELL TOLLED, SLOW AND SOMBER, ACROSS THE free city of Amaveriel, ringing through every alleyway and home. Chasing every watchman's clinking chain mail and every slapping sandal worn by the common folk, it echoed throughout the concave dale, spilling out into the Shining Sea, the Ioun desert, and to the bluff where Aramis stood.

Back where he had been days before. Back on high with the jungle to his back, Aramis stood at the edge of it all. The last time he was here, Aramis thought he had lost everything after the dreaded M'thealquilôk expedition. How foolish he had been. Back then, he had a home, a wife, and people he could trust—treasures far more precious than any jewel. Now, he had nothing but woe.

The clamor of the bells still rang in the air as if the city was pleading, "Stay."

*It is better this way*, he told himself, not for the first time.

There was no doubt that Vanessa would take the tome to the Djinnasi lords, along with all of Amaveriel's secrets. If he leaves now, he might have a chance of catching her trail before the ever-constant Iounese wind swept it away.

*It is better this way,* Aramis repeated to himself, trying to block the bell's droning chime. *Rhyllae wouldn't understand. I cannot bear to let her see this. It's better this way.*

Aramis swore to return once it's all over. When they have long forgotten him, perhaps. He will be a stranger once again, like he was when he first entered the city. He will look around in awe of the changed city while the morning dove, Rhyllae, sings for the dawn high on the minaret. Perhaps moved on from their friendship, and he'll be forgotten.

When that day rises, he shall return. Aramis was sure of that.

The evening bell knelled its last, so he too must be away. Aramis turned his back, tugging on Midnight, the black steed he had stolen, to follow. A few steps away and a sensation of unease overwhelmed him. He wasn't alone. A snap of a twig farther down the slope confirmed it.

In a flash, his wrist snapped one of his twin daggers loose, letting it fly. Its deadly blade landed squarely in the tree trunk, a hair's width from a familiar face.

"Rhyllae? What are you doing here?" Aramis asked once his breath returned to him. For once, he was grateful that his age was creeping up on him.

"I'm here to..." Rhyllae started to say as she pulled on the dirk, but it wouldn't budge. "I'm here..." She growled as she tried again with both hands. Still, the stubborn dagger stayed put. "I'm here to talk to you." She threw her hands up in defeat.

"You mean to stop me."

Flinging the reins over the pommel, Aramis strode over to the sunken dagger. To his surprise, it didn't pull out with a quick tug. He glanced back at Rhyllae. "I told you so" was written all over her perfect, round face. Aramis threw his strength against his knife, feeling his calloused hands rub raw from every pull. He felt her eyes piercing him from behind.

"Where do you think you're going?"

"It's none of your business." Aramis leaned on the hilt for a breather.

Rhyllae's expression turned sour.

"It's not." Aramis turned his back once again to pull the dirk out.

"Since when?"

*Before we met?* Aramis thought, though he doesn't dare say it out loud. *Why are you being stubborn?*

"Why did you do it?" Rhyllae's voice cracked.

He cringed, for there was no escaping it now. Not with that look in Rhyllae's eye.

"Why?" The quiver in Rhyllae's voice wounded him more than any mortal blade.

"What would you have me do?" He threw his arms out wide. "Would you have me let him go? So Mudhi could do this again to someone else?"

"You don't know that." She mirrored his gesture.

"Oh, please. You and I both know that men are creatures of habit. That pig," Aramis spat as he pointed back at the city, "sold his soul so he could gorge himself on a fine meal. If I'd let him free, he would've crawled back and ruined every-thing we have built here. Everything, Rhyllae! He sold us out like a fat butcher with fresh cuts."

"You don't know if he would have done that. Mudhi was an adulterer, sure. But he was also a coward. You could've scared him straight and left him alone. You didn't have to kill him."

"No. If Mudhi could do it again, he would. Rhyllae, he was not worth saving."

"Everyone is worth saving, Aramis."

"Everyone? Ha! Would you have me spare every slaver that met my blade?"

Rhyllae tightened her jaw, her face turning red. "Aramis."

"Oh, maybe I should spare that necromancer back in those ruins?"

"Don't."

"I'm sure our friends will leap up from their graves with joy when we turn the other cheek."

*SLAP*

Aramis fell silent. Stunned as the sting ached on his cheek.

It wasn't because he didn't deserve it—he did. No, he was gobsmacked because it was Rhyllae who dealt the blow. Steadfast, enduring Rhyllae.

"You are not one of them, Aramis." Her words echoed down the dale. "You are not those killers-for-coin we had to face. You are more than any savage beast thirsting for blood. You. Are. Better. Than. That. Better than what they were and what they ever could be. You have something much greater than they ever hope to have."

"And what would that be?"

"That there is some good in you!" Rhyllae emphasized each syllable, tears starting to run down her cheeks. "I know it's there. Somewhere in that black hole you dug yourself in. It's there. That light burning to shine, yearning to be free. Free of the hate that is consuming you."

Rhyllae reached out to him, but Aramis shied away from her. The sting was still fresh on his cheek.

"Let it go, Aramis," she said. "Let it go, and don't be afraid. You are not the monster that you think yourself to be."

"Am I? Maybe I wasn't the man I was supposed to be. Perhaps I was wrong to think I could change what they had done. Created me from that toxic ether to be their pleasure toy. Made broken so they could shatter me over and over again. No matter how hard I've tried, their stain is still tattooed upon my body, and I can never be free of it.

"Don't!" He again shied from her arms reaching out to him. "Don't. I am a broken man. And a fool. I was a fool to believe I could be loved like everyone else. A fool to be lured into Vanessa's embrace, and they played me like a lyre. It was them, Rhyllae. They did it all: the attempt upon Korzha's life, the destruction at the base, hell, even the massacre at the Karatow mountains. Vanessa, if that is their name, was a spy. And I let it happen."

Rhyllae shook her head and, for some reason, let her shawl settle down on her shoulders. Gold shone among her brown tresses as the sun faded. "You can't blame yourself for what they have done. It's not your fault. You wanted to be loved. To be whole. And it's not your fault for them lying to you. They are the one who destroyed it all. Not you."

"But I let them in! I brought Vanessa to Amaveriel. I'm responsible for every death that has happened. And I can end it. There's only one path for me, Rhyllae. If it leads me down there, I must follow it to the end."

"No. Don't throw your life away like this. You seek retribution, but this is not the way."

"No!" Aramis sliced the air between them with his hand. "This is the way. I had played it straight, minded the middle, toed the line—for *what*? So they can betray me as they betray our friends? This is not what I asked for when I made my vows. This is not what I deserve for staying true. I was a good man for far too long."

Aramis paused to catch his breath, dizzy from releasing that anguish. Rhyllae stood there, taking it all in. The curls fringing her face started to stick to the salty rivers streaming down her face. The same rivers welling deep within him.

"If this is the reward we have earned for our good work in M'thealquilôk, I don't want it." The tears he was holding back stung his eyes, forcing him to blink them away. He turned aside so she wouldn't have to see, too ashamed for revealing such weakness. "If I had known this is how it would turn out, I would've died. Oh, Great Sleeper, I should have died with them!"

He couldn't contain it then, no matter how hard he tried. Collapsing to his knees, Aramis heaved and sobbed all that had dwelled within him since that fateful night.

Then, Aramis felt tender hands on his arms. Rhyllae reached around his heaving shoulders and held him tight. For all the times he had wept, he had done it alone, never wanting another person to see him like glass shattered on stone. Yet, here she was with him in his moment of weakness, nuzzling her head in the crook of his neck. Her kinked golden-brown curls tangled with his scruffy beard.

His hands hesitated to embrace her, fearing she would part from such an intimate touch. But she held him tighter as his arms wrapped around her soft frame. They stayed in that embrace for who knows how long. Perhaps a blink. Perhaps a lifetime. Both did not want to part as long as the world held its breath.

"You're more than the sum of your parts." Rhyllae's muffled voice broke the tender quiet. "And you are not alone. You never will be, so long as you have me."

Pulling back, Aramis gazed into her eyes, seeing how the flecks of gold floated in the sea of honey, warm like the sun and pure like starlight. Could there be truth behind such eyes?

Rhyllae placed her hand on his face, wiping a tear away. "*Elyamamen,*" she whispered to him in elvish.

Aramis closed his eyes, drinking in the sound. How he needed to hear that word: "always." The promises he had given but never received until now. To think it was there this whole time, in his hands, no less. Rhyllae, his guiding star, ever casting his shadows far aside with her light as bright as the sun.

He breathed in the subtle smell of roses, letting it fill his lungs as he kissed the top of her forehead. Aramis gently brushed away her hair as he cupped Rhyllae's round face in his rough hands, gazing upon Rhyllae's face as if he were looking at her for the first time. How her cheeks dimpled from her smile, warming like a tender blossom. How the freckles were scattered haphazardly over her button nose. How unique and golden her eyes were—and he had taken them for granted. Aramis would drown in her beauty if he could.

His nose brushed against hers as Aramis leaned in. He felt her breath on his skin before their lips touched. It was timid at best, the tiniest peck, to see if it was too much too soon.

He didn't have to wait to find out.

Rising to the tip of her toes, Rhyllae reciprocated with joy. Of all the kisses in his lifetime, this was the sweetest nectar Aramis had ever drunk, with fireworks bursting inside. Deeply, he drank it in, savoring every sensation. Their hands were trailing with tenderness.

They parted for air. Aramis considered taking her back to the city. To find a safe place from prying eyes and cut loose their longings. But no matter how well-intended, such an act would make him no different than Mudhi and debase fair Rhyllae more than she deserved.

And there was still the matter of Vanessa.

"Come with me, Rhyllae. I must find Vanessa and stop them, but I cannot do that without you. I know that now to be true."

"Aramis... I—"

A whinny from Midnight overtook Rhyllae's words. An alarm Aramis did not want to hear. Running to the bluff's edge, he saw a company of watchmen pounding out of the gate, all fully armored and their swords keen in the fading light.

*I have stayed for far too long.*

Aramis grabbed Rhyllae's shoulders. "Tell me: yes or no?"

Her brown eyes glanced over his shoulder, seeing the dust flying behind the charging company. A quick peck on his lips and a hand on his chest were all Rhyllae could give him for an answer. She pried the dagger from the tree trunk and ran to meet the charging watchmen.

Rhyllae hitched the hem of her robes above her knees as she ran, revealing the yellow pantaloons underneath. Aramis cried out her name, calling her to come back.

She muttered back, "Shut up and run."

She understood now. Vanessa was an enemy spy, not some hapless person caught in a sin. If Rhyllae could distract the watch long enough, Aramis could slip away without losing his head. Of the two of them, he could track down Vanessa in the desert, his home before Amaveriel. Though he wanted her with him, Rhyllae knew she would weigh him down.

*As long as he shows mercy ... I did my job.*

She felt the pounding of the hooves vibrating through her calves when she stepped on the road. Ten watchmen came charging down the gate, whipping their horses faster. The thunderous noise would shake any man standing there. But not her.

Rhyllae closed her eyes. Finding that warmth that brought her there in the first place. Her lips recited words that hadn't been spoken since M'thealquilôk. Aramis's blade in her hand gleamed in the setting sun.

"Stand aside," Captain Tristan called out to her. The thunderous hooves didn't slow.

"No. I won't move, and neither will you," said Sister Rhyllae.

With all of her might, Rhyllae struck the ground before them with the dagger. A flash of golden light sprang forth when the pounding hooves crossed the blade. The horses froze mid-stride in the blink of an eye, causing the guardsmen to fly from their saddles with incredible force.

And the fearful ten came crashing down at her feet.

Aramis looked on in awe, his heart torn. This could be the last opportunity he'd have to leave Amaveriel. The last chance to exact vengeance against Vanessa. And the last time to see Rhyllae.

Not that she would die. No, the Mother Superior would never let one of her own swing for his crimes, let alone allow the watch to slay her. The watch knew better than to murder a sister in cold blood. And if they tried, Rhyllae was a competent fighter in her own right.

Yet, he couldn't turn away as they raised their swords at her.

Captain Tristian pointed his sword at the sister, the filigree on his armor glinting in the sun. "Sister Ghalédale, stand down."

"My place is here, Captain. Between you and him."

The captain of the guard narrowed his blue eyes at the stoic priestess. "He's not worth protecting."

"All the souls who walk under the Light are protected by the Morning Lord."

"Enough of this," said one of the watchmen as he charged forward.

He wielded his blade high to cut her down, too quick for anyone to stop him, let alone allow Rhyllae another prayer. The sister dove to her right, falling onto the silted ground. The blade rang when it hit a stone where she last stood. With the wooden heel of her slipper, Rhyllae kicked at his exposed knee. There was no need for further negotiations.

As he dropped, she grabbed a rock and slammed it on his helm, ringing his bell. Someone grabbed her from behind, lifting her up from the ground. Rhyllae spiked the stone upon his foot and pushed him off when his hold loosened.

Though she had the upper hand, it was dashed in an instant. A watchman whirled her around by the shoulders and kissed her face with their metal fist. The next thing she knew, Rhyllae found herself back on the ground. Everything before her doubled as she felt a swelling welt stinging on her cheekbone.

"All right, Sister Ghalédale," came Captain Tristan's voice. "That's enough for now."

Then there was a whinny from on high. A shadow flitted through the sunlight shining upon Rhyllae's eyelids. The watchmen cried out as a thousand pounds of equine muscle slammed into the encroaching men. Startled, Rhyllae sat up to see them trampled by Midnight's broad hooves as Aramis spun him around.

"I agree. That is enough," Aramis said when he dismounted.

Lifting her up, he wiped something from the corner of her mouth with his thumb. It was then that the sister realized she was bleeding.

A watchman moved to close in on them, but Tristan's blade swung in front of him.

"Feres, this doesn't have to end in bloodshed. Do you surrender?" Captain Tristan asked.

Aramis pointed with his index finger. "Under one condition: no harm comes to her as you take her back to the abbey. My crimes are my own."

"Agreed." With a wave of his hand, the captain ordered his men to arrest the famous Silver Fox.

"What?" Rhyllae shouted with dismay. "I can't let you do this."

"I made my choice, *me'qora*," Aramis told her in a low voice as he unbuckled his belt.

When he presented the reins with his weapon to her, Rhyllae shoved them aside. Holding his weather-worn face in her hands, she begged, "You cannot give up now."

"I had until you came along."

"But—" She began to say, then he laid a kiss upon her lips.

He shoved everything into her hands as he drank her sweet nectar one last time with haste. Trailing kisses to her pointed ears, Aramis whispered a secret, then he was jerked away.

As she watched them carry Aramis back to the city, Rhyllae gripped the blades' handles tightly. It was then she realized he'd snuck something into her hands. Opening her palm, the Morning sister found he had given her his wedding band. The metal looked dented and dingy in the glint of the setting sun.

Words echoed in her ears: "Vanessa has the tome."

# Act 3

"...And I say unto you, look to the East.
In the darkest hour, I shall
return like the Morning Star."
~The Morning Lord
39:70 Gospel of Shutte'el

# Chapter 22

## RIPTIDE

IT DIDN'T TAKE LONG FOR THE CITIZENS OF AMAVERIEL to learn of his arrest. Trickling into the streets from their lit homes, they came in pairs at first, then in groups, until a crowd was gawking at the Silver Fox on his long walk to the Pit.

Most of them gasped and covered their mouths. Some of them whispered among themselves, and others grimly shook their heads. Yet, what hurt Aramis the most were the children looking away in shame. How high were their expectations of him for them to regret such veneration? Can they blame him for taking his revenge?

Someone, he couldn't tell who, spat their chewing tobacco at him. The spit landed on his head, dripping down the back of his neck. Though his hands were bound, Aramis paused to wipe the stain off his back, only to be shoved forward.

"Keep moving, wretch," said the guard.

"Murderer," cried one onlooker.

"Soldier killer," cried another.

Before he knew it, the crowd heckled and jeered. Curses in elvish and dwarfish were heard in the din. Some even used variations of the dragon-kin tongue.

The pace slowed to a crawl when they reached the intersection. Growing tired of throwing slander, the throng pressed in. Hands came out, wanting a piece of the Silver Fox. The guards tried to push them back as some screamed obscenities, curiously demanding their place in heaven.

One set of hands managed to break through, taking hold of his shirt. The force of the pull was enough to jostle Aramis against the guard behind him before his shirt ripped in their grubby hands.

In retaliation, the guard pushed him forward, causing him to fall to his knees. Oblivious to his plight, the watchman holding his rope dragged him along. The broken road sliced and tore Aramis's knees until he managed to get his feet underneath him.

As he surfaced for air, he was pelted with something wet and foul. Aramis had the wits to duck the second volley, this time a rotten date. One by one, fruits, muck, and dung came at them from all directions, coming from those too far to get within arm's reach of the contingency. The pelting became intense, and the watchmen had to use their shields. Only for their sake. They couldn't care less if they left openings for the Silver Fox. All he could do was flinch and duck from the onslaught.

Above the din, a voice cried out his name. Aramis, hoping to see the familiar golden-brown tousled hair in the sea of black and colored scarves, looked through the dense mob. Instead, he found a muscle-bound blonde pushing her way through the maddening crowd.

"Dawn?" Aramis slowed his march, his heart glad to see such a friendly face. When the guard behind him tried to push him forward, the Silver Fox pressed against him. If this was to be his last conversation with her, he would not blow it.

"Aramis, what the hell were you thinking?" Dawn asked when she finally reached the shield wall.

"Well, I thought, 'Gee. It sure is a lovely evening for a stroll,'" Aramis quipped back.

"You know what I mean."

"Sorry, Rhyllae has beat you to that old song and dance."

"Really? Where is she?"

"Back of the buffet line."

Tired of the holdup, the guard in front moved to yank on his bond, but Aramis deftly pulled the rope out of his grip. The watchman turned around and landed a punch on his stomach. The force of the blow knocked the wind out of his sails, and Aramis crumpled to the ground. Through the pain, he saw the whites in Dawn's eyes.

"Don't mind me. Just my age catching up." Aramis forced a smile.

After they resecured his bonds, they moved forward.

"Help Rhyllae," Aramis shouted as they dragged him away. "She needs you. Amaveriel needs you!"

Watching him go, Dawn ruffled her hair in frustration. "Help Rhyllae? What do you think I have been trying to do?"

"Excuse me," someone whispered.

Dawn turned around and didn't see anyone looking her way.

"Down here."

There, before her, the little satyr appeared, waving her arm as if she were removing an invisible cloak. Dawn jumped in her skin. She would've yelled if it wasn't for the leering eyes looking in her direction. Kneeling, she put her shield over the satyr to protect her.

"What's going on?" Dawn asked. "I heard they made Feres and you meat tickets to heaven."

Dido answered back, "It's complicated. If I took the time to explain—"

"Then sum up."

Dido froze for a second, holding her breath until she mustered up the words to say, "Frianul is a baddie. Well, the baddie themself is disguised as the Mother Superior, but that's another tale. We need Aramis's help."

"We have the arms. We can take the superior down."

"No. We need him to flush the doppelgänger out."

"Doppelgänger?" But Dawn saw the little satyr was already flustered. "Okay, okay, I get it. It's complicated. You know the council won't approve if I rough up the watchmen."

"But if we don't act now, the whole city will be doomed."

"Well, this is a fine mess," the lieutenant said, more to herself than to Dido.

"This is all the doppelgänger's doing. The indulgences, the riots, they're to ensnare Aramis in a trap. If we dally any longer, they will kill him."

"Can't you break the spell?"

"Not without an amplifier—Oh!" Then Dido hopped up and down on her cloven hooves. "The sword! The Silver Star is an ancient, magical relic. With the general's help, I can use it to cut through the spell."

"Then, get this to him." Dawn shoved the cloying cloth into Dido's hands. "Tell him it's a message from Mother Myrrh, 'This belongs to the Mother Superior.' I'm going back in to get Feres."

Without waiting for her reply, Dawn waded back into the crowd and didn't see Dido disappear in a flash of light or catch the whiff of smoke and flowers. No, her hazel gaze fell upon the head of the shit-show parade, Captain Tristan himself. Three strides were all it took for the fiery lieutenant to bring herself before the captain. She hurled the shield into the dirt before her, lodging it in the ground.

"Halt!" The word came out of Dawn like a lion's call.

The crowd hushed and parted from the two. Never before had they seen the freedom fighters fight against the city watch. Then again, this was a year of many firsts for the people of Amaveriel.

Captain Tristan ceased the procession with one raised hand. "How dare you interfere with the city's justice?"

"How dare you call it justice when you imprison one of our own? Feres is ours. We will sentence his crimes ourselves."

"I'm flattered," quipped Aramis.

"This is not the time for special treatment, Lieutenant," Tristan said.

"Special treatment?" Oh, how her face turned red. "We bled for your freedoms. Most of us are dead at your door!"

"I've had enough of this Jessenter nonsense. Stand aside!"

The freedom fighter smirked. "Make me."

"So be it." Tristan unsheathed his sword.

The crowd gasped in horror. Some fled to the nearest houses, fearing for their lives; others gave them a wide berth, huddling on patios or behind nearby fences. A year of many firsts, indeed.

Aramis's mind whirled in a panic. *Why is she doing this? Dawn will die. I can't let her risk her life for me.*

Yet, talking sense to a hothead like Dawn was out of the question. If he wanted a bloodless confrontation, there was only one option: escape.

He kicked the inner knee of the guard to his right, loosening the grip on his arm, then slammed against the unbalanced watchman, knocking him prone. With his right arm completely free, Aramis punched the guard on his left, landing right on the windpipe. The Silver Fox drew the officer's sword as the guardsman choked and wheezed.

The watchmen around him went into a tizzy. They lunged to tackle him but backed away when they felt the blade's sting.

The crowd went into an uproar as Aramis parried against the watch. Some shouted, "Kill him," or, "Stop him," but a loyal few shouted in glee and chanted, "Silver Fox," as their numbered, tattooed arms punched in the air. Brawls broke out as the chant grew among those silent during the procession.

*Vanessa has the tome.*

Rhyllae turned the words over in her mind as she was escorted up Uriel Street. A quiet arc away from the swirling chaos of Aramis's procession. Even though two watchmen were taking her to the abbey, she didn't attempt to flee. Her mind was filled with trouble.

Vanessa, the one who left him high and dry, has the deadliest book in all of living creation.

*Why?*

The *how* made sense. If Rhyllae married Aramis for a few years, she, too, would know how to bring the house down with a couple of bombs. But the *why* eluded her. Why would anyone want such a loathsome thing? Why would anyone want to raise the dead into an ever-living nightmare?

*Like Fanteen.*

Remembering how Fanteen's crooked teeth noshed on Mother Celia's throat gave Rhyllae a chill she couldn't shake.

*No. Wait. Fanteen!*

Rhyllae froze in her step. A gasp left her lips.

*How else could Fanteen awake in such a manner? It wasn't Celia's failure in casting the ritual—she rose. Risen by the tome. By Vanessa.*

"Sister Ghalédale?" the young watchman asked her. "Something wrong?"

*She's here! Vanessa is still here in Amaveriel. Somewhere in the abbey.*

Then she heard the familiar chant of "Silver Fox" drifting from the center of the dale.

*He doesn't know.*

"Sister, if you choose to resist..." the older watchman said.

Without thinking, she threw her yellow hijab over their faces and ran off, flying down the street with the two cursing her name.

With a kick, the round shield flew up into the air. In a breath, Dawn snagged it in time to meet Tristan's blade. Kneeling under its cover, she shifted it, letting the edge scrape across the steel. Then Dawn leaped forward, pushing Tristan's sword aside, making him wide open. Usually, she would pierce her enemies with her gladius—but today, she was feeling merciful. A swift uppercut to his jaw was the order of the day.

Dawn had to give the captain credit for taking the hit well. He stumbled a few paces back, spat out some blood, and returned with an overhead strike.

*This will be a good fight.*

A quick step to her right and Dawn dodged the blade cleanly. For good measure, she smashed her shield against his chest, chuckling at how the watch captain stumbled back into the guardsman facing Aramis.

Aramis saw the man shove forward from Tristan's collapse. If it were any other man, he would've taken the opportunity. But not now, not when there was fear in his eyes. Instead, Aramis sidestepped, letting him fall to the dusty earth.

As it was, he was busy dancing against the three men before him. Their swords were drawn—swinging at him in concert. Aramis thanked his lucky stars for his upbringing. If it weren't for him learning how to dance with swords to appease the Djinnasi lords, he wouldn't have been able to block and dodge with such a clumsy weapon. Let alone know how to swing a sword with his wrists bound. That was all it was, a dance of parries to keep his head on his shoulders, waiting for his chance to escape.

With the man behind him kissing the dirt, Aramis made his move. Batting away the nearby swords, he skipped back. While gripping the sword, he cartwheeled onto his bound fists, then rolled along his arm, over his shoulder, and down his back. He flipped to the opposite end and stood next to the faltering captain of the guard. After giving Tristan a wink, Aramis deftly twirled to stand by Dawn's side.

"Ha!" Aramis laughed, triumphant at the turn of fortune.

Dawn and Tristan both blinked with their mouths hinged open. Then their expressions fled when they saw the people in the crowd lurch forward.

They grabbed his torso and his legs—anywhere they could get ahold of him. Aramis brought his sword up and stopped. Mudhi was a traitorous bastard, but these people were the gentle folk of Amaveriel, some of whom he knew by name.

Dropping the sword, Aramis let them drag him away like a riptide in the sea.

"Aramis!" Rhyllae cried out as she waded into the maddening crowd.

The light faded to early twilight. Dark enough for the heavens to be seen, but not enough for them to shine. Yet, Rhyllae could see a few distributing torches among themselves.

"Aramis!"

She continued to press on, jostling with every step she took. She halted when an elderly man fell in front of her. His face was bloodied and toothless, yet still he punched his fist in the air, crying out, "Silver Fox!"

Crouching by his side, Rhyllae brushed her fingertips across his cheeks and nose, seeing them mend under the gory mess. The touch left the man in awe. Then he was dragged away by unseen hands.

"We're not done with you yet, old man," the mob said.

"No! Leave him alone!" Rhyllae shouted.

Try as she may, she couldn't reach him through the wall they had formed. Suddenly, there was a rush of people from the left, and she was swept away, blinded by raised arms and nonsensical shouting. It took every fiber of her being to stay upright.

"Aramis? Aramis?" Rhyllae projected over the crowd, the world spinning out of control.

Then she crashed into someone's arms. Strong and feminine.

"Dawn!" Rhyllae exclaimed, her heady vision clearing to see the lieutenant protecting her with her shield. The crowd parted around them like a river.

"Have you seen him?"

"No. You?"

Dawn shook her head. Then there was a wave of excitement from the center. Where the dead tree loomed, a rope was pulled taut, carrying a heavy load. Once she saw what they were lifting, all she could do was scream.

It boggled Aramis's mind how crazy they were acting. Never in all his years in this Freedom City had he seen them react to the murder of a Jessenter, for it wasn't the first time this had happened. Strange enough, words of "salvation" left some of their lips. The people pushing and pulling him through the crowd came across as demons more than humans or elves. His shirt was gone, exposing his scarred back and the serial number tattooed on his arm. He couldn't recall how he had lost his boots as the sand seeped between his toes.

Try as he might, he couldn't free himself from their clutches. When he thought he had his limb loose, another hand grabbed hold. Lifting his eyes to the sunless sky, dotted by the torchlight raised by the marauding crowd, a rope caught his eye—the noose set for its victim. Aramis stopped struggling and swallowed hard. This may as well be his real punishment, after all.

Closing his eyes, he prayed to the Sleeper, not caring that the clergy claimed the Sleeper had discarded this realm for another. No matter how often others tried to convince him that his deity didn't exist or that their gods were worthier, Aramis needed to say the words. They were for his ears alone.

He was not praying for Them to interfere on his behalf, nor was Aramis asking for Their forgiveness. He was responsible for his actions, and this was his due.

No, he prayed because Aramis Feres, the one who lurked in the shadows and crawled the city's underbelly, was going to die, and he was asking for courage. Courage to be as brave as his friends were when they met their demise. Courageous enough to meet them with his head held high.

When Aramis finished his prayer, his head was in the noose and his limbs were bound. The crowd extended as far back as the eye could see through the scattered torchlight. Near the fringes, the mob frenzied like a swarm of wasps. Those in proximity were packed with glaring eyes.

The man standing next to him asked, "Any last words, vermin?"

Aramis scanned the crowd for Rhyllae. He thought he heard her but couldn't find her beautiful face. Perhaps she left to find help. Perhaps she was in the mob but engulfed by the size of it all. Or perhaps it was a mirage in his mind's eye, knowing they would have taken her to the abbey by now.

"I guess this is how it goes," he said to himself more than to the executioner.

Taking that as his last words, they hoisted him up. The rope painfully bit under his jaw as he felt the ground leave his toes. Aramis struggled to breathe as he was raised in the air like a flag. He couldn't kick since his ankles were bound together, but he felt compelled to try as he surfaced for air—his mind thinking he was drowning in the vast ocean.

Hands pushed him, swinging him around like a ball tethered to a pole. The world spun before him in a sickening seesaw motion while he gagged from his own weight.

Strangely, he spotted a tall, thin man climbing above the sea of souls. Aramis swung around and noticed the man drawing a sword with his left hand. A rare sight to see a lefty. The sword glinted a silver sheen in the torchlight as he twirled it. The base of the blade rested in the palm of his hand. Then Aramis saw him swing back and, oddly, launch the sword like a javelin. As it sailed, it sounded like wind rubbing on the rim of a crystal glass full of pure water. The sound cut through the air, hushing the crowd as the streak of silver came toward him.

*Oh great, I'm going to be pincushioned to death,* were his last thoughts.

# Chapter 23

## THE SILVER STAR

PARTING THE RED CURTAIN, KORZHA FOUND THE fickle Lune nowhere in sight. The rosy lanterns of the Red Pier creaked from the southern sea wind. The raucous jubilee echoed from neighboring establishments catering to Jessenter sailors and pirates alike. But not at Madame Pompadour's Teahouse.

Music, demure laughter, and excitable conversations could be heard through the paper walls. In this establishment, they catered not to sensual desires but to the delicate sense of refined etiquette. Perfume, music, and dance were all they served under Madame Pompadour's roof. A popular choice among the women of Amaveriel who wished to wear their scarves down.

The energy of constrained excitement buzzed all throughout the teahouse. It was not often a general of the freedom fighters came to their establishment. Even the senior artisans acknowledged that their teahouse was the first and only establishment Octavian Augustus Korzha had ever set foot in on the Red Pier.

Which was correct. Korzha never did care for such establishments. Even when he gave his soldiers respite between campaigns, he would dine among the nobles or in the elders' longhouse instead of crawling through pubs or brothel skirts. Even if he had desired it, his code of honor wouldn't allow such a thing.

No, his presence here is merely a tactical move. A cloak to conceal him as he awaited Dido and, hopefully, the Silver Fox.

However, doubt crept into his mind, and he reached for his family's heirloom. Drawing the Silver Star, the blade sang in his left hand when it was free. The faint starlight shone on its keen edge. It had been a hundred years since anyone had wielded the blade. The last thing he wanted was to betray its trust.

"What a beautiful sound. I never heard the like," a young artisan said as she brought in a tray with a bronzed kettle and tiny black cups.

Her adornment was peculiar for these desert climes and unusual for his Töskan tastes. The robin's-egg blue seemed to shimmer against the candlelight, giving the odd sense that the painted morning glories on her gown were swaying in the breeze. Her walk was a slow shuffle due to the lavender sash's binding, embroidered with the same flower. Tiny silver chimes in the corner of her ornate black bun tinkled as she moved to the center table. As the little artist kneeled to set the tray, Korzha saw an impeccable arrangement of tiny painted fans and butterflies all in pastel, gay colors in her dark hair.

Madame Pompadour boasted they exhibited delicate flowers from all around the world. This must be one of her flowers of the Orient from beyond the Chessentari Empire's borders.

"Most never have." Korzha sheathed his sword to join her at the low-lying table. "Only five of the Singing Blades exist in this world. Those who have heard their ethereal song are either their keepers or their victims."

Dreamy brown eyes locked upon him with queer fascination. "Am I to be its next victim, General?"

"Perhaps." He rested the scabbard across his lap. "I did not request tea this late of an hour."

"Late? Why the night is still young." She smiled at him with lips painted with a single drop of red on their bottom. "Look, the Moonflower has yet to unfurl into full bloom."

A quick glance to the right and Korzha saw she was right. The pale trumpet barely separated its five petals. Another oddity of the place was to see such a flower alone in a tall ceramic vase. He didn't know whether to laugh or be insulted, for every Töskan noble knew the flowers and their meanings. In this simple arrangement, it meant a one-night stand. Whether that was Madame Pompadour's intention, the general could not tell.

Korzha saw her sneaking something into the kettle from the corner of his eye. Like a viper, he grabbed her wrist to stop her. Turning it over, he could see a jade ball in the palm of her hand.

"A parlor trick, Madame?" Korzha asked.

"A precaution of such tricks," the maiden answered. "One can never be too careful in serving a renowned noble like yourself." Once let go, she dropped the jade in the pot and swished it around. "If the stone retains its shape, we live to see the dawn. If dissolved, you would have drunk a tonic of endless sleep."

"I doubt it would be as sweet."

"There are many poisons that can be quite as sweet." A wistful smile came to her lips. "Though few of them are to drink."

Then she tipped the pot so he could look inside. The jade bead was still whole. With grace, she poured their tea into the black cups with delicate precision.

"And which poison may you be?"

"Tsuki, if it pleases you." With both hands, the artisan offered him the cup.

"Would any other name be just as sweet?"

His long fingers hovered over the teacup when he felt a disturbance in the air behind him. It could have been the cool breeze from the shift in the coastal wind. Or a brush from death. Twisting in his seat, Tavian Korzha drew the Silver Star and lunged the blade behind him. Stopping short when its tip touched the tender neck of a familiar satyr.

"Am I interrupting something?" Dido asked with a nervous twitch at the corner of her mouth.

Glancing back at Tsuki, he could see her thin eyebrows raised high, still holding the teacup in her porcelain hands. Then again, it was not often one saw a fey creature, let alone a magical one.

"I see you made it back in one piece. Report."

Dido leaped from her hunches and grabbed his collar. "There's no time!"

With a wrinkle of her nose, they were gone in a flash.

"Look at what you made me do!" Mother Superior Frianul scolded Mother Vyreal.

Vyreal, with her bulbous eyes wide open, was mute, stuffed to the brim with the fodder used to feed livestock. The mother also couldn't bend over to help the Mother

Superior pick up the broken glass. She was tied to a rail-thin post with her arms outstretched. A scarecrow to all if anyone could see it. Unlucky for her, the minaret was only used for prayer, and the next one wouldn't be until dawn. Lucky for her, Vyreal didn't feel a thing.

Not the rash forming from the rope pulled too tight on her skin. Not the pain from the long gash running the length of her belly. Or the itchiness of the fodder stuffed within. No smiles, no tears, no horror to change her face; Vyreal had no worries since she had heard a sliver of a noise deep in the crypt. Her last regret was the curious instinct to go down to look for the cause of it.

Frianul came face-to-face with Vyreal. Never had she seen a pair of eyes as vivid of a green. They snarled, then melted into a smirk as they caressed what was left of the poor mother's hair.

"Oh, I see. You desire entertainment."

Then everything toppled over, and she found her face cradled in the white linen that made the robes of their order. The fragrance was overwhelming.

"Here, let me show you a real show."

Held aloft by unseen threads, Vyreal saw the starry indigo sky bob as the minaret wall swayed. Then the Amaveriel skylight opened before them, and lo was there a show. The mass swarm of people spiraled into the very pit of the city. Torchlights glazed their heads with a reddish-orange hue as they encircled a lone tree.

"Fancy my handiwork?" the Mother Superior clucked from behind. "All it took was a little help from my friend."

Then the world turned, and she saw a different woman holding her up. Youthful, pale as the moon, with wondrous black locks cascading down from their head, holding in their hand a tome with a flesh-sewn cover. Yet, those eyes changed not one bit.

"Corrupt the lie with a grain of truth, a dash of magic to push them over the edge, then *voila! Cult brûlée!*"

As they spread their arms out wide, Mother Vyreal saw her own body left behind on the makeshift post. Their pristine robes were dyed in dark maroon from the top down. It was then she numbly realized those weren't threads in the woman's hands but Vyreal's hair.

Then she was yanked in front of the woman's gleeful face. "The Silver Fox must see it now. Yes, that foolish man should understand it by now. Their truth is a lie, and they coveted the reality we all endure. Yes, there's no denying the arms reaching out to him are to tear him down piece by piece. That is what we all are, in the end. Chips, ashes, dust. Nothing more than coal for the fire to consume.

"Look. Look, look, look. See how they are lifting him up? The rising star. To be put on the pedestal so he can fall down, down, down. The only safety net is the noose they prepare him for. Then they ensnare the next shooting star to holster up. That is show business, baby!"

Then Vyreal found herself sailing through the air from the woman's throw. Arcing away from the high tower, down from the Luneless sky into the heart of madness below. All fading into the foggy embrace known as death.

*This is madness!* thought Korzha when his eyes laid upon the maelstrom in front of them. The dead tree loomed over them like a crazed puppet master. He had witnessed much in his long military career, but never had he seen the good citizens of Amaveriel driven to a brutal frenzy. Was this the result of the doppelgänger's spell?

"Tell me you can fix this," Korzha asked of Dido.

"With the Silver Star, I can break it. But you have to make the blade sing."

Then they heard jeers near the tree. They could see them lifting the Silver Fox by the neck in a barbaric display. Even then, Aramis battled death with every fiber of his being, fighting to the bitter end.

Being a skilled swordsman, Korzha could wade among the crowd, hacking a path to reach him. But he saw a quicker alternative. Hopping on the wall near him, he ran on top of the stony division until he came to the street corner, high above the swarm. Aramis was a mere couple yards away, swinging.

There was one way to let the sword sing and to save the man: throw the blade.

The technique was challenging, and the best sword masters debated the effectiveness of the maneuver. It would be the first time he threw any sword, nevertheless the Silver Star, beyond his academic years. He could miss his mark entirely and impale an innocent bystander with one false move. Or worse, kill the very person he was trying to save.

Korzha inhaled and drew the brilliant weapon from his right hip. Exhaling, he let go of any self-doubt and criticism. Then he brought the Silver Star to his lips, whispering, "<Fly straight and true.>"

Hooking his index finger in the ring in front of the hilt, he let gravity drop the blade. With the hilt behind his fingers and the blade in his palm, Tavian Korzha held the sword aloft, high behind his shoulder. Nimbly on the wall, he took a few steps back and strode forward. He propelled it high into the air with all of his skill and might.

Like a meteorite streaking the midnight sky, the Silver Star sailed over the crowd's heads, singing its brilliant and ethereal song. The crowd hushed in awe as they gazed upon its passing, frozen in their movements as they watched it soar.

It was straight.

It was true.

It cut cleanly through the corded hemp fibers and embedded itself into the tree trunk.

Still bound, Aramis dropped to the ground. Coughing as he over inhaled the sweet, sweet air. Those standing next to Aramis reached down and grabbed him. Hoisting him back up on his bound feet.

"Enough!"

All eyes swerved to gaze upon the general. His mouth was fixed in a disgusted scowl as he surveyed them over. His blue eyes were lit by the torchlight, as if his internal flame blazed through them.

"Is this how you repay him? This man who has put his life on the line so you may sleep at night. Some of you were freed by his very hand. Is this how you repay him? Death? Oh, good and gentlefolk you are not. Look at you. Bakers, barbers, tailors. Reduced to mindless beasts—calling out for blood. You are not yourselves!"

Amongst themselves, he could see some shaking their heads as others rubbed their eyes, as if they were waking up from a deep slumber. Glancing back, Dido mouthed at him to continue.

"I know this city and its people. I have walked these streets and breathed its air. I know the tragedies that were laid behind you. A sorrow that we strive to avenge in your honor. I have fought side by side with your best. Their blood spilled on the sands. Their bodies waiting by our gates. You would have disgraced them by killing one of your own."

Here, he heard murmuring among them. A few looked down upon their feet, shifting in nervous twitches. But to his benefit, the animalistic bent in their glazed eyes dissipated, and some were waking up.

"True, this man committed an injustice. A crime that shall be met with punishment. Sentence him to the fullest extent of the law. I care not. So long it is by the law. Laws created not by the Djinnasi lords but by you. You who live here in this city and call it home.

"Amaveriel..." He felt a lump in his throat. He had no choice but to pause until he found his voice again. "The city I have come to call my own. The city which housed me, clothed me, healed me, and lifted my soul. Amaveriel is the house where I place my hearth. If you intend to take his life, here and now, in this fashion, then know I will leave. I shall look elsewhere for my Amaveriel if She is not here."

Puzzled eyes blinked slowly at one another until one of the citizens, he couldn't be sure whom, piped up, "But sir, this here is Amaveriel."

"Then prove it. Prove it to me now, or all hope I have here will be lost."

Once again, they looked at each other. Then, one by one, the crowd let go of their weapons and their opponent's shirt. Those that were holding on to Aramis let him go.

Without hesitation, Aramis doffed the noose from his neck. Using the embedded blade, he cut his bonds from his wrists and undid the rope from his ankles. Fearing he would break and run, Korzha made his way through the stunned crowd. Yet, the Silver Fox did no such thing. Removing the Silver Star from the tree, Aramis presented the blade on open palms. The registry number imprinted on his arm was revealed for all to see.

"I truly don't deserve to be saved."

The sword warbled the moment Korzha reclaimed his heirloom. "Neither do I, but we all have a part to play in this world—including you." Then he sheathed it, quieting the song.

"Thank you, General. I'll take it from here," Captain Tristan said after he pushed through the crowd. He took a strand of rope and bound Aramis's wrists. "Time to put you back where you belong."

"The Iron Lady? I could use a drink," Aramis snarked. He winced when the captain of the guard snugged the bond tight.

"Captain, this man needs to be questioned," Korzha said.

"I don't recall him committing treason, General." Tristan gave him a soured look.

"No. But he has information on Mudhi's informants. I would like to know what he has uncovered."

Korzha saw Aramis squint his eyes at him, perhaps noting the fib he pulled. The general steeled his gaze upon him. Hoping the man would have enough sense to follow through.

Tristan scoffed. "If I was a crackpot, I would say you were in on it from the beginning."

"A good thing you are a man of reason, Captain. When may I see him?"

"You assume too much. You dispatched your hound upon me and waved the olive branch? You can't have your cake and eat it, too."

"Speak for yourself, motherfucker." Dawn nudged her way into the conversation circle. "You can't play buddy with us then shut us out."

The general snapped his fingers toward Dawn. The shock of such a warning rendered the lieutenant silent. Red-faced and stiff-jawed, but silent.

"I had only sent her to seek an arrangement with the prisoner," Korzha said, turning his attention back to the watchman. "Whatever wrong she has committed, I promise to reprimand if you let me speak to Feres tomorrow morn."

"Do I have a say in this arrangement?" Aramis asked.

"No," both Tristan and Korzha said at the same time.

Tristan studied the general with his dark eyes before speaking. "Thirty minutes, and she goes to jail for hitting a watchman."

"Agreed," said Korzha.

Out of the corner of his eye, he could see Dawn quivering to fight back. He leaned to whisper in her ear, "Find all you can from the Silver Fox." Then he backed off, allowing them to bind her. "I expect more restraint from here on out. Clear?"

Dawn nodded. "Crystal."

Korzha waved his arm, allowing her to follow the captain of the watch. Most of the crowd dispersed. The few people left were more concerned with their injuries or gossiping than dealing with the general and, to his surprise, the lady satyr.

Dido gazed upon the departed crowd in equal amazement. "It appears we have broken their spell for now."

"Still does not explain how such a creature can create this type of chaos," Korzha countered.

"Maybe this might help?" Dido pulled out a plain handkerchief from her vest. "It came from Dawn. She said it was the Mother Superior's."

Taking the cloth into his hands, he discovered it was the old handkerchief he had exchanged with her long ago. His initials OAK were still the same as they were on that day. But it smelled peculiar: a sickly, sweet smell wafted into his nostrils. The perfume was not Myrrh's. Unraveling the package, an embroidered red cloth reeked of the pungent scent.

"How did she come by this?" Korzha asked.

"She did not say. What do you think?"

"There are more questions than I care to have right now."

"Maybe I can be of help, general." Sister Rhyllae stepped forward from the disappearing crowd. The twin daggers in her hands seemed to gleam in the growing twilight.

# Chapter 24

## PAPER MOON

"WILL YOU JOIN US?" RUTH HAD ASKED EONS AGO. In the soft glow of the breaking morn, she'd sat by the side of his bed. The steel-forged armor gleamed, and her fiery hair was as red as freshly dyed silk. They were separated by others in the hospice ward with red curtains. Looking back at the memory, Aramis would have choked at the sight. But there in the shadow of dreams, he scoffed and turned his head. Sour from being doused by Rhyllae's "blessing."

"To be another bushel in General Tackett's harvest?" Aramis retorted.

"You reap plenty in your own right," Ruth said with confidence. He never thought he would miss hearing that thick accent of hers. "Some of them were your friends."

"They're no friends of mine," he said, his voice thick with bile.

Ruth nodded in approval. For how can anyone exchange life for gold knowing that weight is priceless in its own right? Still, Aramis kept finding those who would, with no end in sight.

"Why let me live?" he then asked. "You know the elders will have me swing, regardless of what I say or do. Why go through the trouble? Fame?"

"Fame?" She laughed. "True, I could leave you to die and take all the glory for myself. I shall be known as Ruth the Immaculate, forever cleansing the world of evil."

Then she posed with her hand upon her breast, looking out the window. Biting back the laughter on her lips, she gazed out the window looming next to them. Aramis didn't admit it back then, but she looked like the very definition of a knight in shining armor.

"And I shall be known as Aramis 'Faux Face' Feres. Desert nomad, gutter hermit, thief, and murderer. None will miss me when I'm gone."

The mirth left Ruth's face. "Since when have you stopped being the Silver Fox?"

"...Silver Fox... Hey, Silver Fox," a brassy female voice called out in the dark.

Aramis could feel a throbbing sensation on his nose and blood dripping down his lips. His hands were bound in iron-shaped mittens and chained to the ceiling. His shoulders were sore from his dead weight. Finally, it returned to him in a haze: Tristan locked his hands inside the device, and they hung him up in the cell. Then punched him in the face for good measure.

"Look," Dawn barked across the way. "You better wake up, or I'll—"

"Or you'll what, tickle me?" Aramis said.

Squinting his eyes open, he saw the silver pall spill on the cell before him, revealing Dawn, gripping the horizontal bar running along the length of her cell. The warrior was stripped of her shield and sword.

"If that is what you call torture," she said with a smirk.

"I could think of a few who would say so."

Gazing at the ceiling, Aramis saw the chains at the end of the manacles conjoined to a hook that was welded shut. He gave it a yank and found it welded onto a plate secured to the very stone above. This must be the reserved cell Tristan kept threatening about.

"How long was I out?" he asked.

"Since they left? Less than a turn."

"Seems like we have time ... for a spell."

"Wait... That's it? You're giving up?"

Aramis shrugged. Well, the best he could in this setup.

"You're the goddamn Silver Fox. The one who outsmarts the Djinnasi, freeing slaves and guiding them through the desert. You're a fucking hero."

Aramis laughed. "I wasn't always the Silver Fox. Hell, I wasn't always Aramis Feres. That was a name I found in a book during my wanderings. Same thing with your parents when I finally freed them. Hashim and Shayla of Bedouin, right?"

"You know them?" Dawn leaned back on the bars.

"How couldn't I? It took me a while, but I keep seeing both of them in your face. Your father almost crushed me in that bear hug of his. Then your mother popped my bones back into place."

Dawn laughed. "Yeah, he tends to do that. One time, I saw him break a rock this big." She spread her hands out shoulder-wide to demonstrate.

He smiled, but the mirth was brief. "I had been 479241 ever since I was created from the silver model run. No name, no control over my body. I've lost count of how many times they would have their way with me. I wasn't allowed to sleep or eat without permission. No prayers—did they ever tell you that?"

Dawn shook her head, becoming wide-eyed with every word he spoke. Perhaps they hid what they endured to give her a clean slate.

"I didn't even know how to speak this tongue until I found myself outside Bazzuuport." Aramis stopped himself short. His mouth quivered as his eyes danced in his recollection. "I was their puppet. Dancing to their tune from dusk to dawn until I was too damaged to look at. Try as I may, I can't get rid of everything they did to me. I can never forget... Nor can I forgive."

Then his face hardened, and the silver light felt cold on Dawn's skin. "With these bare hands, I killed them. All of them. Those Djinnasi had their last orgy in the high hall. One by one, I felled them all in the shadow of Lune. The ones you're fighting against today are alive because they weren't there that night. I left it all behind with nothing but a bloody shroud upon my back."

Then he looked up at the ceiling, illuminating the chains above him. Tucking in his shins, Aramis sank low, tired of holding himself up. "Say what you will of me being a damn hero. I was a murderer long before the people called me the Silver Fox. No matter what I say or do."

"Then why did you do it?"

"Mudhi? He had it—"

"No, freeing them."

"What?" Aramis once again looked back at the young officer.

"Freeing the slaves. Back then, no one asked you to do it, right? They didn't know what to call you. Anyone who escaped was doing it to save their own hide. So, what led you to do it? Fame?"

"Fame?" That made him chuckle, remembering Ruth's ridiculous pose long ago. "No, I shall be known..." He couldn't repeat the words, knowing she was still there in M'thealquilôk unburied.

Dawn pressed on. "You could've walked away from it all when you escaped—but you didn't. You returned not once, not twice—but fifteen times. And the last time? You trekked through the entire desert of Ioun with everyone in tow. No self-loving bastard would stick his neck out like that for complete strangers. Who would do that but the shepherd himself? You gave them a second chance."

"So I could lead them to their doom? To die a meaningless death?"

Perhaps he had said it too harshly. The young officer stared at him with a cocked-eye tilt of her head for a while. Then she closed her eyes and sighed. "I get it. You lost your friends. So have I. Many times. Sometimes I would wonder if I had done things differently. But I would never have to wonder why we did what we did. It's for freedom." Dawn pointed to herself. "Mine." Then to Aramis. "Yours. Ours. Everyone's. If I have to choose to die free or live in chains, I would rather go out in a blaze of glory and drag those Djinnasi bastards with me. I'm sure your friends feel the same way, too."

For several breaths, Aramis said not a word and closed his eyes. Taking himself back to the fateful day when Ruth sat by his bedside in her gleaming armor.

*She, too, heard his narrative of how he survived the horrors. Ruth took a smooth stone out of her pouch as she listened to his tale.*

*"Why did you join the Jessenters?" he'd asked her back then.*

*To his surprise, Ruth placed the stone into his hand. The painted raven looked as worn as it did that day.*

As she had said back then, Aramis said to Dawn, "'*I would rather live and die by mistakes made by my own hand.*' Ruth. Ruth gave me that second chance, even though I left none for myself." He took a deep breath. "Do you think the Elders would do the same?"

"I would."

Aramis nodded and spilled the bean. "He sold us out. Mudhi. I couldn't let him live."

Upon seeing the whites in Dawn's eyes, he knew he had to tell her everything. The betrayal from Mudhi, Vanessa being a spy, from Korzha's assassination to the base's destruction. Even the odd commentary of her taking on Mudhi's face.

Then Aramis halted. His blood ran cold. "It's too late. The tome. Vanessa could be well into the dunes by now. It's too late."

"It's only a book."

"A book that can raise the dead. A horde of carcasses that cannot die easily. With power like that, the Djinnasi could slaughter all their slaves to create an instant army. Amaveriel and the world would be doomed." Then Aramis closed his eyes, dimming the room once again. "I've become a foolish old man. All this time, I thought she had left me because of Mudhi. Now the fate of the city lies in Rhyllae's hands."

There was silence.

Then Dawn piped up. "Then why Frianul?"

"Why Frianul, what?"

"The Mother Superior. How is she wrapped up in all this? Look, Mother Myrrh gave me this weird-smelling cloth to give to the general. She's in on it, right?"

Aramis raised his head up, the wheels in his mind turning. And oh, how they turned! How could he not have seen it was an act this whole time? Frianul's mannerisms when he interrogated her, her smile, her perfume—even the divorce paper was a prop—all for an audience of one. Vanessa had played him for a fool.

"The world *is* a paper moon!" Aramis exclaimed.

Swinging his legs forward, he hooked them high up around the chain holding his manacles. Transferring his strength into them, he felt it. The manacles loosened when his weight gave way. The spring that was there popped out from the pressure release. With a bit of finagling, Aramis popped his hands out of the iron trap. Soft as a cat, he landed on his bare feet. Then he slipped through the bars with a deftness that made Dawn gasp. Taking two stiff splinters of straw, Aramis crouched to pick at her cell lock.

"Vanessa is still here," he assured Dawn. "She promised to tear down these 'paper walls' and make me see. She would never leave Amaveriel without showing me the grand finale."

Then the gears clicked, and he opened the door, taking care to not let it squeak by pushing the door against its hinges.

Smirking, Dawn put her hands on her hips. "What about your trial, Silver Fox?"

"They can hang me later."

It was a lonely walk back to the abbey for Rhyllae. She was glad, for she felt her bones dragging behind her. It had taken a while to convince Korzha that Aramis was on their side. Even longer to persuade him to save Aramis from the gallows. But her dearest of hearts was safe for now. Deep down, she was glad Aramis wouldn't be there for the procession. Rhyllae had seen that look in his eyes before, and only blood had followed.

*Not this time*, she hoped. *Praise the Morning lord.*

Thinking of which, Rhyllae picked up her pace. Soon the dawn would rise, and the mourning would begin. Come what may, the sister could not neglect her spiritual duties. She never doubted the power of hope to quell anguished hearts. That, in turn, saved lives. Hope. Faith. Breath. All were the same in the collective sigh of awakening, whether in mind or in body. And she would give it to them through song.

Rhyllae padded up the winding stairs of the minaret, rushing past the closed chamber doors and still dew drops. A pilgrimage she often made alone. As she opened the saffron door, she wished she was alone.

A woman with long, raven-dark hair, pale as the moon, danced in a buttoned shirt and dark pantaloons. Their waist sash, dyed in martyrs' blood, made Rhyllae wonder if they were part of the Jessenters. Yet, the crazed glee on their face made her think twice. In a slow parade, they waltzed around an effigy tied to a wooden post. Though it was headless and stuffed to the brim with straw, the scarecrow looked oddly familiar. Then she realized it was wearing the matronly robes of the morn. Rhyllae's stomach sank when she recognized the embroidered hem. Peeking out at a sleeve was an elven hand.

*Mother Vyreal.*

The crazed woman didn't pause in their hypnotic dance as Rhyllae crouched down and stifled her scream. A dark blessing, for there, within reach, was the tome of Tellezard, displaying pages scribbled in odd script, with diagrams and pictures depicting a singer's voice being carried across the land from a metallic stave. The binding in the runed-etched flesh was all too familiar to the Morning sister.

*Vanessa has the tome. This woman is her?*

The Jessenter general mentioned that the spy was an associate of Aramis, but none of them knew it was his dear, loving spouse! All the pieces merged together like a stained glass window.

With one eye on the villain waving their arms over their head, Rhyllae reached for the equally vile thing. The moment her fingertips brushed the blood-stained pages, the book slammed itself shut, quicker than any Venus flytrap.

"Well, about time you came along," the raven-haired woman said.

The woman stopped their crazed movements and turned their head. Their eyes, a fiery green, flickered. Then they smiled in a wicked and twisted manner. Rhyllae's eyes must have been playing tricks, for the grin appeared to stretch to their ears and curl into itself.

"I've heard much about you," the woman continued. "Sister of the gentlefolk. The little songbird that could. Speaking words of wisdom, 'Let it be.' All the while manipulating my hubby's heartstrings."

"You're the manipulator," Rhyllae managed to cut in. "Aramis said you're sick. Broken and shattered like him. But the two of you are nothing alike!"

"Oooh, but we are. More than Aramis would like to admit," Vanessa cooed.

They sauntered toward Rhyllae, letting the straw scratch against the stone from underneath their heels. The look in their green eyes was hungry, like a hyena. To Rhyllae's horror, Vanessa's visage melted. The fiery green eyes dissolved into honeydew—their skin kaleidoscoped into her golden olive-brown. Even their ears broadened and twisted to a stubby point. As they closed in on her, the straight strands curled and bounced into the same kinks that adorned her head.

They were the spitting image of her reflection, down to the same freckles on her nose.

"But don't worry, little tweety bird," the image said in Rhyllae's own melodic voice. "Aramis will soon see that the house of cards and paper dolls are nothing more than flimsy things. Everything he built will burn and blow away like ash in the wind, you along with it. For you see, reality is a broken mirror, and I am what is reflected inside." Vanessa's fingers twisted into dark needles. Raising her hands up high, the edges gleamed from the starlight above. "So, tell me, what is reflected inside of you?"

The strike came quick, but Rhyllae was quicker.

Taking the power of the Morn, Rhyllae willed it into her hands and pressed them against her mirror image. "I'm the light." A flash of brilliance shone forth, blinding the starry night sky. Oh, how the doppelgänger howled and shirked away.

Sister Rhyllae scooped the tome into her arms. The vile energy inside the book screamed in outrage as it had before, back in the Anglorian jungle. Enduring its magical volleys against her, Rhyllae ran for the yellow door. Her feet slipped and slid on the straw before catching traction on the rough stone.

Then a sharp pain pierced her shoulder. Another step, and another pain shot through her hamstring. Long, dark fingers extended past Rhyllae like black arrows as they hit the stone around her. As they retracted, the sister stumbled through the threshold. Her calf gave, and she fell down the spiraling stairs. The book and Aramis's daggers tumbled alongside her, down to the minaret's depths.

Landing back to the first floor, Rhyllae crawled into the hallway. Dragging herself up on the railing overlooking the cloister below. With her being the abbey's prized vocal musician, her voice of alarm filled the slumbering void. She waited, straining her half-elven ears for a cacophony of doors and slippered feet on stone. Yet, none sounded.

"They can't hear you, doll. None of them can," Vanessa called from the shadows, still in Rhyllae's mirror image. A halo of bone-white reflected the red orbs' gaze upon her with alien intensity.

Rhyllae gritted her teeth through the pain. "What did you do to them?"

"I sang the babes a lullaby a little while ago. They're off dancing with sugar plums in their heads."

Vanessa grabbed Sister Rhyllae's neck in a blink, hoisting her up like a kitten. Gasping for breath, Rhyllae could only kick and claw at Vanessa's unearthly hold.

"Now, now, don't you fret. I have something much more enjoyable in store for you. A battle of wits, and you're the lucky contestant."

The doppelgänger queen chuckled deep in their throat as they half-carried and half-dragged the sister to the preparation chamber, heading down into the spiraling depths of the catacombs, past the unblinking Töskan blue eyes of Mother Myrrh frozen by bewitchment.

# Chapter 25

## MORN

A MOURNFUL CRY PIERCED THE MUTE CITY OF Amaveriel.

There were no bystanders in the streets. No street vendors to distribute their rebel flags, no children saluting the fallen, for *all* participated in the dreaded march. All the surviving Jessenter forces, the entirety of the city watch, the widows, and finally, the rest of the depleted city were part of the procession. Even the children and the elderly had a role in the black parade, carrying urns and boxes of the heroes' remains.

*No one this young should carry the weight of their dead,* Korzha lamented when his blue eyes saw a curly-haired boy guided by his mother during their preparations. Even he who had experienced tremendous sorrow at such a young age had never had to suffer such a heavy weight on his shoulders. The thought stayed with him as he and three others carried the late General Tackett.

The unbearable sun beat upon them as the procession stretched from the gate, through Sulmaith Street, and up the winding curve toward the Abbey of the Rising Dawn. Inching ever closer toward the abbey, the procession swayed rhythmically to the somber hymn wailing from the prayer tower on high.

Korzha knew the words well, for Mother Myrrh sang them nightly back home. "Weep no more, Weep no more," she sang, "for we happy few fly free to the Sun's embracing light."

He doubted the souls would fly free as much as he doubted the existence of the Morning Lord. But Korzha did not question the fury of ghosts. In his heart, he knew what he saw was no mirage. He could still feel the torch within his right forearm, stinging him like a writhing, twisted thorn. A reminder of his promise. In a way, he was glad he was carrying General Tackett by his dominant hand, for the unbearable pain antagonized him every step of the journey.

The abbey finally came into view, and all felt relief; they were almost there. However, when General Korzha laid his eyes upon the sight, a strong jolt shot through his arm and punched him in his chest. The electrifying pain halted his march and made him stumble. By sheer luck, he didn't drop the casket on the sandy street.

"Halt," cried the pallbearer behind him, a woman shrouded in cloth of blue and gold. All the way down the line, everyone ceased their march. "Do you need to set the casket down, sir?"

"No. No," came Korzha's response. The last thing he needed was dishonor added to his embarrassment. "We shall carry on through this infernal heat."

Squaring his thin shoulders straight, he barked, "Forward! March!"

The procession inched forward once again. The torch heckled Korzha every step of the way. What it was fore-warning, he didn't know.

All was quiet when Dido approached the abbey. Save for the hymn, nothing stirred. Though cloaked by her own magic, Dido made sure not to let her cloven hooves make a sound. Korzha had given specific orders to scout for Sister Rhyllae. They had both feared the worst when she failed to rendezvous for their plan. Their fears didn't dissipate when they learned of Dawn's disappearance with the Silver Fox. Peering through the entrance, Dido found her answers and muffled a gasp.

There, flanking both lengths of the nave, were the mothers and sisters of the Morn, half-dressed in robes, nightgowns, and rumpled jumpers, lining up between the black-and-white pillars. They raised their monotonous voices to an indistinct chant. Everyone was underneath the thief's spell. Even the regal Mother Myrrh had glazed Töskan blue eyes.

There, before the reddening glow of the chancel, stood the doppelgänger queen. The tome was propped on top of the pulpit. They thumbed through the thick parchment as they hummed the binding spell. Shadows seemed to ooze from its pages with every turn, rising like fanned steam.

Dido raised her hand to cast off the spell they were under, but a thought seized her: how could she capture the doppelgänger by herself, especially with that tome in their hands? When Dido's rosy-pink eyes looked upon the vile thing, her stomach flipped. If she waged a battle of wills, the poor satyr would have to resort to violence upon these inno-cent bystanders. There was no doubt that the doppelgänger would use them as their faithful puppets. Dido shuddered and looked back upon the ladies at a loss.

Then she started counting, a habit of hers that spearheaded her into the treasury office. Every copper coin, every speck of gold dust, and every splinter of every magical artifact was always weighed and noted every dawn and every dusk by her attentive eye. And there before her, unless she was mistaken, one priestess was missing—the one who fought with them against the ghoulish creature a couple nights ago.

*Sister Rhyllae... Where could she be?*

Taking out her wand, she posed the question to the instrument and balanced the focal point on her finger. There it spun to her right and dipped down. Dido whisked it away before it fell. Somewhere in the deep lay Rhyllae. The satyr drummed up her courage and tiptoed past the priestesses into the courtyard, looking for a way down.

The black parade finally shuffled through the entrance, with the general leading the pack. They were colored in the glorious rays of green, yellow, orange, and red from the tall stained glass window. They set their dearly departed in three columns to make the most of the room. Some filtered into the nave, trudging in with their boxes and urns. Most of the procession remained outside, down the sloping street, curving back through the city of Amaveriel. Foremost, all the remaining Jessenters were there in the hall. As soon as General Korzha and the bearers set Tackett's casket down, all kneeled before the chancel with their heads bowed in reverence.

The chancel seemed to cast an unforgiving glow as the Mother Superior stood before them, giving her an evil look.

*Perhaps*, Korzha thought, *it senses they are the imposter.*

Then the hall went silent as she raised her shriveled hands.

"Ladies and gentlemen," the esteemed Mother Superior said to the gloomy crowd. "Boys and girls. Thank you all for coming for our grateful dead. Indeed, they're blessed to have everyone come together in this beautiful mourn. No one deserves such a tearful send-off more than our very own ragtag group of traitors, cutthroats, and thieves.

"But they're not too bright, are they?" She let the question hang in the air for a few seconds. Everyone kept glancing around and shifting their feet.

The Mother Superior chuckled. "Otherwise, why would they be here? They're nothing compared to our newly appointed general." She waved her hands at him, directing everyone's attention. "He knows when to duck his head down like a good coward while the fools rush in."

Korzha was on his feet in a blink, his fists clenched in rage.

The smiling Mother Superior tsked him while waving her finger back and forth. "Now, now, this is their funeral, not yours. Wait your turn."

He was about to signal Captain Felix to attack when he felt a tug on his pant leg. Whipping around, he saw a woman in a royal blue burka. The very one who had been behind him the whole procession. What gave him pause were her hazel eyes glancing to the side repeatedly. Korzha turned his gaze toward the priestesses. His heart sank. Every woman in the holy order was mindlessly chanting in rhythmic gibberish, and their faces were awash in dull expressions. When his eyes laid upon Mother Myrrh, General Korzha sank back down to his knees. She, too, was enthralled by the strange enchantment.

They were surrounded, physically and politically. Korzha knew that the Jessenters would be run out of the city if he commenced such a sacrilegious attack. And where would he go with such a demoralized army?

As the Mother Superior continued her condescending speech, Korzha's mind whirled with possibilities as he recalculated their odds. Then a handkerchief containing the letters "OAK" at the corner flitted into his view.

He patted himself down and realized that the pungent napkin was gone. When she had his attention again, the hazel-eyed woman silently motioned toward the mother while pretending to dab a tear, confirming that it was the superior's perfume.

At first, General Korzha squinted his eyes at the mysterious woman. Then his eyebrows rose high in recognition. *Dawn!* He gave her a scowl before he snatched the cloth back.

Furrowing his brows, he waggled his fingers before his face, "Where's the Fox?"

Looking around, he could tell the answer before she relayed back, "I don't know."

With a roll of his eyes, he sighed. It was a challenge to find good help these days.

Aramis held his breath as Dawn and Korzha happened to look his way. He was in a thinly veiled disguise, after all, dressed as one of the Morning sisters. He found the bloody cloth high on the minaret. He had thought he heard Rhyllae singing and climbed to the top. But none was there save his music box and a carcass stuffed like a scarecrow. Almost as disturbing was finding his weapons at the bottom of the spiral stairs. If any harm came to her, Aramis knew he wouldn't be able to restrain himself. For good or for ill.

But not now. Not when Vanessa had the full view of the entire nave. Aramis inched his way closer to the podium whenever they averted their eyes, bringing him in range of his knives, if need be. Yet, too far to steal her away for questioning.

For the time, he must wait, miming the chant surrounding him like bees protecting a hive.

*Where are you?*

Dawn scanned the crowd, taking care not to step on her burka as she pivoted on the balls of her feet. She saw Captain Felix relaying his strategic opinion to Korzha through their secret hand signals. By the look of it, he wanted to break the giant stained glass window for their escape route.

"They'll be bottlenecked at the entrance!" Felix signed.

The general did not care for that notion of escape; his hand signals were fast and choppy when he relayed, "Retreat is not an option."

Dawn could also see Tristan a little way down. The bruise on his jaw was coming in nicely with blotches of purple and green. Their eyes locked, and he scowled at her upon recognition. She winked and pointed to her jaw before giving Tristan an okay sign. The captain of the watch raised his middle finger at her. That made her grin from ear to ear.

A clap on her shoulder brought her around to face Korzha.

"I still can't find him, sir," Dawn signed.

"We cannot hold the heavens still for him. We have work to do—Ah ungh!" The general grimaced and clutched at his arm, falling forward.

Dawn caught him by his shoulders. "General? General!"

"The torch," he managed to say through his teeth. "It burns."

As he doubled over in pain, Dawn looked at Felix for help. The old salt was at a loss, like her. All around them were sisters of the Morn, and none of them budged an inch to help save him.

Tristan waded over to them. "What's wrong?"

"I don't know," said Dawn.

As those words left her lips—everything happened all at once.

The cry of pain rang out in the hushed congregation. The parishioners and officers all turned to General Korzha, who was on his knees. Sweat beaded on his high forehead as he grimaced and trembled. All but Aramis. His ears are filled with the buzzing chant of the priestesses around him. His lips could not even keep up as they spoke at a faster tempo than him, their language became unintelligible.

*This is not their usual prayer...*

As Aramis turned his gaze to Vanessa, he saw them dramatically waving their hands as they threw their body in the full motions of the chant. Their voice was clear as a bell as they uttered a language he could not comprehend.

*These words... These phrases...*

He had hoped to never hear the enchantment until his last dying breath. After all the horrors of M'thealquilôk, he vowed never again would any living soul suffer the same terror he had experienced. And at that moment, it was going to happen all over again.

With a wave of one arm, Aramis disrobed the sisterly cloth. With the other, Aramis threw one of the borrowed knives past the noses of the priestesses standing by him. There was no need for them, not with his own daggers secured on his person once again.

They turned their glower upon him as soon as the metal's sheen flashed over them. It passed over the heads of the Jessenters and the watch, who, in turn, slowly turned their gaze skyward in confusion. When Korzha bolted up instead of Dawn, Aramis sucked in his breath. Focused was he upon the dagger's flight that he didn't resist when the priestesses tackled him to the ground.

The breath was knocked out of him when he landed on the marble floor. The sisters' weight slammed on him, pinning him to the ground. All he could see was the priestesses falling upon him one by one, grabbing what they could of him.

But the incantation stopped, and he sighed in relief.

Then a voice boomed, "What have you done?!"

A fire within Korzha raged like nothing he had ever experienced. Cold hands held him up as Dawn called out to him. Seizing what shred of human dignity he had, Korzha managed to speak a few words to her without screaming at the top of his lungs.

"The torch ... it burns."

Then it felt like someone grabbed his intestines and yanked them out through his navel. He felt faint—faint! Another sensation that was foreign to him—from the overwhelming pain. The last thing he saw before he closed his eyes was the white veins branching and rejoining in the black marble tile.

In a blink, he found himself knee-deep in the Iounese desert. The sky's colors flew in brilliant hues as the Sun chased the Moon, while the desert remained a constant color of orange and beige.

But nothing striking other than the ghost of General Tackett, as terrifying as ever, appeared before him.

"Spirit. By my life, by my honor, I will avenge you. But why this flame? Is it to forge me to be your new blade?"

Still, the ghost of Tackett made no motion save for his silent lips.

Another roil of pain, and Korzha curled into a low bow and gritted his teeth.

"I care not if this is the blaze of honor or the flames of wrath. I cannot fight if you are killing me."

"The torch... Use the torch." The moan seemed to come between the beating drums in his head.

"How?" Korzha grunted. His face was close to the sand, almost tasting the salted grains of the surreal landscape.

Then he saw the ethereal boots stepping in front of his nose. They didn't indent the shifting grains. Turning his gaze skyward, Korzha saw the naked blade—the Silver Star herself—raised over him.

Is this how he would die? Had he failed a warrior's test? Perhaps he was to never join his mother's forefathers being a Töskan and a widower to a sylvan elf? Doomed to Niflheim? Never before had he questioned his mortal soul and its fate. The thoughts flowed like a river through a busted dam.

All that ceased when the tip of the Silver Star pierced his shoulder. He felt relief as a chilling sensation coursed through his body like the ocean wave, dousing every burning fiber of his being. Though it was rejuvenating, he still felt a queer feeling in his right arm.

The ghostly apparition of General Tackett drew the blade from Korzha's shoulder. His blood spilled down his arm and onto the surreal landscape. Strangely, no pain came from such an act.

"Seize it," the ghost called to him.

At first, Korzha couldn't understand what he was refer-ring to until he looked at his blood-soaked sleeve. Lifting the sleeve, he saw a marking on his arm, glowing like a smithy's ember, writhing like a flag in the high breeze. Korzha tight-ened his fist and saw the torch held still.

A deafening heartbeat thumped in his ears—he let it go with a gasp.

"Seize it."

Embarrassed by his weakness, Korzha clenched his fist again and felt the heartbeat, deep, dark, and malicious com-pared to his own. He could not explain it, but it came from beside him.

General Korzha looked to the apparition for an explana-tion but found he was alone. The ghost was nowhere in sight. A southern wind carrying his name blew sand into his face.

Korzha closed his eyes as he shielded himself from the desert's grit.

When the grit of the sand didn't come, he opened his eyes and found himself face-to-face with Lieutenant Dawn. The young officer mouthed his name again, but the only sound he heard was the sinister heartbeat, still coming from his left, in the casket he had borne.

*No... It cannot be.*

General Korzha stood up in a flash, not heeding the streak of metal flying past the tip of his nose. Or the fact that someone yelped out in pain. It wasn't one beating heart he heard. Three sounded from the neighboring cas-kets. Becoming 9. Then 81. A dozen more with each passing second. A chorus of heartbeats, that should have been silenced forever, coming to life.

"What have you done?!" Korzha bellowed, but it was far too late.

They had heard the call.

# Chapter 26

## THEY ANSWER

E HEARD THE CALL. DRAWN BY THE BEAUTIFUL sound, like a moth to a flame.

He awoke, still in darkness.

With a scrape of his claws, he realized he was sealed in a wooden shelter.

Then he felt the hunger.

Hunger that bites. Hunger that gnaws.

He must get out.

Out to feed.

He knocked. No one responded. He pounded, but the wood didn't give. He kept pounding, turning to thrashing as the need drove him. His nails fell off, and coagulated blood seeped out of the wounds on his hands, but he could not stop.

Feed.

Feed the hunger.

Hunger that bites. Hunger that gnaws.

Down the entire length of the nave, the coffins shook as the dead thrashed in their revival. Civilians scrambled toward the entrance, but it was clogged as people tried to squeeze through the narrow archway.

Felix commanded the officers, Jessenter and the watch alike, to throw lanterns, rocks, anything on hand to break the tall stained glass window. A few young lads created a tiny human pyramid near one of the torches and bashed the metal sconce down. One, none knew who, tossed an urn up, hoping it would smash the window open. But it shattered on the stone sill, and the ashes dusted the crowd below.

Everyone wanted to leave, but Dawn knew it was too late for a retreat. She disrobed herself of the royal blue burka, armored fully in her leather vest and metal guards. In one swift motion, she unhinged her Jessenter shield from her back as she unsheathed her gladius strapped to her thigh.

The coffin lid flew open as the late General Tacket punched his way out. He shrieked in unearthly delight when his glazed eyes met hers.

"Yeah, hello to you, too." Dawn drove the blade home.

The door flew out of Dido's hands, and she leaped back a few feet. It was unhinged from the top, as if some powerful force had knocked it back. Gazing through the wooden portal, she found a raised dais with a desk full of paper, quills, and a bloody set of scales, offset by leaden weights. In the middle of the chamber was a table, clothed in white with unusual lumps underneath. Adjacent was a tray carrying a tidy row of instruments. It must have been the preparation chamber the sisters had mentioned when they escorted her to their library. More important was what lay beyond the shrouded table: the door leading down.

She started to scamper toward it when something, a hair out of the corner of her eyes, moved underneath the white cloth.

Dido froze in place.

*Don't do it. Don't do it.*

Yet she found herself drawn to the motion. Like a cat, her doe eyes were fixated on the wiggling at the end of the table. Every step Dido took created a faint tapping sound. Not loud enough to alert whatever was underneath the sheet. Yet loud enough to create a warning in Dido's heart.

The movement had stopped altogether by the time she reached the pale cloth.

Once again, Dido froze.

She should leave it alone. With the noises echoing the halls, Dido needed to find Sister Rhyllae, fast. Yet, when she turned to go, the most unsettling thought came to her: *what if "it" struck from behind?* Her spine tingled as if someone had breathed on it. Dido hopped back and stared at the shrouded table. Everything was still under the cloth, and nothing flickered in the shadows.

*I need to make sure. I need to make sure.*

Her trembling fingers reached for the cloth's edge. If any-thing leaped out, she had a list of fiery spells ready at her disposal in the back of her mind. After mentally counting down, Dido snapped the covering off, the sheet billowing over to one side.

What she found was not terrifying.

Disturbing. But not terrifying.

There before her was the traitorous Mudhi Nazir, reclined on his stomach with his arms and legs broken by his side as if he were a roast pig. His hairy body was now a shade of green and marbled with purple veins. Out of morbid curi-osity, Dido crept around the edge of the table to where the movement had been. The former officer's face had an apple shoved into his mouth, popping his jaw wide open, a poor match to the massive dent in his skull.

*No sister would prepare a body in this manner. This must be the doppelgänger's doing.*

As she continued to step around, Dido realized his far eye socket was empty of its orb. Peering in, she could make out the pink webbing that connected the eyestalk to the brain.

Then something long and gray leaped out. It clung to Dido's face, knocking her glasses on the floor as it clawed to keep purchase.

"A rat! Oh, a rat!"

Dido shrilled and flailed about. Then her tiny hoof stepped on something round and squishy. It rolled under her, and she fell on the cold stone floor.

The juvenile vermin scampered away, passing by a fat, brown eyeball, bruised and oblique. Dido crab-walked backward, shrieking for her life. When she felt the door on her back, her first instinct was to hide behind it. But the eye was still in her view, looking at her.

"Stop staring at me!"

Then she heard a sickening thud, and a shadow loomed over the orb. Dido couldn't breathe, no matter how hard her lungs pumped for air. Then she held her breath as she watched the clammy hand reach down and pick it up.

"No, no, no, no," squeaked out of her mouth like a wheel needing grease. Her entire body trembled with fright as sparks flew between her stiff hair strands.

Then she grew silent as the light from the garden dimmed. The door creaked wider as the naked Mudhi pushed it open with his broken elbow, his forearm dangling from the joint. The one eye, purple and deformed, bulged from its seat in the right socket.

Mudhi tilted his head at her before he lurched forward, teeth first.

Dido threw her hands up. "*Milost!*" Everything went white.

All looked bleak in Dawn's eye.

The ghouls were leaping onto people like crocodiles in the Hapthos river. Most of them were on the stunned sisters of the Morning Lord, sluggish from the broken spell that had held them. One poor maiden twitched as a raised soldier gnawed at her delicate throat. Felix and his first mate took vengeance on the creature. It was working until Felix was bulldozed by another ghoul, disarmed and thrown about like a rag doll.

"Captain!" Dawn jumped over a casket.

One creature leaped for her. Dawn let it kiss the brunt of her shield. Pinning it to the ground with her boot, she thrust her blade repeatedly until it stopped moving.

A shrill from the left alerted her that another was coming. Dawn moved to block with her shield but found Tristan had stepped in. With one swoop of his longsword, he lopped off the ghoul's head. It flew in front of Dawn, its face in denial of the end it was wreaked. The lieutenant punted it away in disgust.

"We need to get the people out of here," Tristan said when their backs touched.

"No. We need to rally and fight."

"The citizens..." the captain of the watch said, but another ghoul leaped off of the black-and-white striped column. He impaled the creature when it landed on him. With a grunt, Tristan threw it off him. "...need to evacuate."

Dawn retorted that it was no longer an option but was drowned out by a shrill. The impaled ghoul let loose a furious scream. It bellowed low and long, different from all their prior screeches. All around them, the inmorti halted in their fury and joined in the call. Giving it all of their unholy might.

Stepping past Tristan, Dawn held her blade up to strike the ghoul down but stayed her hand. Baying like a dog on all fours was her former captain, Mosul. Her arm trembled, resisting her command to end his suffering.

Tristan was shouting, muted by Mosul's call. By the shape of his mouth and his gesture, she knew he meant to say, "Strike him down. Strike him down!"

With a cry from her gut, Dawn brought her sword down upon him. Piercing through his skull. The tip of the blade cracked the marble underneath. She was no longer deafened by his baying.

Tristan gaped and stared with wide eyes.

Turning away, she bellowed, "Cut them down. Cut them all down!"

Those still with arms jumped into action, swinging their blades, wooden stakes, and whatever was at their disposal upon the creatures. They managed to clear a void of them before the cries ceased.

All the ghouls paused, their heads sideways in a severe tilt, oblivious to the slaughter of their lesser selves, waiting for something.

"What the hell are they doing?" Tristan asked as he continued to kill any nearby ghouls.

Miraculously, those that were freshly slain rose, shambling with new life in their mangled limbs. Then Dawn heard it—the screams of terror outside of the abbey. Not all had the honor of coming inside the cloister. Now they were forced to participate in the same morbid horror they were facing here.

"They're calling for reinforcements," Dawn answered.

"We need backup."

Dawn had to agree. Their numbers were halved. There was no way they could withstand another wave, let alone save Amaveriel.

Her train of thought fled when a ghoul ran past them, screaming in terror. One of the Morning sisters, still doe-eyed despite the long scratches on her face, hobbled next to them.

"Come back. We need to bury you," she said in between pants, then stopped to catch her breath.

Dawn grinned at Tristan and banged the hilt of her sword against her shield, high over her head. Calling for all who could hear her.

Far at the high altar, the Silver Star sang its ethereal song. Korzha parried away one of the ghoul's attacks with grace and skill, pecking and adjusting the creature's swipes with the sting of his silver steel until an opening appeared. With the flick of his wrist, he brought the sword horizontally before him and lunged it through its neck. It jerked wildly as it collapsed to the floor. With one fell swoop, he ended the ghoul's suffering.

Hungry eyes watched him from several feet away, their jaws slack and drooling if not already seized on a fellow Jessenter. The ghouls crouched, unmoving as a tiger in a brush. Then the prickly sensation in Korzha's arm spiked. The unearthly howl filled the nave. And those that surrounded him joined in the unholy chorus.

"You feel it, don't you?" they asked.

The doppelgänger queen chuckled when Korzha brought his sword to bear against them. Once again, they changed. This time he was looking at himself, albeit in the motherly robes. Blood oozed from their shoulder. The imposter was flanked by two of the deceased soldiers. They scratched one behind its ear like a large hunting dog while holding the other at bay by the collar of its burial shirt.

"The call. The hunger. The need to rend your hands through their flesh and bite right in."

"I don't desire the flesh of man, monster," Korzha spat.

"Oh, but you do. We all do." Vanessa's eyes flashed a crazed shade of green, unblinking. "We all desire the destruction of creation. To spill each others' blood until the rivers gush red into the sea. Devouring civilizations like packs of locusts on the wind and letting the world go mad with ignorance."

No warrior, no general, no one—not even the dread Vampire Lord Atanase!—ever desired destruction for destruction's sake. Always, it was for dominance or resources—never this. Korzha found himself staring at evil incarnate.

"You're insane."

"I'm only a consumer 'girl' in a consumer world." Then the doppelgänger let their hands slip. The ghouls bolted at him on all fours with crazed glee on their macabre faces.

Korzha heard a voice ringing clear like a bell. "Now. Light it."

What compelled him to grasp the thick of his blade with his lesser hand, he did not know, but the minute the edge nicked his palm, the blood flowed into grooves on the blade that he never knew existed. The nagging irritation that had plagued him ceased.

It became clear to him what he must do.

Holding the Silver Star erect before him, Korzha met his charging foes, watching them slipping and sliding on the gore-smeared marble. The first launched into the air—saliva trailing behind him.

"*Ilumina*," he commanded, and the torch lit.

A trail of blue flames raced along the Silver Star's blade. It sang a new ethereal song that no tongue could utter. Korzha sidestepped the inmortus, arcing the fiery blade through its midriff as if it were water. Letting the unearthly fire consume it, he lunged the Silver Star forward. The charging ghoul fell upon it, all the way to the diamond-encrusted hilt. Its morbid visage contorted in horror.

Swinging the blade low, Korzha kicked off the creature, watching it convulse from the consuming blue flame until its movements ceased. It smoldered into ash like its kin before it. Then a bite of a flying blade upon his sword arm deprived him of his grim satisfaction, staining the white embroidery on his black funeral silk.

The doppelgänger gave a throaty laugh and spun around, rotating their hands as if they were a dancing dervish, circling to the other side of the chancel, clear of any distracting inmorti.

Korzha sprinted, his long legs narrowing the gap between the two of them. When he came around, he realized he had made an error. For there before him was a knife flying straight for his heart, too fast for him to block.

A streak of silver flashed between his sword and his chest, knocking the knife out of its trajectory. As it clattered on the stone floor, Korzha noted the one that stopped it was a simple, well-worn dagger. High up on the chancel lattice frame was the Silver Fox himself, glowering down upon the imposter through his black mask.

They twitched a half-hearted smile and turned to dash away. Then were halted abruptly by Mariam's imposing presence.

"There's no safe harbor for those who darken the Morning Lord's light, doppelgänger, let alone impersonate our sacred mother of the holy order. For the good of this world, I will not let this pass."

Tumbling down with a double somersault, Aramis Feres landed as the third flank of the three. "It's over, Vanessa. End this madness, and maybe you'll have a taste of mercy."

Myrrh mouthed, *Vanessa?* to Korzha as they exchanged looks.

Vanessa shook their head, covering their face with their hair with each sway. Blond locks darkened into a midnight shade as they lengthened before their eyes. Flicking their hair back, they revealed skin pale as moonlight, lips red like blood, and eyes still that flaming green hue. *Was this the disguise they had used against Feres?* Glancing over to him confirmed it. Oh, how Aramis's eyes longed for them despite his loathsome scowl.

"Oh, Foxy, it's not over until the music stops."

Stepping backward, Vanessa stretched their arms toward him, like a child reaching for a puppy, as they melted into the shadows. Aramis and Korzha sprinted to the spot and found they were no longer there, only a black round fabric slipped to the floor.

"Save the last dance for me," their voice echoed before it faded to the sounds of mayhem.

"Elusive to the last," Korzha sneered.

"Not quite." Aramis's eyes fixed on a spot far off the presbytery's east.

Mother Myrrh said, "Then go with all speed." Korzha's eyebrows knitted in disapproval until she placed her hand on his arm. "We'll destroy the tome once and for all."

At first, the Silver Fox frowned as he glanced between them and the tome. But when she extended her hands, Aramis laid the book across her palms.

The tome gave a ghostly gasp, flipping its pages in rapid succession.

The mother of the Sunset placed her dark hand on its pages, preventing the book from closing. She said in an old tongue, "<You shall remain open. I command it with the blood that runs within me.>"

The book hissed in a dark, guttural language and trembled.

"<You will obey me.>" Flames appeared on her fingertips, melting the ink on the thick parchment.

Finally, the book whimpered and hung limp in her hand. Mother Myrrh then draped it over her arm like a cloak.

"<Tavian,>" Myrrh said, back in the Töskan tongue. "<You will escort me to the catacombs. I require Sister Ghalédale's assistance. Then, you will take me to the high office so I may perform the ritual.>"

"<As you wish, milady, once I acquire one of my officers. They will come for you now that you have the book. You will need protection.>"

The Silver Fox's eyes darted between the two of them. His face screwed up in confusion until he heard the sister's name.

"If you find Rhyllae, tell her—" He paused as he looked at them both, his mouth hung open. Aramis snapped it shut and shook his head. "Tell her I thank her for everything she has done for a wretch like me."

Then he ran, his dark cloak trailing far behind him like a noontime shadow.

"Feres," Korzha called after the Silver Fox, "show no mercy for this doppelgänger. Leave no hope for those who had drunk the Djinnasi's wine with glee."

# Chapter 27

## INTO THE FRAY

DIDO'S HANDS TREMBLED, YET SHE STILL SPLAYED them upward; her nerves were shot from the unexpected magical release. The air reeked of overcooked meat and musty decay from the charred Mudhi. A single flame curled one of his strands of hair as it burned.

Dido breathed as slowly and steadily as she could, letting the tears run down her cheeks and splatter against her lenses. When she tried to move the frames into her kinky brown hair, they fell to her lap and slid to the floor. Dido tried to steady her breath, covering her face with her palms and sucking the air through her fingers.

That was, by far, the worst experience Dido had ever had. A feat, given how terrifying that ghoul had been two nights prior. Surely she had paid back her debt to the Jessenters.

Or she should get a fat raise. Dido deserved that, at least.

Wiping her face dry, Dido realized something was stuck in her hair. Teasing it out, she found another eyeball. She threw it far from her with a shriek and watched it roll down toward the catacombs looming behind her. Then she heard a shrilling call reverberating down the halls and through the cloister garden. She was only a few feet away from the door. Dido could turn around and go back to fight whatever the doppelgänger had summoned.

But as she stared down the spiraling darkness of the catacombs, Dido found she could not leave Rhyllae behind. Yes, it might be the need of one, but she had been in a similar predicament long ago. Alone, trapped, begging for help without anyone hearing her. Ultimately, she couldn't let anyone suffer such a cruel fate again.

"Oh, be brave, Dido, be brave. *Vjeter oko mene, podigni moj teret.*"

Shaping her fingers and thumbs into two *L*'s, she pointed them at the 12 and 6 o'clock positions. A light breeze laced around her ankles. Arcing her fingers wide, she drew a circle in the air and the breeze intensified. Then she brought the index and thumb together to form a square. With a twist of her fingers as if to break a small vial, she pinched and created a thin, shimmering line, stretching it out in a curve.

The wind lifted her up, circling underneath her elbows and cloak. Hanging on to the string like a peddler's handle, Dido floated down the catacomb's spiraling hall. Her goat legs were tucked underneath her so as to not graze the stone floor.

A flit of movement in the shadows led Aramis into the cloister. He had to admit, Vanessa was skilled at melting into the shadows, dancing from one crevice to another. With the sun high in the zenith, there was nowhere to hide in the walkways save where he trod.

Crouching by the corner pillar of the hall, Aramis saw their shadow flew across the floor before dissipating into nothing. He surmised they escaped to the room near the end of the hall. Whether it was to set a trap or to escape, he couldn't tell.

Running from shadow to shadow, he made his way down. Then he heard a woman cry out in terror, mixing in the cacophony of screams of those suffering from the horror behind him. The pitch and tone reminded him of Bagheera's awful descent.

Then the floor rippled as the cloister spun. Drums beat wildly in his ear. Aramis had no choice but to lean on the wall for support. The air thinned as if a constrictor bound his chest.

In a blink, he was back.

*Back in the torch-lit tunnels. Back with sand seeping through the ancient stones. And she's there: Bagheera. Falling away from him. Crying out, she plummets down into the darkness that yawns below.*

*Falling onto his belly, Aramis throws the rope down into the pit. "Grab on!"*

*His legs are heavy from Tamara and Ruth sitting on them, ensuring he doesn't fall in after her. The rope hisses between his leather-gloved hands until he feels a tug.*

*Aramis pulls hard and fast. But the rope is slack. What the—? Aramis peers over the edge; he sees nothing but darkness.*

*"Bagheera? Bagheera!"*

*A horrid face with crooked teeth and no eyes leaps out. The ghoul grabs his neck with its hooked claws and bites into the meat of his shoulder.*

*He cries out in pain and rolls on the ground, shanking the ghoul with his dagger until the monster lets go. When it finally does, he takes his blade in both hands and rains steel upon it until it no longer twitches.*

*Panting, Aramis tilts his head as he looks at their clothes. They aren't garbed in the elven weave but in Jessenter standard armor. Strange to find that here, this deep in M'thealquilôk.*

*"It's not her." He turns back to his companions.*

Only, he doesn't see Ruth, Tamara, or anyone. The sun blazed high in the sky, shining down on the limestone roof and arched windows of the abbey. Aramis knitted his brows in confusion as he strained his vision against the light. Turning back to the ground before him, the same creature lay on the freshly tilled earth of the cloister garden.

Out in the open.

Staggering to his feet, Aramis ran to the shadows of the walkways, leaping over the low railing of the hall onto the marble floor. Crouching in the corner of the wall and pillar, he looked around. None followed him. What random dead that lurked in the shadows hadn't noticed him thus far.

Closing his eyes, he concentrated on the heartbeat in his ears, thumping at a calmer pace than earlier.

*A nightmare, it was a nightmare.*

He leaned his head against the wall. He couldn't believe he let himself be vulnerable at such a critical time. Nor did he want to think about how lucky he was to survive that encounter. As he steadied his breath, Aramis heard the battle in the nave.

"Oh, what's the matter, dear?" a mocking voice echoed down the hall. "Had a bad dream?"

Aramis thought he heard a step behind the pillar. Yet, when he whirled around with his blades flashing, no one was there.

"Don't worry, I'll make you feel all better."

Then a dark cackle greeted him from every side.

At first, it wasn't as scary as Dido had thought it would be, even when she passed well into the darkness. Dido conjured a simple flame at the head of the curve to light her way. Even though it is a form of a graveyard, the Morning priestesses of old looked peaceful, reposed in their recesses.

Then a bang echoed from above. Followed by a tapping sound growing louder behind the satyr. Dido looked back to see nothing stirring in the shadows and sighed.

Turning her eyes back to the front, she noticed that the dead faced the hall, their skeletal jaws hanging open.

*How odd they would bury this group in this manner.*

But that wasn't as odd as the one stepping out of her crypt. Her head cracked and popped as she turned to see her with hollow eyes.

Dido veered far to the right to avoid her, close to the wall's inner curve. It was fine until bony hands jutted out from the alcoves of their graves, clawing at her as they clamored out. Curling into a little ball as she flew, Dido bobbed and weaved from their groping fingers. She yelped when one snagged their bony fingers in her hair. Another swiped at her elbow, forcing her to fly toward the middle of the curved hall.

"*Brže, brže!*" she commanded. The wind roared beneath her.

Speeding with all of her magical might, Dido tilted so that the walls became her ceiling and floor. Space narrowed as the ancient priestesses of old awoke from their slumber. Making herself as small as she could, Dido accelerated until their bony appendages blurred together like one large shadow. Her little flame highlighted contorted faces as the darkness swallowed her view and snuffed it out.

Yet, she didn't fly in utter darkness. There was a warm glow behind their grotesque silhouettes, a heat hotter than their friable skin and bones.

*Torchlight! I've reached the bottom.*

Releasing the magical propulsion, Dido sailed through the air by momentum alone. Drawing from the flame's power, Dido chanted the most potent fire spell she could conjure, safe from any innocent's harm.

> "<Ye who consume Air and whelps Dust
> "<Ye who scorch a Thousand Plains
> "<And melt a Thousand Swords
> "<I call upon Thee and bind ye to me
> "<To incinerate all who stand before Thee
> "<To the very Earth from whence they came.>
> "Midas Touch!"

Her skin glowed like molten steel, her hair and fur the color of spun gold, her eyes burning like a thousand suns. Her clothes peeled away. Time held its breath as Dido descended into their arms. The moment they touched her, their flesh, their bone, any fiber of their being, a brilliant spark lit upon them. It trailed up their bodies in a bright line, leaving soot in its wake.

Then Dido blinked, and time released its hold. A deafening boom clapped as the air rushed to fill the void she had wrought from the fiery burst. When she opened her eyes, they returned to her warm brown color. Dido found herself in a snowfall of ash and without clothes.

Dido shivered and wrapped her arms around her bare chest, carefully tiptoeing through the gathered ash.

*I hope Sister Ghalédale won't be offended by such indecency, or the cremation of her saints...*

Two torches with glowing embers flanked the large portal. Upon the sturdy door was a plaque that read, "Here lies Justiania, Mother to us all." The blood smeared upon it read, "PARADISE." Dido clapped her hands in front of her, then quickly covered her bosom. The heavy door swung open.

It was the sister herself! Sister Rhyllae was covered in soot as she coughed.

"You're alive!" Dido scurried over to her side.

"Yes." Then Rhyllae gasped for air and rocked herself from coughing.

With a wave of her hands, Dido cleared the air of ash and debris. Finally, the sister breathed freely.

"Why did they leave you down here?" Dido asked.

"Vanessa thought I was dead. Yes, Vanessa, Aramis's spouse." Rhyllae interjected when she raised her eyebrows. "It was poison. They made a twisted game and forced me to choose. I chose poorly and was left alone. But..." Shaking her golden-brown curls, Rhyllae pulled out a pendant made of jasper and two fangs. "This jewel saved me. I was trying to figure out how to get out when I felt I couldn't breathe. It was as if the very air was sucked out of this room."

At this remark, Dido shifted her weight from one hoof to the other as she twiddled her thumbs. The spell would consume the oxygen to fuel its flame. It simply slipped her mind how limited that was deep in the catacombs.

"Well, thank goodness you made it," was all the little satyr could say.

Rhyllae cocked her eyebrow at her. To which Dido gave a nervous chuckle. Then Rhyllae, ever the sister of gentle folk, took off her outer robe and draped it over the satyr's shoulders, daring to wear her under tunic and pantaloons brazenly.

"I'm glad you came. *Shaka un.*"

Feeling the heat creep to her cheeks, Dido shied away. "With everyone fighting the ghouls, I knew I would have to get you."

"It started?!" The morning sister grabbed her shoulders. Before Dido could utter a word, Rhyllae grabbed her hand and bolted out the door.

The dead kept coming, scrabbling from the archway like a swarm of spiders. Leaping over freshly fallen warriors as they dashed toward them. Peering through a crack in the shield dome, Dawn saw more jumping from the pillars to join the fray.

"Hold," she told the soldiers and watchmen. They overlapped what shields they could find, forming a dome of steel. Dawn exchanged glances with Tristan. Beads of sweat formed on his forehead.

"Hold."

The inmorti yelped in joy as they closed in, their jaws slack, trailing strings of spit in their wake as they bounded forward on their hands and feet. Their glazed eyes were wide, showing the whites of their orbs.

"Now!"

A dozen voices buzzed into the chant. "Though I walk through the Shadow, I will raise my candle high..."

The ghoulish creatures threw themselves on their shields, thrashing and pounding their arms. Punching dents into the metal. Their fingers sought an opening through their edges.

"...For the Light within me shall shine, like Fire of the Sun."

There was a flash of light, and the weight was lifted. Dust seeped through the shields, slipping onto their hair and the floor. Peering through the choking cloud, Dawn could see those far away falling hard on their heels, screeching to a halt.

"Break!"

They unlocked their shields. Bolting down the hall, the survivors cried out for Amaveriel and all of their loved ones, running past their recent dead, covered in the thin veil of ash. They closed upon the monsters, their blades and make-shift cudgels making short work of them.

Pausing in her handiwork, Dawn could see the back of their line breaking. Some of the ghouls fled through the constricting entrance, and others scampered into the abbey.

"It worked. We have them on the run!" Tristan said as he skewered one.

Dawn smiled, then she was knocked to the ground. The creature, the one with flaming red hair, tore at her side with its bony fingers, going into a frenzy with streaks of red blazed through the skin.

Gritting through the pain, Dawn slammed the edge of her shield against the temple of the risen soldier. After dislodging him from her side, she dove for her gladius. Rolling to her knees, Dawn brought her shield to bear, with her sword up high.

Then she gasped.

It was Falçion. His skin was sallow, and the blood from his throat dried and crusted—but it was him. He popped his jaw back into place and gave her a hateful glare—never in her life had she seen him giving her such a look. Falçion screamed for her blood before he leaped to strike at her.

And Dawn couldn't strike back.

She couldn't do it.

Not against her friend, the one she had called "brother." Not against the one who helped make Amaveriel home for a disinherited lesbian. Dawn would rather die than lay a blade upon him. Thus, she let her sword slip through her fingers, and it clattered on the floor. Her shield arm drooped, not caring if she left herself exposed.

*I'm sorry. I'm sorry I let you die.*

Then came a voice, singing as clear as a glass bell. Falçion's spine went rigid, and his movements jerked about. As suddenly as it happened, he stopped. His malice faded and he fell into Dawn's arms. In shock, she flipped him over and found his pocked-covered face serene again.

"By Lune's glow," Tristan said under his breath.

All the ghouls that were cowering from them dropped to the floor, back to the gentle repose, all from the soft warble of the famous songbird.

"Rhyllae!" Dawn rushed to the priestess and embraced her. "I thought you were dead. Where were you? And why are you covered in soot?"

"It's a long story." She half-smiled and nodded toward Dido.

Yet the little satyr gave a mournful look as she took in the scene. "We're too late."

"It's never too late," came Mother Myrrh's voice. She soon joined the small reunion, accompanied by the general. "Not while there's still hope left. There's another way to be rid of these vile creatures. A prayer as old as the land of Ur."

Dido gasped and Korzha raised his eyebrows. The mother simply gave a silent nod to them all. The young lieutenant ruffled her sandy blonde hair in confusion. For there in Mother Myrrh's arms was the vile tome, draped like a rag doll.

"But you got the book. Summon the ghouls away," Dawn said.

"No! No," Myrrh said again to still the panic in her eyes. "The book can only bring about further destruction. Besides, we have another power far greater at our disposal."

Rhyllae tilted her head at her mentor, then raised her eyebrows in understanding. "You mean to consecrate the ground? By summoning help from the Heavenly Court?"

Dido interjected, "Such a thing hasn't been done since the treaty between the Fey and the Heavenly Court. Almost fifteen hundred years ago!" She whirled on the Sunset mother. "You can't possibly think of doing such a thing. It would break the treaty—there will be war!"

"I must, madame satyr. For none shall survive from this madness," Mother Myrrh replied.

Then the howl renewed, somewhere beyond the abbey. The dead rose up once again, hunger in their glazed-over eyes.

The following words from the Sunset mother sent shivers down Dawn's spine. "Sacrifices must be made."

# Chapter 28

## HOUSE OF CARDS

THE LAUGHTER WAS ALL-CONSUMING, AND THE shadows closed in. Leering faces loomed with twisted sneers, cutting off any chance of escape. Whirling the daggers in his hands, Aramis turned slowly on the balls of his feet, lowering one knee to the floor. From what he could see, there were six of them—three in the north and three in the south. Spread out like rays of a lonely star.

"Well, what are you waiting for, Foxy?" came Vanessa's voice. "Tuck in."

The ghouls launched themselves at him, one by one, like a wave. The first, whom Aramis deemed North, was impaled through the eye socket with his right knife. He swung himself over their corpse, slashing Northeast a new smile as he went. Aramis dislodged the blade he had in North as he came to a landing behind Northwest, greeting that ghoul with it before they had a chance to face him.

Southwest was nonplussed by the sudden loss. They swung their arms at him with wild abandon, with South closing in pursuit. All Aramis could do was parry their blows away, fast on his heels as they continued their onslaught. Then he saw Southeast leaping high toward him from the pillar.

Giving one final pushback with his twin daggers, Aramis ducked, letting the foul thing crash into its fellows. They clawed and bit each other like territorial hyenas. If it weren't for Northeast, he would wade in to finish them off one by one. Their nearly severed head lolled from side to side as they waddled toward him.

Running to one of the striated pillars, Aramis let the grotesque creature chase him. Then he jumped high and grabbed the pillar. With the fueled momentum, he swung around and snagged the ghoul with his legs. Aramis crossed them into a grip on Northeast's bloody shoulders. He ran steel upon its swollen head as his weight tipped their balance. Once they hit the floor, Aramis rolled into a low crouch, steeling himself for another bout.

"Don't you see how it'll always end?" Vanessa's disembodied voice echoed from every shadow.

The other three were crouched as well, stalking toward Aramis with bony hands and slacked jaws. Their Jessenter uniforms were ragged and loose from their desiccated limbs. But something caught his eye—something on their blue-veined arms.

"You play the hero and fall..."

Then he saw it. Faded tattoos on their arms. A series of numbers like his. Free people.

"...Only to have them bury you dead."

He remembered their names. Aramis was there when they chose them on the first steps of freedom. Fletcher, Hawk, Cassius. Now mindless beasts with hollowed eyes and unhallowed hearts. Enslaved once again.

Crying out the rage in his gut, his sight turned to crimson. Crimson, like the stain on his hands as his blade rained down upon them. Crimson, like their tattered sashes, falling to the floor. All became a blur of crimson as his body danced to the wild beat of the drums in his ears.

One by one, they all fell back into the cool embrace of death—a chilled, frosted blue.

He panted and wobbled over to lean on the pillar. With every breath, the drums faded away. Glancing down at his shaky, tremoring arms, he couldn't tell if the blood was his or theirs. Through it all, Aramis saw his scripted numbers of 479421, as if they were freshly inked that day.

"Aww, why so glum?" their insidious voice cooed. "Thought they could still be saved?"

Aramis clenched his fist as he glared down the hall. What Vanessa was doing was a mere parlor trick. If only he could find a shift in the shadows.

"Are you going to be their savior, Aramis?" they cackled.

"I wouldn't have to do this if it weren't for you."

"Oh, please, you always want to be the hero. To be a god among men. Can you choose who lives or who dies?"

Then down the hall, one of the pillars' shadows became slender, and a flicker of a shade moved around the corner. Easing down the striated hall, Aramis followed. Leaving the gory mess behind.

Aramis came to the checkered hall overlooking the cloister garden. Strewn about were cots and blankets long since discarded. Perhaps, with fleeting optimism, the injured from the blast were able to heal and evacuate the premises. Yet, the sickening weight in his belly told him some may have turned, or worse.

Then a sob broke his thoughts.

*A trick?*

He leaned against the wall near the door, holding the knives to his chest. Aramis listened for any sound. A creak of the door. A giggle. A step. Anything to indicate it was his vicious Vanessa. For a few heartbeats, there was nothing but soft murmurs and weeping.

Quiet as a viper, Aramis peered through the threshold. A large room with a series of tall windows took up the entire length of the hall—filled with rows of cots and separation screens with blankets, clothing, and toys interspersed in between. The high vaulted ceiling held lines of clothing long since dry.

The hospice ward for the sick and poor.

It was odd for Aramis to see this place vacant. Whenever he had visited Rhyllae here, it was always crowded with muttering family members and moaning patients. Children would run to play their games as the priestesses dodged them with trays of salves and bandages. Now a cluster of bed-ridden Jessenters lingered, lost in the poppy's healing stupor.

Then he spotted the source of the pitiful cries: a little girl kneeling next to a lifeless figure on the floor, mewling, "Mama, wake up," as she rocked the limp corpse with her tiny hands.

*Was this what Vanessa meant by choosing life or death? Did they spare this child to prove a point? To be a god among men?*

Shaking his head free of such thoughts, Aramis stooped down next to the little girl, who gasped when she noticed him.

Putting a finger to his lips, Aramis hushed the child. "Do you know where they went? The shadow person?"

The girl pointed behind her to a window smashed open with a clothesline tied to one of their hooks. Looking out to the city, Aramis cursed under his breath when he found

Vanessa was nowhere in sight. He would have to hunt them through the city.

An unearthly howl echoed down the hall, all too familiar to the seasoned Silver Fox. In a few short strides, Aramis kicked the door closed. Then moved the medicinal cabinet in front of it for good measure.

"What was that?" The little girl's face was etched with fear. "What are they?"

Aramis glanced between her and those still bedridden. He knew the longer he stayed, the colder the trail would be. Yet, if he abandoned the people, all would perish by the inmorti's tooth and claw. However, Aramis was only one man; if he stayed and fought, he would die from the sheer number of the coming horde. Or maybe he doesn't need to.

Looking out, Aramis scanned the wall above. It had been beaten by the ever-persistent wind, exposing grooves between the bricks big enough for him to climb upon. He knew he could not take them all. He could carry one and one alone. The rest were lost in their medicinal stupor.

The door pounded, rattling the vials inside the cabinet. The child shrieked and clung to him.

*So be it.*

Taking out the vial labeled "Beeswax," Aramis slapped a dab on the cabinet and left the whole container on top of the cabinet. He wouldn't be needing it where he was going. Then he lit his last cigarette and puffed on it, creating a trail of smoke as he picked up the girl. He kicked out the rest of the glass and stood on the windowsill. The ground was three stories below. The quickest way to get her to safety had to be up.

Clenching the cigarette at the corner of his mouth, he asked between puffs, "What's your name?"

"Za... Zaporrah."

"Okay, Zaporrah. I need you to be brave. We have to climb up to get away from the monsters. I want you to hang on tight."

"Like a monkey?"

"Yes, can you do that?"

Zaporrah nodded, wrapping her arms around his neck and her legs underneath his arms, cradled under his chin as a lemur babe. Still puffing away on his cigarette, Aramis found his footholds and handholds. Inching off to the side of the window, he felt the breeze whipping his cloak like a flag. Not wanting the wind to drag him down, Aramis untied the cape with one hand, letting it fly out to the sea.

The banging on the door intensified. He held the smoldering paper as he took one last inhale. "I'm sorry," escaped his lips with the smoke. Then Aramis flicked the cigarette inside.

The cigarette landed in the room, rolling on the stone tile floor, stopping halfway to the cabinet. The crushed herb from Valentra continued to smolder, eating away the paper encasing it.

The inmorti clamored against the door until it popped out of its hinge. It banged against the cabinet, knocking its doors open. Vials of precious medicinal herbs and salves shattered on the marble floor. The shards of glass skittered across the surface, past the burning cigarette.

The inmorti smelled human flesh through the door and redoubled their efforts. In their frenzy, they slammed their bodies as they attempted to claw through, bumping the container of beeswax toward the edge until it sat precariously over the lip of the cabinet.

The first in line gripped the upper frame of the door, shoving their way through, tipping the cabinet over, sending it and the beeswax toppling onto the smoldering cigarette.

The concussive force from the blast vibrated through the stone into Aramis's hands. He braced himself while shielding Zaporrah from the debris flying out of the windows next to them. Glass shards tinkled as they fell to the streets below. Then all was silent. Aramis bowed his head, knowing that the two of them were safe, while those within were all dead.

The high breeze freed his senses from the suffocating smell of poppies and iodine. Yet, as he bowed his head low, another scent tantalized his nostrils. A lingering fragrance from Zaporrah's scalp. Sickly sweet as an Anglorian jasmine flower.

*It can't be.* His mind raced. *There's no possible way. Vanessa can't shrink themselves down to be this small... Can they?*

Craning his head to overlook the dale, he could see the crazed horde swarming through the gates. People raced through the rubble in the market square while a remarkable few stood their ground. It could be possible that Vanessa was mingling among them, had managed to avoid the blast debris, thrown on a disguise in the nick of time, and disappeared amidst the chaos, slinking away to deliver the loathsome tome to her Djinnasi masters.

Yet, her words rang in his ears, *Save the last dance for me...*

"Silver Fox, sir, my arms are getting tired," Zaporrah moaned as her tiny brows peaked in worry.

"Hold on," he said without forethought.

Training his eyes up for any handholds to grab, he found they were directly below the next story's window. It was smaller than the one below and sheltered by shutters, and simpler to break in than the stained glass windows. He climbed, rising from the tip of his toes for the next crevice to cling to. Yet, with every step he took, an insidious thought flirted in his mind. *Drop the girl into the rocky depths.*

For all he knew, she could be Vanessa disguised, save by their natural odor, manipulating his heart once again with no care for those he loved and protected, not even the wounded he'd sacrificed to escape from the crazed inmorti. The very inmorti Vanessa created from the bodies of his former friends.

Aramis froze in his ascent. His fingers trembled—not by excursion or fear. But by the evil, twisted thoughts that would lead him to kill a possibly innocent child. How could he honestly know? Vanessa was devious enough to lay such a cruel trick before him, rubbing their scent upon a child and sending the hungry horde after them. If he tossed her aside to her doom, could he bear the burden if he was wrong?

Dashing the insidious thoughts, Aramis concentrated on the climb. Nothing would matter if he perished from the stunt. Aramis inserted his right toe between the stone layers and pushed himself up to grip the next foothold. Grabbing hold, he shifted his weight onto the right foot to find the next foothold—the window ledge a handhold away.

Then, the limestone groaned.

*Oh, that's not good…*

Soon after, the groan ceased. Aramis would have to hurry before the quake intensified. If they could get under a sturdy frame, one made of cedar and stone…

Rising to the tip of his toes, Aramis reached for the next hold.

A pop snapped in his ears like a whip. Before his very eyes, a crack sprang forth high above them, and the wall slipped. He braced Zaporrah against the stone, fearing the worst.

Then it stopped.

They dropped an inch—a good inch. The fissure ran high above the window. No doubt that floor would give underneath their feet with the next shift. They needed to get to the roof, fast. Aramis would not stoop to their level and sacrifice the child, Vanessa be damn. If it was them the whole time, then he would rather fight them fair and square than in this compromising situation.

A foothold, a push up, a handhold. Another foothold, another push, another handheld. Over and over, Aramis carried Zaporrah toward the top. They were halfway toward the fissure line when another loud pop sounded.

Another slide.

Zaporrah shrieked into his ear until they halted again. The gap had widened considerably. Aramis felt the footholds giving underneath him as the stone underneath him sagged.

"On my back. Whatever you do, don't let go."

As quickly as she dared to move, Zaporrah swung over to his shoulders, still giving him the vise-like squeeze on his neck. Not that he minded. It was risky, even for him. Aramis tucked his arms and legs underneath him and doubled his pace. He didn't search for any secure holds. As long as it was enough to use, he moved on to the next. He raced against time with each breath he took.

Aramis's fingertips hovered over the fissure line, reaching for the stones above it.

*Almost there...*

With a gasp, he felt as the wall plummeted.

Instinct took hold.

In a blink, Aramis found himself leaping up.

Regaining inches lost.

His fingertips hovered over the broken edge.

That was the moment—if he failed there, they would free-fall to the rubble below.

He reached.

He grasped the stone.

It broke from the mortar.

Scrambling, he grabbed the second stone. That, too, crumbled from his weight.

So, he clamored for the third, the fourth, and the next. Until, at last, he found a firm enough hold. Then all was still save for his breath. Blood trickled down from his scraped fingertips, reminding him that he never should have left his gloves behind at the Eagle's Nest.

"Are you okay?" Aramis asked Zaporrah.

When she nodded, he sighed in relief. If this was truly Vanessa, they would've done something by now. It was a sleight of hand to cover their trail. Securing a foothold, Aramis maneuvered up toward the rooftop, leaving specks of red behind. When they reached the flat roof, Aramis heaved her up to safety.

Looking back down, he saw most of the abbey's eastern wall had slipped down to the streets below. Dust billowed from the wall's path. A twinge of guilt hit him as he looked on—another disaster for the people to suffer from.

Aramis pulled himself over the edge and rolled onto his back. "There you go, kid, safe and sound."

"Yes, but you're not."

# Chapter 29

## TILL DEATH DO US PART

LIGHT FLASHED OFF OF THE BLADE AS IT HURTLED for Aramis.

He rolled to the side, letting the blade clatter on the stone roof. He moved to his knees, unhooking his knife while doing so. As he landed, he extended his arm but didn't let it go.

It was Zaporrah herself who threw the blade at him.

The girl smirked at him, her hands on her hips. "Well, what are you waiting for, Aramis?"

At first, he couldn't believe it. Then, as he watched how she held herself with that twisted smile, Aramis couldn't deny it. Vanessa. Oh, how it sickened him to his core.

As he stood up, Aramis took out another knife, flicking both points toward his elbows. The blood from his thumb smeared on the metal pommel.

"Clever. You should've been an actress," said Aramis.

"Oh, please. Aren't we both actors on this wonderful stage?" asked Vanessa.

They waved their arms out and twirled around, transforming into a full-bloom woman, like they did before he left for that forsaken mission. Vanessa sauntered to the roof's edge, looking over the ravaged city, all in their naked glory.

"Amaveriel—the City of Freedom. Refuge to the refuse, homeless, and tempest-tossed. A plague of locusts on a high wind. Yet, a stage is only a stage, no matter the dressing. There comes a time when we actors must return to reality." Vanessa glanced back at Aramis, their vivid green eyes gleaming. "A time to go back home."

Aramis thought the wind played tricks with his ears. Was that what they were seeking this whole time? The reason for this madness?

"Yes," Vanessa answered his unspoken question. Sauntering back to him, their raven hair danced against their bare curves from the breeze. "Home, Aramis. Back to Bazzuuport. Let the dolls burn in their paper world. We can escape this fantasy and return to what is real. Back to the way we had it. Just you and me." They drew close, and he felt their hot breath on his neck. "Together. Forever."

That last word echoed in his mind as Vanessa nibbled on his ear. He closed his eyes as they smooched along his jawbone to his lips, tantalizing his tongue before they parted. Sweet as poison.

Gathering his blades in his off-hand, Aramis caressed their cheek down to their neck. "Is this what you wanted me to come back for?" Then he squeezed, threatening to crush their windpipe. "To an empty home? A broken marriage?"

Though they gagged, Vanessa still maintained a toothy grin. "Oh, my sweet hubby. You weren't married to me. You married the idea of me."

Enraged, Aramis threw them down onto the stone, tossing his dagger back into his hand. The blade curved down to deal a fatal blow. And yet, they still mocked him with their derisive grin.

"You didn't want an equal. Oh no! You wanted to play hero, with a capital H." Vanessa put the back of their hand to their forehead, pretending to faint. "Saving the sweet, innocent damsel too weak to defend herself. Like many slaves. Like all of Amaveriel. Pathetic."

He could've pierced their black-hearted breast right then and there. He should have! For all the good in the world, Aramis should have ended it all here. Yet, he stayed his hand. For there was a ring of truth in their words.

With a smirk, Vanessa dusted themselves off. "You honestly believe you're the hero they desperately wanted? Look at you! Shredded and tattered at the seams. Hung together by a single thread. Throwing yourself upon the wheel over again until bent and broken. A wheel they created themselves. News flash: they never wanted you in the first place.

"Why continue to bleed for those who wanted to bury you? Those who never have been bent themselves? Never shaped by another hand." He felt Vanessa snaking their hand down his arm to clasp his hand. Why was he too numb to move? "Then be told to fit in the same mold they come from. You and I... Don't you see? We were made by the same hand."

Vanessa took that hand to their lips as if to kiss his knuckles. It took all of his mental effort to yank it away from them.

"Deny it all you want, but you know it to be true. All of this," Vanessa waved their slender fingers over their face, "this is nothing more than a mask. A costume to blend into their charade. Layers and layers of normalities perpetuated by simple minds to rule with simple designs. A veneer slathered on thick to suffocate the true visage inside."

"A mask, you say?" Aramis took the black cloth off his face. "Then what, pray tell, is underneath mine?"

Vanessa crept close to his face, studying it with quiet consideration. Then closer still to say a single word. "Nothing."

It was a simple word. Harmless within itself. Yet, it brought everything back to Aramis. *Back to Bazzuuport. Back to the grand pleasure halls. Back to the sticky bedsheets of Azurl. Back to a name he thought dead. Back to his previous body, chained and starving. Bent over, with his head smothered into the pillow. Feeling every humiliating thrust from his master's rod. That singular word brought him so far back he could feel the spit on his ear as the vile air Djinnasi told him, "You are nothing. You came from nothing. You'll die as nothing. There's no escape. You. Are. Mine."*

With a jolt, Aramis shuddered awake. His daggers raised in each hand toward Vanessa. Yet, his hands trembled as he choked back the hopelessness welling within him, focusing his murky sight on their pale visage.

"You're like me," they said. "We're empty vessels—"

"Shut up!" Aramis shouted.

"—shaped and formed—"

"We're nothing alike."

"—to hold a higher purpose."

"I'm more than a sum of my parts!"

For once, Vanessa stood there with their head in a tilt, at a loss for words.

"I am a man." The tears came to sting him, but Aramis rubbed his arm against his eyes for a quick second. "More than mere property. All my life, I thought I was nothing but a broken person beyond repair. Deserving of a broken home or a broken spouse like you. Doomed to be the scum under their boot. But I was wrong! I was wrong long before I saw Amaveriel."

"If you're going to tell me you're the people's savior, I'm going to vomit."

"No. No, you're right," Aramis said, drawing a raised eyebrow from Vanessa. "I'm no savior. I'm an inbred monkey made to do Cirque du Soleil in bed. What do I know about how to be a hero? But the people of Amaveriel do—they know. They are the true heroes. They endured in that hell-pit you call home. Not once had they thrown themselves off a cliff to end their suffering or maim each other over scraps. They persevered through the worst hardships one could imagine on this Earth.

"Look." Aramis waved his arm out toward the city, encouraging them to see. "They created this—all of this. The only building here before them was the Abbey of the Rising Dawn. The rest they made themselves. Their own homes, their own laws, their own life. To live as equals, for themselves, by themselves. No matter who they were or where they had come from. All I ever did was give them a second chance at life. I'm a guide." A laugh escaped his lips. "The Silver Fox, the shepherd of the desert. That's all I am. They don't need saving—they can save themselves. I'm only there to set them free."

Then Aramis crossed his arms and gave them a good look over. Part of him would laugh at how ridiculous Vanessa looked, cocking their head as if he had grown two heads. Aramis doubted they could ever be redeemed. Then again, who was he to judge? He was just beginning to understand what Rhyllae had been trying to tell him: he could save himself from this dark path. If Rhyllae took a gamble on him, so too could he on Vanessa. Thus, Aramis threw the dice.

"I could offer you the same if you want," Aramis offered. "I know what it's like serving the Djinnasi. 'Throwing yourself over and over on the wheel they created' to use your words.

I could break those bonds tying you. Could break that wheel and set you free." Then he held up two fingers while holding on to his dagger. "You have two options: leave Amaveriel and return to the Magionni tribe. You're too far away from the Djinnasi for them to know. It would be a peaceful life with an adopted family. They obviously couldn't tell the difference. Why the hell not? Or you stay in Amaveriel and join the Jessenters. Pay for the damages you've done. Give all the intel you can and fight back. Vengeance and redemption: two for the price of one. In any case, you won't be kissing the dirt six feet under. Both will free you from the Djinnasi lords and your Shadowhand. So what will it be?"

Vanessa gave a longing look at the city. The wind whipped their long dark hair as tears welled in their eyes. "To live and die free?"

In his gut, he thought they might be playing another trick. Yet, the single tear trickling down their perfect cheek made him doubt. Though divorced, though they almost slew him, though they created this destruction, his instinct was to draw near to their side, caressing his knuckles on their biceps. He knew the most formidable chain to break was the one in the mind.

With eyes swimming in tears, Vanessa turned to him with a pout. "Like Rhyllae?"

All the color on his face washed away. His stomach dropped low between his knees, trembling from the weight.

Then Vanessa giggled mercilessly, wiping away those crocodile tears. "Oh, Foxy." They caressed his cheek down to his scruffy chin with the tip of their nail. "After all of these years together, you didn't think I wouldn't sort your laundry?" Then they backed away after leaving a cut from the flick of their finger.

At first, Aramis didn't know, his mind whirling until it clicked: *Rhyllae*.

"What did you do?" he asked.

Vanessa smiled like a cat that caught a mouse. "Why, we had a heart-to-heart. Mano a mano. She completely opened up after a few drinks, and everything came pouring out. The way she pines for you—"

Aramis seized them by the shoulders and shook them. "Where is she?"

"Picnicking in Paradise, no doubt."

"You didn't."

"Why wouldn't I? She was filling your head with images of grandeur. Stroking your ego so she could stoke your fire."

He let Vanessa go like hot coal. His trembling hands ran through his salt-and-pepper hair. Rhyllae. His darling friend. Rhyllae. His guiding star. Gone. The air thinned, and his legs crumbled underneath him. What was there left for him?

"Oh, Foxy," Vanessa cooed. "If only you can see what I see..."

When they placed their hand on his shoulder, he laughed, backing away as he rose. Never had he laughed this way before.

"I can see it now. I see that you must pay for what you've fucking done."

With that, he let his knife fly, slicing through the air as it aimed for Vanessa's heart.

Yet, they merely smiled as the blade came toward them. Stepping forward, Vanessa took the knife in hand, pirouetted, and threw it back at Aramis without hindering its speed.

Taking a sharp inhale, Aramis rolled to the side, hearing it clatter next to him. Coming up to his knees, he braced for their next strike. But it didn't come. His face twisted in confusion as Vanessa stood there with that ridiculous grin of theirs.

"I appreciate the offer, but I brought my own." Vanessa's voice shifted to a deeper tone.

Before his eyes, their fingers elongated into long black claws, their edges glinting in the sunlight. Darkness spread from those lethal points, creeping up their arm, devouring their body, no longer curved or angled into any gender. Their hair fell out, blowing away in the wind, as the obsidian color crept up to their head. Vanessa had utterly transformed into that black shade, except for their face: still as white as porcelain, with lips as red as blood and eyes green with madness.

The Vanessa he knew was but a shell.

Taking the clothes they discarded, Aramis wrapped them around his left forearm. Then he charged, his dagger keen for their blood.

Vanessa, for Aramis had nothing else to call them, waved their hands before themselves like a pair of fans as they swayed their hips, dancing as they battled. He, in turn, fell into the deadly rhythm, dodging and weaving to the beat. Those keen finger blades never gave as they parried his furious strikes, constantly flicking the daggers away by the wave of their wrist.

Aramis soon realized how futile his efforts were. Vanessa mercilessly chuckled at every failed attempt as he delivered blow after blow, never daring to strike out at him. They were toying with him, waiting for him to wear out so they could come in for the kill. He needed to draw them out if he were to win.

Slowing down his strikes, Aramis backed off his strength, belaboring his breath as he flailed at them in a slipshod fashion. He even shook his hands on his last two strikes upon them before dropping his guard and wobbling in his gait before he crouched down.

Their chartreuse eyes widened in glee, swinging their hands wide across their hips in the form of an *X*.

*Gotcha.*

He snapped into Vanessa's personal space and blocked their strike with the cloth-bound arm. Aramis stabbed Vanessa thrice: once at the right bicep and twice at the left shoulder. Finally, he slashed at the back of their left wrist for good measure.

Oh, how they howled.

In retaliation, they raked at his side as he attempted to jump away, cutting into the grooves between his ribs. Making him howl in return. Then, Vanessa dropped to their knee, spinning low to kick at his kneecaps.

Gritting through the pain, Aramis jumped, his feet hovering over the deadly claws. Then he saw them spin around again, this time swinging their obsidian claws high. He arched his back, grunting from the burning sensation from his chest wounds as he reached for the ground behind him.

The cool breeze was a small victory for his quick thinking. Once it passed by, Aramis swung his legs over his center for a handspring. Then he tucked into a roll, collecting his second blade, and hopped into a crouch, guarding his forearms with his twin daggers.

His left forearm ached and felt empty. Glancing down, Aramis found the protective clothing stripped from his hold, left with nothing but long red grooves down his forearm. A frustrated cry brought his vision to the fore. Vanessa struggled with the cloth, tearing it apart with their scissor-like fingers, getting nowhere fast.

It was his chance.

Pinching the tips of his daggers, he skipped forward, launching one. Another few steps, and he threw the other. He held his breath as the hilt left his torn fingertips. The daggers sailed through the air straight like an arrow, shredding through the garments before sinking into their flesh. One thud followed by the second. A grunt came before the third thud.

Then silence.

After the fabric drifted down, Aramis saw Vanessa's body limp on the rooftop. Still as stone.

*Sleeper be praised.* Aramis collapsed to his knees and bowed.

A sound escaped his lips, part laughter, part sniffling. Sweat mingled with tears as it dripped from the tip of his nose. Sitting on the heels of his boots, he gazed upon their still corpse as an ooze of maroon pooled around them.

*It truly is over.*

With tender care, Aramis picked himself up and made his slow walk to collect his daggers. He bit his bottom lip as his wounds reminded him of his mortality. All the wounds he had accumulated were finally catching up to him. He hoped that Mother Myrrh found a solution to the ghouls quick.

He looked over their obsidian backside with pity when he finally made it over.

Three years. They were one soul for three years. In a way, Aramis had killed a part of himself, making him wonder if there was anything worthy in his life to salvage. He was alone once again. With Rhyllae gone, Aramis was the only one left of Ruth's company. A hefty price. But finally, he understood that it was a price they were all willing to pay, for the people of Amaveriel and for their future. And so must he, until his own mortal end.

"That was for Rhyllae," Aramis said as he collected the first dagger lodged in their back.

The moment he dislodged it, Vanessa's eyes popped wide open. Ruby red with a tiny black orb swiveling inside. They fixated on him.

Aramis gasped as he felt his chest and belly pop. Looking down, he was stunned to see their black obsidian fingers plunged into him. When they mercifully retracted them, Aramis hobbled back, choking and sputtering from the fresh blood that was filling his lungs. He was too shocked and too feeble to avoid their grasp as Vanessa grabbed his neck. Once again, he was in the noose. This time, there would be no Silver Star to cut him free. He clawed at his neck as Vanessa dragged him over to the roof's edge. They held him aloft, despite his dagger embedded in their chest.

"And so this is how it ends…" Vanessa mused, tightening their grip as they brought him to their face. Their alien black orbs swiveled as they relished in his misery. "Not with a bang," Vanessa poised their other hand high, ready to deal the final blow, "but with a whimper."

"'Til death do us part," he gurgled before he removed the embedded dagger, relocating it into their exposed armpit.

They cried out in pain as Vanessa released their grip, as he expected. Using the dagger as a peg, he swung over to their side. Locking his leg around their knee to stabilize himself, Aramis pried the knife free, then kidney punched them with the blade.

They howled in fury and twisted to see him. Amid their contortion, Aramis saw an opportunity. He slammed his entire weight against Vanessa's body, pushing them both over the edge. The city of Amaveriel closing in.

# Chapter 30

## MESSENGER OF FIRE

"**F**OR AMAVERIEL!" DAWN BELLOWED.

Dawn shoved the ghoul against the wall with her shoulder, still biting and flailing at her up until she dealt the final blow. Another came down the stairs, heading for her flank. A streak of lightning dumbfounded the creature in its place. Growling through the pain, Dawn swung her gladius through its neck—ending it.

Dawn panted, taking a slight breather. "Thanks, Dido."

"Anytime," came the meek voice from behind.

When the young officer looked down at her shield arm, she cursed—blotches of red seeped through her sleeve.

"Here, let me get that." Sister Rhyllae patted her arm, mending her torn shoulder.

"Keep going!" Mother Myrrh called out to the three of them.

Looking back, they were surprised at the density of the ghouls the general and the mother were holding back. Korzha parried, slashed, and stabbed at the vile creatures with expert skill, all while moving backward without glancing back, lighting the spiral stairway with blazes of blue fire. Through it all, the Sunset mother patched him up and, whenever he was overwhelmed, pushed them back with holy light, like at this moment. Dissipating the ghouls into dust, coating those that dared to replace them. It was as if they knew they were the ones who would bring them a swift end.

"Go, go, go!" Rhyllae relayed the message to Dawn.

The archway for the floor was blocked by another group of risen soldiers. "Get out of the way!" the lady lieutenant screamed as she charged up the stairs. Dawn bulldozed through them with her shield, impaling one with her blade as she punched through the archway.

"Clear out!" Dido squeaked back at them.

All five fled the claustrophobic stairway. Then Dido formed a flame out of the air and shaped it into a ball. She tossed it in and ducked out of the way. Flames shot out from the archway as if straight from the bowels of Hell itself. The blaze licked the backs of the ghoul impaled by Dawn's sword.

Together, Dawn and Korzha hacked down the rest of the torched creatures. Then the sister and mother raised their ward to prevent further mayhem. They had a reprieve for a moment.

"This way." Mother Myrrh pointed down the hall toward the superior's office.

They ran. But when it opened on their left, everyone slowed down. The entire structural wing had buckled with a gaping hole in the center.

*That was the medical wing!* Rhyllae wondered, *What's happening over there?*

Then the shadows behind the pillars rolled. Ghouls howled as they caught their scent.

"We have to keep moving," encouraged Mother Myrrh.

As everyone picked up the pace, Rhyllae halted. Something caught the corner of her eye. Something dark looming on the rooftop. Her heart sank when it lifted up a man by his neck.

A broken, "Aramis?" escaped Rhyllae's lips. She couldn't fathom how he had escaped from the watch or how long he'd been there in the chaos. All she knew was that he was out of her reach.

Someone, she couldn't tell who, tried to pry her away. Numbly, Rhyllae waved them off, rooted to the spot. Her golden-brown eyes were glued to the scene. She held her breath when Aramis managed to get out of the being's grasp. Swinging himself behind the masked figure, out of her sight. Surely, he would escape from it once and for all.

But it was not to be.

The foul being twisted and fell with the Silver Fox in tow.

"Aramis!" The cry came deep from the gut, echoing throughout the cloister.

Dear, steadfast Rhyllae would've, without a second thought, run the whole stretch of the abbey to be at Aramis's side. As she cried out his name, the ghouls answered in kind; howling, baying, cackling like hyenas on the prowl. Hearing them echo throughout her home rooted her to the spot.

"Rhyllae, let's go!" Dawn came to her side.

"There's no time. Take her," came Korzha's order.

And take her she did. Dawn lifted Rhyllae by her legs, letting her drape over her shoulder, carrying her away from the sight, ignoring the pounding on her back from Rhyllae's fists.

"No! It's Aramis. We have to go save him. What are you doing?"

Then she became mute as she saw the ghouls scrambling up whence she stood, clamoring over the stone edge with wicked delight. In seconds, they were mowed down by Korzha's fiery blade and Dido's fey magic.

Then Dawn crouched under a threshold and set Rhyllae down in the late Mother Superior's office.

"We'll keep them busy." Then Dawn slammed the wooden portal shut before Rhyllae could get a word in.

Rhyllae whirled to Mother Myrrh, her eyes pleading to that sphinxlike gaze.

She held out her palm. "It's not over. Come, we must prepare. Bar the door."

For once in her half-elven lifetime, Rhyllae gave a scolding look at her superior.

Yet, Myrrh didn't deter. "Not all is lost."

Without another word, the mother raced around the office, plucking randomly from the bookshelves lining the walls. Finally, she swooped in before Rhyllae and strewed her harvest on the floor: lava stones, quartz, pyrite, jasper, obsidian, bismuth, turquoise, all the size of her thumb; incense of sandalwood, clove, sage, and the most coveted, dragon's blood. A jar of the Shining Sea's salt was laid aside as the mother kneeled and produced a small wooden box. She pulled out a hairpin left behind in her thick locks. She blew out centuries of dust from the keyhole, then impaled it with the pin.

Seeing how she was struggling with the lock, Rhyllae crouched next to her. Silently, she gestured with her open palms, and silently, Myrrh placed the box in her hands.

They had to end the madness, with or without Aramis.

Rhyllae twitched the hairpin with each click until the lid popped open, revealing a thin shaving of parchment with faded ink and a fist-sized garnet. The Philosopher's stone. The anvil of all creation and destruction.

Korzha leaned against the door for a minor respite. The area was empty of the ravaging ghouls until a new crop rose. He saw Dido looking back toward the open vista, covering the bottom half of her face with her hands. Glancing at Dawn beside him, he saw that the shock of Aramis's death echoed in her hazel eyes.

Part of him wanted to snap them to attention or give a little word of encouragement. Yet, he found that he, too, was taken aback by such a noble sacrifice. The shrills of the coming horde snapped him out of it. He needed to steel their hearts for the new wave.

"Ladies. We make our stand here," Korzha said. "If anything gets past us, all will be for naught. We will not budge. We will not break. We will not be moved until they are dust in the wind. We. Hold. Here."

The ladies nodded, accepting the grim task.

"For Feres." Dawn held out her gladius between the three of them.

Through her incantation, Dido produced a long gnarled medlar twig in the air in front of her. Firmly, she placed the thick, crooked branch on Dawn's sword. "For Feres."

"And for all of Amaveriel." Korzha crossed their weapons with the flaming Silver Star.

They broke from the formation, the fire in their hearts lit once more. Korzha took the left, Dawn faced the right, and Dido the center of their hurricane. Out poured the inmorti from both sides. Their slack jaws drooled as they galloped on all fours. Echoes of their shrieking enjoyment of finding new flesh to gnaw upon surrounded them.

Saluting with the flaming Silver Star, Tavian Korzha muttered to himself, "For Feres."

There was a vigorous rattle at the door, enough to unsettle the books in the shelving that barred it. Rhyllae closed her eyes and breathed, refocusing her efforts on the task at hand. The ritual circle, with its interwoven petals, had to be precise. Each petal design correlated to a heavenly constellation, made precarious by the blessed salt.

Meanwhile, Myrrh placed the precious stones where the lines crossed. Each had a part to play in the ritual. Some of them were to cleanse the evil surrounding them, others to grant a protective shield greater than the one they currently had. Though the use of the large garnet mystified Rhyllae. How such a rare gem came to play in this consecration, the Sunset mother would not explain.

Once the Sunset mother placed the rough-hewn crimson in the center, she pointed toward the incense. "Quick, light them and set them at the cardinal points."

Rhyllae snapped to it, lighting in order: sandalwood to the north for the heavenly court, dragon's blood to the south for humanity on earth, myrrh to the west for mortal men to die, then frankincense to the east for those born to rise.

All the while, Rhyllae could not help but sneak a glance at her mentor, solemnly gazing upon the frail, centuries-old parchment with a beeswax candle in one hand. Once done, Rhyllae gave her a nod and a silent prayer everything would go well.

Mother Myrrh produced a single flame with a snap of her long, black fingers. Fluttering like a butterfly inches from the candle wick, the flame was held in the palm of her hand.

"Oh, Precious Gift. Keeper of all Secrets. I beseech you to assist us and light the fires within. Restore this dwelling to its beauty, radiance, and wonder. In the name of our Morning Lord, we pray for this to be so."

Lowering her hand, the hovering fire zipped to the wick. In a blink, a yellow tongue flame swirled around Mother Myrrh, becoming a column of beautiful latticework. Engulfing her entirely.

"Mother Myrrh!"

Rhyllae ran to step into the circle but ducked away when the cardinal incenses crackled and popped like firecrackers. An arc of fire, like a solar flare, zipped along the salt lines, dancing in its intricate pattern, dazzling Rhyllae into stillness. Peering through the inferno, Rhyllae could only see a dark silhouette in the shield of dancing flames, hardly writhing at all from the intense heat.

"Please." Tears welled in her eyes to protect her sight.

It was then she heard it, a whistle of something hurtling down from on high. Rhyllae dove behind the former Mother Superior's desk, crouching with her arms covering the back of her neck. The sound escalated into a singular clap that echoed all around her. Then breath. Something was breathing.

Peeking around the mahogany corner, Rhyllae saw the flames emerge from the circle's edge, becoming brighter than the midday sun and whiter than the purest midnight star. Rhyllae had no choice but to duck back once again, daring not to open her eyes until the roar of the fire died.

Then all was silent save for the rustle of feathers.

She thought her half-elven ears had, for once, deceived her, and she emerged from her hiding spot. She was amazed to find Mother Myrrh whole and unharmed, floating a foot above the glinting garnet jewel, held aloft by numerous white wings: a pair on her back, from her hips, from her elbows, from her ankles, from the collarbones, and from the arch of her temples. What was even more stunning were the white flames in her eyes, and a rainbow arc of light poured forth from her ebony brow like a sun flare.

In a heartbeat, Rhyllae ran for the nearest candle stand and wielded it before her as if it were a quarterstaff. "In the name of the Morning Lord, I command you to speak. Who are you, and what have you done to Mariam Myrrh?"

Despite the aggression, the mother's face remained placid. She lifted her dark palm. "*Bhayam matsu. Mama nama Nathaniel, agniuta.*" Then, Rhyllae heard a quiet voice in her head, overlapping what was said. Gentle, but a deep baritone. *<Do not be afraid. I am Nathaniel, the messenger of fire.>*

Immediately, she dropped the gilded stand and kneeled down. Her head bowed while her hands trembled. The angel continued to talk to her in the same manner, speaking the foreign tongue while the translation overlapped in her mind.

*<Why bow to me? I am a servant like you. Stand. There's much to do.>*

"What do you mean?"

*<I feel the dead crawl.>* As they spoke, the wings ruffled in agitation.

Rhyllae couldn't help but glance at Tellezard's tome, laid far in the corner so the vile thing wouldn't disrupt their holy work. Did her eyes deceive her? She thought she saw it quake.

*<I feel the desecration upon these grounds. Broken, stained, violated. Despair reeks in the air. Hope drawing on its last breath while mortal beings make their last stand.>*

"You're going to help us?" Rhyllae staggered to her feet. "Destroy the book? Destroy the ghouls?"

Nathaniel tilted their head. *<Do you think we are callous, seeing you mortals as nothing more than grains of sand? Filed away like a bookkeeper and never thought of again? A soul is a treasure beyond measure.>*

"Every soul? No matter the choices they made?" Rhyllae blurted.

Then they sighed and shook their head as if a mother with a child. The act made Rhyllae avert her eyes in shame. She couldn't help being skeptical, considering what had transpired these past few days. Yet, she felt warm hands cupping her face, gentle as they turned her face to look upon them. The feathers beat as if reeds in a breeze.

<*Oh, sweet mourning dove, can one ask a mother to choose the world over the babe in her arms? Can a father sacrifice their son for the world? How one chooses is not based on any mathematical method. There is no equation or value system to measure a soul's worth. For a soul is a jewel, whether pristine or flawed. All are worthy of love.*>

"Love?"

<*Yes. Love is sacred.*> Then Nathaniel laughed as Rhyllae's cheeks flushed in a ruddy color. <*Why you daughters of the Sun and Moon think of procreation more than any mortal, I can never comprehend. Creation can be done out of love, true. As the Sleeper hath done many a time. Love in all forms is a sacred tenet beheld by all. It is the fire within. Pure and bright as a star.*>

Then Nathaniel touched her forehead with their index finger. Rhyllae found her mind encapsulated in a wondrous image. There in the velvet indigo was nothing as far as she could see. Then, a flash. A blossom of light bloomed in a flourish. A ripple escaped, streaking across in a brilliant bow. In that flower, her mind's eye beheld galaxies, stars, planets, and moons. All swirling, dancing in a miraculous concert. Everything was brilliant and beautiful to see, grander than any nighttime vision she had ever witnessed. Then the image faded, and she found herself again in the Mother Superior's office. Her face was still in the warm embrace of the angel. When they let go, a tear fell down her cheek.

Nathaniel smiled broadly, perhaps satisfied that Rhyllae finally understood it all. Seemingly from nowhere, they placed the garnet jewel in her palms. It was rough, as if it was chiseled right from the earth. Flicking their numerous wings, they floated away from her with the grace of a swan.

<Now, what dost thou want of me?>

Rhyllae brought the garnet to her chest. "Nathaniel, messenger of fire, save us all from this evil. Take us back to the beauty that we once were. In the name of the Morning Lord, let it be done."

<And so it shall be.>

They curled into a ball, letting their wings cover them. Then the wings glowed hot white with brilliant light. Ribbons of color pulsed from them as if steaming the vapors of the stars above, then zoomed around them as they, too, became a shining light, bathing Rhyllae and the entire office in rainbow hues, pulsing faster with each passing second until they burst into flames of brilliant white.

Rhyllae had to shield her eyes. All she felt was this tremendous joy washing over her. So magnificent was the power that she wanted to dance, sing, and laugh all at once.

Then she heard the ring of a single clear bell.

She took a peek and saw a brilliant supernova with white flames jettisoning outward. The book curled into itself when the fire passed it over, becoming cinder and dust. Rhyllae gasped when it came to her but felt no harm. Nor was it hot. The sensation was relieving, like being washed by a mint sprig.

When the wave extended past her and through the walls, Rhyllae ran to the window. Down below, she could see all the Jessenters and her sisters fighting in arms at the entrance. When the ring extended over them, the ghoulish creatures were turned to dust, and all that had risen fell. Then the brilliant arc was gone.

Rhyllae heard another whistle behind her, ascending higher in register until fading to silence. When she turned, she found Mother Myrrh floating down, deprived of the numerous wings. Her head lolled from the weight of her dark, rippling locks. Her priestly vestments were tattered.

Rhyllae gave a smile. *She's going to feel that tomorrow, I'm sure.*

Her mirth was then wiped from her face when her honey-brown eyes caught a giant looming shadow heading toward the stained glass window.

With a leap, Rhyllae tackled Mother Myrrh as her entire world shattered.

# Chapter 31

## CHANCEL

THE WIND WHIPPED ARAMIS'S SHIRT AS THEY HURtled down. Floors flashed by as the wails of terror echoed from within. The abbey looked like an open dollhouse, all thanks to him. And he thought he was saving someone innocent.

He grimaced and shut his eyes. He was too tired to do anything else. It was all up to Korzha and Mother Myrrh to end the ghouls. He had ended Vanessa. They would crash to the earth, and he along with them. What else could he do? It was over.

"Aramis!" the wind howled.

His eyes snapped wide open. *Rhyllae? Screaming from the grave? Why?*

Then he saw feathers, long and dark, unfurling next to him. Vanessa was changing. Their arms grew into tarblack wings, and their feet hooked into talons. Their porcelain-masked face gave a derisive smile before they unfurled their wings. Then she kicked him aside and snapped their wings wide. They stayed aloft by the wind's buffeting as he continued to free-fall.

Aramis scrambled for the rope tied around his waist. He didn't know if it would hold—it was only for a disguise. But it was better than nothing. Tying his shoes at the frayed ends, he made the rope into a makeshift bolas. Whipping it back, Aramis forced it into a spin. Releasing it back toward the heavens. Hoping against hope. It wrapped around their waist, then slipped. Slinking down their leg until he could snag it tight on their talon.

"Oh? You still want to play?" Vanessa queried, grasping the rope with both of their talons.

Yanking on the sash, they rolled over, pulling as they flew. Then Vanessa caught an airlift and sailed skyward. They sang about flying to numerous islands in a smooth, masculine tenor as they climbed ever higher into the sky. A song from the Ancients' time.

Poor Aramis hung on for dear life. His eyes trailed over the string of corpses in front of the abbey's entrance. Most of the horde clung to the abbey, bottlenecked at the doorway. Farther away, those who had slipped past chased the frightened citizens throughout the city. He could see them running in the alleyways like mice in a puzzle box. Above all of their cries for help was Vanessa's archaic song—the whole situation disgusted him. With grim determination, Aramis snaked his way up the rope.

Through the chilling clouds, Vanessa paused in their singing and flashed a wicked smile at him. "If I fall, would you catch me? Let's find out."

They tucked their wings back. Aramis's stomach twisted into a knot as they pivoted in the air to fully face him. The line yanked him as Vanessa beat their mighty wings down toward the ground below. The wind stung his eyes and deafened his ears with its roar. All of a sudden, they opened their wings wide, parachuting their descent. Using their talons, Vanessa tugged at the rope like a whip, flinging him toward the battle at the abbey threshold.

Seeing what was coming, Aramis braced himself. Wrapping the rope around his entire arm. Praying it would prevent his fall. It worked. Much to his regret. A sickening pop cracked over the western side of the city. Then a gut-wrenching cry followed. Dizzy from it all, Aramis hung from his dislocated shoulder, whimpering as he swayed to and fro.

"I guess what they say is true—marriage is like a ball on a chain," Vanessa commented, their voice clearly unamused.

Still woozy from the pain, Aramis merely scowled at them.

"But like mommy used to say, 'If you don't first succeed—try, try again.'"

Once again, they ascended into the sky. Climbing higher than before, with Aramis in tow. Aramis could not afford another whiplash. He had to take out Vanessa with one arm down. But how? He was only one man.

Aramis looked at his dislocated arm, still entangled in his impromptu snare. He saw the numbers 479241 clearly in their ornate Djinnasian scrawl through all the tears in his shirt. Like the free people, like Shayla and Hashim. They prayed every dawn and night for any salvation from that hell. No one heard them save for him—a miracle from the blue.

*Yes,* he reminded himself. *I've done it before. I can do it again. The secret of Amaveriel will be kept to our graves.*

Aramis took one of his daggers and set it between his teeth. Steeling himself, he gripped the rope with his left hand and slowly unraveled his limped arm. It flopped down to his side, and a wave of sickening pain coursed through his body—causing him to faint.

Almost.

Grunting through it all, Aramis hung on for dear life as they reached the peak of their ascent. Vanessa tucked their wings back again, allowing themself to fall back to earth. Aramis watched them dive past him, letting the rope tug him around, sailing through the air below, trying to position himself behind them to the best of his ability. Vanessa increased their speed, and Aramis's eyes watered from the cruel wind.

Blinking through the tears, he saw their talons reaching back to whip him around. He let go, sailing down. Taking the dagger out of his mouth, Aramis poised it high. Vanessa opened their dark wings out wide—rapidly slowing their descent. They slammed together, and Aramis drove the dagger home between their shoulder blades. This time, it was their turn to cry out in pain.

Vanessa clawed at their neck for air, gagging on the blood flowing into their punctured lung. Flapping upward as if they were drowning in the ocean, trying to reach the surface. One of the wings receded back into its obsidian body, causing them to barrel roll.

Determined to hang on, Aramis wrapped his legs around their waist as he twisted the knife farther. He didn't care; they were falling back toward the abbey. He didn't care that a brilliant burst of light decimated the dead to dust. Nor that the cheers of joy had turned into gasps of horror. Nor that they were aiming for the towering stained glass window.

This was the end of them.

The end of Amaveriel's suffering.

The end of his pain.

He was going back home.

Back into Rhyllae's embrace.

And he didn't intend to leave anytime soon.

Shattered.

Rhyllae's world was shattered like the stained glass window high above. She cautiously lifted herself off of Mother Myrrh. The colorful shards broke into smaller pieces as they fell off her shoulders. Not too far from them were two figures, lying still among the broken colored glass. One of them was a misshapen black mound. The second, limp as a rag doll, Rhyllae knew all too well.

"Aramis?" Rhyllae called out to him as she crawled through the delicate shrapnel.

The shards crack under the weight of her knees. The glass tinkled as it was brushed aside in her wake. But all she heard was silence.

Aramis didn't stir, not even to breathe.

Rhyllae grabbed hold of his limp arm and shook him. "Aramis, wake up. It's over. We won. The ghouls are gone. Aramis?"

Rolling him over to see his face, Rhyllae lost her breath. Aramis's skin was dramatically paler than his usual tan shade. A yellow shard jutted out of his chest, right where his heart should be. When she eased the delicate fragment out, a trickle of his blood spilled and then ceased.

"No..." Her voice cracked as she stroked his ragged cheek, brushing his blood-soaked bangs clinging to his face. "No. You weren't supposed to die. I made a promise to save you. Please, don't make me break it."

Yet, no matter how much she begged, his eyes wouldn't flutter open. Tears streamed down Rhyllae's cheeks, washing Aramis's face. She placed her hand on his chest. Drawing from the Lord's light, trying to push it into him. Yet, her mind was a jumble, and all she could do was recite the first line over and over in her mind.

*In what Grace that's within me...*

Rhyllae let go of the verse and shook him with what little strength she had. "You can't let me break it. Not now. Aramis, you have to wake up. Please, wake up."

Crumbling on top of him, Rhyllae cradled his lifeless body in her arms, weeping as she rocked him back and forth. Her shoulders heaved with each heavy sob.

"Please," her voice barely whispered. "I love you."

Then she placed her lips upon his. Feeling how cruel it was to only be met with stiffness, left with a memory of his warmth.

There was a banging on the barricaded door—a muffled cry calling out, "Mariam," and, "Rhyllae."

Rhyllae clung to Aramis tightly. She didn't want them to come in. Not the real world. Not the unfixable, unchangeable real world. This placid, peaceful face covered in grit and blood could not be his death mask. It could not be the last time his numb, unmoving lips received her kiss. It couldn't be real.

Yet, they finally blasted their way through with Dido's magic, knocking aside the barricade they put up before they did the ritual. They ran in, their boots snapping the scattered glass until they slowed to a stop.

They must have been stunned to see that the entire office was littered with glass shards. Or that there was a gaping hole in the tall window, showing the grandeur of the setting sun. Perhaps they were taken aback by the weird black mound of indescribable flesh and bone nearby. Or, perhaps, they were shattered like her when their eyes fell on Aramis in her arms. Dumbfounded to be sure that he would end up here when they all witnessed him falling moments before.

Dido gave out a quiet, mournful, "No," before she turned her back from the scene. Dawn bent low to embrace the tiny satyr, letting her use the maroon sash as a handkerchief. She, too, turned her head as she shed her tears. Another martyr to the cause.

Only one dared to move from the stillness.

Muttering, "Mariam," under his breath, Korzha quickly strode over to the still-collapsed priestess. Holding Mother Myrrh in his arms, he patted her cheek. When she fluttered her Töskan blue eyes at him, Korzha let out a sigh of relief.

"Did it work?" Her voice was drowsy from sleep.

"Yes. Very well," he whispered to her with half a smile. Then a frown returned to his features. "Though at a cost."

Myrrh furrowed her dark eyebrows at him, following his gaze upon Rhyllae, cradling the Silver Fox. With Korzha's aid, the mother walked over to the brokenhearted sister.

"Tell me, what can I do to fix this?" Rhyllae asked her when she kneeled by her side. "Don't tell me this is forever."

"Why don't you ask him yourself?" Myrrh stated.

"What? How?" Rhyllae said as she rubbed the salt from her eyes, to no avail.

Cupping her dark-brown hands around Rhyllae's round cheeks, Mother Myrrh rubbed off Rhyllae's tears with her thumb. "We are daughters of Light. We stitch their wounds, lance their boils, and, when need be, sew their life back together." Seeing hope renewed in her eyes, the mother's smile grew wider. "Let go of the grief in your heart. Listen to the love within you. Crystalize it and light it as a torch. Let it be a fire that burns all shadow of doubt. When you find him, offer the flame to him. Only he can let it in."

"What if he refuses?"

"He won't," Dawn told her matter-of-factly, despite her ruddy eyes. "Aramis loves you."

"Don't be too sure, Lieutenant," Korzha cautioned. "Though one can have the grandest love that there is in this world, such beauty pales in comparison to the mysteries of the other side."

Mother Myrrh nodded. "All souls are governed by the choices they make. All you can do is ask. It's always no if you don't."

Sister Rhyllae turned her gaze to each one of them, from the gentle expression of Myrrh to the reserved Korzha, to the pleading, teary eyes of Dido, then at last to the confident lieutenant.

"Well, what are you waiting for?" Dawn encouraged.

Sister Rhyllae looked at them all one last time before taking a deep breath. Closing her eyes, she formed the images in her mind.

It was dark at first.

Then a spark. A sliver of light.

Rhyllae cupped her flame. It was tiny and feeble in the darkness surrounding her. She looked in the inky pitch space. The mother told her to let go of all of her doubts, but how could she? What if he didn't want to come back? What if he was happy with their friends? Happy away from this painful world?

*Happy away from me?*

The flame flickered, threatening to go out. Rhyllae brought it to her breast, shielding it with her fingers.

Then she heard it, a song. It was low, barely audible. Somber, raw, and gentle.

Shielding her flame, Rhyllae moved toward the source. She recognized the words; she sang them when greeting the Sun every morning.

As the sister moved through the space, she discovered she was walking through a mirror of their world. It looked like the Mother Superior's office, but all the colors were drained, and everything had a smoky haze. Yet, as Rhyllae approached the window, the broken panes revealed infinite stars, swirling in a stream of colors and smoke. Part of her felt drawn to it, like a moth to a flame. Let everything go and be part of the eternal splendor and wonder.

Then she saw a cloaked man sitting on the stone sill. Hunched over as he cradled a broken string. One that was attached to his navel. The other was limp on the floor, trailing to who knows where. Fat tears fell from his hooded face as he sang the song like a broken music box until he choked, sobbing as he brought his palm to his face.

With a voice pure as a lark, Rhyllae picked up where he left off. As she sang, her flame fanned to life, illuminating the shadows surrounding them, giving them the same color as the starlight beyond, splashing upon the cloaked man.

Lowly, he sang in harmony with her, hesitantly at first, growing stronger as he drew in her light. When he pulled back his hood, Rhyllae felt her heart leap.

It was her beloved Aramis. Whole. With nary a scratch upon him.

They reached out for each other with music on their lips. Aramis swung her in the air, then brought her into his embrace. Resting his forehead against hers as they finished the song. Ending it with a kiss, warm and bright.

All turned to a misty white.

Opening her eyes, Rhyllae found her lips still locked on Aramis's frozen lips. She could taste the copper tang of his blood as she drew back. Aramis looked as he had before, the blood dried into cracks, and his eyes were still closed. She could not tell the color of his pallor. The room was unusually dim.

Looking about, she saw it was well into the night. The room was lit by the soft illumination of candles. Dawn was kneeling in prayer beside Dido, who also clasped her hands in kind. They both were a little wide-eyed as they gazed at her.

*Did they see me kiss him?*

Rhyllae turned to her superior. Mother Myrrh was covering her mouth, trying to hide her mirth. Though there was a twinkle in her eyes as she glanced at Korzha. Rhyllae had never seen the general's cheeks turn a garish red. His blue eyes looked away from the mother as he cleared his throat.

*Oh, by the Morning Light, they did!*

Before Rhyllae could explain what happened, she felt Aramis's breath underneath her fingers.

"Aramis?" Rhyllae could see his eyelids twitch, but he didn't utter a word. "Aramis, wake up."

Aramis's lips twitched into a smile. He mouthed something that even Rhyllae couldn't hear. She leaned farther down to listen to him better. Then, his lips pressed against hers, holding the back of her head so she couldn't back out. He moaned as his tongue mingled with hers.

Rhyllae's eyes bugged out. Aramis was a fantastic kisser—there was never a doubt. But not in front of an audience.

"Aramuff." Her voice was muffled by his passionate kiss. The more she pulled away, the more Aramis pressed on. Rhyllae heard chuckling.

Finally, he broke away and huskily told her, "I said, 'Please, ma'am, I'd like to have some more.'"

Dawn hooted. "Haha! The son of a bitch lives."

"Language," Rhyllae blurted out, feeling the heat in her round cheeks.

"Yes, he's recuperating quite well," Mother Myrrh teased, letting the faux pas slide.

"Let's escort Dido out before she faints from such infatuations," Korzha equally teased.

The lady satyr pouted at them. "Hey, this is nothing compared to Valor Kirshna's *Sacred 7*. Hmm, that was some spicy material."

The general did a double-take. Dawn doubled over in laughter.

Rhyllae looked down at Aramis. "Do I need to know?"

"If you have the time, I can give you a good summary." Aramis waggled his eyebrows.

Rhyllae laughed and kissed him again. Parting with a sigh and a smile on her lips, she patted his chest. "C'mon. Let's get you cleaned up."

Gingerly, they picked him up from the floor and made their way over the colored shards. As they all came out of the doorway, they were greeted by cheers of "Huzzah" and "Hosanna."

# Chapter 32

## EULOGY

THE PRAYER CHANT ROSE ONCE AGAIN—THIS TIME over the Shining Sea.

The people gathered at the sandy inlets with candles and songs. Part bittersweet, for many had fallen during the dreadful event. Part relief, for they could now give them their proper due. Underneath it all was titillation, for nothing they were about to witness had ever been done in their living history.

There, lining the beaches, were barges laden with urns, flowers, and unleavened bread. Those fortunate to be whole, such as Lady Ruth, Bagheera, and Joel, were laid in freshly made boats. It had taken three treacherous weeks to cut through the jungle to retrieve the trio. Even longer to haul back the treasure of the ancient city. But finally, they were home, washed and dressed in clean linen with all their worldly belongings about them. Tamira was returned to the stone, as a dwarf should be when called home. Thus her name and possessions were part of the dwarven barge in memoriam.

Kneeling in front of the trio, Aramis tended to them with care, placing weeping asters on top of their combed hair, while Rhyllae nestled their goods in the grooves between them. Bagheera's broken neck was covered with jungle flowers, giving her a royal look. Ruth's sister, Naomi, hummed a psalm sung by her family as she held Ruth's hand. The tiny flowers looked like the stars shining through the night.

They all rose when Korzha came forward, dressed all in black velvet, presenting Lady Ruth's sword. The decorated quills of raven feathers sparkled in the setting sun.

"She would never dare enter Valhalla without Gleamwood. Though she is in peace, the blade will still be needed to protect and defend her people."

Naomi's lips sputtered when her quaking arms received the glorious weapon.

"Ruth wouldn't have it any other way." Rhyllae spoke up, seeing how Naomi could only nod in acceptance, tears flooding her cheeks.

A smile flickered across Korzha's face as he watched Naomi kneel before Ruth's barge. Rhyllae crouched by her side, offering words of comfort. The general and the Silver Fox stepped away to give her space.

"She was strong in life. I have no fear of her strength in spirit." Korzha spoke, at first to himself, then to Aramis. "Though, it's been too long... Too long."

Aramis looked off to the horizon, seeing the families and friends casting off their barges. The candles decorating the floating pyres looked like the stars emerging in the sky.

"Better late than never," Aramis finally said.

Both of them locked eyes. What animosity had been there had cooled to a simple understanding—a truce of sorts and, perhaps, respect.

Korzha broke the silence. "In many ways, you remind me of her. Did Ruth ever tell you she was once a concubine to the emperor?" When Aramis shook his head, Korzha continued, "That was how we met. I made a bet with him after my conquest in the North. 'If you can train my harem to be your soldiers, you can take them wherever you like.' And so I did. I made them the women of war they were always meant to be."

"You set them free?"

"In a way, depending on your views of conscription. Of all the phalanxes under my charge, they were the apex. I could take them through icy tundras to the fae's forest—even the shores of Trimbaline. I could always count on their mettle as I could always count on Lady Ruth. I knew whichever deadliest mission I gave would be met with success. Even in death."

Aramis rocked onto the back of his heels and was stunned silent. He didn't even notice that Rhyllae left to finish preparations with her sisters.

For reasons unknown, that put a smile on Korzha's face. "When I opened her letter, I was not at all surprised who she put forward as the new company leader."

Aramis knew. As did everyone in their company before that fateful trip. He kicked the sand under his boots. "You know the Council of Elders put me on probation—"

"To pay off your crimes and serve the community, yes."

"Under your watchful eye."

"That never changed." Then he pulled out a slip of paper from the inner pocket of his velvet doublet without taking his eyes away. "Your next expedition, Silver Fox."

The paper was blue and etched with white designs. Flicking the flap open, Aramis focused the light from his eyes on the faded scrawl: "SILO 51."

"Treasure?" Aramis asked.

"A weapon. One that can end it all."

Before Aramis could get a word in, the funeral bell tolled. It was time for the dead to set sail. Together, Aramis and Korzha pushed Bagheera and Joel, trailing after Ruth, who was set off by Naomi. Straightening his doublet, Korzha signaled the archers high on the rocky knoll. They knocked back their short bows and let loose the first volley. Everyone gasped when the flames sprouted up from the floating vessels. Soon, the crowd settled in awe as the second volley lit more of their kin.

Absorbed in the sight, Aramis flinched when Rhyllae put her hand on his arm. As an apology, he wrapped her in his arms, using his cloak as a blanket against the coastal breeze.

"Did they light them yet?" Aramis asked. Her eyes could see farther than his.

Rhyllae shook her head. "They're switching to the longbows."

"Tristan can't get to them all. He'll wear out."

"He's not alone."

Aramis dropped his mouth, then smirked, for he knew who she spoke of.

The air gently thrummed from loosed bowstrings. The archers, martial and civilian alike, were illuminated by the braziers at their feet. Higher up on the rockier inlet, Dawn could see the arrows arcing toward their targets as a rosy meteor shower. Those that were hit blazed into life. Sparks fled heavenward as they cruised toward the horizon. If it weren't for the singing, Dawn would have thought she was back in the fight.

*But not yet,* she reminded herself, for they always take the time to recollect their efforts during the cold season. Yet, there was worry in her heart; with the new general in charge, who knew when the deployment would come.

"It's time," Tristan announced by giving her a long bow.

Few could string such sturdy wood, and even fewer knock it back. But the two of them did so in a fluid motion. Their arrows flew toward the sun itself.

"Did we get them all?" Dawn asked.

Tristan turned and looked behind them. Even higher on the rocky precipice was Dido. In her hand was a silver mirror, and it illuminated her face and curled horns.

"One more, to the far right. Captain Felix's and Captain Mosul's barge."

*Friends to the bitter end.*

Dawn pulled the string back as far as the wood would allow it without breaking and let the fiery arrow loose. Everyone held their breath, scanning the horizon. Finally, a new light shone among the indigo waters, leading the way for the sparkling fleet.

Tristan gave a silent nod to the ladies and made his way down the slope. Yet, Dawn found herself standing still. Her hazel eyes took in the sight. Then she felt a gentle touch on her arm from Dido. It took everything not to break down in front of her.

Dawn asked her, "All those promises made, Dido, were they for nothing? Was it empty comfort to fill in the meantime? I can't help but feel I let them down somehow."

Dido paused in thought and eventually spoke in the growing twilight. "I don't find it's wrong to seek comfort in the present moment. Nor should we deprive ourselves of such things to steel our resolve in times of crisis. Nay, it should be something to strive toward and make it more readily at hand, no matter the weather. This humble flame of hearth and home that kindles our spirits is the same flame we find in companionship. Those promises we make in hushed whispers as storms roll over are just as mighty as the careless laughter made in summer. And though they are not with us, we feel their flame alight in our hearts even in the dead of winter. For every laughter we shared, every kindness granted, and all promises made will not be forgotten, lest we will be forgotten ourselves. Better to have comfort that we so readily wish to receive—that they themselves so wish to give—than to cast it aside in the cold, harsh wind."

With that, Dido gave a soft smile and a pat on Dawn's arm. They looked at each other with glassy eyes. Then Dawn coughed and sniffled back a tear. "Thanks, Dido. I think there's one more promise I have to keep, or I shall regret it."

And so Dawn headed down from the rocky slope, her gaze seeking the singing maiden she had met not too long ago.

Two flaming arrows streaked across the night sky like shooting stars. Then four, and six. All hitting their mark, and the pyres sailed out farther to sea. One such star flared down toward the barge of Captain Felix, holding General Tackett and all the high officers. It lit with a blaze greater than the fading sun—a beacon to all rafts sailing to their heavenly home.

Rhyllae gasped and pointed when one landed on their beloved friends. A small constellation among the sea of stars. Her fingers then touched her lips as silent tears rolled down her cheek.

Kissing the top of her head, Aramis then snugged her into a warm embrace. Aramis remembered such a beacon from his short trip. Within that halo was everyone he knew and loved. They waved for him to join. If it weren't for his grief, he would've walked out of that window into the stellar beyond.

Strange that Vanessa wasn't there. Not that he saw them as part of his beloved people—far from it. There was no hell, and no Devil, no matter how often the priestesses trumpet the notion. From what the Reaper of Souls said, there's a Heaven and an Earth, all thanks to the Morning Lord. If Vanessa were dead, they would've been there with him, gloating over his misery. When he told Rhyllae all he had witnessed, she was equally relieved and confused.

Aramis tried to shake the unsettling feeling in his stomach. There was a charred body, a hulking mass of flesh and bone smoldering in the room. He and everyone else watched the newly anointed Mother Superior Myrrh bury Vanessa's misshapen corpse in the earth. Vanessa couldn't be hiding among them in the crowd. Truly?

The burning pyre passed by the late captain's fleet. In his honor, they fired their cannons in a salute. Gunpowder and smoke curled into the darkening sky.

Aramis shuddered in the wake of their boom.

The glasses shuddered from the fists banging on the tables.

"Speech! Speech!" they roared.

It was the height of the wake at the Iron Lady, and all the Jessenters had their fill of drink and song. Aramis and Rhyllae came in time to see Dawn shove the spindly Korzha up to a table. Little Dido guffawed into her glass when he nearly flipped the furniture.

Rhyllae tsked at the poor taste while she laid white roses on Falçion's seat. Meanwhile, Aramis bummed a smoke, away from her distracted eye. Every year, there had been a wake for those they lost during their summer campaigns. Though, it was normally a handful that showed up, never this many. The poor inn was filled to the brim, with some loitering outside.

"My fellow compatriots," the general raised his voice. "Here we are, once again, standing side by side in honor of our brethren and sisters."

"Hear, hear!" some replied.

Sticking the cigarette between his lips, Aramis patted down his pockets, a dimming realization that he went through all the matchsticks he had just bought.

"Fallen—but not forgotten. We shall write their names among the martyrs who came before us. Let us dye our sashes in their spilled blood, light their fires in our torches..."

To Aramis's amazement, the cigarette was lit by a magical flame at the end. Peering through the curling smoke, Dido waggled her fingers in greeting as she slurped down her drink. The little satyr was already flushed.

"...and bring their swords crashing upon the Djinnasi's heads."

With a gallant flair, Korzha stepped down to a chair, then to the floor. Everyone hooted and hollered. Glasses and steins clanked. Tables rattled from banging fists once again. Rhyllae smiled back at Aramis, then took a double-take.

"Tomorrow," he whispered, smoke spilling forth.

Rhyllae gave him a glare.

"I'll quit tomorrow. Come on, let me get you a drink."

All of a sudden, Dawn hopped to her feet and raised her glass. Though her voice cracked in some parts, her spirit shone through. One by one, all had the song on their lips:

"Join me, my Amaveriel,
"Where I run free
"Stand beside me and fight with me
"Emancipate who I left behind."

Soon, she was drowned out by all—yes, even Aramis—as their voice raised as one:

"Through the mountains, through the valleys
"To the hurricanes, crashing on the shore.
"Stand by me, Amaveriel
"Where I run free..."

Then the crowd broke as Rhyllae raised her voice to a higher octave. She held it there, her eyes closed as the cup pulled close to her bosom. Then she alone finished it, as if in a closing hymn:

"Stand by me, Amaveriel
"Where I run free."

Everyone applauded, and a few, namely Dawn, whistled. Rhyllae flew her eyes open wide. Her cheeks flushed red as she took in her drink. Her honeydew eyes darted for an escape.

And Aramis provided one. He guided her through the crowd toward the back. All the meanwhile, muttering that he had to pay off a debt to poor Bashir. Ducking under strings of garlic, they found themselves alone in the root cellar.

Abashed, Rhyllae looked down into her cup. "I was moved, I..." But she stopped when he lifted her chin.

"So was I." Aramis leaned into the kiss.

He tasted the honey mead on her tongue as they mingled. This time, it was Rhyllae who broke away from the kiss. "There's something I have to tell you."

He held his breath as grim thoughts raced through his mind.

"The mothers—well, the Mother Superior—they..." Then she sighed and brushed her hand over her head, unknowingly pulling back her hijab an inch from her forehead.

"They changed their minds about us?"

Aramis had heard the gossip behind their back. A few of the surviving members refused to call Rhyllae their own sister, still believing that a priestess of the Lord must remain celibate in all manners. Most of them supported Rhyllae. Thus, they threatened to snuff out the Silver Fox if he left her behind. The one they called Gertrude crushed a fresh melon to solidify the threat. All calmed down when the Mother Superior gave everyone in the abbey the option to be courted. If approved by the superior, of course.

"Huh? No. As far as I know," Rhyllae said.

"Then it must be the mischevious ferrets in the laundry."

"No, it's about—wait. What?"

"They're frisky when they're hungry."

"Oooh, theywantmeasamother," Rhyllae blurted out.

"What was that?"

"I'm getting promoted to be a mother." She cleared her throat. "They've wanted me to join for a long while now, but I didn't want to stop helping the Jessenters. This time, I couldn't say no. There are so few of us now in the abbey. With no one else on the way, I couldn't put it off any longer."

Aramis looked her in the eye. "What happens now?"

"I don't know. The mothers were talking about trials to test my faith."

"Trials? That's new."

"Well, they haven't had anyone raised in the church like me for ages. They want to make sure I 'earn my keep.'"

"And get you out of the Jessenters."

Rhyllae bit her bottom lip and looked into her cup, watching the liquid swirl by her hand. When she spoke, there was an unmistakable crack in her voice. "When are you leaving?"

"I'm not."

She flew her eyes up at him, wide-eyed despite a tear streaking down.

"I'm not," he repeated, wiping that drop with his thumb. "Not without you. As the company leader, I conscript you into service."

Rhyllae snorted and chuckled at the same time. "And how many years do I have to serve?"

"'Til the end of our days?"

A smile as warm as the sun splayed across her face. "Yes, 'til the end of our days. Come, I have to greet the dawn."

They passed Dawn smooching a black-haired foreign beauty in the corner, too engrossed to notice. Aramis raised his eyebrows. He knew the woman as Tsuki, a famous artist on the red pier. How Dawn landed such a dish was baffling. But he was proud of her, nonetheless.

It was a quiet walk to the abbey. Most people had turned in for the night, all shuttered in their homes with their loved ones. It would've been a lonely stroll for the Silver Fox if it weren't for Rhyllae's hand to hold.

"Come to me tired. I shall give you rest.
Come to me hungry. I shall give you a feast.
Come to me lonely. I shall comfort you upon my breast."
~Psalm 79 of Lune

# THE END

# Book Club Questions

1. The statement "Everyone is worth saving" was used often by Sister Rhyllae in this book. What does she mean by it? Do you believe that this applies to criminals like Aramis and those whom society considers lost? Without the spiritual concept of a soul, is this statement still valid?

2. Aramis Feres is a jhasin transman, a person who transitioned to become male, past 50 years of age. In the 2016 *Indian Journal of Psychological Medicine* article "Suicide and suicidal behavior among transgender persons," suicidal attempts range from 32% to 50% across the globe, trending higher among youth. How likely is it now for trans people to make it to age 50? If not, what would have to change?

3. Aramis Feres had often mentioned he was "shattered" and "broken" from childhood abuse and child slavery. If he never had experienced this during his youth, would he have been able to have a stable life in Amaveriel? Would he have ever left Bazzuuport?

4. Masking is a term used by the autistic and neurodivergent communities for trying to blend with society outside of their home and safe spaces and appear normal by curtailing their idiosyncrasies. If the doppelgänger queen had been able to "unmask" and be their true self, would they have been accepted in Amaveriel? If not, what conditions would allow them to live in co-existence with the people of the city?

5. The doppelgänger queen told Aramis Feres that both of them were shaped by a different hand. What do they mean by this? Do you think this applies to Aramis as posed by them?

6. In Ancient Greek philosophy, there are at least six types of love: agape (selfless, universal), eros (romantic, passionate), philia (friendly), storge (familial), philautia (self), and pragma (enduring). How are they showcased in this book?

7. Dido had mentioned that goodness can only come from goodness alone, yet Aramis used his blades against his enemies, who were considered evil. When discussing good versus evil, violence is thrown into the equation. Is violence evil even if it is used against evil? Are there other non-violent methods that can right wrongs? Are those methods applicable to this story?

8. Violence has been used in story mediums such as books, movies, tv shows, and video games. By showcasing violence in stories, are we perpetuating it in our culture? Or is depicting violence an artistic snapshot of the darker side of the human condition? What would it take to live in a violence-free society? Would we be comfortable living in it?

9. There have been references to the Ancients, a high-tech society similar to our current world. What would it look like if the Ancients had not fallen? Would this story still have occurred?

10. We see the Abbey of the Rising Dawn and the holy order being integral to the city of Amaveriel. If the elders decided to have a separation of religion and government, how would that change the citizens' relationship with the abbey?

11. The doppelgänger queen had been a dark mirror of the characters they transformed into. However, they could not showcase Aramis Feres despite being the most familiar of all characters. Why?

12. Dawn is a lesbian yet worships the Morning Lord. Is there a place for LGBTQ+ people in religion? Should everyone be allowed to worship no matter who they are? What would it take to allow a safe space for LGBTQ+ people in religious institutions?

TEASER

# The MANNEQUIN QUEEN

# Chapter 1

## HEWN

JOSIAH WAS BORN YESTERDAY, FULLY FORMED AND hairy. A dwarf newly hewn, as the term was used, would have all the musculature and nerves of any stout adult; but with the wide wonder of a child taking in the world around him. And his eyes were quite wide in the world he had emerged in for many reasons.

For one, it was smooth. All surfaces, walls, ceiling, and floor, were flatter than slate, with no etched markings of the skilled maker. For another, it was all metal. Leagues and leagues of shiny alloy stretched onward. He had been walking down an everlasting tunnel for his first whole day, wondering about its making. For he knew the purpose of his own making.

All dwarves were hewn from the stone for a single purpose: to know.

To know all the world, as much as they could. Of the civilizations that lived in it. Of the food. Of its people. What they had known to be true and the lies they told themselves to sleep at night. That was why they were made small, hairy, and with an archaic accent: so all would embrace them wherever they went. Once they knew as much as they could obtain, they were called back into the living stone. For that was their true home and family—the mountain that birthed them.

Josiah's purpose was more finite. His was to know what this strange place was—this place of steel. For that was what he had been treading upon. Steel pressed and shaped not by flesh but cut with fire and screwed into place by something beyond understanding. But he must understand, he must know. Otherwise, he wouldn't be able to return to the stone.

And so he traipsed on and on, peering into diversions such as broken glass that had sheltered rooms of tables and chairs. Soon, the hall ended with a door. It had no handle and was smooth as the walls it was framed in. There was a square relief on the wall next to it, with numerous slits that formed a circle.

*Curiouser and curiouser*, thought Josiah, as his broad fingers brushed against the device.

He recalled from what the stone had given to him that this was a speaker. But was this something that received speech or gave it?

"Ello?" He spoke into the cold device.

The only response was his voice echoing in the hollow hall that stretched behind him.

*Oh, of course! I must consider the recipient of this query. How inconsiderate I am.*

"Ello, computer."

A *sh-chk* sounded and the door was lowered before him in its vertical slot. A massive void stretched before him.

*Chk.*

*Chk.*

*Chk.*

One by one, conical lights illuminated from the expansive ceiling to reveal highways of metal platforms that crisscrossed each other at different elevations, all upheld by metal cords as thick as his bare arms. Below was a red glow of light. Gears from beyond his sight clicked and whirred. The platforms started moving. Some of them rose and fell, some of them rotated around.

Enamored by the display, Josiah stepped forward. The moment he crossed the threshold, the door slammed shut.

"Test subject 479240 has been acquired," boomed a calming voice that sounded too perfect to Josiah's ears. "Test 7099 shall commence in 5... 4... 3... 2..."

A horn blared and the ground shook. The dust falling on his bare shoulders led him to look up. The ceiling had parted to allow for rows of perfectly cut metal blades shaped like a shark's teeth. They whirred in place, feeding the chains that held the platforms into its vicious mouth.

While as alarming as this situation was, Josiah was not too troubled by it. All dwarves knew that when the world rocks, you roll. Thus, Josiah couched low, tucking hard against his legs, and rolled like a boulder off a cliff. He slammed against every steel platform in his way. When stalled, he simply shifted his mass and barreled over the edge. On and on, he made his descent, not caring about the wreckage he made on his way down, until at last he dropped to the bottom.

There, a single sliver of a podium stood with a red button that shone. Josiah unrolled himself and casually investigated it. There were no indentions or etchings. It was made of the same material as all that surrounded him save for the button. It was of an unnatural make that imitated glass. Regardless, he saw nothing else and pressed it.

Another horn blared. The destruction roaring above him ceased.

"Congratulations. Test 7099 has been completed by a margin of 15 seconds. Patient 479240 shall be integrated into the menagerie."

*Menagerie? A collection of monsters?* he wondered. *What sort of monsters are these?*

He found his answer soon enough. A door slid down nearby to reveal a doll. Life-size for human standards and pristine. Pristine porcelain skin. Pristine of nicks or blemishes. A pristine golden ratio on its figure and face. There was no paint and no clothing adorned to mask the feminine stature bearing before him. No emotion came from its mold-press mask for a face.

*Incredible*, he thought, until it moved.

Faster than anyone should move, it ambled toward him as the gears within its chassis whirred. It was joined by another perfect copy. They moved to flank Josiah on both sides and pointed their perfect, slender fingers at him. The fingers flipped backward on their joints to reveal four barrel chambers.

"Wait, where am I? What is this place? I'm just a visitor here."

"Designation?" Their voice box rattled.

"Yes? Yes! What is this designation?"

"SILO 51."

Josiah nodded slowly, then tucked and rolled between their legs. He knew he wouldn't be able to survive them. But if he was going to die, he was going to die on living stone. He barreled down the hall, knocking down all these perfect dolls standing at dainty attention. Soon, he came to a wall with exposed sandstone. Blood was scrawled on it by a finger, trying to spell out something in a language he couldn't read.

Josiah unrolled and touched the earth and felt the pull. The call to go home. He pressed the palm hard and willed the stone to know what he knew. When he removed his hand, the words 15 OLIS were hewn.

The sound of grinding gears drew near. Solemnly, he turned to face his attackers. Blank, symmetrical, oval faces stared him down with empty, plastered eyes, silent as ever. Four barrel guns fired manufactured bullets, piercing into his flesh. The pain was quick, for he felt the call home.

Josiah melted back into the stone, taking the etched words with him.

"Patient 479240 has been deleted," boomed the calm voice from earlier. "Please obtain patient 479241 for testing."

# Author Bio

K.N. FITZWATER WAS BORN AND RAISED IN THE heart of Kentucky. Raised in a fantasy-loving home, she had always wished she could travel, so she dreamed of tales of adventure and magic. The stories swam in her head until they spilled out on paper and were bound together by twine. This is one of them.

If you want to join her on her adventures, you can follow her on Threads, Instagram, and TikTok by @knfitzwater and on Twitch by ArduousSpark912.

# Trigger Warnings

9/11 effect

In chapter 11, buildings collapsed and the scene was describes in detail of the chaotic aftermath.

Abuse

Domestic violence, gaslighting and manipulation was showcased in chapter 14. Emotional manipulation and sexual assault (the latter recalled as a triggered memory) occurs in 29.

Cannalbalism

The ghouls eat people as they attack. This occurs in chapter 1, 16, and 26.

Child death

The bodies of the children who passed away were shown respectfully in chapter 16. No killing or death were shown.

Gore

Depictions of gore or body horror occurs in chapters 2, 10, at the end of 11, 16, 23, 26

Lynching

Hanging from an angry mob occurs in chapter 11 through a dream, 22, and 23

Mysogyny

Sexism was metioned in chapter 11

Religion

The majority of the Amaveriel citizens follow the Morning Lord and Lune, which was based on the Abrahamic religions. Aramis and Korzha don't follow this religion and they received microaggressions in chapters 3 and 9.

Smoking

Aramis is a smoker in this book. This occurs in chapter 1, 4, 28, and 33

Torture

A quick depiction occurs in chapter 8, 17, 18.

# Glossary And Translations

### Glossary

Amaveriel: A secret city that lies in Ioun, far to the east. Also-known as the city of freedom. It's nestled in the caldera of a dormant volcano where the mountain meets the sea. Due to its unique topical layout, most homes were built verti-cally as the city slopes steeply to the town's center, known as the Pit. No one says they're Amavarielian unless within the confines of the city walls.

Anglora Jungle: This jungle nation lies between Ioun and the Chessentari Empire to the east. A vast jungle safeguarded by elves and dwarves alike. The ruins of M'thealquilôk were found here. Those who hail from here are Anglorian.

Bazzuuport: Capital of Ioun, which houses the Djinnasi lords. Located far to the west of the nation. Named after the demon djinn, Bazzuu.

Chessentari Empire: Another empire that lies east of the Anglorian jungle, known for its spices and gold. Those that hail from here are Chessentarian.

Djinnasi: Born of djinn, these are the lords that rule Ioun.

Dwarves: These people are elemental beings of the mountains made into living flesh. Their sole purpose is to obtain vast amounts of knowledge and take it back when their time has come. Some can live for a few days, some have lived for centuries. Curious and strong-hearted, they are accepted into every corner of the world for trade and knowledge.

Fey: A group of magical beings who came into this material plane from a fantastical dimension known as the Seelie Court. When the Ancients fell, they tore open a rift as a way of opening their borders. As payment for the drastic change in landscape, they taught magic to those who wish it and constructed schools around the world. Satyrs are part of the fey court and rarely enter into the material plane.

Humans: Once the main populace of the world until the devastating fall of the Ancients. The cult of the Morning Lord and Lune originated from them and has spread worldwide. They have limited magic and limited technology compared to their living peers, and not all humans know their history. But they are quick learners, and many humans have adapted to the changing environment and have created empires. Maybe too quickly, for in their hubris, the demon djinn Bazzuu was summoned to the detriment of the Iounese.

Ioun: The name of the desert nation. This nation lies south of the Gallileah mountain range and the Töskan empire. The

Shining Sea is along their southern coast. If someone hails from here, they're called Iounese.

Jessenter: The official name of Ioun's freedom fighter. They have many stations throughout Ioun and at sea; Amaveriel is their core base.

Jhasin: Magically created homunculi made for the sole purpose of sexual service and entertainment to the Djinnasi lords. Their default model is intersex, but some lords can request a custom gender appearance. Aramis is a jhasin and is of the Silver model, an old formulation that is geared toward dancing and acrobatics. All Silver models had been considered out of date and had been destroyed for the newer models.

Moon Elves: As the story of their creation goes, all elves emerged into this material plane when the light struck the surface of this planet. Moon elves are such beings that hail from vast tundras and deserts of the planet. They used to congregate in tribes until the demon djinn Bazzuu was summoned. By the time of this book, the Iounese moon elves are dispersed widely, some are enslaved, some escaped into the Anglorian jungle, and some live in Amaveriel.

M'thealquilôk: Elvish for "Our City of Stout Hearts." The city, now in ruins, was instrumental in uniting elves and dwarves into a common union.

Nagano: A nation of islands that came together for a common union. Located beyond the Chessentari Empire. Known for their silks.

Sun Elves: As the story of their creation goes, all elves emerged into this material plane when the light struck the surface of this planet. Sun elves are such beings that hail from the open oceans. Not much is known about them in Ioun as they never do trade with the island people far away. Not even with Sister Rhyllae, whose father by the ship records is a sun elf.

Sylvan Elves: They were the ones who emerged from the light that struck through the dapple leaves of forests. Mottled skin and regal, they were the first elves to lay the groundwork with the dwarves for peace and prosperity. Most of their cities fell into ruins over the ages as they retreated from the world in their own crafted dimensional plane. Due to the vigorous expansion of the Töskan empire, they were rediscovered. A marriage between a human general and an elven prince helped broker peace between the two nations. None know of their fate since that fateful union.

Töska: An empire that stretches from the Gallileah mountain range all the way into the Great North. They're always seeking to expand their borders. Those that hail from here are Töskan.

Valentra: A nation that lies across the ocean to the west. They are known for their smoked products.

Zemzem waters: A collection of springs that has magical transformative powers and lies hidden somewhere in Ioun.


## Elvish Translations

*A'nim khashra:* "I faltered."

*A'nim shurri:* "I sorry."

*Elyamamen:* "For all time," "for every moment," "always," "infinity," and "eternity."

*Li'nim me'khatra:* "It was my fault."

*Me'qora:* "My heart."

*Muel lausel sa'wauji:* "What is lost will be found." A common phrase of comfort.

*Shaka un:* "Thank you," informal

*Theliad:* "Fox"

## Latin

*Est mea culpa:* "It's my fault."

*Mea maxima culpa:* "My grievous fault."

*Paeniteo:* "I am sorry."

## Magical Incantations

The Seelie Court had cut through Croatia and its neighboring countries when it opened into the material plane. Most fey speak the locals' original language and have incorporated it into their magic. Dido hails from the epicenter and thus speaks Croatian.

*Brže:* "Faster"

*Milost:* "Grace"

*Vatrena ptìca:* "Firebird"

*Vjetar oko mene, podigni moj teret:* "Wind around me, lift my burdens."

## Misc.

*Bhayam matsu. Mama nama Nathaniel, agniuta:* Sanskrit for "Fear not. My name is Nathaniel, angel of fire."

*Ilumina:* Romanian for "Iluminate."

Discover more at
**4HorsemenPublications.com**

10% off using HORSEMEN10